Death on the Railway

Second Edition 2022

A horror thriller novel by

Manuel Rose

$15.99 USD
$17.99 Canada

DEDICATION

To my family,
thank you for all your support
in all of my ventures.

Published by MMRproductions.com &
Ingram Spark a Lightning Source Company

Copyright © 2019, 2021, 2022 Manuel Rose
MMRproductions.com
815 Route 82 # 51
Hopewell Junction, New York 12533

Cover designed by Robynne Alexander of Damonza.com © 2021
Edited by Melissa Rose and Mark Meyer

Printed in the United States of America

PUBLISHER'S NOTE
This is a work of fiction. Names, characters, places, and incidents either
are the product of the author's imagination or are used fictitiously,
and any resemblance to actual persons, living or dead, business
establishments, events, or locales is entirely coincidental.
This novel is not intended to insult, discriminate, embarrass, or degrade
any group of people in any way.

Books and audio books can be ordered.
For information please write to:
MMRproductions.com
815 Route 82 # 51
Hopewell Junction, New York 12533

Author's Note

This novel was not intended to insult, discriminate, embarrass, or degrade any group of people in any way. This novel was written purely from my own imagination, and from experiences around me from some close-minded people I have known in my lifetime. If I offended anyone, it was totally unintentional and I do apologize. I do firmly believe that we should all be open-minded in everything, and be respectful of everyone's beliefs.

CONTENTS

ACKNOWLEDGMENTS

To my beautiful daughter, Melissa Rose, thank you for all your help editing and formatting this book; and to Mark Meyer for final editing. I also want to thank Robynne Alexander and Damon Freeman of Damonza.com for the fabulous cover design.

PROLOGUE

She had left the house feeling very confused, not knowing where to go. Carina knew that what she did was wrong. They were both wrong, but she clearly took advantage of the entire situation. Carina decided to walk on over to the railway station; the girl thought she could just sit on the bench there to think. It was a little cool out, but it certainly didn't feel like mid-March weather. Carina noticed her picture on the cover of the latest bathing suit magazine, as she had passed by the newsstand. The young lady thought it was really cool being a model. Her beautiful flawless face, long blonde hair, and bright green eyes were practically on every magazine, tabloid, and TV commercial. *Not bad for a twenty-six-year-old chick,* she thought to herself, but Carina didn't know that her future was coming to an abrupt end. She sat down on the bench of the Morton Town outdoor train station, to contemplate the whole scenario that just happened. Suddenly, without any warning at all, a figure emerged from the darkness. Carina was so startled that she dropped her expensive smartphone on the concrete platform.

"Oh, it's just you," Carina said. "I didn't expect to see you, of all people, here tonight. Are you working a late shift or something?" she curiously asked.

But the figure said nothing to her and just kept on advancing toward her. Carina picked up her phone to see if it was all right and to check out the time. It was 12:55 a.m. The last train to the city had left well over a half an hour ago. There shouldn't be anyone here, but there was. She knew this person.

"I'm sure you know that there's no more train service here tonight. So what are you doing here?" Carina asked.

The figure still said nothing and kept coming closer to her. Carina was getting very nervous. Her long blonde hair was shining in the fluorescent lights of the station, making her look sexy, but she sure didn't feel sexy, not now anyway; she felt afraid, very afraid. The figure was standing right next to her now in an intimidating fashion. A long, sharp, stainless-steel knife had quickly emerged from its hand, glistening eerily in the nighttime lights.

"Hey! What the hell are you doing?" Carina said with a shriek.

The figure quickly grabbed the girl from behind and proceeded to cover her mouth with a black gloved hand. Carina screamed, but it was quickly stifled as the long stainless-steel blade of the butcher's knife severed her throat and larynx with a swift movement of its hand. The only sound that she made, the only sound that was audible, was the gurgling of blood. Carina slumped down from her killer's arms onto the cold, hard concrete of the train station's platform, as her spirit exited her body. The poor young girl never stood a chance from her attacker; she didn't expect that from someone she knew, but the killer wasn't through with her yet…oh, no. The cold-hearted attacker stared at her for a bit and knew that it had to have something else, something as a perpetual reminder of this once very attractive girl, a souvenir from the kill…her head.

You know, there are a lot of psychos here in this highly stressed, fast-paced world that we live in today. For some of us, it really doesn't take much at all to reach our breaking point. As you read this book, ask yourself this one question: How many of us are always one hundred percent truly normal? Think about it.

1

WHAT WILL I DO NOW?

Monday morning, April 1. Angelo Russo was getting ready to go for a job interview. He had to take a morning train to Morton City. *What will I do now?* Angelo had thought. The young man was truly all alone in his family's two-story, white colonial home in Morton Town, Massachusetts. It's been about three months since his parents died in a horrific automobile accident on the parkway. He remembered it as if it were yesterday. A snow storm had dumped over a foot of snow in Morton Town. Angelo and his sister were playing video games in the family room when the doorbell rang. It was ten o'clock at night. The state troopers were at the front door. When Angelo opened the door and saw them, he knew something was wrong. The troopers had told him and his sister the bad news. Their parents were killed when a tractor-trailer slammed into the couple's SUV. Angelo and his sister were both devastated. Now, all of the money that his parents had left them was running out. The bills were piling up. Angelo was only twenty years old, working as a pizza delivery boy. He needed a real job to pay the property taxes, oil bill, electric bill, phone bill, not to mention food and cable TV. His sister wasn't even with him now; she had left over two weeks ago. *I'll bet she went back to her boyfriend,* he thought. Now it was just him. *How could she leave me now when I need her most?* Angelo sat down at his kitchen table eating a bowl of cereal. He remembered what Carina used to make him for breakfast, ham and eggs. It had quickly become his favorite, especially the way she would make it. Carina would scramble the eggs, chop up the ham, mix it up with chopped tomatoes, basil, then add cayenne pepper with garlic and fry it up in a pan. Angelo thought it was to die for.

"I wanna have this every morning, Carina," he had told her.

One good thing: the train station was only a five-block walk away from his house. Angelo put on his brown leather jacket and left. It was a little chilly out, but it was supposed to get warmer later on in the day; at least the sun was shining. Angelo knew how to drive, but he couldn't afford a car, nor did he need one right now. Angelo got his ticket from the vending machine at the Morton Town train station. After paying twenty-four dollars for a peak round-trip ticket, he got upset. *This is pretty expensive,* the young man thought to himself. Angelo put the ticket in his pocket and looked at his phone; it was seven fifteen a.m. *I have to get down to the city by nine,* he thought. The express train to Morton City was just pulling into the station.

"Whew! I made it just in time," Angelo said out loud.

The train came to a full stop and Angelo boarded. He grabbed a seat by the window. Within a couple of minutes, the train started pulling out of the station. As it picked up speed, the train's engines began spewing out diesel exhaust into the air. The conductor was coming around toward Angelo.

"Tickets, please," she said.

Angelo searched his pockets for the train ticket, and then he handed it to the conductor. The conductor punched a hole in his ticket and handed it back to him. There was something quite familiar to him about the female conductor, but Angelo couldn't place it. Instead, he wondered about working for the railroad as a conductor. Angelo stared at the conductor in her blue uniform for a moment, and then he said, "Excuse me, Miss, are they hiring here? I mean, how can I get a job with the railroad?"

"You have to take a test, but you look kind of young," she said. "The minimum age they'll hire is twenty-one."

"I'm going to be twenty-one next month," Angelo said.

The conductor gave him a look and said, "They're giving the test at the town hall next Friday. It's just a basic aptitude test. You just got to pay the fifteen-dollar filing fee, and you are in."

"Great!" Angelo said. "By the way, do you know what the starting salary is?"

"I believe it's about twenty dollars an hour for a conductor. You'll get a raise after a year," she said.

"Wow! That's way more than I'm getting now," he replied.

Angelo Russo was getting very excited. He looked at the conductor, thinking, *I could do this!* Angelo decided to ask her some more questions.

"Is it a hard job, or do I just have to punch tickets like you do?"

"It's a little more than that," she said to him.

"For starters, you're responsible for all of the passengers and the safe operation of your train," she told him.

"Do they train you for the position?" Angelo asked.

"Sure they do! You get three months of training. First, you'll go to the training school, then, you'll work in the yard, and finally, you'll work out in the field," the conductor replied.

"Thank you for all the info, I really do appreciate it."

The train conductor had been checking him out. Angelo was a handsome young man with his baby face, curly blond hair, and bright green eyes. She thought he looked like a rock star from the seventies. The conductor had to get back to work, but she certainly didn't mind talking to him.

"I'm off next Friday, I wouldn't mind going with you, just to show you where it is," she said with a smile.

"That's ok, I know where the town hall is," Angelo replied.

"Are you sure?" the train conductor said while sounding disappointed.

"Yes, I'm sure, thanks anyway," he said.

The conductor took one last look at Angelo. She then proceeded to go down the aisle of the train car checking everyone's tickets. Angelo was happy for the tip, but at the same time he couldn't wait for her to leave. She was hitting on him, making him feel very uncomfortable. *Maybe if she were attractive, it would have been ok,* he thought to himself, *but she's creepy looking.* Angelo thought the conductor was a drag queen or maybe a transsexual; the husky voice pretty much said it all to him. She was tall and thin with long blonde hair, but that was about it. The conductor was anything but attractive; still, there sure was something very familiar about her. She had definitely reminded him of someone, but Angelo couldn't place it. He reflected on it for a while and then gave up.

Angelo had an hour-and-forty-five-minute ride to get into the city. He was practically going from one end of the line to the other. The young man was cutting it close for his job interview. *I'll just blame it on the train, everyone else does,* he thought. Angelo picked up his newspaper and began to read the headlines while the train whizzed past all of the local stops.

Railway Butcher Strikes Again

Another young woman was found slain and dismembered at the South Park railway station, for the second time in two weeks. Her body was left on the tracks. The Morton Town police were baffled. "This psycho serial killer has to be caught and brought to justice soon, so that we can bring peace back to our little town. It's just disgusting. If anyone's got any information, please contact us soon," said Chief Brady.

I can't believe they didn't catch him yet, thought Angelo. *They suck!* The papers had now dubbed him the "Railway Butcher," since he only strikes at the railroad stations, and then cuts up his victims like a butcher. *The killer seems to be going down the railway line,* thought Angelo. South Park was in two stops. Angelo read some more of the article:

> The killer had the same method of operation: killing young women at railway stations. He then mutilates them. The butcher also takes a souvenir. This time the victim's heart was removed and taken. The police had identified the body as twenty-five-year-old Sharon Jones, a librarian at the Morton Town Library.

Angelo could not read anymore; it was too unnerving for him.

"Next stop: South Park," the conductor said over the public address system.

"Shit!" Angelo exclaimed.

Angelo didn't realize how loud he said it until the young man noticed the passengers were all looking at him. Angelo decided to check his email on his smartphone, but there was nothing except solicitations in his inbox. The train was pulling into the South Park station when he noticed the police presence. Two uniformed officers got on the train and the rest remained there. One cop went toward the front of the train, while the other went toward the back. The officers were asking everyone out loud if anyone had any information leading to the railway killer. Clearly, the police were beginning to get desperate. They seemed to be running out of options.

The train started to move again, and all Angelo thought about was getting off. He was getting very uneasy. The Morton City express train was barreling down the tracks at seventy miles per hour. It was trying its best to get to the city by nine a.m. Angelo thought about how lucky he was that this was an express train. If the train made local stops, the young man would not be able to make his nine-a.m. interview. They passed by town after town and after a while, the towns all looked alike. The sun was brightly shining over the trees and lawns, which helped melt the remaining snow. The train was now cruising by at seventy-five miles per hour. A little while later, Angelo looked at his phone and he noticed it was eight fifty-eight a.m.

"Morton City will be the next and last stop everyone. Please take all of your personal belongings with you and thank you for riding with the Morton City Railroad," the conductor said over the public address system.

We made great time, Angelo thought. The train started pulling into the terminal and everyone started to head toward the doors. Angelo followed everyone else toward the exit doors. He noticed the conductor was winking at him, which made him feel queasy. *Jesus*, he thought, *let me get the hell out of here!*

Angelo hurried over to the advertising agency, walking as fast as his legs could carry him down the street. It was the tail end of rush hour, but the streets were still very crowded with people running late. At least it was only a two-block walk to the agency. Angelo didn't know anything about advertising, but the young man thought he would give it a shot. He got into the building and went onto the elevator. Angelo prepared to exit the elevator on the second floor. When the elevator doors opened, he saw a large sign that read: "Tate Advertising Agency." Angelo walked in through the glass doors and was greeted by a young receptionist at her desk.

"Good morning. May I help you, sir?" the young girl asked.

"I'm here for the job interview," Angelo replied.

The pretty, young brunette told him to have a seat, while she made a call on the intercom to her superior. Angelo sat down on one of the brown leather chairs in the waiting room. He wondered if he should even be there. Angelo clearly wanted the railroad job instead, but he wasn't taking any chances. Angelo needed money. If he did get this job, the young man would still apply to the railroad, anyway. Angelo looked around in the waiting room; *nothing fancy here,* he thought. The waiting room was rather small, painted light gray, with dark gray commercial carpet. There were four brown leather chairs and the secretary's walnut-colored desk. Two large outdoor scenery pictures hung on the walls. The secretary picked up her phone after it rang, said a few words, and then hung it back up.

"Mr. Harrison will see you now, sir," she said.

Angelo followed the secretary into her supervisor's office, while checking out her ass. He was then greeted by the supervisor.

"Mr. Russo, I'm Mr. Harrison; have a seat," he said.

Angelo sat down into the plush black leather chair and prepared himself to get grilled by the supervisor. He got a bad feeling about working for this man. Mr. Harrison was an overweight, balding, middle-aged man that looked like he wouldn't take shit from anybody. What little black hair the man did have was already turning gray, from stress no doubt.

"After looking over your résumé, young man, I see that you don't have any experience in the advertising business," Mr. Harrison said to him, "but I also see that you have some creativity," he added while looking at Angelo's résumé.

"Now, tell me, what sort of value could you bring here to our advertising agency?" Mr. Harrison asked him.

Angelo sat there and thought about the question for a bit, and then he replied, "I know pretty much what people want to hear and see about a product, sir, before they even consider buying it."

But Mr. Harrison did not seem very impressed at all. *What would this snot-nosed, young punk know about advertising?* Harrison thought. *He's just wasting my time and his.*

"We've been in business for over fifty years now, son, and we want to continue to be the number-one advertising agency around here. I have to tell you that I don't tolerate slackers around here. You have to push, push, and push. I want progress. I want results! You have to be able to convince our future clients that they have chosen the right advertising agency. If you don't, they'll go somewhere else and you'll be out of a job. This is a far cry from being just a lowly pizza delivery boy. Do you understand what I'm getting at, son?" Mr. Harrison said sneering.

Angelo knew where this was going, and it sure wasn't going in his favor at all. *This guy doesn't seem to be impressed with me at all,* he was thinking. *Why is he even wasting his time with me?* Angelo really wanted the railroad job, anyway. He knew the benefits and the pay would be much better there. Angelo felt that Mr. Harrison was belittling him. He also figured that job security would sure be much better working for the Morton City Railroad. However, Angelo knew that his work hours would probably be unstable working as a rookie, until he gained enough seniority. *I might as well tell him to go take a hike,* Angelo thought. Besides, he knew that working in the advertising industry was very competitive. *You're here today, gone tomorrow,* he thought. Angelo kept thinking about the starting salary on the railroad. *Twenty dollars an hour to start is a real no-brainer,* he thought to himself. The young man also remembered the conductor saying that they get a raise after a year of service. Angelo wondered how much of a raise he'd get after working a year, but the starting salary was more than enough, for now. Where else could he go to make that kind of money and have job security like that? Working for the Morton City Railroad would be a great-paying steady job, with great benefits, *if* Angelo got the job. Angelo knew that the competition was fierce. Practically everyone wanted to work there.

Meanwhile, back on the northern part of town, a human heart from Sharon Jones and a pair of kidneys from the victim before her were temporarily being stored inside a basement refrigerator of their assassin. The killer had been collecting all of its victims' organs, a grotesquely bone-chilling exhibition of the destruction of youth and innocence. Were they all just trophies, or were they something…*more?*

2

WHERE'S MY SISTER?

The police were waiting for him at the front door. They thought they had a suspect, or at least a lead in the killings. It was just a hunch, but it was better than nothing.

Angelo got off the train and was walking back home. It was nice outside. The sun was shining brighter and bringing more warmth. *Wow, twelve o'clock in the afternoon,* Angelo thought. *What a damn waste of my time and money that was.* He knew he didn't get the job.

As Angelo Russo approached his home, he noticed a patrol car in his driveway. There were two police officers waiting for him at his front door. One was a uniformed cop. The other man was taller and dressed in a gray suit, wearing a gray derby, *probably a detective,* he thought. *What the hell?! What are they doing here?* Angelo's mind was spinning like a top as he approached them.

"Are you Angelo Russo?"

"Yes, I am," he replied to the officer.

"I'm Lieutenant Collins," said the man.

Lieutenant Collins towered over young Angelo with his impressive height of six foot six inches. He had a slender build. His salt and pepper hair and rough face showed he had been around for a while.

"This is Officer Ireland," the lieutenant stated.

"We'd like to ask you some questions," said the short, stocky, red-headed police officer.

Angelo took his keys, unlocked the front door, and ushered the two men inside his home. He then closed the door behind them, not knowing what to expect next. The police officer and the lieutenant were standing in the foyer trying to analyze Angelo.

"What's this all about?" Angelo asked.

Collins stood there, staring down at Angelo with icy-cold blue eyes for a moment, and then he asked, "When was the last time you've seen your sister, Mr. Russo?"

"It's been over two weeks."

"Well, how come you didn't report her missing?" Officer Ireland asked.

"She was living right here with you, wasn't she?" asked Lieutenant Collins.

Angelo explained to the men that his sister came and went as she pleased.

"She stayed here sometimes, then she'd go back with her boyfriend," he said.

"I'm not her keeper you know. She *is* older than me," Angelo declared.

"Did you have any contact with her at all since she left?" the lieutenant asked.

"No," Angelo said. "We had a little fight, nothing big, but she said she had to leave. I just assumed she went back to her boyfriend's house, she never called me," he stated.

"On what day was that, exactly?" Collins asked.

"It was on Monday night, March 11, which was twenty-one days ago," Angelo said.

"Did you say night? About what time?" the lieutenant asked.

"It was close to midnight."

"And you didn't find it strange she left that late at night, didn't contact you at all, and has been missing for over two weeks?" asked Officer Ireland.

"I called her cell once and just got her voicemail. I did leave a message, but she never called me back. I thought she was still mad. Isn't she back with her boyfriend?" Angelo curiously asked.

"We've spoken to Michael Alfonzo, he hasn't seen her in over a month," stated Collins. "In fact, he has an alibi. He was in Texas visiting his mother *and* we checked it out. Her photographer reported her missing when she didn't show up for work three days ago. Her vacation was over and it wasn't like her to be unreliable," said Lieutenant Collins.

"Yeah, you see, her photographer first called her cell several times and got her voicemail, and then he called her boyfriend. When her boyfriend said he was away and hadn't seen her, he tried to call you, but your phone was disconnected," said Officer Ireland.

Angelo was getting worried now; he had clearly taken his sister for granted.

"Then, where's my sister?" Angelo cried out.

"We think she's been murdered," the lieutenant said.

Angelo collapsed to his knees.

"No! No, not my beautiful sister!" cried Angelo.

Collins helped Angelo back up on his feet as he analyzed him.

"Mr. Russo, we have a body down at the morgue we'd like for you to try and identify," Collins declared. "You see the problem is, the victim's head, hands, and kidneys were all removed. She was found naked with no ID," the lieutenant stated in a matter-of-fact tone.

"Oh, my God, no!" Angelo sobbed.

"Didn't you read about it in the papers? It's been all over the news, Mr. Russo," said Officer Ireland.

"No, I didn't. I just read today's paper and I haven't watched much TV lately," Angelo said.

"You seem to be living a sheltered life here, Mr. Russo. We now suspect that she may have been the first murder victim of the Railway Butcher," the lieutenant said.

"How do you know it's my sister?"

"We don't know for sure, we were hoping you could shed a little light on this for us," said Lieutenant Collins. "This body was discovered on the railroad tracks of the Morton Town train station five blocks away from here, Tuesday morning March the twelfth."

"The engineer on the first train out discovered it," said Officer Ireland.

"That coincides with the fact that you last saw her the night before on the eleventh, and *you* are the last person to have seen her alive," said the Lieutenant. "It also seems to fit the MO of our so-called 'Railway Butcher,' Mr. Russo."

Angelo felt like shit; he just wanted to roll over and die. First his parents and now his only sibling, his beloved sister, was gone.

"Well then, do you think you can vouch for your complete whereabouts on March eleventh, Mr. Russo?" the lieutenant asked.

"I was here all along, upset," he said.

"Can anyone verify that, sir?"

"No sir, I was all alone."

"Why was your telephone disconnected?" Officer Ireland asked.

"I couldn't afford the bill, so I guess they just cut it off on me," Angelo replied. "I have my cellphone, but no one has my number except my parents and my sister. It's been tight around here ever since my parents died in that car accident," he cried.

"Yeah, we know about that, Mr. Russo," Lieutenant Collins replied.

The lieutenant had thought that Angelo looked like a pitiful sight, squatting there and sobbing.

"Are you ready to come downtown with us, Mr. Russo?" asked the lieutenant.

"Yes, just let me go to the bathroom really quick please," he replied as he stood up.

Soon after, Angelo went in the patrol car with the two officers. He felt like a suspect. Angelo didn't know how he was going to identify his so-called sister's body without a head. *The killer had thought of everything,* he thought. *Not only removing her head, but also her hands, so they couldn't check her fingerprints.* His mind was racing faster than the patrol car he was in.

On the other part of town, the Railway Butcher was coming back home. Its human souvenirs were there waiting in the basement refrigerator. The killer began contemplating the next murder. *I need a good pair of lungs,* the killer thought while placing its mask in the jar.

It was lunch time and the slaughterer was getting hungry, knowing it was almost time to get back to work. *I better hurry up and eat something; I haven't much time,* thought the butcher.

Back at the police station, Angelo was being questioned again by the lieutenant in the interrogation room. The room resembled a recording studio, with large soundproofing materials on the walls. There was a table and two small chairs in the room. A camera and microphone were also available in there. This time, Chief Kevin Brady and two other officers were watching and listening in the other room, while the interview was being recorded.

"He's got a very strong attachment to his sister," said Chief Brady.

"A little too strong, if you ask me," said one of the officers.

Chief Kevin Brady had been with the police force for over thirty years. Brady was almost ready to retire; he had five more years to go. Brady loved his job, but at fifty-seven years old, balding, and being overweight, he feared that the department would soon be forcing him out.

"I thought you brought me down here to ID a body," Angelo said. "You're treating me like a suspect, while the *real* killer is still out there!" he exclaimed. "I loved my sister dearly and I'd never do anything to hurt her!"

After almost two hours of questioning, the lieutenant decided to take Angelo to the morgue to identify the female body. *Another tense car ride,* thought Angelo. *Oh, God, please don't let it be her. I can't deal with anymore death.* Angelo kept wondering how he was supposed to identify a headless body, and then he remembered something. There was a way; it was something she showed him long ago.

After fifteen minutes, they arrived at the town morgue. Angelo and Lieutenant Collins got out of the white Chevy Caprice and started walking into the building. They took the elevator up to the second floor.

"Come this way, Mr. Russo," said the lieutenant.

After walking down the left corridor to the end, the lieutenant pressed the intercom button near the door.

"Yeah," said a voice on the speaker.

"It's Lieutenant Collins with Mr. Russo," said the lieutenant.

A loud buzzer sounded and the two men went inside. The room was painted a sterile white, with light gray commercial floor tiles. There were stainless-steel doors in the walls, which led to the individual body drawers. The cold, fluorescent ceiling lights casted an eerie glow in the room.

"Hey, Charlie, how's it been?" asked the lieutenant.

"Same ole, same ole, Mike," replied a short, African-American man wearing a lab coat.

"This is Mr. Russo; he's here to ID the butcher's first victim," Collins stated.

"This is our medical examiner, Charles Boyd," the lieutenant stated as he looked at Angelo.

"It's not a pretty sight, Mr. Russo, follow me," said the medical examiner.

The two men followed Mr. Boyd to the last freezer door on the bottom. The medical examiner turned the cold, stainless-steel handle to open the door. Then, he pulled open the drawer to expose what was left of the woman's body. Tears welled up in Angelo's eyes as he looked at the pale but shapely body of the female victim. There was a Y-shaped incision measuring the length of the torso that was held together by staples. Angelo got all choked up.

"Well, is this your sister, sir?" Collins asked.

"I-I think so. There's-there's one way to-to know for sure," Angelo stammered. "My sister had a birthmark under her left breast that was kind of shaped like a star. She had showed it to me years ago."

The medical examiner put on a pair of blue latex gloves. He carefully maneuvered the frigid victim's left breast the best he could.

"Is this what you're looking for, sir?"

"Oh, my God, yes, yes it's her. It is Carina," Angelo said with great difficulty.

Angelo completely fell apart, collapsing right onto the cold tiled floor. Collins, with help from the medical examiner, picked him back up. After that, they escorted Angelo out to the car.

Lieutenant Collins drove Angelo back home and told him not to leave town in case they had further questions for him.

"You'd better catch him before I do, because if I find him first, I'll cut this sucker up," Angelo managed to say to the lieutenant.

"Mr. Russo, if I were you, I'd watch what you say and do. Do you understand?"

Angelo shook his head yes, then he closed the door as the lieutenant was leaving his home. His anger was getting the best of him. The young man was going to have to take it easy, knowing he was still a suspect.

Back over at the police precinct, Lieutenant Collins was consulting with Chief Brady.

"I don't know what to make of it, Chief. I mean, you should have seen him down at the morgue. He literally just fell apart when he identified the body," said Collins.

"Really?" Chief Brady questioned.

"Yeah, really! I tell you, he's either innocent or he's putting on a great act."

"I have noticed that Mr. Russo seems to have a *real* strong attachment to his sister," the chief replied.

"I picked up on that too, Chief."

"Well, until we have any more leads, we'll have to keep a very close eye on Mr. Angelo Russo," said Chief Brady.

Meanwhile, just a few miles away, the Railway Butcher was planning its next move. *When I get off work tonight, I'll start scouting for my next victim,* the killer thought. *I have a few ladies in mind already. Just have to find the right one, at the right time.* The killer was drooling while thinking. A crazed look was forming on its face. *Only two more hours to go. Only two more hours.* The murderer couldn't wait, making sure all the knives and scalpels were really sharp and ready to go. *Must keep them all together in my bag. I'm gonna need my little saw for this one. Only two more damn hours; can't wait, I just can't wait,* the assassin kept thinking.

Angelo was back at his home fixing himself a ham and cheese sandwich with mustard. It was almost five o'clock and he was getting hungry. *I've got to pull myself together,* he thought. *The cops suck in this little hick town. I'm gonna have to find this piece-of-shit myself.*

Angelo pondered the idea, but then reality set in. He was going to have to find a job; first, the money was dwindling away. Angelo thought about the train conductor position at the railroad. *That's the perfect job for me. The money's good, the benefits are great, and I'll be close to home. I just hope I can get the job,* he contemplated.

Four hours later at the Kensington train station, the butcher was getting ready to claim its next victim. The killer had donned a mask and wig. It was dark, cloudy, and cool out—the perfect setting for the killer. The train was just pulling into the Kensington station. The slayer waited patiently for the train to come to a full stop. Then, the murderer scanned the train to see who was getting off. The butcher savored the idea of committing another unspeakable act of evil, devoid of any conscience.

Joanna Helms was just getting off the train; she was the only one getting off that stop at that time of the evening. Joanna was pretty and young. She was always flaunting her girlish figure to her male co-workers. Her striking, long red hair was another great feature she had, coupled with her crystal-blue eyes. Jerry from payroll had told her he had a dream about her.

"Lots of guys dream about me," she had replied.

The slayer waited for the train to pull out of the station, making sure that no one else was around, besides its prey. It then slowly started to follow its next victim. Joanna stopped walking so that she could send a quick text to her girlfriend, not knowing she was in trouble. The killer was watching her like a hawk. Joanna put her cellphone back in her purse and took out her car keys. Then, she closed her purse. Before Joanna got a chance to start walking again toward the parking lot, she was overcome from behind. With one swift stroke of a sharp stainless-steel blade, her throat had been slashed open. Joanna was now gurgling and drowning in her own blood. The rest of Joanna's blood was spewing out all over her and the cutting knife. She was losing blood fast. Her whole life began flashing in front of her. Joanna tried to beg for her life, but couldn't. Suddenly, everything went dark. Within a few diminutive minutes, Joanna had lost consciousness. She collapsed down onto the cold, hard, concrete train station platform. The young woman died right in front of her killer.

The butcher just dragged her limp body down on the station platform toward the northbound tracks. *She's got a beautiful pair of legs, like a fricking stallion,* thought the killer. *Let me get my little cordless saw out of my bag and finish the job.* The butcher proceeded to saw off the victim's legs with great precision. The killer thought about taking her legs, but it was not on the list. *What a shame, what a damn shame,* the murderer thought to itself.

After removing both of Joanna's legs, her assassin took them and placed them alongside her body. *Well, will you look at that, she's more compact now,* the killer thought. The slaughterer then surgically removed her lungs and liver. Then, the assassin placed the human parts into a cooler, packed with ice. *I love that fiery red hair, I think I'll take that with me too,* the murderer thought. He took his scalpel and made an incision completely around the top of her cranium. Then, the butcher that he was completely peeled off the woman's scalp. The killer had no conscience, just a fiendish intellect. No one was around to see what had happened to Joanna. Not one person was around to save her life. No one would know, until the first train came around the following morning.

Joanna Helms was now victim number three. She was just one day away from her twenty-fourth birthday. Joanna never made it to the big surprise party that was waiting for her at home. All of Joanna's family and friends were waiting for her, but she never showed up.

Joanna Helms never got to fulfill her lifelong dream of becoming a prosecuting attorney for the town. Her life had been snuffed out, cut short prematurely by a deranged serial killer. Joanna's death had left her family and friends totally devastated. She had become yet another tragedy, another statistic, from a horrible monstrous crime. This was just another senseless killing from the town's own infamous railway killer, waiting to strike again.

3

WRONGFUL SEX

Monday evening, March 11, over two weeks earlier…

Angelo had just finished taking a shower. He got out of the bathtub and pulled the light blue floral shower curtain closed. After drying himself off, he put on his light blue pajamas and walked out into the tan painted hallway. While Angelo was passing by his sister's room, he heard some noises emanating from behind her door. It sounded like she was in pain, or something. He slowly turned the door knob and cracked her door open to get a look. Angelo couldn't believe what he had seen. Carina was on her bed naked, with what appeared to be a pink vibrator between her legs. Carina was writhing and moaning, grabbing the white bed sheet with every climax that she had. Angelo watched in awe while thinking, *Mom was right about her, Carina really is a fricking nymphomaniac.* He remembered the conversation Carina had with Mom a while back in the kitchen. Jenny Russo, their mom, had given Carina a lecture on boys and sex.

"You can't just have sex with every boy you want to, just to please yourself," she said to Carina.

But Carina didn't listen. Instead, she became extremely defensive.

"I don't want to be like you and dad, sleeping in separate rooms," she said.

But Mom was very adamant about Carina saving herself for the right man.

"You've got to be careful, Carina! You don't want to get pregnant. You also need to watch out for sexually transmitted diseases," she said.

Carina told her mother that she just couldn't live without sex.

"Maybe you could, mom, but I can't!" Carina shouted.

"And just what do you mean by that remark, young lady?!" questioned Mrs. Russo.

"Let's just say, I've heard Dad complain over the phone to his friends that it's been over ten years since he got laid. Dad said he had more sex when he was single. If it's true, I'm surprised he's still with you, Mom," Carina retorted.

Carina's mother was so stunned by her remark that she became speechless. Jenny Russo had stormed out of the kitchen. Mrs. Russo became very angry; she even turned beat red. Jenny had told everyone to fend for themselves for dinner. Mrs. Russo left the house by herself and came back home extremely late.

Now, Angelo was watching his sister getting off on a vibrator. His penis was getting engorged with blood, growing and getting harder in his pajama pants. *Wow! She's so damn hot, I didn't think Carina was so fine*, he had thought to himself.

Angelo closed her door quietly. He then went back to his room and took off all of his clothes, including his underwear. Angelo was extremely horny. He just couldn't stop thinking about her. Angelo got on his bed and started to masturbate while thinking about Carina.

"Aha!" Carina had said as she came into his room wearing a sexy white nightgown.

"I caught you red-handed, literally. You were watching me, weren't you?" she said.

Angelo didn't know what to say. He was too stunned, lying there on the bed with his big dick in his hands. Carina took off her gown, got on the bed, and straddled him.

"I'll make a man out of you yet, little brother," she said.

"No! It's not right," he said.

"This is wrongful sex; you're my sister, for Christ's sake!"

"Oh, God, you feel so good inside of me. I didn't know you were so damn big!" she said.

Angelo watched her as she rode him. Carina was bouncing up and down on him, while she tossed her waist-long hair around. Her blonde hair was so shiny that it looked like strands of gold. Carina's shapely, succulent breasts were crowned with nipples as hard as little rocks. Angelo wanted to suck on her breasts so bad, but Carina clearly took hold over the situation.

"You're making me so wet, baby," she said as she arched her back.

Angelo was struggling not to climax; he wanted to please his sister, even though he knew that this was dead wrong. Then, Angelo remembered something he had seen in one of his porno movies. Angelo took both of his hands to his mouth, licked his fingers, and grabbed hold of Carina's breasts, massaging her nipples. This put her over the edge as she screamed in ecstasy with her first climax. Carina gave Angelo a loving look.

"Oh, shit! Oh, shit, yeah! Mother!" Carina screamed with her second and more powerful climax.

Angelo enjoyed making his sister have multiple orgasms. Carina kept going after having three of them. But Angelo was losing control fast. His sister was way too hot and way too experienced for him.

"I can't hold out much longer, Carina," Angelo had said while doing his best to maintain his control.

She jumped off of him, grabbed his member, and stroked him until he shot his big load. Angelo pumped his semen all over her pretty face and breasts, one blast after another.

"Oh, my God! Oh, my God!" Angelo exclaimed while breathing hard and thinking he was about to have a heart attack.

"Wow! That's a lot, baby brother! Shit! You sure were all bottled up inside, weren't you?" Carina said.

Carina had kissed his shrinking penis and gave him a loving look.

"That was so much fun, wasn't it, Angelo?" she asked him.

"Yes, it was," he said while catching his breath.

They laid in bed together for a while, feeling completely satisfied.

"Not bad for a virgin, little brother," Carina said.

"How did you know?" Angelo asked.

"I just knew, that's all," she said.

"Come on now, how did you know?"

"Well, I knew you only had one girlfriend and you told me she didn't believe in pre-marital sex, right?" asked Carina.

"Yeah, that's true," Angelo shamefully admitted.

"It's really nothing to be ashamed of, little brother," she said.

Angelo gave her a subdued look.

"Come here, little brother, let's take a shower."

"Together?" Angelo innocently asked.

"Yes, together. You never took a shower with a girl before?" Carina asked, already knowing the answer.

"No," he barely said.

"Well there's always a first time for everything," she said.

They went into the bathtub together, knowing it wasn't the right thing to do. Carina lovingly sponged his body with warm soapy water, going ever so gently and slowly around his private parts. Angelo was already getting aroused. She bent down and started kissing his penis until he reached over and pulled her close to him. They made love again, in the shower.

Carina knew deep down inside that this was really wrong, but it felt so right. *What if someone found out about us?* Carina thought. Her reputation and career as a model would be ruined. She could have told Angelo the truth, maybe it would have helped, but then Carina thought that it might hurt him. *I've got to leave here,* she thought to herself. Carina went to her room and got dressed. Angelo followed her.

"Where are you going?" he asked her.

"I have to leave. I just need some time to think," she said.

"It's almost midnight!" Angelo said while raising his voice.

"I just need a little space for a bit, that's all, bro."

"You're going back to your boyfriend, aren't you?!" shrieked Angelo.

"No! I just need some time to think this through."

"You used me!" he stated in a wounded tone. "You, you took advantage of your own brother!"

"No. I didn't!"

"Screw you!" Angelo screamed.

"I just need some time to myself, that's all!"

"Go already!" he yelled out.

With that, Carina just stepped out of the house, leaving Angelo all alone. They were both hurt. It was the last time he'd seen her alive…

Back in the present time, Angelo was preparing himself for the railroad test. *It's just an aptitude test,* she had said, remembering what the conductor had told him. The test was Friday. *That's tomorrow, damn,* he thought to himself.

It was getting late. Angelo decided to sit down and watch the evening news. He wanted to see if they caught the killer. Angelo went into the oak wood paneled family room. He sat down in front of the television set. When Angelo turned on the TV, he got nothing but a blue screen. The young man tried changing the channel, but it was no use, his cable TV service was disconnected. Angelo was one pissed off puppy. He had no entertainment. No way to find out what was happening in the world. Angelo had no one to talk to. He still had his smartphone, but the boy had a very limited data plan. Not enough gigabytes to watch the news online, that's for sure.

"Shit!" he yelled out loud. "They don't fricking play when they say they're gonna cut you off, do they? The hell with them!" he said, thinking they could hear him.

Angelo didn't have any money to pay the cable TV company. The last bill was over a hundred and sixty dollars and was past due. He had to budget his money for much more important things right now. Food, electricity, and his cellphone bill were Angelo's biggest priorities. Angelo was also putting money away for the town property taxes that were due next month. He was lucky his parents had paid off the mortgage on the house, or he'd really be up shit's creek.

Angelo sat down on the sofa, thinking, and remembering the last time he'd seen Carina. He regretted the last thing he said to her. *She would still be alive today, if she'd only stayed home,* he thought. Carina was all he had left in the big ole house; now Angelo was all alone.

Angelo remembered screwing Carina on that fateful night. He was already getting aroused thinking about that. Angelo used to have to depend on porn to get him off; Lord knows he had plenty of that on his phone and on his computer. Now, all he had to do was think of his sister on that night, and he was hard as a rock. Angelo's penis was literally throbbing in his pants. A wet spot began to form in Angelo's pants where his member bulged. He was going to have to do something about that.

Across town, the police department was receiving an anonymous phone call about another murder. Someone had spotted a slaughtered woman near the train tracks again. Apparently, the killer was trying to hide the body from being seen.

"What the hell?!" shouted Chief Brady.

"That's the fourth victim in less than a month! Shit!" bellowed the chief.

Then, the chief looked at his men in disbelief.

"Johnson, Rose, you two head on over to the Meryl Street station, northbound tracks, on the double!" Brady ordered.

"Yes sir," said Officer Rose.

"Yeah, you got it, Chief," Officer Johnson added.

The two officers flew down the road in their black-and-white squad car, with the lights flashing and the siren blaring. When they arrived at the Meryl Street station, the officers found what was left of twenty-five-year-old Laura Ashford. Her body was sliced open from top to bottom. The remains of the poor girl were lying there on the cold ground, as the sun was setting.

"Jesus H. Christ! Who the hell would do such a horrible thing?" asked Officer Johnson.

"Poor girl, she never stood a chance. It's really disgusting, I tell you," Officer Rose said repulsed.

"This is the work of some seriously sick-ass puppy," Officer Johnson added.

Laura Ashford's remains were barely covered with brush. It was as if her assassin didn't want her to be found, at least, not right away. The wind from the movement of all the trains passing by during the day had finally uncovered her enough to be seen by the passengers; one of them had called it in.

Laura was engaged to be married to Joe Hardy. Joe was her co-worker at the medical center. The two of them had been dating for over a year now. Joe had finally popped the question to her. She thought he would never ask. They had just set up a date for the wedding at Laura's church. Laura will still be at her church, only this time, instead of her wedding, it will be her funeral. Poor Laura was another victim of a heinous crime. Rest in peace, Laura, rest in peace.

4

WHY?

Monday morning, May 20. Spring was in full bloom. The sky was bright blue; flowers were growing everywhere, along with weeds and grass. It was a comfortable seventy-two degrees outside. It had been over two months since the Railway Butcher struck its last victim in Morton Town, Massachusetts. Police Chief Brady was holding a meeting at the police precinct.

"Why?" said Chief Brady.

"Why did he stop killing?"

"He has killed and dismembered four women in less than a damn month, and he just stopped for no apparent reason at all," the chief stated.

"Forensics couldn't even come up with anything, except that this butcher must have some medical knowledge. He removes body parts with such precision, obviously using a scalpel and other medical tools," Chief Brady stated.

"We don't even know what the hell he's doing with all the stolen body parts," said Lieutenant Collins.

Just then, Officer Ireland entered into the room.

"Excuse me!"

"What is it, Ireland?!" barked Brady.

"We just got a big tip from an anonymous caller, someone stumbled upon a gruesome discovery," Ireland stated.

"What the hell is it already, Ireland? I haven't got time for riddles!"

"Well sir, the caller claims to have found a human head…or what was left of it," the officer explained.

"Where was it?" Brady asked.

"In a wooded area, near Clayton Road, just right off the highway," responded Ireland.

"Looks like we've got ourselves a lead. Get down there and bring forensics with you," the chief commanded.

Two police squad cars (one carrying a forensics team) went barreling down the road with blaring lights and sirens. When they all arrived at Clayton Road, the officers prepared themselves for a horrible sight. Officer Ireland spotted it first.

"There it is!" shouted Officer Ireland.

The forensics officers took out all their cameras and sample kits. The female head was lying there on the grass. Sunlight exposed the maggots and worms crawling out of the eye sockets and mouth. There were flies buzzing all over it. The head was also completely scalped, leaving no hair to frame the once beautiful face of a young woman. Officer Rose got so disgusted that he went into the field to vomit. The head was brought back to the police lab, along with some other evidence that was recovered.

"I want dental records checked, but I've got a feeling I know who this head belongs to," Chief Brady told the men in the lab.

The Chief had his hunches and so did Lieutenant Collins.

On the other side of town, Angelo was opening up his mailbox to retrieve his mail.

"Nothing but fricking bills," he said to himself.

Then, Angelo came upon a letter that was from the Morton City Railroad. He opened the letter and read it.

Dear Mr. Angelo Russo:

You are required to come down to the Morton City Railroad Office of Human Resources at 51 West Montague St., Morton City, Massachusetts, 3rd floor on June 1st at 9 a.m.

You will be interviewed and required to submit to a drug and alcohol screening. You'll also be fingerprinted, and a background check will be performed on you.

Should you not arrive at the specified place and time, you will forfeit your chance at the position of "Railroad Conductor," and we will move on to the next applicant.
Please be prompt.

Yours truly,
James Cohen
Manager of the Dept. of Personnel
Morton City Railroad

Angelo couldn't believe it.

"All right, man!" he screamed out loud. "Things are finally looking up for me!"

Angelo took his mail and went inside the house. *This calls for a celebration,* Angelo thought to himself. He went to his bar in the family room to pour himself a glass of apricot brandy, knowing it may be the last time he could drink, for a while at least. *I've got to stay sober for that drug-alcohol test,* he thought. But in the meantime, Angelo wanted to get stoned, or at least high enough to feel nice. He had a lot of shit on his mind. Right now it was time to celebrate and feel nice.

In a dimly lit basement, not too far away, the killer was looking at its prized possessions in the large refrigerator. All the body parts of the butcher's victims lay there for some devious plan, but what? What could the killer want with all those body parts? Why would any serial killer want to keep that kind of incriminating evidence? The butcher enjoyed its little collection, but realized the box was full. There was no more room. *I've got to get rid of them*, the killer thought.

The butcher decided to go for a ride. *I'm going to find my connection*, he thought. The butcher got in the car and drove downtown, passing by the police precinct. *They'll never catch me. They're not smart enough. Never, never, never, never, never*, thought the killer. *Way too stupid, especially the chief of police himself.*

Back at the Russo residence, Angelo was so drunk that he fell asleep in his black leather recliner, holding an empty glass in his hand until it fell on the carpet. Angelo dreamed the same dream he always did, of his beloved sister, Carina. The night she made a man out of him had changed him forever. Angelo grew up big time that night, in more ways than one. He could see her in his dream, a memory that's been ingrained in his brain. The sex was so good and yet so wrong. Angelo never got to make love to a woman, until his sister took him. *It was all her fault. She used me*, Angelo thought in his dream, but he didn't do much to repel her at all, even knowing it was incest. Angelo could still see her riding him, up and down, tossing her beautiful, long blonde hair.

It was late in the evening, about eleven p.m. when Angelo awoke to a peculiar sound; it was a low moan emanating from upstairs.

"Who's there?" Angelo yelled out.

"A-n-g-e-l-o," a ghostly female voice cried out from a room upstairs.

"Wha-what the hell was that?" Angelo stammered.

"They found my head, A-n-g-e-l-o," the spirit said.

"Carina? Is that really you?" Angelo questioned.

Angelo ran upstairs. The moaning was coming from inside Carina's bedroom. Angelo had kept Carina's bedroom locked up as a shrine. He missed his dear sister so much, but now Angelo was afraid to see her spirit, if that's what it really was. He stayed right in front of her locked door listening. The moaning continued.

"I want you, baby brother. I want to feel you inside of me," Carina's spirit called out.

"I want you, I want you now!" Carina was taunting and calling him from her grave.

"They found my head, Angelo! They—found—my—head!"

As much as he wanted to, Angelo was simply afraid, afraid to go downstairs and get the key to her room.

"Come to me, Angelo," the spirit called out to him.

"No! I'm afraid! I won't go in there!" he cried out loud. "You can't make me!"

Angelo was on the verge of tears. He was really scared. Suddenly, the door burst wide open. Carina's body was on the bed.

Maggots had emerged from the eye sockets and mouth of her detached, scalped head.

"L-o-o-k, baby! They found my head!" the detached head said while rising in front of him.

It was more than Angelo could bear. He ran down the stairs while screaming in horror. Angelo was so distraught that he didn't see the skateboard in the middle of the kitchen floor that had mysteriously appeared. Angelo Russo tripped on it and flew across the floor, crashing into the wall. He was knocked out cold.

What do you think, reader? Was it really an apparition, or was Angelo's mind playing tricks on him? Only time will tell, read on…

A few miles away, Daphne Greenberg was getting ready to get off her train.

"Next stop, Williams Port. Exit in the first two cars please," the conductor said over the public address system.

That's my stop, thought Daphne. She made her way toward the front of the train as it began slowing down. Daphne was the only one departing. She walked off the train and looked at her cell.

"Shit!" Daphne said out loud.

It was eleven thirty p.m. Daphne was already regretting working overtime. *It's friggin dark out,* she thought to herself. *This is way too late.* Daphne thought it would be nice to do her handsome young boss a favor. She finished those reports for him. Charles was so tired and just wanted to go home, so Daphne volunteered to stay late for him. She would do anything for Charles. *His wife doesn't even appreciate him, not like I do,* she thought to herself. Daphne believed she was a formidable opponent; after all, the woman was only twenty-seven years old. Daphne was very attractive with her long black hair and shapely figure. *I've seen him gazing at my breasts, typical male,* she thought. But Daphne really did enjoy his attention.

The local train started to pull out of the station, leaving her all alone. She decided to check her email; unfortunately, the phone slipped out of her hands and fell onto the concrete station platform. Daphne was pissed off.

"Shit!" she exclaimed. "That's what I get for putting too much lotion on my hands."

Before Daphne could bend down to grab her smartphone, a stranger's foot came out of nowhere, stepped on it, and shattered it to pieces.

"Hey! That's my phone, asshole!" Daphne screamed.

The stranger punched her in the face. Daphne then regained her composure and ran. The killer chased her. The butcher finally grabbed Daphne from behind and slit her lovely throat. Daphne Greenberg collapsed onto the platform, drowning in her own blood. She became the Railway Butcher's fifth victim after over two months of abstinence.

The butcher proceeded to dismember her with a cordless saw, using a very fine blade. *She sure was a hottie, that's for sure,* the killer thought. Then the assassin took out its scalpel. *I have got to have this beautiful long black hair for my collection,* the killer was thinking. The butcher then proceeded to scalp her with its scalpel. The last thing the slayer did was to remove Daphne's heart. Then, it placed it into its cooler.

The following morning, Angelo woke up on the cold, tiled kitchen floor, wondering how he even got there. *It must have been a*

dream, he thought. *No, maybe a nightmare. Yeah, that's what it was, a fricking nightmare.*

Angelo picked himself up and dusted himself off. He had a lump on his head from crashing into the wall the night before. On the floor was the skateboard Angelo tripped over; it belonged to Carina. *But how did it get there?* he wondered. The last time Angelo remembered Carina playing with it was last summer, but it's been in her closet ever since then. He begrudgingly decided to go upstairs to Carina's room, just to make sure it was still locked up. Angelo walked up the stairs slowly and cautiously. His heart was pounding a mile a minute. When he got to her room, Angelo was horrified. Carina's room was open. The smell of death was in her room; her bed spread was covered in blood.

Suddenly, the doorbell rang. Angelo tore off the sheet, stuffed it in the dresser drawer, and ran downstairs to open the door. When he opened it, Angelo was surprised to see Lieutenant Collins standing there.

"Hello there, Mr. Russo," the lieutenant sharply said.

"What can I do for you, Mr. Lieutenant?"

"May I come in?"

"Sure," replied Angelo.

Angelo let the lieutenant into the foyer, and then closed the door behind him.

"We think we have finally recovered your sister's head, Mr. Russo."

"What?"

"We'd like you to come downtown and try to identify it, but I'm gonna level with you, Mr. Russo; it's not a pretty sight."

"I-I just buried her, M-Mr. Lieutenant," Angelo stammered.

"I'm sorry, Mr. Russo, but we still need you to come downtown."

"Did you find her hands, too?"

"No, Mr. Russo, just her head."

Angelo grabbed his sweater and left with the police lieutenant in his white Chevy Caprice. The sun was shining and what could have been a nice day out, was going to be nothing but turmoil. While riding in the car, Angelo kept playing last night's scene over and over again in his head like a DVD on repeat. "They found my head," that's what Carina kept saying, he remembered. Now he knew what her spirit meant. The lieutenant drove his car through the downtown traffic with ease. Every time that they got stuck, Lieutenant Collins just turned on the police lights that were hidden behind the front grill. Angelo was in no hurry to see his sister's head if it really was her head.

They finally arrived back at the morgue. By now, Angelo was trembling. Collins parked the car in the first available spot and turned the engine off.

"Well, we're here again, Mr. Russo," the lieutenant stated.

Angelo followed Lieutenant Collins into the building and into the elevator. Again, they got off on the second floor and went all the way down to the end of the left corridor. The lieutenant buzzed the intercom system to gain admittance.

"Yeah," said the voice on the speaker.

"It's Lieutenant Collins again with Mr. Russo."

A loud buzzer sounded and the two men went on inside again.

"Hey, Charlie!" said the lieutenant.

"Hey, what's up Mike? You must l-o-v-e comin' here," said the attendant.

"Yeah, sure I do."

"Show him the head, will you!"

"All right, but it's…"

"I know, I know! It's not a pretty sight. Just show it to him, will you please, Charlie?"

The man opened up the third freezer drawer on the upper right corner to reveal the hideous sight. Angelo got choked up when he saw what was left of his sister's head.

"Who did this to her?!" Angelo cried out. "What happened to her lovely hair?!"

"So, it is your sister then, isn't it, Mr. Russo?" the lieutenant asked.

"Yes, yes. It is. Oh, God, I wish it weren't, but it is."

"I'm sorry, Mr. Russo, but we still don't know who the killer is, or what his motive is."

"How many more?!" Angelo screamed out. "How many more have to die like this before you find him?!" Angelo buried his face in his hands and sobbed.

Collins reached for his cellphone to report in. He told Chief Brady that Angelo Russo had cleared up their suspicions about the head.

"Not only did he ID the head, chief, but you should have seen his reaction."

"I think you better get on back here, Collins, we've got another victim," said the chief.

The lieutenant couldn't believe what he just heard.

"Another victim, after two months of playing possum, why?" he asked himself aloud.

Collins drove Angelo back home on his way to the precinct. When he arrived at the chief's office, the detective was told to go to the Williams Port train station.

"I want you there right on the double! Forensics is already there!" Brady hollered.

The scene of the crime was like a media circus, there were reporters and camera crews everywhere. When Collins arrived, he was bombarded with microphones and cameras in his face from all of the local networks. The reporters were so relentless; they barely gave him enough room to get out of his vehicle.

"Lieutenant, is this the work of the Railway Butcher?"

"Why did he strike now after two long months of being dormant?"

"Have you got any leads?"

"Who is he and what is his motive?" asked the reporters one by one.

When Lieutenant Collins had reached the forensics team, he was livid.

"What's with all the reporters? This is a friggin crime scene!"

"We don't know, Mr. Collins, somebody leaked," one of the forensics officers told him.

Collins grabbed a bullhorn and turned toward the crowd of reporters.

"All right, everybody get out of here, this is a crime scene investigation! come on, let's go everyone!" Collins yelled at the herd of reporters as camera flashes sparkled.

"Has anything been compromised or tampered with since you guys got here?" Collins asked the forensics team.

"No sir, not since we've been here," one of the men responded.

The body was starting to decay in the warm sunlight. The once attractive single girl of only twenty-seven years old was now just a memory. Daphne Greenberg's destroyed body laid on the concrete train station platform in pieces. Her throat was slashed and full of dried blood. The young woman's arms and legs were severed. A tall young man with dark hair rushed over to see her.

"Oh, my God, no! No, it's Daphne! Who would do such a thing to her?" asked the man.

The once happy-go-lucky fine young businessman was now disheveled. His brown hair was all in his face, hiding the tears that started to emerge.

"Excuse me, sir, but this is a police crime scene," Lieutenant Collins stated.

"I'm sorry, officer, but I know that girl."

"Really?"

"Well, suppose you tell me who you are and what's your relation to her."

"Officer, my name is Charles B. Davis; I have been her supervisor at B & B Publishing for the past five years."

"I'm Lieutenant Michael Collins. You said her name was Daphne?"

"Yes, It's Daphne Greenberg. She didn't show up for work so I had a hunch something happened to her, that's why I'm here."

"You wouldn't mind coming down to the station to answer some questions, would you?"

"Uh, no, I mean sure, but just as long as you don't consider me a suspect. I *do* have a legitimate alibi, sir."

"No, Mr. Davis, it's just a preliminary routine questioning, being that you're familiar with the victim."

Collins escorted Mr. Davis to his car and drove off to the station, leaving the forensics team behind at the scene of the crime. Charles Davis had a lot to think about while he was riding in the back of the lieutenant's car. *She was absolutely gorgeous,* he had thought. *I was falling in love with her. I'll never forget her beautiful face smiling every morning, as she brought me a cappuccino and a buttered roll, out of her own money.*

Charles was getting angry. Daphne was more than defiled, she was destroyed. He never got to tell her how much she had meant to him or how his marriage was on the rocks. Charles had thought about leaving his wife of over three years for her. *That beautiful, shiny, long black hair of hers. How I longed to taste her sweet lips,* he thought. *Oh, how I wanted to please her.* But Daphne's assassin had deprived him of all that.

"Are you doing all right back there, Mr. Davis?" asked the lieutenant.

"Yes, as well as I *can* be, Lieutenant, but I was wondering…"

"Wondering what?"

"What kind of sick bastard would do such a horrible thing to such a sweet and considerate young woman like her?"

"Your guess is as good as mine, Mr. Davis. It kind of sounds like you were sweet on her. Were you?"

"I won't lie to you, Lieutenant. I did have feelings for her."

"So it wasn't just business then."

"Nothing ever happened between us, if that's what you're implying."

"Well, I just wondered if maybe there's a jealous spouse or something…I noticed you have a wedding band on your finger."

"That is very observant of you, Lieutenant. It shows that you really know your job," Charles Davis sarcastically added.

"So, are you married, Mr. Davis?"

"Yes, I am, sir."

"Did your wife know about her?"

"I know what you're getting at and the answer is no. Look, even if my wife knew I had feelings for Daphne, my wife's not a murderer. Nor could she even do something that sick, Lieutenant."

"I'll never put anything past anyone, especially a woman. What is it they say? 'Hell hath no fury like a woman scorned,'" the lieutenant went on to say. "Remember that female that cut off her husband's penis years ago?"

Charles Davis knew what the lieutenant was trying to say. He remembered the case. It was in all the headlines.

"Let's see now, Lorene something…I don't remember her last name but…" the lieutenant just stopped in mid-sentence, while trying to remember. "She had cut off his penis while he was asleep and threw it into a field."

"That was an extreme case and you know it, Lieutenant. Like I said before, my wife is not a murderer," Charles snapped back.

They finally arrived back at the police precinct. Lieutenant Collins parked the car and escorted Charles Davis inside. Collins brought Mr. Davis into the interrogation room for questioning. The lieutenant turned on the video and audio recording equipment, and then he closed the door.

Later on in the afternoon, Chief Brady was in the classroom giving another lecture.

"All right, men, what do we really know about this so-called butcher?"

The fifteen police officers sat in a small classroom watching the chief intently, as he stood in front of the blackboard. They were all hoping that Brady had some insight as to who the serial killer was, and what his motive might be.

"I'll tell you…" Chief Brady said as he proceeded to write on the blackboard.

"First off, we now have five young female victims. All of them were in their twenties and all were very attractive. All of them were single. No real attachments, except for Carina Russo. Every one of them was mutilated. Every victim had at least one body part missing, as if the killer wanted souvenirs from his prey. None of them were sexually assaulted. There was no evidence of penetration, no signs of semen on any of them, anywhere. We still don't know the answer to that very important question: Why? Why does he or she do these things? What's his or her motive? What's their method of operation, besides what we already know?"

Brady turned around to face the men in blue sitting in the room.

"Obviously, this bastard has got some kind of fetish with the railroad. Each victim was slain at a train station along the Morton line, one stop at a time. And what is this sick puppy doing with all of those body parts?"

"Excuse me, Chief?" Officer Rose asked while raising his hand up.

"Yeah what is it, Rose? Do you have something you'd like to contribute to this?"

"Yes, I'm a little confused, sir."

"Confused about what, Rose?"

"Well for one thing, sir, why do you keep referring to the killer as he or she? I mean, I thought we've established that the butcher was a male, sir."

"We can't just assume anything, Rose. Women are just as capable as men are when it comes to certain things, especially murder. Do I make myself clear?"

"Yes, sir."

"Does everyone here understand what the hell I'm talking about?"

The whole classroom had answered with a resounding, "Yes, sir."

"Good, now let's get out there and find this son of a bitch, so that we can restore law and order around this here town again.

We have got to stop all of this death on the railway! You're all dismissed," the chief concluded.

They all left the classroom, one by one, not knowing any more than they did before. Not knowing who or where the killer was and when he or she would strike again. But more importantly, who would fall prey to the butcher next? Who would be the next unlucky soul to succumb to its horrible wrath and be slaughtered? Only time will tell. One thing was for sure though; death had come to their small town, and it was not about to leave them anytime soon.

5

ANGELO THE CONDUCTOR

Monday, early in the morning, June 24. Summer arrived with hazy, hot, and humid weather. Angelo had his sister's body exhumed and reburied with her head. He wanted to keep her together. Angelo was so happy; the Morton City Railroad had needed conductors badly, there was a big turnover. Senior conductors were retiring and others were being promoted to engineers. Angelo got hired sooner than he thought. He was getting prepared to go to his first day in school car training when the doorbell rang. *It's only seven o'clock in the morning,* the young man thought. *Who could that be?* Angelo ran down the stairs barely dressed to answer the door—it was a floral delivery man.

"Mr. Angelo Russo?" asked the man.

"Yes, that's me," Angelo responded.

"Sign here, please."

Angelo signed the receipt.

"Have a good one," the man said as he handed Angelo a long box.

I wonder who sent it, Angelo thought. He opened up the box to find a dozen long stem red roses. A card was inside that read:

Congratulations and welcome aboard, my love.

I know you'll make a great conductor.

There was no name on the card or package, nothing to indicate who sent it, or where it was from.

"What the hell? I didn't even start yet and already I have a secret admirer?" he shouted out to no one's ears.

Angelo didn't know what to make of it. He only knew that he had to hurry up and get to the training school. *It's my first day, I can't be late,* Angelo thought as he put the flowers down on the kitchen table. Angelo had to be there by nine, so there wasn't much time. He finished getting dressed and left.

Angelo took the next southbound train into the city, thinking soon he'd be able to ride for free. He arrived there ten minutes late. The training center was actually an old public-school building from the fifties that the railroad bought in an auction. The building was updated and retrofitted by the Morton City Railroad to be used as a training center.

Room 310, that's what the paper said, Angelo thought to himself. He quickly took the stairs up to the third floor and went down the hall looking for room 310. The room was toward the end of the hall. When he entered the classroom, class was already in session. The instructor gave Angelo a dirty look.

"Sir, you're fifteen minutes late to my class," the instructor irritably stated.

"I'm sorry, sir," Angelo replied.

"Let this be a warning to you, I do not tolerate lateness in my class. This one's on me. If you come in here late again, you will be sent back home and your time will be cut. Do you understand?"

"Yes, sir."

"Good! I'm really glad. Now that we understand each other, take a seat and fill out this form with your name and address."

"Yes, sir," Angelo replied, knowing he did not make a good first impression in class.

After a while, the instructor introduced himself as Train Service Supervisor Elliot Jones. Mr. Jones was a pudgy middle-aged man with mostly gray hair and a bad attitude. He had become set in his ways, with plenty of seniority under his belt. TSS Jones had his pension and was going to retire next year. *I've just got to get all of my ducks in a row,* he thought to himself.

"Ladies and gentlemen, I would like to point out that we run two different types of equipment down here, diesel and electric. We refer to our trains as equipment. Out in the burbs we run diesel. When we get to the city limits, we switch on over to electric power. Any questions so far?" TSS Jones asked.

Angelo shot his hand right up.

"Yes, Russo, what's your question?"

"What train stop do we switch over to electric?"

"At the 125th Street station, any more questions?" Jones asked the class.

The class of thirty, consisting of mainly men, said nothing.

"Good! Now we all can proceed. Today, we're going to take a trip to the Morton south train yard. Make sure you have all of your safety gear with you while we walk the tracks and structures."

"Excuse me, sir," Angelo said while he raised his hand up again.

"Yes, Russo, what is it now?"

"Well, I was wondering what safety gear you were talking about, sir."

"If you would have gotten here on time, you would have

gotten your gear, Russo!"

The instructor then went back into the classroom closet to get Angelo his gear.

"Ok, Russo, here's your flashlight and safety vest."

Angelo thanked the man and sat back down at his desk.

"Ok everyone, listen up!" Instructor Jones commanded. "Tomorrow, you will be issued your train keys and your photo ID cards. Now, everyone put your safety vests on and follow me."

Not too far away, the butcher was devising its next move. Who will be the next victim? Where would it take place? And more importantly, what body parts would be taken? The killer was in the basement admiring the new refrigerator it had just purchased. *I like my new refrigerator,* thought the slayer. *It's got so much more room. It just needs to be filled. I want more parts. It would make it more interesting, yes, very interesting indeed.* The killer formed a great big smile on its face, while thinking about the possibilities at hand. The murderer was getting ready to go to work.

Back at the train yard, Angelo Russo was walking with the rest of the group. The instructor had just stopped walking to explain safety measures.

"Ok, listen up, everyone!" Mr. Jones stated. "First off, you can call me TSS Jones, instead of Train Service Supervisor Jones. Now, let me explain the safe way of walking in the yard. Always look both ways before any crossing to see if there's a train coming. Secondly, always carefully step over the third rail. This is an active yard and all tracks are hot. The third rail carries six hundred volts of electricity at ten thousand amps. If you step on it, instead of stepping over it, you will fry. If, God forbid, some unfortunate person is making contact with the third rail, do not touch them! Your body will act as a conductor of electricity, and then you will also get electrocuted. Instead, try to knock them off the rail with any object that doesn't conduct electricity, such as a wooden stick, like a shoe paddle. If you can't safely help the person, immediately get assistance. Do I make myself clear everyone?"

A resounding "yes" was loudly heard from everyone in the group.

"We are going over to track forty-nine to get to our school car. Let's go everyone, move it!"

They all walked out in the hot June sun. Angelo took a drink from his water bottle while wondering how much further they had to go. It was already eighty-five degrees out, but the sticky humidity made it feel worse. Finally, they arrived at an old 1960 railcar that was converted to a classroom. The car was painted red with white lettering on it that read: "School Car." There was a small box of wooden stairs made to lead from the ground up to the railcar. Sharon White, one of the female students, had asked why there was gravel on the ground. TSS Jones stopped and turned around to face the group of students.

"That's a good question, young lady. That's called track ballast," the instructor responded. "It's used under, over, and around the ties to bear the load of the tracks and the trains. It also facilitates water drainage and keeps down vegetation. Now, let's all climb aboard our school car."

Everyone started climbing up on the wooden stairs to the old railcar, after the instructor had gone up to open the storm door. When they all got inside, the class started to complain.

"Man, it's hot in here," Angelo Russo said, followed by the same exact remark from everyone else.

"This railcar has been retrofitted with air conditioning," TSS Jones stated. "Just give me a minute to turn on the A/C breakers."

After turning on the air conditioning system, Mr. Jones told everyone to take a seat. Then, he called everyone's attention to the blackboard. After a few hours of boring, yet informative, safety lectures, Angelo was getting sleepy.

"Ok, everyone! That about wraps it up for today. Now, our newly revised itinerary will go like this…" the train instructor said. "On Wednesday, we'll be heading out to the uniform center to get you guys sized up. On Thursday, you'll be getting your photo ID passes and your badges."

"You mean we get to wear badges like the cops do?" Angelo asked.

"Yes, but they're for transit only, so don't start playing police officers. We'll meet back here tomorrow at eight thirty sharp. Do I make myself clear, Mr. Russo?"

"Yes, Mr. Jones," replied Angelo.

The class of students started to leave the train, following TSS Jones down the tracks. After a while, Angelo realized that he left his notebook on the seat. He decided to go back and get it. No one paid any attention to him; they all had one thing in mind—getting home.

Angelo snuck back to the school car to get his notebook. He decided to copy the rest of the notes on the blackboard. It was going on five o'clock. Angelo had to hurry before it got too dark out, since he didn't really know his way around the yard. Angelo was so tired. Before long, he fell asleep on the seat. His pencil and notebook fell from his hands and onto the floor.

After a moment or two, someone came aboard the school

car; it was the blonde female train conductor that had creeped him out on the train. She stood over Angelo as he slept in his chair. *He sure looks cute, a regular Sleeping Beauty,* she thought, knowing she had to wake him up.

"Hey sleepyhead, time to wake up. No sleeping on the job, you know," the conductor told him.

Angelo was slowly waking up, trying hard to focus his eyes.

"Wh-what are you doing here?" Angelo asked her.

"I was just bringing our train back to the yard with my engineer, and I saw you come in here. You're not supposed to be in here all by yourself, did you get lost?"

"No. I'm in training. I came back here to finish taking my notes; I guess I just fell asleep."

"I could walk you out of the yard if you want, it's no biggie."

"No-no, thanks, it quite all right. I can find my way back."

Angelo slowly got up out of his seat and left the school car. He carefully navigated himself out of the train yard while thinking to himself. Angelo had just observed something that made him feel very uncomfortable. The female conductor he had just spoken to was sporting a massive bulge in her pants, right between her legs. *Oh, my God, I was right. That was no female, she's a he,* Angelo thought.

Back on the train ride home, Angelo's mind was racing. *Damn, I think that conductor likes me, Shit!* he thought. *What am I going to do? I'm not gay.* Angelo couldn't wait to get back home. He felt so confused, but also very tired; it was a long day. The young man just wanted to go home and relax.

Back at the school car, Taylor, the conductor, was feeling sad and lonely. She wanted Angelo. *I want him so bad, but I think he resents me,* Taylor thought. *I'm a woman. I can't help it if I'm trapped in a man's body. I must make Angelo understand. I must win him over.* Taylor was falling in love with him. She realized it was getting late and decided to leave the train car. Taylor stared one last time at the seat where Angelo sat only a little while ago, before leaving to go home.

Angelo was drying himself off in the shower, thinking how good it was to be clean and be back at home again. He turned the air conditioner on and went straight off to bed. While Angelo slept, his thoughts were of all that happened in the day. His mind had replayed the training school session, but mostly the encounter he had with the conductor, all alone in the school car.

Suddenly he awoke to a haunting voice that was moaning.

"A-n-g-e-l-o," the voice cried out.

"Wh-what the hell is that?" he asked groggily.

"A-n-g-e-l-o," the ghostly voice called out to him again.

"Carina, is that you again?"

Angelo got up and fearfully went back to Carina's room. He unlocked the door and opened it. Angelo put on the light and stared in awe. Carina was lying on her bed, completely naked and looking extremely sexy.

"Carina, you look as beautiful as ever," he said to the apparition.

"I came to warn you," Carina's ghost said to him. "I came to warn you, baby brother."

"Warn me? Warn me about what, Carina?"

"S-t-a-y a-w-a-y. Stay away, and be careful."

"Stay away from what, Carina?"

Then, as quickly as she came, Carina disappeared.

"No! Come back here!" he bawled. "Come back to me, honey, I miss you! I need you, please come back to me," Angelo cried out as he collapsed on her bed.

Two days later, Angelo was there at the uniform center getting sized up. He looked at himself in the mirror, admiring his reflection. *I look good in a blue uniform,* he thought. *Angelo the conductor.* The other student conductors were just as happy. One of Angelo's classmates came over to him and told him how cool it was going to be wearing uniforms.

"Man, don't you know? Uniforms are a magnet to women," Josh told him.

"Yeah, I heard," replied Angelo.

But Angelo wasn't really looking for a girlfriend right now. He was still trying to get over his sister. All Angelo wanted to do was to get his life back in order, and the best way to do that was to keep working.

A week later, Angelo was back in the classroom. The train instructor was putting something down on the blackboard, and then he turned around and said, "Attention everyone! We all have been asked by the state police department to keep a diligent lookout for any suspicious activity. Also, keep an eye out for any suspicious-looking person. The police need our help in locating this so-called 'Railway Butcher.' If anyone has any information whatsoever, please call the number up on the blackboard."

He put his chalk back down on the blackboard tray and turned around to face his class.

"Now, has everyone here got all of their uniforms?"

"Yes, sir," the class responded.

"All of your tools, including your train keys, safety vest, and flashlight?"

"Yes, sir," the class stated.

"Your train photo IDs and badges?" Mr. Jones asked.

"Yes, sir," they all said again in unison.

"Ok, today we're going to have a quiz to see how much you all have learned."

They all started to moan in fear; the students didn't expect a quiz today.

TSS Jones picked up a stack of papers from his desk drawer. He handed the papers to the first student in front of him and said, "Mitchel, pass these out, please."

Everyone in the classroom had a worried look on their face. No one expected a test so soon in the course. Everyone started passing quiz papers to each other. TSS Jones told the class they must be finished by nine thirty. Angelo looked at the old analog clock up on the wall; it was five after nine in the morning. They only had twenty-five minutes to complete the exam.

Angelo tried very hard to concentrate on the quiz, but he had something else on his mind. *What did Carina mean by saying stay away and be careful?* Angelo thought to himself. *She looked so beautiful last night. It couldn't have been a dream, could it?*

Carina, like her mother, had a gift. They both practiced witchcraft. Their father knew all about it, but he didn't want to be a part of it. Daddy told Angelo not to mess with it either. If you don't know what you're doing, you could screw yourself and others up, he said. Angelo didn't believe in it anyway, but now, Angelo thought differently. *She really was a witch. How else could Carina come back?* Angelo kept thinking.

Not too far away, the Railway Butcher was sitting at home, thinking. *It's time to fill my refrigerators,* it thought. But the killer didn't have much desire to slaughter another victim at the time. *Not now. I'm just not ready. I need more time,* the murderer thought, while sitting there in its dark and gloomy basement, alone with two empty refrigerators that were recently full of body parts. Body parts from the poor, unfortunate souls that had fallen prey to its wrath.

Back at the training center, Angelo was upset, he barely passed the quiz. *Sixty-five? That's all I got is a sixty-five?* Angelo thought.

"Hey, Russo!" TSS Jones said in a very commanding voice. "You have to focus. You got the lowest score in the whole class."

Angelo looked embarrassed. He knew the whole class was staring at him.

"I expect you will do better next time, right?"

"Yes, sir," Angelo solemnly replied.

The training instructor spent the rest of the day reviewing the quiz, even showing films of safety situations. Angelo fell asleep during one of the films and was caught by TSS Jones.

"Russo!" the train instructor yelled out. "That's why you got a sixty-five. You sleep at home, Russo, not in my class," the instructor sternly warned him.

At around four o'clock, Train Service Supervisor Jones was wrapping things up.

"Listen up everyone, for tonight's homework assignment, study the first five chapters of the rule book. Tomorrow, we go to fire school. You're all gonna learn how to put out fires. You'll learn the different types of fire extinguishers you could use for each type of fire. You will also learn how to evacuate a train and to bring your passengers to safety. Class dismissed."

Angelo couldn't wait to get back home; he was so tired. There was a lot of information to absorb. Angelo had walked out of the building with the rest of the students. Someone was waiting for him outside by the gate. It was Taylor.

"Hey, you need a lift, Angelo?" Taylor asked him.

"What the hell?!" Angelo screamed out. "Are you stalking me?!"

Some of the other students had turned around to see what the commotion was all about.

"I just thought you were tired and that you needed a lift, that's all," the drag queen conductor innocently replied.

"Well, you thought wrong," Angelo replied as he continued walking home.

Taylor got back into his car and left, feeling embarrassed and hurt.

The next day at fire school, Angelo was having lunch at the

pizza parlor across the street. Tanya, one of his classmates, came over to join him.

"Hey, Russo, what do you think of the class so far?" she asked him.

"I think it's pretty cool," he replied.

Tanya was a pretty, young, African-American girl, but Angelo wasn't really interested in her. Josh, his friend, did say he noticed that Tanya was sweet on him. "You don't have to marry the chick," he had said, "just have some fun with her!" But Angelo only had one thing on his mind right now—becoming a railroad conductor.

Of course, Angelo did have another reason, Carina. Although Carina was gone, he still mourned her. Angelo felt guilty for having sex with his own sister. *I wish she weren't really my sister, I would have married her*, he had thought. Everything changed when she made love to him, but even before that, Angelo had a crush on her. He just wouldn't admit it to her, or himself.

"Are you still with me, Russo?" Tanya asked him.

"Yeah man, I'm here," he replied. "Just thinking to myself," he added.

"I saw you had some trouble yesterday with some girl."

"That was no real girl. That was a drag queen."

"A what?"

"You've never heard of that phrase before?"

"No, I haven't," she replied.

"It means a man who dresses up to look like a woman and wants to be a woman."

"Oh, shit, you mean…"

"Yeah, he's gay and wants to go all the way. I feel like he's stalking me."

"If she or he keeps bothering you, why don't you just go down to the police department and file a restraining order on him?"

"It's a little more complicated than that; he's a conductor."

"Here?"

"Yeah, he works here and I bet he must have some seniority. I'm just a rookie here and I don't want to rock the boat, if you know what I mean?"

"Yeah, I do," Tanya answered.

They finished their pizza and returned back to the fire training safety school. Angelo wished the drag queen conductor would pick on someone else and leave him alone. All he cared about was being a conductor for the railroad. *Maybe if I just tell him I'm not gay he'll go away,* Angelo thought.

It was early Friday morning, September twenty-seventh. Summer had come and gone. TSS Jones was congratulating the entire class.

"Everyone here passed the final exams on troubleshooting mechanical difficulties, track safety, train and passenger safety, and train operation. Again, congratulations, you are all now certified railroad train conductors!"

The whole class happily applauded themselves.

"Ok, ok, now please listen up, listen up everyone!" the

instructor shouted. "This is the last weekend you will have off. You are rookies now and you belong to the system. As soon as you get home, call the crew office for your assignments. The number is right up there on the blackboard. You all will be posting with a trained, seasoned railroad conductor for the next week, then you'll be on your own."

Josh Vincitore, who had gotten close to Angelo, raised his hand with a question.

"Yes, Vincitore, what is it?" TSS Jones asked.

"Sir, I heard that some conductors don't like to take on students, is that true?" Josh asked him.

"Yes, it's true, Vincitore. You're a safety liability to them. If you screw up, they can lose their job. If a conductor refuses to take on students, just ask the dispatcher if you can go out with someone else, that's all."

With that, TSS Jones gave out radio code cards to everyone in the class. There were ten emergency codes on the wallet-sized cards.

"I explained the proper way to use your two-way radios, but these cards will help you remember all the emergency codes. You sign in and out your radio at the terminal every day."

"Any questions?" he asked.

No one said a word. TSS Jones wished everyone good luck, then he dismissed the class.

Angelo got on the next northbound train heading home. Josh Vincitore, his classmate and friend, was with him. The two of them looked like brothers, except Josh had slightly darker blond hair and a larger nose.

"You know, we could almost be twins," Angelo jokingly said.

"Yeah, two pizanos," replied Josh.

The two of them laughed and talked about their training instructor.

"If you screw up, they can lose their job, ha, ha, ha," Angelo laughed while mocking TSS Jones.

They really hit it off, until Josh had to get off at South Park station.

"You live here, Josh?" Angelo asked.

"Yeah," Josh replied.

"Be careful, man."

"Why should I be careful?"

"Because, a girl got killed around here."

"Yeah, I know. 'The Railway Butcher strikes again,'" Josh said jokingly.

"I'm serious! Be careful."

"I don't have to worry, I'm a dude and he only attacks girls, you know."

Josh really played it off, but Angelo was really concerned about him. Josh was his only friend. The train was slowing down as it was entering the South Park station. Angelo said goodbye to his friend, not knowing he would never see him again.

The next morning, Josh Vincitore was found slaughtered at

the very same train station he got off the day before. His throat had been slashed. His face had been destroyed beyond recognition. Josh's kidneys and liver had been removed, leaving his other organs intact. The only thing that had identified him was his new railroad ID pass and badge he had on him. Josh was not robbed, his wallet and cellphone were also left untouched. The police were puzzled, since this was the first male that was murdered in this fashion.

"Now this was definitely a hate crime, it had to be," Chief Brady said.

"This doesn't fit the butcher's MO," said Lieutenant Collins. "For one thing, this was a male victim, unless he's changing his style."

The chief paused for a moment as he thought about the details of the case.

"You're forgetting something," the chief replied. "The victim was found slain at a railroad station, just like the others. I want a full investigation and the medical examiner's report on my desk ASAP, do you hear me, Collins?"

"Yes, sir," Collins replied.

Later on in the day, the lieutenant had decided to pay Angelo Russo a visit. Angelo had come down the stairs to answer the front door thinking, *who could be ringing my doorbell on a Saturday afternoon?* When he got downstairs, Angelo saw the lieutenant through the sidelight window. *Oh, no,* he thought. *What could he possibly want now?* Angelo hesitantly opened the door.

"Good afternoon, Mr. Russo. May I come in?" Collins asked.

"Sure Mr. Lieutenant, you come on in," Angelo hesitantly replied.

Collins came in and took off his hat as he towered over Angelo.

"Did you find my sister's killer yet?"

"No, and that's not why I'm here, Mr. Russo."

"Then, what's up?"

"I guess you haven't heard then?"

"Heard what?"

"One of your railroad classmates was murdered yesterday," the lieutenant stated.

"What? Who?" Angelo nervously asked him.

"Josh Vincitore," the lieutenant replied.

"No! No! It can't be!"

Angelo was so shocked, he started sliding down the wall he was leaning on and tears welled up in his eyes.

"I'm sorry, Mr. Russo," the lieutenant said with genuine sympathy. "I heard you boys were pretty tight."

"We, we were all going to get together tonight, to celebrate our..."

Angelo couldn't talk anymore; he just sat on the floor and moaned.

"Mr. Russo, will you please get yourself together."

Angelo looked up at the man, wishing he weren't there at all, wishing he would just go and leave him alone to grieve. But the detective *was* there and Collins wasn't leaving until he got some answers.

"I'd like to ask you some questions," the lieutenant stated as he pulled out his little notebook.

One by one, Lieutenant Collins rattled off questions to Angelo Russo.

"Do you know who might have done this to him? Did he have any enemies in training school? Was there any animosity toward him from anyone that you know of?"

"No. Not that I know of," Angelo barely said.

"Ok, I can see you're upset, so I'll leave you for now. Here's my card again. If you remember anything, please give me a call, Mr. Russo."

"Ok, I will," Angelo replied.

With that, the lieutenant let himself out and closed the door behind him. Angelo's cellphone started ringing in his pocket. He tried to pull himself together to answer it, wondering who it could be. Angelo looked at the display screen on his smartphone; it was Mrs. Vincitore. He pressed the send button on his phone to answer it.

"Hello," Angelo uttered softly.

"Hello, Angelo?" Mrs. Vincitore asked him.

"Yes, it's me."

"This is Mrs. Vincitore, Josh's mother. I'm sure you heard by now what, what…"

She broke off crying and desperately tried to regain her composure.

"I'm so, so sorry, Mrs. Vincitore," Angelo solemnly said. "He was my best friend."

"I know. Josh spoke very highly of you, Angelo. He was my only child, did you know that?"

"Yes, yes I did."

"Listen, all of his family members, friends, and railroad classmates are going to get together tonight for a candlelight vigil. Would you like to come?"

"Where is it going to be, Mrs. Vincitore?"

"It'll be where he was murdered, the South Park train station."

Angelo had warned Josh about that station. He recalled telling him to be careful around there, but he obviously didn't heed his warning.

"Will you please be there tonight at eight o'clock, Angelo?"

Angelo wondered what good it would do. Angelo knew nothing they did could bring Josh back again, but he had to pay his respects to Josh. Angelo had to go.

"It would sure mean a lot to us all," Mrs. Vincitore added.

"Sh-sure, Mrs. Vincitore, I'll be there."

Angelo said goodbye to Mrs. Vincitore and hung up the phone. He wondered why. *Why did this happen? Who would be next?* Angelo thought and pondered. *What if I'm next?*

6

A REVELATION

Over three weeks had passed. It was now mid-October. Autumn was in full session with all of its colorful foliage. There were leaves everywhere. The police department thought they had another killer on their hands. Josh Vincitore's death did not completely fit the pattern of the other victims. The medical examiner couldn't be one hundred percent certain in connecting his death with any of the others. The main difference was that this victim was a male. The others were all female. But he wasn't ready to rule out the butcher, in any case. One thing was for sure, the chief had said, the way his face was sliced apart, this was definitely a hate crime. Somebody had it in for him. Josh was the youngest victim. He was only twenty-two years old.

Angelo had just finished cutting the grass and picking up the leaves in his yard. He was getting ready for his dinner date tonight. Angelo had invited Tanya Wright, his former classmate, over to dinner. It was Tuesday afternoon and both of them were off Tuesday and Wednesday this week. After finally getting himself back together again, it was time to unwind. He had been working real hard doing plenty of overtime. Angelo was working six days a week and sometimes doing double shifts, just to keep his mind off of Josh's death. He did need the money to pay the bills, but the real reason was to keep him occupied.

It was starting to get dark out. Angelo looked at his phone and noticed it was six o'clock. He went inside to take a shower. Tanya was coming over at seven, which left him an hour to shower. Angelo also needed time to re-heat the large pepperoni pizza he had picked up earlier.

A little while later, Tanya was pulling up in Angelo's long driveway. She was driving a red four-door sedan. It was an old, worn-out car that spent more time in the repair shop than being out on the road. Tanya was saving up for a new car; she liked the Nissans, but for now, this was all she could afford.

Tanya had straightened up her hair. She also painstakingly applied just the right amount of makeup to her pretty young face. The young lady was looking very hot. She was wearing a brand-new pink dress that was tight enough to accentuate her hourglass figure.

Tanya didn't wear a bra tonight. Her nipples were popping right out of her sheer dress as the cool autumn breeze hit them. She wanted to look sexy for Angelo. Tanya had a crush on him since they were in class together at the railroad training center. The young lady checked out her surroundings and was very impressed by Angelo's two-story colonial house and finely trimmed lawn. *Nice piece of property*, she thought. *He even has a two-car garage. I can't believe Angelo lives here all by himself.* Tanya began to daydream. *I sure could get used to living here with him. A fine, sexy young man and a nice ass house,* Tanya kept thinking to herself. *This sure is nicer than that cramped apartment in the city we live in.* Tanya was tired of living with her parents. She was twenty-three years old, had a great job with the railroad, and was ready to start her own life, a life she now wanted with Angelo. The problem was her parents. Tanya's parents, especially her father, were not happy about her hanging out with a white boy. "He's gonna use you and throw your ass away when he's done with you, mark my words," her father had told her.

What Tanya didn't realize was that Angelo's inquisitive next-door neighbor was watching her through the venetian blinds. Tanya rang Angelo's doorbell. Angelo opened the door and gave her a wolf whistle.

"Boy, someone looks real fine tonight," he said.

Tanya blushed and gave him a hug.

"You didn't have to go through all that," Angelo said to her. "We're just gonna hang out, that's all."

"You don't like the way I look?" she asked.

"Well, of course I do, we're friends, remember?"

Tanya looked disappointed, she was hoping for something a little more than just friendship with him.

"Aren't you going to invite me in?" Tanya asked.

"Sure, I'm sorry. Come on in."

Angelo ushered her into the foyer and closed the door behind her. After talking for a bit, they had their pizza dinner in the kitchen. Then, the two of them sat down together on the sofa in the family room.

"Wow!" she exclaimed. "This is really nice!"

"Thank you," he replied.

"Man! You even have a fireplace and everything. I still can't believe you live here all by yourself."

"Yeah, but I'd trade it all away if I could have my family back."

They talked about Josh. Angelo brought up that Josh was only a year older than him. Tanya moved closer to him on the sofa to console him. She gave him a hug. Tanya pulled away to gaze into his green eyes. Then, she pulled him close to kiss his lips, but Angelo turned away.

"What's wrong?" Tanya sadly asked.

She was on the verge of tears.

"Is it because I'm black?" Tanya asked.

"No! No!" he replied defensively.

"I, I'm just not ready for a romantic relationship right now. Can't we just be friends for now?" he pleaded. "Please?"

"You don't even want to have sex with me, Angelo?"

"I just think it'll ruin what we have right now, that's all. Look, you're very pretty and smoking hot, but I'm just not ready yet. I really don't want to take advantage of you. You deserve better than that, Tanya," he added.

She got all teared up and gave him a big kiss on the forehead. *Boy, what a gentleman,* she thought. Soon they were just talking and laughing again about their adventures on the job.

Time was flying by and neither one of them seemed to care.

"Gee, I wonder what time it is." Tanya said as she looked at her phone in horror.

It was 12:40 a.m. There were three texts from her parents there on her smartphone: one from her mom and two from her dad. They were both worried. She had her phone on vibrate and since it was in her bag, Tanya never heard it.

"Oh, my God, I got to go!" she exclaimed.

"What time is it, Tanya?" Angelo asked her.

"It's 12:40 and my parents are livid. I told them I'd be home by eleven."

"How long does it take you to get home?" he asked.

"If I take the expressway, I can get home by 1:10. I should send them a text to let them know I'm all right, but they're probably sleeping by now. I should just go."

"Come, I'll take you through the garage."

Angelo took the girl down the stairs, through the basement, and into the garage.

"You really don't have a car, do you?" she asked.

"No, I don't. I walk to the train station and the supermarket is near there also. My parents had an SUV; they died in it when they got in an accident. I guess now I can save up for a car."

Angelo opened up the garage door and put on the outside lights for her. Then, he noticed her car.

"Hey! Nice ride!"

"Yeah, right, that's my hoopty."

"Hoopty? What's a hoopty?"

She laughed and then explained that it was just a raggedy, old car.

"At least you have wheels, Tanya, I don't."

He kissed her goodbye on the cheek, then he walked Tanya to her car.

"Hey, maybe someday we can go to Martha's Vineyard or even Cape Cod?" Angelo asked her.

"I'd like that," she replied.

Tanya started her old car and warmed it up. Angelo hoped she wouldn't get in trouble with her folks. Tanya gave him a goodbye kiss on his lips; this time, Angelo didn't turn away. It was the first girl he had kissed since Carina. He told her to get home safe and then he watched her leave down the driveway.

Tanya went down the road and got on the expressway, not knowing she was being followed. Angelo went back upstairs after closing the garage door. Again, he heard Carina call to him.

"A-n-g-e-l-o," her haunting voice called. "A-n-g-e-l-o."

Angelo went back to Carina's bedroom. This time, she was fully clothed. Carina was wearing the same exact clothes she wore the last time he'd seen her alive. Carina's spirit was sitting up on her bed calling to him.

"I've seen your friend, Angelo," she said in her ghostly voice. "Are you going to marry her?"

"No," he said. "There can only be one woman for me. You! If we weren't brother and sister, I would have married you, Carina."

"You need to move on; I'm not a part of your world anymore."

"I can't. I love you, Carina. I just feel so guilty having sex with you. Why did you force yourself upon me?" he solemnly asked her spirit. "I forgive you and I wish you were truly here with me," Angelo tearfully said.

"I have a revelation to share with you, Angelo."

"What is it, sis?"

"I'm not really your sister."

"What are you saying, Carina, of course you were."

"Look in Mom's wall safe in her room."

"A wall safe? What wall safe?" Angelo asked.

"It's just behind her painting in her bedroom."

Angelo didn't even know his parents kept a safe. If he found it, how would he even open it up?

"A-n-g-e-l-o. Your friend."

"My friend?"

"Your girlfriend is in trouble."

"Yes, I know. She's in trouble with her folks."

"No! She's in real trouble."

"What do you mean, Carina? What kind of trouble? Is she in danger?"

"I have to go."

"Wait!"

"I love you, Angelo."

"I love you, too."

"I'll always love you, but you have to move on," her ghost added.

Then, she started to fade away.

"Wait, come back!"

He went to reach for her, but she disappeared.

"Come back to me!" he cried out.

Carina was gone, again. He sobbed on her bed, wishing she never left. Wishing she were still alive. Angelo cried himself to sleep on Carina's bed.

Back on the expressway, a strange vehicle had been tailing Tanya. She noticed the high beam headlights in her rear-view mirror, getting closer and closer. *Why is this guy up my butt? I'm doing the speed limit,* she thought to herself. Tanya accelerated her car to seventy miles per hour, but the big, black Ford pickup truck was revving its engine and closing in on her. She went into the other lane, but to no avail. The truck followed her every move, pushing her faster and faster. Soon, they were both doing close to a hundred miles per hour. The red engine warning light was illuminated in Tanya's dashboard. Her engine was overheating. *Oh, no,* she thought. *He's out to get me, but why? What did I do to him? Lord, please help me!* They went faster and faster. Tanya and the stranger were the only ones out on the road at that time of the night. Tanya's engine was failing. Smoke began billowing out from under her hood as her car was slowing down. The stranger finally went around her. They were going neck and neck, then, the truck side-swiped her. Tanya started crying as the smoke just poured out of her engine compartment. She tried to regain control, but the truck slammed into her again. This time, Tanya was pushed over the guard rail. Her car was thrown down off the overpass, and over a hundred feet down to the road below. She died instantly.

The next morning, Angelo was woken up by the sound of the front doorbell. He got himself together and went downstairs to answer it. Angelo looked out the sidelight window to see who it was. When he saw the middle-aged African-American couple outside, Angelo immediately thought it was the Jehovah's Witnesses again.

"Who is it?" he asked.

"We're Mr. and Mrs. Wright, Tanya's parents," answered Mr. Wright.

Angelo opened the door.

"You Angelo Russo?" the big, husky man asked, as he got up in Angelo's face.

"Yes, I am."

"Where's my daughter?" Mr. Wright angrily asked.

"I don't know," Angelo replied.

"Wrong answer," he said as he grabbed Angelo by the shirt.

Angelo was getting nervous; he wasn't very good at confrontations and Mr. Wright was furious.

"You know something, I done told ma baby daughter about you damn white boys just wanting to use her, but she just wouldn't listen," he angrily said while staring down into Angelo's eyes. "Give me one good reason why I shouldn't just kick your ass right now?!" Mr. Wright shouted as he towered over Angelo.

"Ben! Stop it!" Martha Wright told her husband. "I think he's telling the truth," she added.

"Is you, boy?"

"Yes, s-sir, Mr. Wright, I am," Angelo stammered.

"She was here with you yesterday, right?" Ben asked as he released Angelo's shirt.

"Yes, sir. She came by at seven last night," he nervously added. "We had dinner and talked. Nothing happened between us, Mr. Wright, I swear."

"What time did she leave?" Ben asked him.

"It was around one o'clock when she left. I'm sorry; we just got to talking and didn't realize how late it was, sir."

"We sent her three texts and she never replied," Mr. Wright told him.

"I know, Tanya had told me that you were worried," Angelo said.

"We just want our daughter back, that's all," Mrs. Wright added.

"I understand," replied Angelo.

Suddenly, another car was pulling up in Angelo's driveway. It was Lieutenant Collins. They all watched as he got out of the car.

"Good morning there Mr. Russo," the lieutenant said.

"Good morning Mr. Lieutenant Collins," Angelo replied.

"Oh, I see you finally remembered my name, Mr. Russo."

"Did you say, 'Lieutenant?'" Mr. Wright asked.

"Yes, I'm Lieutenant Collins. I'm with the Morton Town Police Department. Are you two Mr. and Mrs. Wright?"

Yes, we are," Martha Wright fearfully answered, expecting bad news.

The lieutenant took his hat off and gave them a sorrowful look.

"Did you find my daughter, Lieutenant?" Mrs. Wright asked him.

"Yes, ma'am, we did. We found her car upside-down under the overpass on I-90," the lieutenant gravely responded.

"Oh, my God!" she exclaimed in shock.

"Is she all right?" Ben Wright asked.

"I'm afraid not, she was pronounced dead on the scene. I'm sorry," Collins added. "I came to tell you first, but you weren't home."

By now, Angelo felt guilty, thinking it was partially his fault. Carina's ghost was right; Tanya was in trouble.

"Oh, no! Not my baby! My baby!" Martha Wright kept saying while she cried.

"What happened to her?! How did it happen?!" Ben Wright asked.

"We initially thought she fell asleep at the wheel, but then we found some scrape marks with black paint on the driver's side of her car. It looks like she was run off the road at high speed."

"Oh, my God," Mr. Wright gravely said.

"Do any of you know if she had any enemies?" the lieutenant asked them.

"Not that I know of," Ben replied.

"What about you, Russo? Did she have any enemies in training, or on the job?"

"No, Mr. Collins, she was well-liked, as far as I know," Angelo replied.

Tanya's parents left with the lieutenant as Angelo went back inside his home, feeling all alone. *Everyone that gets close to me, gets killed,* he thought to himself. Tears welled up in his eyes as he looked at his sofa, the same sofa that he and Tanya shared just a few short hours ago. *I should have listened to Carina,* he thought. *But what was all that nonsense about her not being my sister?* Angelo remembered something else she said. Carina said there was a wall safe in their parents' bedroom.

Angelo made his way upstairs to his parents' room. He opened the door and looked for the portrait. Angelo went inside the room. There on the right wall hung a large painting of his mother. The painting was very old. It depicted her as a young teenager in a field of flowers. Angelo carefully lifted the painting off its hook. Low and behold, there was a gray wall safe behind it. *I never knew they had a safe,* Angelo thought. *This is something like in one of those old movies, but how can I open it?*

It was now two o'clock in the afternoon. Angelo had been in his parents' room for over an hour trying to open the safe, with no success at all. Angelo was ready to call it quits until he remembered how forgetful his mother was. Jenny Russo was always writing things down in her little notebook that she kept in her purse. After the accident, the police gave him all of his parents' belongings. Angelo looked in their dresser drawers where he put all of their belongings. Angelo found his mother's purse just where he had put it after the accident. Inside were house keys, makeup, a change purse, tissues, and a small pink notebook. Angelo opened the book and started to read it. Most of the information in it were people's names and addresses. There were doctor appointments and to-do lists. Finally, he came across some random alpha numeric numbers. 24L 3X, 76R 2X, 12L 1X. *That's got to be the combination; what else could it be?* Angelo thought.

Angelo tried the numbers on the wall safe after he set it to zero. Twenty-four left three times, seventy-six right two times, then he turned the dial to twelve left one time. Angelo pulled on the dial and then the door opened. Inside there were two envelopes and some jewelry. He opened one of the envelopes and found a large sum of money. After counting it, Angelo realized he had over five thousand dollars at his disposal. *This would definitely come in handy to pay the bills,* he happily thought to himself. Angelo also considered selling the jewelry in the safe, but not now. The money is more than he needed to get some big bills out of the way. For one thing, the school tax was due and then the property tax would come next. There was also one other bill he forgot about: the house fire insurance, which was due in three weeks. *It's not easy being a homeowner. You never really own your own home, even after the mortgage is paid in full,* thought Angelo. But he was lucky his parents had paid off the mortgage on the house, the young man would not be able to afford it on his salary alone.

There was one more envelope left in the wall safe and it was sealed. Angelo reluctantly opened it, afraid of what he might find. *I have a revelation to share with you, Angelo. I'm not really your sister,* he remembered his sister's spirit telling him. Angelo unfolded the papers in his hand and began to read them. The papers were from an adoption agency; they were dated twenty-one years ago. The documents were all about the adoption of a male baby boy. Angelo was that boy.

"Oh, my God, no; I was adopted!" he exclaimed in horror.

Angelo collapsed on his parents' bed, clutching the adoption papers in his hands. Tears started to well up in his eyes.

"All this time! All this time and they never said anything to me! Why? Why didn't they tell me? Oh, Lord, why didn't they tell me? Carina knew. Carina knew all along," he said as he wept on the bed.

7

THE BUTCHER'S REVENGE

Police Chief Brady had just devised a plan to trap the Railway Butcher. The chief wanted an undercover female police officer to pose as a passenger on a night train. She was to get off at different stops in the evening. The officer would be riding the trains undercover for at least a week. She would also be fitted with a hidden communicator and recorder.

The chief called in Officer Rivera. Kathy Rivera had been with the force for over three years and was no stranger to the covert operations. She was also the most attractive woman on the force. Kathy had a very shapely build and was on the tall side. Her long, light brown hair had a nice shine that would catch the sun. Kathy also had deep blue eyes. Being an attractive female on the police force was not easy for her. She constantly had all the men hitting on her. Now, after three long years, the men had finally come to respect her. Officer Rivera went into the chief's office, not knowing what was in store for her. Chief Brady filled her in on the assignment. Officer Rivera was not pleased at all.

"Why does it have to be me? Why not Avila or Cho?" she asked.

"Because you are the most attractive woman on the force and that's what our killer likes. You're also the most experienced here with underground operations," the chief replied.

"But you're sending me on a suicide mission. You know that, don't you?"

"Look, Rivera. You'll be wearing a wire, and we'll have men stationed nearby listening in. But I got to tell you this, you can't be armed."

"Are you for real? Why?"

"Because, I don't want you to blow your damn cover. If the butcher even suspects that you're packing a piece, he'll flee."

"I don't like it, I don't like it one bit, Chief."

"Like it or not, this *is* your assignment, Rivera, and you *will* follow orders! Do your job and it'll be all right!" Brady bellowed. "Now, go see Ritter at the end of the hall, so he can outfit you for the job tonight. You're dismissed, Rivera."

With that, Officer Rivera went over to get wired up for tonight. She wasn't happy about it, but she didn't have a choice in the matter. Kathy really wanted to carry her service pistol with her; she would have felt a little safer with it, but the chief advised her against it. *Shit! It's not fair,* Rivera thought.

Angelo had woken up in his parents' bedroom, with the adoption papers still in his hand. He thought it was all a dream, until the young man looked at the papers he'd been holding. Angelo felt like his whole life was just a lie. The only good thing was he no longer felt guilty about screwing his sister. *Carina was never really my sister, at all,* he thought to himself. *We grew up together, but that was it.*

Today was Thursday. Angelo Russo had remembered that he had to go to work today. His two days off had gone by so fast. So much had happened. So much had changed. *Who am I really? Who are my real parents? Will I ever find out?* He had pondered all of these questions and more. Angelo put everything back in the safe, except for the money; he was going to drop it off at the bank on his way to work.

Angelo went to his room and opened his black work bag to look at his schedule for today. Angelo noticed that he had to be in at Morton City terminal at three p.m. This was an evening shift that would last until eleven p.m. *Man, it's tough being a rookie,* Angelo thought. *I ain't getting home until twelve forty-five at night, or later. Shit!* He looked at the clock on the wall. It was now eleven twenty. Angelo thought about leaving home at twelve thirty, that would give him time to go to the bank. The young man went to the bathroom to take a shower. Then, he had a bowl of cereal, wishing it were ham and eggs, the way Carina would make it. Angelo stayed in his underwear until the last minute. He didn't want to put on his uniform until it was almost time to leave.

A few hours later in the evening, Angelo was onboard a northbound train punching tickets. When he got to Officer Rivera, she flashed her badge and photo ID at him.

"Hey conductor, have you seen any suspicious characters on board?" she softly asked him.

"No, not yet," Angelo quietly replied. "But nothing for nothing, I think you're much too pretty to be a cop. I thought you were a model or something."

"A model, like your sister was? No thank you, look where it got her."

Rivera saw the sad expression form on his face.

"I'm sorry, that was uncalled for," Kathy replied.

"You seem to know a lot about me, Officer."

"I try to make it a point to completely familiarize myself with any case I'm working on."

"Am I the case you're currently working on?"

"Let's just say, you're a small part of it. Is this your regular run, Mr. Russo?"

"No, I work the extra list. I'm a rookie. I thought you knew that."

"Mr. Russo, I'm just trying to establish what interval you usually work on, that's all. Now, I need you to keep working so you don't blow my cover."

"Ok, Officer. I can take a hint. Tickets, please!" Angelo said aloud, as he walked down the aisle of the railcar.

Officer Rivera watched as Angelo walked away. *He really is cute,* she thought. *He's got a nice little ass, too.* A middle-aged balding man asked her if the seat next to her was taken. She knew where this was going. *Why would he want to sit next to me, when there are plenty of other seats available on this train?* The man didn't fit the profile of her suspect. For one thing, he had a wedding band on his finger. The last thing she needed now was another man hitting on her, especially a married man.

"I'm waiting for my friend to return back from the restroom," Kathy replied.

The man turned and walked away. Officer Rivera thought she'd keep an eye on him, just in case. Rivera noticed another person staring at her and she decided to make her move. Officer Rivera quietly announced on her radio that she was getting off at the next stop.

"Next stop, Rockaway Circle," Angelo announced over the train's public address system.

The officer got up and started making her way toward the front of the car. The train started slowing down as it was pulling into the station. After the train had stopped, Officer Rivera left through one of the opening doors.

Officer Kathy Rivera looked around as she walked down the platform. The train started pulling out of the station, making a lot of noise in the process. This particular train had slow-releasing brakes that squealed as it took off again. Kathy looked at her watch and noticed it was ten after nine. It was dark outside. She started to inform her superiors of her whereabouts over her wire.

All of a sudden, a stranger snuck up behind Officer Rivera and subdued her. The butcher was choking her with a rope around her neck. She desperately tried to break free, but her assailant was way too strong for her. She was gasping for some air. Kathy finally collapsed in front of her attacker, onto the cold concrete platform. The butcher released her, then it noticed something shiny protruding from Kathy's black jacket. It was her police badge.

"The bitch is a cop and I've seen her around," her assaulter said in a low gravelly voice.

Officer Rivera started to open up her eyes as she slowly regained consciousness.

"You? I know you," Kathy barely said, while she gasped for air.

"Not for long, bitch."

With that remark, the butcher sliced open her pretty little throat. Officer Rivera laid there gasping for oxygen and losing blood fast. The killer ripped open her shirt and began slicing her open with a cold stainless-steel knife. One cut after another, showing no mercy at all. Kathy was in so much agony, but she couldn't scream. Her assailant relentlessly slashed her over and over again out of pure hatred, spilling her blood everywhere. Then, the slaughterer took a special souvenir.

"I hate female cops; they think they're hot shit. Die, bitch, die!" it said to the dying police officer.

A police car was now approaching with flashing lights. The butcher ran for its life, just barely escaping. Officer Paul Flanigan arrived at the scene and got on his police radio. Kathy Rivera was barely alive.

"All units, attention all units! Officer down, officer down!" Flanigan shouted over the radio. "Stay with me, Rivera! Stay with me!" Flanigan told the dying officer as he held her in his arms. "Stay with me! Look at me, Rivera! Who did this to you?"

But Kathy couldn't survive any longer. Her wounds were way too extensive. Officer Kathy Rivera closed her eyes and passed away right in Officer Flanigan's arms. She was only twenty-five years old. Rivera had her whole life ahead of her. She didn't deserve to die so young.

Officer Kathy Rivera did bring a small, personal hand gun with her. She always kept one hidden in her boot, but Kathy never got a chance to use it. Her attacker had spotted the gun sticking out of her boot and had taken it. *This may come in very handy,* the killer had thought.

Officer Paul Flanigan was with the force for only a year and a half. The twenty-five-year-old Irish male had never seen anyone die before him, up until now. His bright red hair looked astray as he sobbed over Kathy's body. The officer felt so helpless. He wished he could have gotten to her sooner. *I could have saved her,* he thought, as he held her limp body close to himself. Officer Flanigan really did have feelings for her, but he was always afraid to ask her out. Now, it was too late. *I must avenge her death. Mark my words, I will find you,* the officer was thinking to himself. *You better hope someone else finds you, because if I find you first, I'll kill you.*

Angelo was "deadheading" back home on the last train back, which meant he was riding as a passenger instead of operating the train. When the train stopped at Rockaway Circle, Angelo noticed all of the police presence at the station. *I wonder what happened. What's all the commotion for?* his mind started reeling. *I hope nobody else got killed.* The train started to move again. Angelo only had a few more stops to go. He was tired and just wanted to get home and go right to bed. After a while, the train was approaching Angelo's stop.

"The next stop is Morton Town. Please exit in the first two cars only," the conductor shouted right over the train's public address system.

Angelo got himself up and then started heading to the front of the train. He spotted one of his classmates, James Mitchel, riding in the front.

"Hey, Mitchel! What's up?" Angelo asked him.

"I'm going home," Mitchel replied.

"Yeah, so am I. This is my stop, man. Hey, maybe we could hang out together someday."

"Cool man, cool," said Mitchel.

"All right, take it light," Angelo said as he waited for the conductor to open the doors.

Angelo started walking down the platform, down the stairs, and onto the street below. He looked at his phone and noticed it was almost one in the morning. The weather had become cooler than it was when he started work in the afternoon. It was also pitch-black outside and for the first time in his life, Angelo was fearful walking at night. He knew now that no one was safe here anymore. Women weren't the only ones being murdered any longer. His best friend, Josh, was evidence of that. It was a horrible feeling for him to be constantly looking around and over his shoulders while walking. Angelo nervously started walking faster. *Got to get home,* he thought. *Got to get home quick!*

Finally, Angelo arrived at his driveway. He walked right up the one-hundred-foot-long driveway. Then, he went up the pathway steps and to his front door. The wind was so strong, it snapped a branch from a tree and sent it crashing down in front of him. Angelo was so terrified that he dropped his house keys.

"Shit!" He yelled out. "I'll never find them now!"

Angelo reached into his black laptop bag. He purchased the bag to keep his work papers and tools together. Angelo also carried his lunch in it. Everyone on the job carried a bag for work-related items. He sifted through his overtime forms, train keys, and finally, Angelo found what he was looking for—his flashlight. Angelo shined his flashlight down on the lawn, frantically looking for his keys. He searched and searched, but found nothing. The man was getting desperate. A big storm was approaching. Lightning had struck and illuminated something shiny in the bushes.

"My keys!" Angelo screamed out.

Soon, it began to rain. Angelo ran right over to the bushes with his flashlight on, desperately looking for his keys.

"I found them, all right!" he exclaimed victoriously.

The rain was coming down harder now. Angelo was getting drenched. The young man knew he had to get inside quick before he got sick. Angelo grabbed his keys and ran back up to the front door steps. He unlocked his door, opened it, and quickly ran inside, closing the front door behind him.

Back over at the police precinct, Chief Brady was feeling extremely guilty. He knew the killer took out a personal vendetta on Officer Kathy Rivera. Her body was so bloodily torn up that anyone could tell it was done out of pure hatred for her. *Poor girl*, he thought. The chief had sent Collins over to inform her parents of her demise.

The butcher had taken its revenge on the police force. *He's one pissed off puppy,* the chief thought. *He sure knows how to hold a grudge.* Officer Kathy Rivera's right hand had been removed from her, probably as a souvenir. Brady kept thinking about it. He felt responsible for what had happened to Rivera. *The butcher even bent Officer Rivera's badge and placed it in a pool of her own blood,* the chief remembered.

Angelo had just come out of the shower and was getting ready for bed. The October storm was really hitting solid. The rain was coming down so hard, it almost sounded like sleet. The young man was wondering how he was going to sleep with all that noise. Lightning flashed through his window, casting an eerie shadow around him. Thunder followed shortly after, making him wish he weren't all alone. Suddenly, right there in front of him appeared an all too familiar apparition. Angelo's sister was standing there with open arms, wearing absolutely nothing. Angelo now believed that Carina was a perfect example of ageless, timeless beauty. *Too bad she isn't real,* he thought.

"Are you still mad at me, little brother?" Carina asked in her ghostly voice.

"No," he replied. "I could never be mad at you. I love you."

Angelo went over to her. He wanted desperately to hold her in his arms again, but when he reached for her, Carina simply just disappeared. Tears began to well up in his eyes again, as he realized she is nothing more than a spirit. *Carina is not among the living anymore…I must realize that…and move on,* Angelo sadly thought to himself.

Angelo became depressed again, but he was also very tired. He could have slept in any room he wanted. It was a big house, much too large for any single person. Out of habit and of pure comfort, Angelo went to his own bed, in his own little room.

The storm made it quite difficult for Angelo to fall asleep. When Angelo finally succumbed to slumber, his mind raced into a very chaotic state. He had visions of all of the terrible things that recently happened to him.

There were scenes of his parents' death, Carina's death, Josh, and Tanya. Then, he had an additional nightmare of the drag queen conductor chasing him. Angelo woke up in the middle of the night, hyperventilating and in a cold sweat.

"What the hell?!" he screamed out loud. "Man, what a fricking nightmare."

Angelo went to relieve himself in the bathroom and returned to bed to go back to sleep. This time, his mind was clear. Angelo finally got the restful night sleep he was longing for. Sweet dreams…for now.

The storm had knocked out all of the nearby power lines, rendering Angelo's home completely dark. He was lucky it wasn't too cold outside or inside his house. Angelo was also lucky that his alarm clock ran on batteries and not on electric. Unbeknownst to him, Carina was keeping a watchful eye over Angelo as he slept. She wanted to help him, but there was only so much that she could do. Angelo was in such a deep sleep; he began to snore.

The storm was relentless and showed no sign of easing up. The emergency electrical crews were out trying to restore service for everyone affected in the area. Trees were down, along with any nearby power lines. There was flooding in many areas.

Not too far away, the butcher was in the basement looking at its two refrigerators, worrying about the power outage.

"My parts! My body parts will spoil! Must have electricity," the killer said to itself.

The Railway Butcher was concerned about the body parts it had recently collected. Without electricity, its precious collection of human body parts would all be ruined. All of a sudden, the power was restored to the slayer's home.

"Right on!" the killer shouted. "I'm going to have to invest in an emergency standby generator."

The butcher went over to a mannequin it had in the corner of its basement. The mannequin was wearing a scalped head of black hair that had once belonged to Daphne Greenberg. The butcher stared at the lifeless head.

"She had the best pair of tits I ever laid my eyes on," the slaughterer said.

Angelo Russo was just waking up to the beeping sound of his battery-operated alarm clock. It was nine a.m. He looked around and noticed his night light was off. *Must have burned out*, he thought. Angelo reached for his TV remote. *I want to check out the news before I get ready for work*, he thought to himself. Angelo pointed the remote to the television set he had on his dresser and pressed the power button, but nothing happened.

"What the hell?!" he shouted. "I paid the bills. What's up?"

Angelo got up to put his stereo on and noticed it too didn't work. After going to the wall and flipping on the light switch with no results, he determined the power was out. Without power, there was no hot water to bathe in. Actually, Angelo knew there was no water available to him at all. His house had well water, instead of town water. Without electricity, there was no power to run his underground water pump.

"What the hell am I going to do?" he said aloud to no one's ears. "I've got to get ready for work! I can't even cook breakfast. The stove's electric. Shit!"

Within a moment, the power came back on. His prayers were answered.

"All right!" he shouted.

At one forty p.m., Angelo left for work. He liked walking around the streets in his uniform, at least, in broad daylight. It made him feel important. The conductor he was covering for was going to be out for a week. Angelo found out the man was on vacation. It was nice outside. The sun was shining with just a little brisk breeze occasionally blowing.

The southbound train was arriving at the Morton Town train station. Angelo quickly ran up the stairs to catch the train. He reached for his railroad ID after getting on board. Angelo grabbed a seat and waited for the conductor to come around. The locomotive revved its engines back up and began to move again. *It sure is nice to ride for free,* he thought. *Who needs a car when I get to ride for free?* The conductor came around to check tickets and Angelo recognized him immediately.

"Hey, Mitchel! What's up?" Angelo asked the conductor.

"Yo, Angelo! Where are you heading off to?" Mitchel replied.

"I'm deadheading down to the city to pick up that evening job that starts at three p.m."

"Yeah, I know which one. The guy is on vacation. I got this run just for today. The dude's coming back tomorrow."

"Cool! I guess you don't need to see my train pass," Angelo laughingly said.

"Nah! But you do have it with you, right?"

"Yeah I do, here it is," Angelo proudly displayed it to Mitchel.

"Hey, did you hear what happened last night?" Mitchel asked.

"Yeah, the freak storm had knocked out everyone's juice."

"Besides the storm, there was another murder."

"No shit? Is that why all the cop cars were out at Rockaway Circle last night?"

"Yup. And you'll never guess who the victim was."

"Who?" Angelo asked.

"A police officer."

"What?! A cop?!"

"Yup, a female cop. She was sliced and diced."

"Man, that's ballsy. I wouldn't wanna be in his shoes when the cops catch him."

"Oh, yeah. They're on a witch hunt for his ass now, that's for sure," Mitchel replied.

"Wait, there was a beautiful cop on my train yesterday; she was undercover."

"Did she have long, light brown hair and looked like a fashion model?"

"Yeah! Her name was Rivera."

"That was her."

"Oh, man, what a damn waste. She was so gorgeous," Angelo said sorrowfully.

"Listen, I'd like to chat some more, but I've got to get back to work. Here's my number, give me a call someday," Mitchel said as he handed Angelo a business card that read: *Mitchel's Car Audio Installations (800) 555-2424.*

"Wow! You've got your own business on the side?"

"Yeah, I install car stereos on the side, spread the word."

"Ok, cool," Angelo told him.

Mitchel left Angelo and proceeded to check the passengers' tickets. He was also checking out the female passengers, but none of them seemed interested in him. Angelo thought that if Mitchel lost weight, he'd have a better shot at them. The man looked like he weighed close to three hundred pounds. Mitchel barely passed the physical exam.

Mitchel always had trouble climbing up and down on the trains in the yard. He at least looked decent with a full head of black hair neatly trimmed and combed. The man had soft brown eyes and was always clean shaven. Mitchel was on the short side, which made him look even heavier. Angelo was considering giving him a call later on. Mitchel was cool. He was also one of the brightest pupils in the class, with a nice personality. Almost everyone had asked him for help before taking an exam.

Shortly after, the train was now going through the tunnel. It was only a matter of time before they arrived in the city. Angelo kept thinking about the female cop. *I was just talking to her yesterday*, he thought to himself. *What a waste; she was gorgeous.*

⁂

Back at the police precinct, Chief Brady was consulting with Lieutenant Collins.

"I want this guy's ass, Collins! You hear me?"

"We all do, Chief, but it's not that easy. The son of a bitch leaves no trace. No trace at all!"

"I know. Forensics hasn't come up with any shit yet! They just don't have anything concrete to nail this bastard or bitch."

"You still think it could be a female?"

"Like I said before, Collins, we can't assume anything. Women are just as capable as men are when it comes to murder."

"I hear you, boss."

"Well, one thing's for certain, Collins, the killer's gonna slip up sooner or later. They always do and when that happens, we'll be right there to crucify this monster. He or she has got to pay for what the hell it did to Officer Rivera and everyone else."

"You got any more plans, Chief?"

"I'm working on it, Collins. I'm working on it real hard."

Collins had stepped out of Chief Brady's office. He knew everyone on the force wanted this serial killer caught ASAP. He could still see Mrs. Rivera falling apart in front of him, as he informed her of her daughter's death. She had collapsed in his arms, hysterically crying. *No! Not my baby. She was my only child. Sweet Jesus, no!* She kept on saying, over and over again. Of course, Collins didn't give a shit about Officer Rivera; he thought she was a stuck-up bitch.

Screw her. I couldn't care less about her ass. She had it coming, he coldly thought to himself.

Later on, Angelo was finally coming back home from a long, hard shift. *Almost one o'clock in the morning again,* Angelo thought. It really sucks being a rookie. He remembered what they told him in the school car. Angelo could still hear the train service supervisor say that it would take a few years before they all get a steady picked job. Even the old-timers said the same thing. Forget being off Saturday and Sunday and forget working day-time hours for at least five years, they all said.

"Well, I can dream, can't I?" he said to no one, as he went through the front door.

The next morning, Angelo was woken up by his cellphone. It was Mitchel.

"Yo, Mitchel, what's up?" Angelo asked.

"I was wondering when we could hang out, or something," Mitchel asked.

"You woke me up for that? Man, it's only seven thirty in the morning. I had at least another hour of sleep left you know."

"I'm sorry, man; I thought you'd be up. You want me to call you back later?" Mitchel asked.

"Nah, I'm up now."

"What are your days off, man?"

"I got Tuesdays and Wednesdays off."

"I got Wednesdays and Thursdays off. So you wanna hang out on Wednesday, Angelo?"

"Sure! Where do you want to go?"

Angelo did not get any response from Mitchel.

"I said, where do you want to go, man?"

The line went completely dead. Angelo was concerned. He looked at the caller ID number on his smartphone and called Mitchel right back. The call went straight to his voicemail. *Maybe his cellphone battery died,* he thought. *I'll try to call him back later.* Angelo decided to shave and take a shower.

Later on, while having breakfast, he decided to try and call his friend back. Mitchel could not be reached. All Angelo kept getting was his voicemail. Angelo figured he would see him on the train going to work, anyway, providing Mitchel had the same run as yesterday. After relaxing for a bit, Angelo put his uniform on, grabbed his bag, and left for work.

Later on, the southbound train was pulling into the Morton Town station again. Angelo waited for the train to stop and open its doors. He then boarded, expecting to see Mitchel; instead, another conductor was on the train. Angelo recognized the pretty female conductor. Sharon White, a former classmate from the training center, was on board checking tickets. Angelo admired her for a while. Although Sharon was one of the oldest students in class, she was still very pretty. He stared at her while she punched tickets. *Not bad for a thirty-five-year-old chick,* Angelo thought. Conductor Sharon White had a nice lean figure, long auburn hair, and a great smile. Her fellow classmates also appreciated her sweet disposition. Sharon was tall. The woman towered over Angelo by seven inches. She was six-foot-two. He was often intimidated by her height. Sharon made her way over toward Angelo. Her bright green eyes seemed to hypnotize him as he stood there watching her.

"Angelo! How are you doing?" Sharon asked as she gave him a hug.

"Hello, gorgeous! How the hell are you?" Angelo replied back.

"I'm doing all right. Where you heading off to?"

"The end of the line. I got to pick up that three to eleven job in the city."

"Oh, that one. I hate the late shift, don't you, Angelo?"

"Yeah. It's part of being a rookie, what are you gonna do?"

"Deal with it, I guess."

"Hey, listen, wasn't this supposed to be Mitchel's run?"

"Yeah, the crew office has him AWOL."

"What? I was just talking to him on the phone this morning."

"Yeah, well, he never showed up for the job this morning. I was sitting on the board waiting for a job. The dispatcher told me to get on this train. So here I am."

"Wow. That's not like him at all. He was always 'Mr. Dependable.' He came in to class early every single day."

"Yeah, I know. Mitchel loves his job. What did you guys talk about in the morning?"

"He called me up at seven thirty this morning, asking me if we could hang out. He asked me what my days off were."

"Did he sound sick, like he wanted to take off or something?"

"No, he didn't," Angelo replied. "Funny thing though…"

"What?" Sharon asked him.

"We agreed on hanging out together on Wednesday, but when I asked him where, he never answered. I tried calling him back a few times, but all I ever got was his damn voicemail."

"Maybe his phone died or he got in a dead spot."

"That's what I thought, Sharon."

"What time did you say he called?"

"He called me up at seven thirty. I was a little upset with him. I told him, 'You woke my ass up early just to see when we could hang out?' I kind of regret saying that to him, now," Angelo regretfully said.

"It's not your fault, Angelo, but I think something may have happened to him. Mitchel was supposed to be at Hyde Park terminal at 8:05 this morning. He never showed up and never called the crew office, or the terminal."

An elderly woman started making her way toward them as they chatted.

"Excuse me please. Which one of you conductors are in charge of this train?" she asked.

"Is there something I could help you with, Miss?" Sharon asked her back.

"Are you in charge, Miss?"

"Yes ma'am, what seems to be the problem?"

"Well, I just thought you'd like to know that there's another conductor in the back, sleeping."

"And?"

"Well, he doesn't look too good at all. He doesn't smell too good either. I think he's sick," the elderly passenger stated to them both.

"Where did you say he was, again?" Sharon asked.

"He's in the last car, all by himself," she answered.

They all started heading back to the last car of the ten-car train, hanging on, as the train took a sharp turn on the track. When they got to the last car, they knew something was wrong. In the corner, on a double seat, sat conductor James Mitchel, looking very pale. He smelled as if he defecated on himself. The elderly lady had pointed him out before she left the two conductors alone. Sharon and Angelo approached Mitchel, while holding their noses.

The train took another sharp turn, which made Mitchel fall forward on his seat.

"Wow, this engineer's a friggin cowboy," Sharon said.

Angelo tried to straighten Mitchel up in his seat, while asking him if he was all right.

"He's cold and stiff, like rigor-mortis had set in."

"Oh, God, no, Angelo, what the hell are you saying?"

"I think he's dead, Sharon."

Mitchel *was* dead. He was strangled and left on the train. There was no one else there in the railcar but Sharon, Angelo, and now-deceased conductor Mitchel. The two of them looked at each other in horror. Conductor James Mitchel was only twenty-six years old. Sharon started to get hysterical. Angelo tried to calm her down.

"We've got to call this in to Command Center and get some help!" he told Sharon.

But Sharon just sat there on the seat with her face buried in her hands and cried.

"Sharon! Give me your radio so I can call Command Center! Please!"

Sharon grabbed her radio and gave it to him.

"What's your call letters?" Angelo asked her.

"We… We're the eight twenty express out, out of Hyde Park terminal," she barely replied.

Angelo got on the radio and called for help.

"Hello, Command Center? Come in to the eight twenty express out of Hyde Park terminal, please."

"Who's calling Command please?" the supervisor replied.

"Command, this is the eight twenty express out of Hyde Park terminal."

"State the nature of your problem, sir."

"Command, we really need immediate assistance with a possible deceased passenger on our train."

"Are you sure the passenger is deceased, or maybe just sleeping?"

"I'm not a doctor, sir, but I think he's deceased and one other thing, sir, he's an employee."

"Did you say an employee?"

"Yes, sir, he's a conductor."

"Are you the conductor of the train, or the engineer, sir?"

"I'm a deadheading conductor, sir. The conductor in charge is with the passenger."

"Where are you now, Conductor?"

"We are now approaching 125th Street, sir."

"Ok, Conductor. Make your next and last stop at Morton City. Don't forget to make your appropriate PA announcements to all your passengers. We'll have police meet you there. That train is to be taken out of service pending police investigation. Make sure that everyone gets off the train safely."

"Ok, Command, that's a copy," Angelo told the supervisor over the radio.

Angelo gave Sharon back her radio and gave her a hug.

"We have to make sure everyone gets off this train at Morton City," Angelo told Sharon.

"I know," she replied.

"I'll go and make the PA announcements to let everyone know our next and last stop is Morton City."

"Thanks for all your help, Angelo. I owe you one."

"Don't mention it. What are friends for?"

"No, really, you covered for me, thanks."

She gave Angelo a quick kiss on the mouth. Angelo blushed, and then he stepped into the cabin to make his announcement over the train's public address system.

"Attention, passengers! Due to police action, the next and last stop on this train will be Morton City! The next and last stop will be Morton City! We really do apologize for the inconvenience!" Angelo stated.

The train flew by 125th Street, leaving angry passengers on the platform. However, the riders on board were happy. They were getting to work earlier.

After passing all of their scheduled stops, the train was finally arriving at Morton City terminal.

"Let's get everyone off this train," Sharon said.

They both headed toward the front of the train as it was entering the terminal.

8

WHO WILL BE NEXT?

Angelo was waking up in a strange room, wondering where he was. The bedroom was painted a pale green, with mahogany wood furniture. It didn't look like any room in his house. The sun was beaming through the light-blue-colored curtains, in the windows of the very unfamiliar room. There barely was enough light to see everything there. Angelo turned his head and realized that he wasn't alone in the bed. A very attractive young woman with long red hair laid next to him, under the green-colored blanket. *Where am I?* Angelo thought to himself. *What the hell happened?* His head was spinning like a carousel. Angelo looked closely at the woman lying there next to him. Her beauty was simply exquisite. He began to remember; it was Sharon White, his co-worker.

Sharon was so distraught over finding her friend and co-worker, James Mitchel, dead on the train, she had asked Angelo if he could come over for a while to comfort her. The two of them had drinks and talked about training school days. One thing had led to another and they both wound up in bed together. Angelo began to feel guilty, thinking he might have taken advantage of her. He remembered the two of them being grilled by the police and their supervisors. After filling out a bunch of forms, the two of them got the customary three days off to recuperate from a death on the job. Sharon was beginning to wake up.

"Good morning, Angelo," she said in a groggy voice.

"Hey, Sharon, listen, I don't remember much about last night. I hope I didn't get fresh with you."

She started to laugh before she replied.

"You? You got shit-faced drunk last night," she laughingly replied.

"I did?"

"Yeah, you did. You clearly can't hold your liquor, Angelo. I wanted to make love to you, but you fell out."

"I'm sorry."

"Don't be, some other time, perhaps."

Angelo took off his blanket and then realized he was in his underwear.

"Hey! Where are my clothes?" he asked.

"Your uniform? I took it off of you before I put you to bed. You didn't want it to get all wrinkled up, did you?"

"No, no. Thanks."

"I'm going to take a shower. Care to join me?" Sharon asked him as she pulled off her blanket.

Angelo was flabbergasted; she was now completely naked. He admired her body for a bit. Angelo's eyes were fixated on her breasts. *Nice and firm,* he thought.

"I, I don't know."

"Oh, come on now. You're not scared are you?"

"No"

"Have you ever taken a shower with a girl before?"

"Yeah, I have."

"Well then, come on now, let's go," she told him.

Angelo got out of the bed and took off his underwear in front of her.

"Nice body," Sharon told him as she got out of her bed.

"Thanks, you too," he replied.

***

After admiring each other's body, they both stepped into the light blue bathtub together. Sharon made the first move. She soaped up a wash rag with warm water and started to wash him from top to bottom. Angelo started to get aroused.

"Hey, look what we have here," she said flirtatiously.

Sharon started to stroke his now-rigid penis with her bare hand, until he bent down and took her in his arms. Angelo tenderly kissed her lips. He then started to kiss her neck. She began to moan. Sharon was getting very horny. Angelo started licking and sucking on her left breast nipple and then her right one. Her nipples were getting hard in his mouth. The warm water from the shower head felt good on them.

"I want you, Angelo," she said in a very sensual voice, while gazing into his green eyes.

Angelo took his free hand and tentatively inserted some of his fingers into her vagina, preparing her for what was next. She moaned again. Then, Angelo inserted his erect penis into her. Sharon raked her fingers on his back with her first climax.

"Oh, shit!" she screamed.

Angelo began pumping her with his member.

"Oh, God! Oh, shit. Don't stop..." she said breathlessly.

"Just like that, keep doing... Oh, my God. I-I'm gonna—" Sharon screamed with her second and more powerful orgasm.

The woman climaxed so hard that she shuddered in his arms. Angelo quickly pulled his member out of her. He stroked himself off until he shot his all-inclusive load all over her and the bath tub. After that, they both hugged and kissed.

"You see, that wasn't so bad now, was it?" Sharon asked him.

"No, that was fun," Angelo replied.

"Nothing like a little stress reduction, right Angelo?"

He just kissed her again, while grabbing her ass. The two of them dried each other off, got out of the tub, and got dressed.

"We must do this again sometime," she told Angelo.

"Yes, we must."

"I haven't felt like this in a long time," Sharon said to him.

"Me neither. I'd like to see you again. Maybe we could hang out some time," Angelo said as he kissed her goodbye.

"I'd like that," she replied.

Angelo left her house. He walked to the nearest train station and looked at his phone; it was twelve noon. The sun was shining, but it was a little chilly out. Angelo dreaded the winter and he knew it would be here soon. *I guess I'll have to get me some wheels if I go out on a date,* Angelo thought. *I better start saving up.* The train was approaching. Angelo got his train ID out of his pocket. He was in uniform, but Angelo knew the conductor might ask for his photo ID anyway. The train finally came to a complete stop and he boarded. Angelo grabbed a seat and waited for the conductor to come around. As the train picked up speed again, Angelo began thinking about everything that happened yesterday. *Another one of my*

classmates was gone. Was Mitchel murdered, or did he die naturally? One thing was for certain, Angelo was tired. He just wanted to go home and rest in his own bed. Angelo only had three more stops to go.

Back at the police precinct, the chief was reviewing the medical examiner's report on Conductor James Mitchel's body.

"He was murdered! James Mitchel died of strangulation," Brady told Lieutenant Collins.

"You know, I figured that. He was kind of young to just drop dead like that."

"Anything's possible, Collins. You're forgetting something, you know."

"What?" Collins asked.

"Conductor James Mitchel was really overweight. He could have dropped dead of a heart attack right there in his chair. But that's not the case here, is it? Don't just jump to conclusions until you have all of the facts."

"Hey, Chief, do you think this is the work of our butcher?"

"I can't say for sure yet, Collins. It certainly doesn't fit his MO."

***

Later on, Sharon White was brushing her hair in front of her bedroom mirror. She thought about how hot Angelo was. She couldn't wait to see him again. Sharon was lonely ever since her divorce. Her ex-husband had let her have the house they bought together. All he wanted from her was his freedom. Suddenly, her front doorbell rang.

"He's back!" she said aloud to no one's ears.

Sharon quickly went down the stairs of her two-story home to answer the door. When she opened it, there was no one there.

"Hello?! Hello is anybody there?!" Sharon shouted as she stepped outside. "Is that you, Angelo?! Are you coming back for some more fun?" she asked, but no one answered. "You don't have to hide from me, honey. Come out, come out, wherever you are!" Sharon called out.

After a while, she gave up, went inside, and closed the door. Sharon didn't see the stranger behind her in her home as she locked the front door. Before she could turn around, the large stainless-steel knife came from behind and severed her throat. Sharon White collapsed to the floor as her killer stood there watching her die. The butcher took its knife and sliced her open from top to bottom, exposing her organs. It drew its fingers into her chest cavity. Then, her executioner removed her heart, liver, and kidneys, and placed them in its cooler. This was the first time the butcher had killed someone in broad daylight, in its victim's own home. Sharon's slayer looked at her one last time. *Mm nice red hair,* it thought. The butcher decided to scalp her, before leaving her lifeless body all alone in her foyer. Sharon's blood was pouring out all over the oak wood floor as she laid there.

Angelo had just gotten off the train and was heading home. As he walked, Angelo began to think about Sharon. She was the first woman who took his mind off all of his problems. For once, he didn't think about his sister. *Sharon could be the one for me,* he thought to himself. *She may be older than me, but I think I'm falling for her.* Angelo thought about how sexy and experienced she was. Angelo thought about giving her a call as soon as he got back home, but maybe after a little nap. The sexual encounter had also given him an appetite. Angelo was hungry. He figured he'd make himself a ham and cheese sandwich with mustard first and then take a nap. Angelo stepped into his home at (12:50) in the afternoon. He made himself a sandwich and then the man decided to call his new love. The phone rang a few times before the voicemail recording kicked in.

"Hi! You've reached Sharon. I'm not available now, so please leave your name and number and I'll call you back later. Bye," her voicemail played.

"Hello, Sharon, it's Angelo. Just wanted to see how you were doing. I'd like to hang out with you again, you know, like on a date. I'm not good at talking to machines, but just wanted to say, I really like you. Call me when you get back, you know my number. Bye," Angelo said before making a kissing sound.

But poor Conductor Sharon White would never get to hear that message. Sharon would never know what an impression she made on Angelo. He kept thinking about her, then, Angelo decided to do something he hadn't done since his parents passed away. Angelo went into the living room and sat down in front of the shiny black grand piano. His father was the pianist in the family. Angelo remembered sitting at the piano with his father and taking lessons. *This is how you make a chord, son.* Angelo could still hear his father telling him as he showed him finger placement on the keyboard. Angelo loved making up his own tunes. He thought about writing a song for his new love. Angelo played around with a simple melody. He soon discovered the piano was seriously out of tune and gave up on it. After a while, Angelo was feeling lonely and tired. The young man had decided to take that nap after all, until he heard something. It was his sister calling him from beyond the grave.

"A-n-g-e-l-o," Carina's ghostly voice called him. "A-n-g-e-l-o."

"Carina?" Angelo cried out.

He went upstairs to where the voice came from.

"A-n-g-e-l-o."

The voice was emanating from Carina's room. Angelo had unlocked the door leading to his sister's bedroom. Carina's spirit was sitting on the bed, wearing a white gown. Angelo ran to her with open arms. He tried to hug her, but his arms went right through her.

"Carina! I found someone. Someone I think I could start over with. She's lovely, but not as beautiful as you. You'll still be my first love."

"I'm happy for you, Angelo. What's her name?"

"Her name is Sharon, Sharon White, and she's got beautiful, long red hair."

Carina's spirit looked up, and then she looked down shaking her head no.

"No, Angelo, not for you," Carina sadly responded.

"Why? You don't think that she's good enough for me?" he sternly replied.

"No! Angelo, that's not what I really meant. You don't understand."

"Yeah, I do. You're just jealous of her, that's all."

"But, but, Angelo."

"No. You just don't want me to be happy. I deserve to be happy! Look, baby, you told me to move on, so I'm moving on."

"Angelo, wait."

"No! End of discussion!" he roared. "Goodbye, Carina."

Angelo left Carina's old bedroom and he locked the door behind him. He decided not to wait for Sharon's call after all.

Angelo Russo left the house and headed straight over to the flower shop by the train station. He picked up a dozen long stem roses and then got on the next downtown train. *I'll surprise her with these flowers and take her out to dinner,* Angelo thought while thinking about her. He just couldn't believe that his deceased sister was jealous of his new girl. *She's only a ghost!* Angelo thought. *What could she do?*

A while later, Angelo Russo was ringing Sharon's doorbell. When he got no response, he decided to call her phone. He heard her cellphone ringing from inside her house; it sounded really close, like it was right on the other side of the door. Then, like before, the voicemail recording played. Angelo hung up his smartphone without leaving a message. He knocked on the door while calling out for Sharon. The man was getting worried. Angelo decided to look through the sidelight window, near the door. He was horrified. Angelo could see a pair of legs lying there on the floor. Angelo tried the doorknob to see if it was open. After realizing that the door was obviously locked, he then reached for his smartphone and called 911. After a short while, two patrol cars came onto the scene. A familiar face had approached Angelo; it was Lieutenant Michael Collins.

"Boy, you just can't stay out of trouble, can you, Russo?" the lieutenant sarcastically said.

"That's not fair," Angelo replied.

Two police officers joined the lieutenant. Collins knocked hard on the door, shouting, "Police! Open up!" When there was no reply, he peered through the sidelight window.

"All right boys, there's a body in there lying down on the floor. Let's break it down!" Collins yelled out.

Then, the two police officers proceeded to break down the front door. After three tries, the door finally gave way.

"Jesus H. Christ!" one officer shouted.

"Good Lord, this is brutal! She's been gutted and scalped!" Officer Ireland said.

Angelo dropped his roses in the pool of blood emanating from Sharon's body.

"No! No! Please not again!" Angelo screamed.

"Get him out of here!" Lieutenant Collins shouted to the two officers.

Officer Ireland escorted a now panic-stricken Angelo Russo to one of the squad cars. Angelo was blaming himself. *Everyone that gets close to me dies,* he thought quietly to himself. Collins got on his radio and called for assistance.

*
**

Later on at the police precinct, Angelo Russo was being questioned again by Lieutenant Collins.

"You feeling all right now, Mr. Russo?" the lieutenant asked.

"I, I guess so, sir," replied Angelo.

"Good! Now maybe you could tell me what you were doing at Sharon White's home today?"

"I wanted to ask her out to dinner. I tried calling her several times, but all I ever got was her voicemail, so I decided to go visit her."

"The flowers you had with you, were they for her, Mr. Russo?"

"Yes, I brought her a dozen roses."

"Was that sort of a peace offering?"

"I don't understand, Lieutenant. What are you driving at?"

"I'm just trying to get the facts here, that's all."

"We didn't have a fight, sir."

"When was the last time you saw Miss White alive?"

"I had left her house a little before noon. I remembered looking at my phone at the train station, it was twelve o'clock."

"You were visiting her after the incident on the train?"

"Yes, sir. She was feeling kind of down and needed some company."

"That was yesterday, correct?"

"Yes, sir."

"So, you stayed the night, right?"

"Yes, sir."

"I just find it very hard to believe your whole story."

"Well, I…"

"I'll tell you what happened, Mr. Russo. Now the way I see it, is you came over to your girl's house. You found out she was seeing someone else. You got jealous and killed her."

"No! No!" Angelo screamed.

"Let me finish! You went back home and got her some flowers, just to make it look good. It was all just a cover up. Isn't that the way it happened, Mr. Russo? Tell me the truth!"

"No! I tell you, that's not the way it happened!"

"Oh, come on now, Russo, you staged this whole fricking thing. Didn't you?"

"No, no, no," Angelo said as he wept in his hands.

"Pull yourself together, Russo! Man up!"

Angelo picked his head back up as the tears streamed down from his eyes.

"I-I was beginning to fall in love with her, Lieutenant. I would never do anything to hurt her, honest."

"So, tell me then, why'd you leave, then come back?"

"I was tired and just wanted to go home and sleep in my own bed. But then when I got home, I was feeling lonely. All I kept thinking about was Sharon. So, I called her up to see if she was free for dinner. When I couldn't get ahold of her, I decided to go and surprise her with some flowers. When I arrived at her house, I rang the doorbell several times and no one answered."

"How did you even know she was dead? That's what you said when you called us."

"What I *did* say, sir, is I see a body on the floor. I think it's her and I think she's dead. That's what I said, Mr. Lieutenant, sir."

"But how did you see her?"

"I looked through the long window near the door."

"The sidelight window, right?"

"Yes, I guess that's what you call it, sir."

"But what made you look through the window? Are you playing peeping Tom?"

"No! I called her cell and I heard it ring in her house. It sounded really close, like it was just on the other side of the door."

"Yes, well it was, Mr. Russo. We've all established that, haven't we?"

"Yes, we have, sir."

"So you heard the phone ringing, then what?"

"Well, when she didn't answer, you see, after it rang a bit, her voicemail recording played. I knocked on the door and asked if she was all right. I decided to look through her window and that's, that's…"

Angelo could not finish his sentence; he was getting all choked up again.

"I know, that's when you saw Sharon White lying there dead on the floor, right?"

"Yes, sir," Angelo said while sniffling.

"I'm curious about something you said at the scene of the crime, though."

"What's that?"

"You said, and I quote: 'Oh, no, not again.' Just what did you mean by that remark, Russo?"

"I just feel that every time someone gets close to me, they get killed. Who will be next?"

"You tell me, Mr. Russo, who will be next?!" the lieutenant asked in an accusatory manor. "Oh, and just one other thing, Mr. Russo…"

"What?"

"The report from the medical examiner showed that your friend, Conductor Mitchel, was murdered."

"What? Are you sure?"

"Yes, he died of strangulation. You know anything about that, Russo?"

"No, no, I don't," Angelo nervously said.

The lieutenant got up and stepped out of the interrogation room. Then, he proceeded into the monitoring room to see the chief.

"I've been here watching the whole damn show, Collins," Brady stated.

"I know you have, Chief."

"Well, what do you think, is he guilty or innocent?" the chief asked.

"I think he's guilty."

"Really? I don't think so."

"Well, I think he's putting on a good act, or at least holding something back, Chief."

"One thing's for sure, Collins…"

"What's that, Chief?"

"This is definitely the work of the damn butcher. It fits his MO completely, but all we've got on Russo is just circumstantial evidence, if any. That's not enough to hold him."

"Oh, come on now, Chief," the lieutenant pleaded.

"Let him go, but we'll all be keeping a very close eye on Mr. Angelo Russo," Brady retorted.

Collins went back to the interrogation room to take Angelo home.

While Angelo was riding back home with the lieutenant, his mind was racing. *Carina knew she was dead, didn't she?* Angelo kept thinking over and over again. *That's why she gave me that look and said, 'No Angelo, not for you.' Now, I know what she really meant by that.* He couldn't wait to get back home and confront her.

Collins was finally arriving at Angelo's home. He reminded Angelo not to leave town in case they still had some more questions for him. It was now six o'clock in the evening, darkness was settling in. Angelo waited for the lieutenant to leave before closing his front door behind him. He kept thinking about how the day had gone sour. It was not the day off Angelo had hoped for. The only fun he had was short lived with the death of his female friend.

Angelo took the keys that were hanging on the hook in the kitchen. He went back upstairs and unlocked the room that once belonged to his late sister. Angelo called out to her while looking at her bed.

"Carina! Carina! Where are you my love?!"

Carina's spirit materialized on her bed. She was dressed in a sheer white gown looking very sexy.

"Angelo, my darling," she replied in her ghostly voice.

"You knew. You knew, didn't you? You knew all along that Sharon was dead, right?"

"Yes Angelo, I did."

"Why didn't you tell me?"

"I tried to tell you, Angelo, but you just wouldn't listen to me. I'm sorry."

"It's not fair. I was falling for her."

"She was just a little too old for you, anyway."

"She was sweet and beautiful."

"But you didn't really love her, did you?"

"I was starting to."

"You haven't known her long enough, Angelo."

"Do you know who killed her?"

"Yes."

"Who?"

"It's the same one who took my life away. The same one who stole my beautiful hair. You have to be careful, my love."

"The police think I did it."

"They couldn't be more wrong."

"Who is it?"

"I don't know his name. He has changed his looks and he's very dangerous. Please be very careful when you walk home at night. I don't want to lose you."

"I'm all alone again, Carina."

"You still have me, honey. Do you remember when I first taught you how to French kiss?"

"Yes, Carina, I remember."

"It was a day before your tenth birthday. I was fifteen at the time. When I first kissed you, we both laughed at first. Then, we kissed again and we both felt something special. Do you remember, Angelo?"

"Yes, but I knew it could never be. You were my sister, for Christ's sake."

"But I knew that you weren't really my brother, I knew it all along, but I dared not say. Mom and Dad would have killed me if I did."

"It must have been hard for you."

"Yes, it was, Angelo. I helped change your diapers, bathe you, and helped dress you. I still remember the day they brought you home from the adoption agency. You were only three months old."

"Who are my real parents?"

"No one knows. Mom and Dad had never cared to find out."

"I just feel so all alone, Carina. I really don't have anyone to love. Nobody loves me."

"You still have me, Angelo. I will always love you," Carina passionately replied.

"I love you with all of my heart, and I miss you dearly, but you're not really here. You're just a ghost."

"Someday, we will be together again, Angelo. I promise."

"How?"

"I still do have some of my witchcraft powers. I just need a vehicle, that's all."

"A vehicle?"

"Yes."

"Oh, Carina, please, will you stay with me," Angelo pleaded.

"I have to go now," she said as she began to fade away.

"Wait! Wait, don't leave me again! I love you! I need you," Angelo pleaded to her as she disappeared.

He stayed in her room feeling sad and confused, wondering what she had meant. *What did she mean about a vehicle? Who was the killer? What did it all mean?* Angelo wondered, trying to make sense of it all. After a short while, he simply just gave in to his exhaustion. Angelo fell asleep on Carina's bed.

Angelo dreamt about Carina. His mind was playing back memories of them playing together as kids in the backyard. He could always talk to his big sister about all the problems he had in school. Angelo always had a special bond with her that he didn't share with his adopted parents.

Carina Russo was very special. She was always more understanding. Angelo idolized her. In his mind, she could do no wrong. When Carina went off to college, he was devastated. Angelo got extremely happy when Carina came back home to stay, but when her modeling career took off, he saw less and less of her. Angelo really became distraught when Carina showed up with her new boyfriend. *He's not good enough for you; I don't trust him,* Angelo angrily told her.

Carina knew he was jealous of her boyfriend, but she enjoyed the extra attention. Carina loved to tease him. When their parents had perished in the car accident, they became closer together. Carina would still go back and forth to her boyfriend's house. Angelo thought that would all change after they made love together on that fateful night, but it didn't. She had left him on that night, but why? *I have to leave. I need time to think,* is what Carina had said when she left. It was the last time he had seen his beloved sister alive. Angelo Russo wished that he could turn back the hands of time and change things.

Angelo woke up the next morning in Carina's room, knowing that his three-day vacation was over. It was time to get back to work. He went downstairs to the family room to watch the morning news. Angelo grabbed the remote and turned on the TV. The news came on after a few commercials. He was so happy to have his cable TV service back on. Angelo went to the kitchen to fix himself a bowl of cereal and some orange juice. The young man would have to call the crew office for his assignment tonight. Angelo hoped he would have a job close to home. The boy wasn't crazy about going all the way downtown, but it was part of being a rookie. You had to take the good with the bad. Those were the rules.

A few miles away, the butcher was on the phone making some arrangements with its contact.

"I've got my new price list for you, Muhammad. Are you ready for it?" the butcher asked the West Indian man on the phone.

"What is it now? I'm ready," Muhammad asked.

"These are my new prices as follows:

"Heart: $120,000.

"Liver: $160,000.

"Pint of blood: $337.

"Spleen: $508.

"Stomach: $508.

"Small intestine: $2,520.

"Kidney: $270,000.

"Gallbladder: $1,320.

"Scalp: $650.

"You got it?"

"Yes, I have it here. It appears to be a significant increase in your prices. I take it they are all fresh, as before?"

"Yes, guaranteed fresh."

"Question: where are you getting them from?"

"Ask me no questions, and I'll tell you no lies."

"Why do you always have to have cash?"

"Yours is not to question why, yours is but to do or die."

"Oh, you are a tough guy, eh?" Muhammad replied.

"Yes, very tough. Now, do we have a deal, or what?" the butcher asked.

"We have a deal," Muhammad said as he hung up the phone on the slaughterer.

Clearly, Muhammad was not happy at all about the recent price increase on the organs.

9

BODY PARTS FOR YOU

Thursday afternoon, October 31. Halloween arrived bringing out the usual trick-or-treaters. Children started walking around in their costumes at four o'clock. It was cool outside, so they had to wear jackets over their scary get-ups. Leaves were falling all around in the little suburban town of Morton, Massachusetts. Some of the folks had already started their Christmas shopping.

Chief Brady was just hanging up the phone. An irate man was complaining about someone being parked right in front of his driveway. *I'm blocked in and I can't get out,* the man had complained. Officer Ireland had walked into the chief's office with a package in his hand.

"You've got a package here, Chief!" Officer Ireland stated.

"Who's it from?" Brady asked.

"It doesn't say, sir."

"What are you, stupid or something?! You brought me an unmarked package?! It could be a bomb and you just brought it right into my office!" he bellowed.

"Well, it doesn't look like a bomb, sir," Ireland said as he accidently dropped the box on the floor.

"You idiot! That could have blown us all up!"

The box was now partially open from the fall on the floor. Officer Ireland picked it up and tried to look inside.

"It wasn't packed very well, sir," he said while opening up the rest of the box.

"Jesus H. Christ!" Brady exclaimed.

"It's a human hand, Chief!"

"No shit Sherlock! A right hand, it looks like it belonged to a woman," Chief Brady said.

"That ring on the index finger, it looks familiar, Chief," Officer Ireland plainly stated.

"Yeah, I know. Two guesses at whom it belongs to, but we've got to be sure. Send it down to the lab and check its prints, Ireland."

"Yes, sir," he said as he took the small box containing the hand with him.

*
**

A little while later at the station, the chief's suspicions had been confirmed. The hand belonged to Officer Kathy Rivera. The butcher kept it well preserved in his freezer. He had waited for Halloween, just to send it to the chief. Officer Paul Flanigan had arrived in time to hear most of the conversation. Flanigan was with Kathy Rivera while she passed away in his arms.

"She deserved better than that," Flanigan miserably said.

"I'm sorry, Flanigan. I knew you were fond of her," Chief Brady said.

"I've been trying to put it behind me. Now, after all this time, another part of her shows up," Officer Flanigan sadly stated as he walked out of the chief's office.

Chief Brady told Lieutenant Collins to try and locate where the package originated from. He was convinced beyond a shadow of a doubt that it came from the butcher. Brady wanted this scumbag bad; it had now become a personal vendetta to him.

Angelo Russo was sitting at the table in the downtown crew room eating his lunch. He had only one more round trip to make before getting off of work. His co-workers were all watching the five o'clock news on TV. The dispatcher walked in and was looking for Conductor Russo.

"Hey Russo!" the dispatcher called out.

"Yes, sir, that's me!"

"I need you to jump ahead on the five-o-five. Jones didn't show up."

"But, sir, I'm on lunch," Angelo stated.

"Put in for a 'no lunch!' Your train is on the stand! Hurry up!" the dispatcher bellowed.

Angelo grabbed his sandwich and his bag, and he left. He ran down the platform to get into his operating position. Angelo unlocked the cabin door and got inside. He got on the public address system to check if it was functioning.

"Hello, Engineer, can I get a PA check?" Angelo asked.

"Loud and clear, Conductor!" the train engineer responded.

"Ok, welcome aboard the Hyde Park Express, everyone! Please stand clear of the closing doors," Angelo announced over the public address system.

He then proceeded to close the doors by pressing the appropriate buttons. The train made a ding-dong chime sound while the doors were closing. Angelo checked his indication lights, turned the master door controller lock, and removed the key. Then, he gave his engineer two long buzzer signals to proceed. The train started to move, while Angelo observed the platform for three car lengths.

Afterwards, Conductor Angelo Russo started checking tickets. He came across a blonde woman sitting in one of the seats. Angelo became upset when he noticed who the passenger was. Taylor turned toward Angelo to show his ID.

"Well hello, baby," Taylor said to him.

"What the hell are you doing here now?" Angelo said while raising his voice.

"I work here, remember? And I've got every bit as much right to be here as you do."

"Yeah, I know. You could put your pass away now. What are you doing on my train?"

"I'm going home after a hard day's work. You care to join me for dinner, lovey?"

"Hell no! You stay away from me; you hear?"

"Baby, that's no way to talk to a fellow co-worker, is it?"

"Listen up, I'm trying really hard to keep my cool. Don't push me."

"Oh, yeah, we both know how hard headed you can be, don't we, Angelo?" Taylor responded in a flirtatious manner.

"Why do you keep bothering me? Listen, I'm not gay, I like girls, real girls. Maybe you got the wrong impression or something, but I don't owe you an explanation. I don't owe you anything."

"Oh, but you *do*, baby. You owe me your job."

"What? You must be high! You gave me a tip and thanks for that, but I got this job all by myself. End of story."

"Well, that's not entirely true, baby. You would still be waiting for the railroad to call you if it weren't for me."

"No! I don't believe you. I passed the test, legally!"

"Yes you did. You got an eighty-five. With that kind of a score and with no military backing, they would have called you in two, maybe three years, probably closer to three. I know the superintendent downtown and asked him to give you a break. I told him you were a hard worker and that you needed a job. He knew the story about your parents dying in that car accident, everyone knew it, heck, it was even in the news. I told him that you and your sister were all alone and had to fend for yourselves. Superintendent James felt sorry for you and pushed you up on the waiting list. So you see, Angelo, baby, you owe me big time, and *don't* you forget it."

Angelo was now speechless. He didn't like to owe anyone anything, especially him. Angelo was angry at Taylor, even though his story sounded logical. It was all just too much for him to bear.

"What's the matter, baby, cat got your tongue?" Taylor sarcastically asked him.

"If you call me 'baby' one more time, I'll…"

"Kick my ass? I don't think so. Listen, I've taken very good care of you. I even sent you those roses and this is how you treat me?"

"You're the one?" Angelo asked.

"That's right. I've liked you ever since you delivered pizza to my house. I kept requesting you as my delivery boy from the pizza parlor. I know I looked different then, but look at me. Don't you remember me, Angelo?"

Angelo stared at Taylor for a moment. Then, he started to remember him, but he did look different. Back then, Taylor had short black hair and a mustache. He looked like an average young man. Now, he looks very feminine, indeed. *Where did he get this beautiful, long blond hair from? It must be a wig,* he thought to himself. Angelo was feeling very uncomfortable near Taylor. He wanted to leave there as fast as he could. The nearby passengers were staring and listening to everything they said to each other. They kept looking at them while they spoke. One woman said to her friend, "This is like a soap opera, isn't it?" There was a time and a place for everything, and this was neither the time nor the place for this conversation. Angelo was feeling very embarrassed.

"Look, I don't even know your name, and…"

"Taylor."

"What?"

"I said it's Taylor. My name is Taylor. If you took the time to actually look at my pass, you would have known that."

"All right, Taylor, I've got to get back to work. Excuse me," Angelo said to him as he continued to punch the passengers' tickets.

Angelo was so confused and upset. He now felt like he owed Taylor a favor. The question was: How was he going to pay him? Taylor clearly wanted him, but Angelo was not gay.

"Shit," he said to himself. "What the hell am I gonna do?"

The train finally arrived at the Hyde Park terminal at 6:55 p.m. Angelo was only one stop away from his hometown. He wished he could just get off and walk home, but Angelo had to bring the train back downtown to complete his run. Angelo closed down the train and walked to the dispatcher's office. The dispatcher told him he had a twenty-minute layover break.

"So what time am I leaving, sir?" Angelo asked him.

"You'll be going out at 7:15, on track two, Russo!" the dispatcher replied.

"Boy, just barely enough time to go to the bathroom."

"That's what the schedule says and I don't have anyone else to make the interval."

"Question, sir: what's really up with Conductor Taylor?"

"You mean Parker?"

"Parker, sir?"

"Yeah, Taylor Parker, 'pretty boy.' He giving you a hard time, Russo?"

Angelo decided not to rock the boat. He didn't want to complain, especially since he was new around there.

"No, no. I was just wondering if he was a rookie like me, that's all."

"Rookie? He's here about ten years now. I wouldn't rub him the wrong way if I were you. Parker's got friends in high places."

"Yeah, I heard."

"He's real tight with the big superintendent downtown, so watch your Ps and Qs around him."

"Taylor didn't always look like that, right?"

"Between you and me, he's thinking about a sex change operation, but he hasn't got the dough for the surgery. Our health insurance won't cover it, you know."

"I wouldn't know about that, sir. I'm not gay."

"I hear ya. Well, if he goes through with it, Parker wants an updated pass and female bathroom privileges."

"He doesn't ask for much, does he?" Angelo said jokingly.

"Listen; don't get me wrong, Parker's a good worker. He shows up here on time and he hardly ever takes off. He's just a little weird, that's all. When he gets off work, you'll see him dressed in women's clothing. I'll tell you this though; he looks good with that blond wig. From behind, he looks just like a woman. I don't know where the hell he got it from, but he must have paid a pretty penny for it."

Angelo went to the bathroom and got ready to make his last trip down to the city. He thought about what the dispatcher had said, especially about Parker's hair. *Where did he get that hair from? It looks so real! So familiar…*Angelo kept thinking.

A few miles away, the Railway Butcher was in the basement of its home. The butcher had gingerly wrapped each body part. The killer proceeded to place ice cubes all over the parts and place them into the coolers.

"Body parts for you, ha, ha, ha, ha. Cha-ching, cha-ching, cha-ching," the slaughterer said to no one's ears.

"I can't take a chance of another storm knocking out my damn power."

The butcher had closed up both of its refrigerators and went upstairs to eat. The fiend was thinking about its next victim. *I've got to see what other parts I'll need for next time,* it thought. The killer was getting ready to meet its contact downtown.

Later that evening back at the police precinct, Lieutenant Collins was in the chief's office. He was desperately trying to convince Chief Brady to bring Angelo Russo in.

"Are you for real? On what grounds, Collins?" Brady asked the lieutenant.

"I think he's guilty, Chief!"

"We can't just bring a man in and lock him up because you think he's guilty!"

"I'll bet my badge on it. If we lock his ass up, the killings will stop!"

"You better be careful what the hell you bet on, Mike, you just might lose."

"Look, Chief, I've got a gut feeling about this. Just trust me on this, will you?"

"Until you go and find me some real incriminating evidence on Mr. Russo, the answer is *no*! Now, go out there and see what the hell you can find, Collins!"

"Yes boss."

Collins stormed out of Chief Brady's office like a child that's had his favorite toy stepped on, but Collins wasn't about to give up that easily. He had a plan. The lieutenant just had to find a way to implement it.

⁎⁎

Angelo finally stepped into his home at 11:20 p.m. He was tired and confused. Angelo had asked his co-workers at the downtown terminal about Conductor Taylor Parker. Everyone basically said the same thing: Parker was a real weirdo and not to be trusted.

He went upstairs, got undressed, and went to take a shower. When Angelo pulled open the light blue floral shower curtain, he was shocked to see his dead sister's ghost standing in the tub, naked. Carina's spirit had given him another warning.

"Be very careful now, A-n-g-e-l-o," the apparition said in a spooky voice.

"Ca-Carina! You just scared the shit out of me!" Angelo stammered.

"You must be careful, my love."

"Yeah, yeah. I get that. Now will you please let me take a shower, Carina? I'm so tired. I just wanna get cleaned up and go to bed."

"Choose your friends very wisely, my love."

Angelo tried to give her a hug, but Carina faded away.

"I wish you would just stop doing that, Carina," he said to the empty bathtub.

Angelo wished he knew exactly what she meant about "being careful." He thought of her while taking his shower. The warm water felt good on his body, but Angelo was tired; the young man just wanted to go to sleep after his shower. Angelo dried himself off and put on his pajamas. He would normally sleep with just his underwear, but it was a little too chilly for that.

Angelo had decided to sleep in Carina's old room tonight; he wanted to be close to her. Sleep came over him quickly, so did the dreams. Angelo saw Carina with Taylor. They were both talking about him. The two of them were just sitting there in the dining room, having a pleasant conversation, until Taylor gave his sister a strange-looking large knife. *You have to do it while he's sleeping,* he had said. *You must kill Angelo tonight.* Carina was coming after Angelo with the knife over him while he slept. Angelo woke up screaming.

"Nooo! Don't kill me, Carina! I love you!"

Angelo Russo woke up in a cold sweat, hyperventilating.

"It was a dream, that's all, just a damn dream…or maybe a nightmare. Why would Carina try to kill me? She loves me," he said in the empty room to himself.

Angelo felt something hard in the bed. He pulled off the blanket and to his horror, there it was. In between his legs, there was the same knife that Angelo had seen in his dreams. The knife looked like an antique with its long, curved blade. The handle was solid mahogany with fancy curved lines engraved on it. Aside from the dream he had, Angelo had never seen that knife before in his life.

"What the hell? How the hell did that get in here? Where did it come from?!" he screamed out loud.

Angelo got out of bed and out of Carina's room. He went back to his room and locked the bedroom door behind him. *Is Carina mad at me?* Angelo thought. *Is she really trying to kill me? If so, why? What did I do to her?* Angelo struggled to fall asleep again, feeling scared and hurt.

The next morning, Angelo awoke to the doorbell ringing. He looked out of his window and immediately recognized the man outside. Angelo glanced at his clock radio on the night stand; it was eight o'clock in the morning. He went down the stairs to let Lieutenant Collins in.

"Lieutenant Collins, what brings you here on a Friday morning?" Angelo asked.

"I was hoping you were ready to confess, Russo, are you?" Collins asked with a smirk on his face.

"Confess? Confess to what?"

"Listen, I think we ought to take this conversation inside. That is unless you care to have your neighbors know what's really going on with you," the lieutenant stated.

Angelo begrudgingly asked the police lieutenant to come inside. He closed the door behind him and prepared himself for the worst.

"Now, suppose you tell me what I should confess to?" Angelo asked him.

"Come on now, Russo, you can knock off that innocent act with me. We both know you orchestrated this entire charade. Now, why don't you just come clean with me and I'll see that they go easy on you."

"You still think I killed my sister?"

"I think you killed them all, Russo!"

"You're crazy!"

"Maybe, but I'm not the one going on trial here, you are!"

"On what grounds, Lieutenant? What evidence could you possibly have on me?" Angelo asked him.

"I know you killed your sister to get her out of your way. You wanted this whole house all to yourself, that way you and you alone would collect all of your inheritance."

Angelo was on the verge of tears. *How could this asinine lieutenant think that I killed the only love of my life?* Angelo thought. The accusation alone was ludicrous. He got very defensive with that remark.

"I loved my sister very dearly. I would never do anything to hurt her," Angelo's voice cracked.

"Yeah, I see. You sure had a very strange relationship with your sister, didn't you?"

"I'm afraid I don't understand."

"Oh, yeah, you do. What were you really doing…banging her?"

"That's none of your damn business!" Angelo cried out.

"Oh, I see I hit a nerve, didn't I?"

"You're sick, Lieutenant! You think that I killed everyone, all by myself. Well, what damn reason would I have? You tell me, Lieutenant!"

"You did it to get rid of your classmates, so that you could move up on your seniority ladder, that's why. You wanted to be up on top as quickly as possible. My only question is, why so messy, Russo? You could have just killed them. Why'd you tear them up like that? And the missing body parts, where'd you hide them?"

"Do you have any evidence against me?"

"Not yet, but I'm working on it."

"For the record, Lieutenant, I really think I know who the real killer is!"

"You do? Who is it?"

"I'm not telling you until I'm sure."

"Listen Russo, I could just lock you up for withholding information, you know."

"When I'm sure, you'll know. Now, get the hell out of my house!" Angelo shouted.

"I'll be back, Russo, you can bet on it."

"I said: get out!"

With that, Angelo slammed the door behind him, went to the family room, and cried on the sofa. He truly hated the lieutenant. He wished Collins would get the hell off his back and find the real killer. *This was no way to be woken up early in the morning,* Angelo thought.

"Don't cry, A-n-g-e-l-o," Carina's ghostly voice called out.

"Wh-what?" Angelo asked as he looked up in the room.

"Don't cry, ba-by."

"Carina? Where are you?"

"Over here, my love."

Angelo turned his head toward the doorway and saw Carina's ghost just standing there. She was dressed in white again, looking like an angel. He got up and approached her.

"The lieutenant thinks I committed all the murders. What am I going to do, Carina? Help me, please!"

"He has nothing on you, Angelo. He's trying to intimidate you; that's all."

"I'm afraid, Carina. I don't want to go to jail."

"The lieutenant has no evidence on you. He's grasping at straws, my love."

"I didn't do it! I didn't do any of it! I swear to you!"

"I know. I know you're innocent, baby."

"It really means a lot to me to hear you say that, sis, but, I had a bad dream. I thought you wanted to kill me."

"Never, never, my love, don't ever think that."

"I found a strange knife in my bed. Did you put it there?"

"Yes love, I did."

"Why?"

"I want you to have it for protection."

"Protection?"

"Yes, from my killer. Keep it with you always, love."

"Where did you get such a strange knife from? I've never seen it before in my life, except in my dream, you had it in your hand. You had it when you were trying to kill me."

"It belongs to my killer. I stole it. I stole it for you, Angelo. How ironic it would be, if you killed my assassin, using his very own weapon."

"But that dream. That dream seemed so real."

"I told you, I would never do anything to hurt you, Angelo. You are and always will be the love of my life."

He tried to put his arms around her, but they just went right through her.

"I wish I could just hold you in my arms again, Carina."

"You will, someday soon. You will, I promise you that."

Angelo gazed into her translucent green eyes and tried to kiss her. Carina started glowing. She tried to completely materialize, even for a bit, but her powers just weren't strong enough.

"I have to go now, my love," she said.

"I will always love you, Carina."

She faded away again. Angelo wished to God that she never died.

"Why was she taken from me, oh, Lord, why?" he cried out. "It isn't fair. It just isn't fair."

Angelo went back upstairs to his room. He wanted to get another look at that strange knife. The knife that killed his sister. The knife that probably killed all of the others, too.

On the other part of town, just a few miles away, the Railway Butcher was in its house, looking for something that was very important to its existence.

"Shit! Where the hell is it?!" the killer screamed out alone.

The butcher had been searching the house for well over two hours for its prized killing knife. A knife it had used to slice open the throats of its many victims. The knife that was handed down to it by its father.

"I can't find it! Where the hell could it be? Shit! It's got to be here! That knife's an antique. It's got to be at least fifty years old!" it said while feeling baffled.

Earlier in the night, Carina's spirit had used her powers to remove the knife from the killer's vehicle where it kept it. Carina's apparition was at the scene of its last kill. The butcher was going to have to find another weapon to use for its next victim. *It won't be the same. It just won't be the same without it,* the murderer pondered.

A little while later, Kevin Croce was on the southbound train approaching Morton Town. He had been conducting the trains all night, working overtime. The young conductor needed the money.

"Next stop, Morton Town. Morton Town is the next stop," Kevin said over the train's public address system.

The train began slowing down as it was entering the station. After it came to a complete stop, Kevin opened the doors for the passengers. Conductor Kevin Croce observed the platform and then he closed the doors. He turned the master key to give the engineer indication to proceed. The train began to move out of the station and Kevin stuck his head back inside.

Angelo Russo got on board the train and grabbed a seat by the window. *I wonder who's operating this train,* he thought. Angelo took out his train ID and waited for the conductor to come around. Kevin was busy answering a passenger's question, so he couldn't check tickets right away. Before long, the train was arriving in the next station. Conductor Croce knew he had to get back into the cabin to operate the passenger doors.

"Next stop, South Street! South Street next stop," Kevin said over the public address system.

Conductor Croce waited for the train to come to a complete stop before opening the doors. After the passengers entered the train, Kevin closed the doors. Once they were moving again, he proceeded to check the passengers' tickets again.

"Tickets, please," Conductor Croce said as he greeted the new passengers.

"Yo, Kevin! What's up, man?" Angelo asked.

"Angelo! Angelo Russo! How the hell are you?! I haven't seen you since training school!" Conductor Croce replied.

They gave each other a half-hug.

"So, how do like the job so far?" Angelo asked.

"It's cool," replied Kevin.

"Did you hear about what happened to Sharon White?" asked Angelo.

"Yeah, that sucks. I also know about Mitchel and Tanya."

"You forgot one."

"Who?" Kevin asked.

"My best friend, Josh Vincitore. We're all dropping like flies down here," said Angelo.

"Yeah, I know. I did hear about Josh. I'm sorry; I knew you two were very tight. I sure hope the police have some leads by now."

"The police? Shit, they suck! They think I freaking did it!"

"What? No way, man!"

"It's true, man. I am the lieutenant's primary suspect in all of the murders," Angelo solemnly stated.

"I can't believe that. I know it's not you, bro. That is so wrong."

"Well, in any case, I think I better start shopping around for an attorney."

"Yeah, I would, if it were me. You don't wanna get locked up for something you didn't do."

"No I don't."

"Listen, you take care, all right? I got to get back to work."

"All right, later man, take it light," Angelo said while grabbing Kevin's hand.

Kevin Croce resumed his job of checking the passengers' tickets.

"Tickets, please," Conductor Croce said while he was walking down the aisle of the railcar. "Tickets, tickets please!"

Conductor Taylor Parker was in full uniform a few seats down watching Angelo and Kevin. Taylor wanted to talk with Angelo, but decided not to cause another scene.

"Tickets; oh, you're one of us! I still need to see your ID."

"Here it is," Taylor said while showing Kevin his ID pass.

Angelo was watching from his seat. *Oh, no! It can't be,* he thought to himself. He saw the back of his blonde hair, and a uniformed arm handing Kevin her ID pass. *What the hell?! Is he following me?* Angelo asked himself. He resisted the temptation of starting a fight. They were both in full uniform. Angelo knew that everyone carries cellphones that had high-definition cameras nowadays. It was way too easy for anyone to shoot a video, upload it to social media, and then the news. He did not need that kind of attention. If a fight had broken out between the two of them, they both would then be dismissed from the railroad…permanently. He decided to keep his cool.

Soon after, the train was finally pulling into Morton City terminal. Everyone was getting off the train, everyone had to since it was the last stop. Angelo waited for Taylor to get off before he went to the exit doors. Angelo did not want an altercation, not now, not on the train, and not while he was in full uniform. Heck, he remembered the rules of conduct while being in uniform. You couldn't even go to a bar for a drink while you were in railroad clothing. You really couldn't do anything that would be detrimental to the railroad. It just wasn't worth losing your job. It was in the rule book. The rules stated, whenever an employee of the railroad was in full uniform, he or she had to behave properly and act diplomatically. The employee had to use discretion at *all* times. An employee in uniform could not be seen drinking any kind of alcoholic beverage. Angelo worked way too hard to get the job on the railroad. He wasn't about to lose it for some dumb bullshit like this. Angelo was not about to go looking for a new job all over again. It just wasn't worth it. Taylor wasn't worth it. He took down Kevin's phone number and vowed to give him a call later on, whenever he got a chance to.

10

A NEW LOVE

Saturday, November 2. Angelo Russo was checking his passengers' tickets on the northbound local train. There was no express train service on the weekends or holidays. He liked going express, it was less work. There was one good thing though: this was his last run. He was so happy to have a morning job that started and finished uptown for a change. The train had just left 125th Street. Since there was no more third rail power, the train had to switch over to diesel power. A very attractive young woman with long blonde hair had just boarded and caught Angelo's eye. He thought she was drop-dead gorgeous with her deep blue eyes, inviting smile, and her shapely figure showed very well through her ever so tight dress. Angelo had never seen her before in his life, but this was his first time on this particular run. He went over to check her ticket.

"Tickets, please," he asked in a gentle voice while trying desperately to remain calm.

"Here you go. It's the first time I'm taking a train since my car broke down," she said.

"Oh, I'm so sorry to hear that, Miss. What happened to your car?" Angelo asked.

"I got into a car accident. It's in the shop."

"Wow, are you all right?"

"Yes, thank you. It was just my car, that's all."

"Was it badly damaged?" Angelo asked.

"No, it's mostly body work. Some fool was texting instead of paying attention to the road and cut me off at an intersection. Luckily, none of us were going very fast," she replied.

"Well, at least you didn't get hurt. It sure would have been a crime for such a beautiful young woman like you to get hurt."

"Oh, that's so sweet of you to say," she said with a smile on her pretty face.

Angelo was now blushing beet red. The woman was in her mid-twenties. Angelo thought she reminded him of his sister, Carina.

"I see here you purchased a round-trip ticket for today," Angelo said as he punched her ticket.

"Is that a problem, sir?" she asked.

"No, no, as long as you use the rest of it today."

"Today?" she asked nervously.

"Yes, today."

"I was going to use it Monday morning when I returned to work."

"I'm sorry, Miss, but this ticket is only good for today. You're not going back to the city today?"

"No! I was planning on going to work with it and buying a weekly ticket in the city. I, I don't know how long it's going to take to fix my car," she said sadly.

Angelo started to feel really sorry for the woman. He didn't mean to upset her, but rules were rules. *Maybe, this time, there could be an exception to the rules,* he thought.

"What time were you planning to leave for work on Monday?"

"I figured I would take the eight o'clock train out of South Park in the morning."

Angelo took out his little black pocket book and checked his schedule for Monday.

"You're in luck, Miss; I'll be operating that train on Monday. Just bring this ticket on board with you and I'll let you ride."

"Oh, thank you, thank you so much. You're a doll. By the way, what's your name, sir?"

"Angelo, it's Angelo, and yours?"

"You can call me, Carla," she happily replied.

"Ok, Carla, I'll see you then. I've got to get back to work, we're approaching the next station," he told her.

Angelo went back into his cabin to prepare for the next train stop.

"The next stop is Berry Road! Please exit in the first two cars only! Don't forget your personal belongings and have a good evening," Angelo said over the public address system.

After a half hour, the train was pulling into the South Park train station. Angelo remembered that South Park was Carla's stop. He quickly went over to her to say goodbye and to remind her about Monday. Carla thanked him again before getting up from her seat. Angelo was in love again, but he was a little apprehensive. *Every time I fall in love, my girl gets murdered,* he dismally thought to himself. *I must be cautious this time and take it slow.* Soon after that, the train was pulling in to the terminal.

"The next and last stop is Hyde Park! Ladies and gentlemen, please take all of your personal belongings with you. Have a great evening, and thank you for riding with the Morton City Railroad!" Angelo had happily announced.

Angelo went over to the dispatcher's office to sign out and go to the bathroom. It was 5:25 p.m. He had to hurry up to catch the 5:30 train that was going southbound. Angelo only had to go one stop to Morton Town to get back home. He ran out of the bathroom and onto the train as the doors began to close. Angelo barely made it. The young man was trying desperately to catch his breath.

Not too far away, the butcher was sitting at home thinking. The killer thought about all of the body parts it had collected and sold since March 11. Not to mention, all the cash the butcher had collected. Its first victim had been Carina Russo, Angelo's beloved sister. The big question now was: What was this crazy lunatic going to do with all of that money? Was that the only reason for the killings? What were its plans?

It was almost six p.m. when Angelo finally stepped into his home. He was upset. There were track workers doing work outside of the Morton Town train station. His train had been detained for over fifteen minutes from entering the station.

"Shit! One stop, just one damn stop to get home and I get stuck!" he said to an empty house.

Angelo went upstairs to take a shower. He wanted to get cleaned up before having dinner.

"A-n-g-e-l-o," a ghostly voice called.

"Carina? Is that you again?" Angelo asked.

"I'm in my room. My powers are strongest here."

Angelo Russo stepped into his sister's bedroom. He left her door unlocked and open from now on. Carina was just about fully materialized. Her apparition was lying down on the bed, naked.

"Well, hello, sexy," said Angelo.

"I was waiting for you to come home, love, Carina's spirit said to him."

"It's so nice to see you, even though you're not really here, Carina."

"You seem so happy, my love."

"I am. I found a new love."

"Who is it this time, honey?"

"A girl I met on my train; she was a passenger in distress."

"What do you mean by that remark?"

"She bought a round-trip ticket for today and wanted to use the other half for Monday. I told her she couldn't do that, but if she saw me on the train, I would hook her up."

"What does she look like, Angelo?"

"She's blonde and beautiful, just like you."

"What's her name?"

"She said I could call her, Carla."

"Carla? Did she have blue eyes and was around my height and build?"

"Yes, yes! How did you know?"

"Stay away from that bitch, Angelo!"

"Why? Why do you always seem to find something wrong with every girl I meet?"

"Her real name is Carlita Gomez. She's an opportunist. She will use you and abuse you. You deserve better than that, my love."

"How do you know so much about her, Carina?"

"I met her in college. We took some classes together. She's a piece of shit. I can't even count how many people she's hurt."

"Really? She seemed so sweet to me on the train."

"It's just an act. Carlita Gomez is even ashamed of her own Puerto Rican heritage, including her name. She's a phony. Carlita tries to be white and won't even speak Spanish to any other Latino."

"I'm sorry you disapprove of her, but I haven't even asked her out yet."

"You will, I know you. Tell me the truth, are you attracted to her because she reminds you of me?"

"Maybe…maybe I just got a thing for blondes."

"I'm trying my best to look out for you. Someday, I will come back to you, I promise. Until then, please be careful of who you befriend, my love."

"I still can't believe Carla is as devious as you say she is."

"You have been warned!" Carina shouted as she dematerialized.

Angelo got undressed and went to take his shower. He thought about Carla while bathing, but he also thought about what Carina's spirit had said about her. Carla did look a little like Carina. The main difference between the two girls was that Carina had green eyes, while Carla had blue eyes. Other than that, they could almost pass for sisters.

The next morning, Angelo was having his breakfast while watching television in the family room. The network had interrupted the old movie they were showing for a breaking news flash. The news reporter said there was another body found by the railroad tracks. The body was identified as twenty-five-year-old Kevin Croce, a railroad conductor. Croce's body was found mutilated, while in full uniform at the Hickory Road train station this morning. Kevin's picture was being shown on the split screen with the reporter. Angelo's jaw dropped as he heard the news. The news reporter went on to say that the police believe it to be the work of the Railway Butcher.

"Oh, my God, no!" Angelo said to the television set.

"I don't believe this shit!" he said while choking back the tears. "This is so damn screwed up!"

The doorbell rang and Angelo had a feeling he knew who it was. Sure enough, Lieutenant Collins was at the front door, again. Angelo opened up the door and yelled at him.

"What do you want now?! Are you going to arrest me for Kevin's murder, too?!" Angelo screamed at the lieutenant.

"If you don't calm down, sir, I will have to bring you in as an emotionally disturbed person!" Lieutenant Collins told him.

Angelo tried his best to keep it together.

"Now, do you think you can calm down enough so that I can ask you some questions, or do I have to just bring you in, Mr. Russo?"

"Come on in, sir. I'll tell you all I know," he begrudgingly said.

The lieutenant walked into the foyer and Angelo closed the door behind him.

"Now, suppose you tell me, when was the last time you've seen Kevin Croce alive?" Lieutenant Collins asked him.

"It was yesterday, Friday morning. I was going to work and Kevin was working the morning train."

"About what time was that, Russo?"

"It was about eight thirty in the morning, sir."

"And you were going downtown into the city, right?"

"Yes, sir, that's right."

"Now, Mr. Russo, do you know off hand if Conductor Croce had any enemies?"

"Not to my knowledge, Lieutenant."

"The dispatcher at the Morton City terminal said his train arrived eight minutes late. He called Conductor Croce over the radio and the station's public address system, but he never responded. Croce was supposed to go to lunch, but he was never seen again."

"You mean he never made his second trip?"

"Nope. It looks as if you were the last person, outside of the passengers, to see Kevin Croce still alive."

"Wait! There was someone else who saw him!" Angelo exclaimed.

"And who might that be, Russo?"

"Conductor Taylor… I can't think of his last name. He's a drag queen with long, blond hair. I think it's a wig."

"You mean, Taylor Parker?"

"Yes! That's right, that's his full name, Taylor Parker!"

"Ok, we'll check it out. In the meantime, don't go anywhere, in case we have some more questions for you, Mr. Russo."

"All right, Lieutenant, I am not going anywhere," said Angelo.

"I'll be seeing you around, Russo," the lieutenant said while leaving Angelo's home.

Angelo was really worried. He knew the lieutenant was out for his ass. Somehow, he had to prove his innocence. One thing was for sure, there were not many classmates left from the railroad training school. Angelo went back to the family room to finish his bowl of cereal, which had gone soggy by now. Soon after he finished his food, Angelo got ready for work.

At about 10:30 p.m., the northbound train was pulling into the Allen Park train station. Jessica Klein was getting off. Jessica was going to visit her boyfriend for the night. Tony, her lover, was all alone and waiting for her. His wife was out of town on a business trip and wouldn't be back for five days. "We'll have the whole house all to ourselves," he had told her.

Jessica wanted to come over early, but she had to wait for her husband to go to work. "He works nights, as soon as he leaves, I'll be on the next train to see you," she had said over the phone. Jessica was extremely attractive. Her curly blonde hair, hazel-colored eyes, and charming personality are what attracted her to him. She loved to work out in the gym to retain her sexy figure. Jessica's primary problem was that she was a nymphomaniac. She had to have sex at least twice a day. Her husband couldn't keep up with her, so Jessica masturbated quite frequently. Jessica was sorry she married Joseph; he was always tired. He frequently complained about her wearing him out. One complication was of course the age difference between them. Jessica was twenty-four years old, but Joseph was over thirty years her senior. The other problem was that Joe was very overweight and out of shape. Everyone knew she married him for his money. Joseph owned a large shipping port. He always liked to be there at night, to make sure his workers weren't goofing off on the job.

Jessica started walking down the train station platform, wishing it weren't so dark and cold out. She was nervous because of all the murders in the area. *He better make it worth my while, making me come out here like this*, she thought to herself as she walked.

The train station was rather dark. There were some burned out lights on the outdoor platform and a crescent moon. Only one other person had departed with her and he had already gone in his car. Jessica stopped walking to reach for her cellphone in her bag. She wanted to call Tony to come pick her up. *I guess I should have called him while I was on the train,* she thought. Jessica pulled out her phone and tried to turn it on. The young lady realized her battery was so low that her phone couldn't even power up. What Jessica didn't realize was that she was being followed.

Jessica Klein walked right over to the only payphone on the platform. She dug into her purse for some change, until Jessica felt a tight rope being pulled around her neck. The butcher was trying hard to cut off her air supply. Jessica was frantically trying to break free, while still clutching her bag. She quickly reached for her can of mace. Jessica aimed the spray behind her neck and right into the assailant's face. The butcher released its hold on Jessica. The butcher was screaming from the pepper spray as it burned its eyes and face.

Jessica ran for her life. She flew down the station platform and down the stairs, as fast as the young woman's long legs could carry her.

"Help me! Somebody, please help me!" Jessica screamed when she got to the parking lot.

A middle-aged man had overheard her screaming and got out of his black BMW sedan. It was the same man that got off the train with her.

"Over here, miss! Come over here!" the man yelled back.

Jessica Klein ran over to the man's car.

"Oh, please mister, help me! Help me!" she frantically yelled.

"Are you all right?" he asked her.

"Someone tried to kill me!"

"Just now?"

"Yes, yes!"

"Where? Right here?"

"Yes, by the payphone! We've got to call the police!"

"Get in! I'll take you to the nearest precinct!"

They started to drive off. The butcher was running behind her in the parking lot. *She's a witness, I've got to kill her,* the killer thought. The butcher's eyes were still burning from the pepper spray. The killer took out the gun it had stolen from Officer Rivera after killing her last month. The killer fired several rounds at the moving car. One of the bullets went through the back window of the moving car. Then, another bullet struck the driver in the back of his head. The Good Samaritan that was helping Jessica was instantly killed.

Jessica screamed as the car lost control and crashed into a parked van.

A nearby police officer was driving by in his cruiser. He heard the gunfire and was approaching the scene with his lights flashing. The butcher realized it was in trouble and ran the other way. Officer Rose pulled into the train station parking lot and saw the accident. He immediately got out of the car to assist the victims. Smoke was rising from underneath the smashed hood of the black BMW. The officer also noticed the bullet holes in the rear window of the vehicle.

"Sir, are you all right?!" Officer Rose asked the man.

There was blood gushing from the back of his head where the bullet entered. The officer figured there wasn't much he could do for him. He quickly moved on to the woman. Her face was smashed into the windshield. She wasn't wearing a seatbelt.

"Ma'am, are you all right?!" he asked while gently pulling her back into her seat. There was no response from either one of them. Officer Rose called for assistance over his two-way radio.

"Hello, Central, come in to unit nine please!"

"Go unit nine. What's your twenty and problem?" the female dispatcher replied.

"We've got a situation over here at the parking lot of the Allen Park train station."

"What kind of situation, officer?"

"I have two victims in a car accident, one male and one female, unconscious. The male has a bullet wound in the back of his head. I'm requesting medical assistance."

"Ok unit nine, assistance is on the way. Stay with the victims."

"Ten-four," Officer Rose replied.

The next day, Monday morning at eight o'clock, Angelo was working the southbound express train. He was pulling into the South Park station. Angelo spotted his new love, Carla, getting on board while he observed the platform. She had long, blonde hair, down to her behind, just like his sister had. Angelo closed down the train after everyone boarded. He turned the master door key to give the engineer indication to proceed. The train began to pull out of the station. Angelo pulled his head in and closed the window. He then proceeded to check the passengers' tickets. Carla was looking for him; she was in the next car. When Angelo finally got to her, she gave him a big smile.

"Well good morning, Carla," Angelo greeted her.

"I'm impressed, you remembered my name," she said with a big grin on her face.

"I make it a point to never forget a beautiful woman."

Some of the male passengers turned around to see them after that remark.

"I have my ticket. You said it was…"

"Yes, yes. Let me see it, please."

Carla smiled and handed Angelo the expired train ticket. Angelo punched an acceptance hole into her ticket. He then clipped it onto the back of her seat. Despite the warning he got from his sister's ghost, Angelo decided to ask her out.

"Say, this is not like me, but…what are you doing this Thursday or Friday night?"

"Are you asking me out on a date, Mr. Conductor?"

"Yes, and do you remember *my name?*"

"It's…it's…don't tell me…"

She thought about it for a minute and then replied, "It's Angelo, right?"

"Yup! You just won the grand prize: me! That's if you want me, of course."

"You don't give yourself enough credit. I'm free Friday night, if that's all right by you."

"It sure is," he said with a big, fat grin.

"Fine, here's my number. Call me," Carla said as she wrote down her number and gave it to him.

"Thanks! Good luck with your car!"

"Thank you, Angelo. See you later."

"You sure will. Goodbye for now."

Angelo left her and thought about how fine and gorgeous she was. *Man, that there is a 'blonde-delicious.' She is so luscious,* he thought to himself. After daydreaming about her for a little while, he returned to the other passengers on board.

"Tickets please!" he said to the elderly man sitting opposite Carla.

"You sure got yourself a real nice catch there, young man," the man said as he handed Angelo his ticket.

"Thank you," he replied while blushing.

Angelo felt as though he was walking on air. He hadn't been this happy in a long time. *I don't believe what Carina said about her, she was dead wrong. Carla's a nice girl,* he tried to tell himself. He couldn't wait for tonight to call her. *That chick is so smoking hot,* he thought. Angelo went to the next car to check some more tickets. The train was cruising down the tracks at about seventy-five miles per hour. It was a nice, bright, November morning. Some of the passengers were looking out of their windows, taking in the scenery, while others were either sleeping or looking at their smartphones.

"Tickets please!" Angelo shouted.

Angelo had to hurry up. He had only five minutes left before the train would be pulling into the next station. The train was already getting packed. It was, after all, rush hour.

"Tickets please!" he kept shouting while walking down the aisle.

Angelo waved to a few of his co-workers. He started making his way back to his operating position. The train was getting close to the next station. Angelo unlocked the cabin door and went inside to make his service announcement to the passengers.

"Martin Road next! The next stop here will be Martin Road, everyone!" Conductor Russo had announced over the train's public address system.

Angelo got his keys ready to activate the door controller for the next stop. He really liked his job. The pay and benefits were great. Angelo also liked to mingle with the people on board, especially the women.

A few miles away, the butcher was sitting in its basement. The killer was worried, wondering, and hoping that the woman it attacked was dead.

"That bitch has got to be dead," the killer said to itself. "It would figure, the one time I forget to wear my mask and wig, and I get spotted. Shit! I know I shot the driver. He's got to be dead, but I don't know about the woman," the killer said to itself.

The killer didn't know if Jessica Klein was still alive, or if she got a really good look at her assailant. The killer couldn't risk being identified by anyone.

"It was dark outside. Some of the station lights were out. She couldn't have gotten a good look at me…if she's even alive," the butcher said.

But still, the assassin remained worried. There was that pang of uncertainty. That's what was gnawing at it—the doubt. The killer wanted an insurance policy. The murderer needed to know whether or not it would be recognized.

"I've got to pay a visit to that damn hospital to see if she's alive or dead. The bitch might be in a coma or something," the butcher said while thinking of a plan.

The butcher had friends, friends that could help. The killer had to be cool about it, though. The assassin had to know, one way or the other. If the woman were still alive, she'd have to be killed. *I mustn't have any witnesses. No loose ends to incriminate me,* the killer thought. The murderer sat there in its dark and dingy basement. The assassin kept thinking about what it was going to do next, just like a professional chess player strategically planning its next move.

11

THE WITNESS

It had been five days since the attack on Jessica Klein and the car accident that followed. She had been lying in a coma in the hospital, hooked up with IV fluids and monitoring equipment since then. Joseph Klein, her husband, was in the hospital room, waiting for her to awaken. He had been back and forth between checking on his business and visiting his wife in the hospital. Jessica Klein had undergone facial reconstruction to repair her damaged face. Jessica's face was all bandaged up with only openings for her eyes, mouth, nostrils, and her ears. She also suffered three fractured ribs. Her beauty was just a memory now. There were glass fragments from the windshield stuck in her face that had to be cautiously removed. The doctor said she was very lucky to be alive. Unfortunately, Ishmael Rosenberg, the Good Samaritan that tried to save her life, didn't make it. He was found dead on the scene from the gunshot wound to the back of his head. Jessica was finally opening her eyes. She tried to look around her surroundings, but her vision was blurred. Jessica tried to focus her eyes.

"Joe, is that you?" she managed to say in a voice that was barely audible.

"Jess? You've come back to me," Joseph said in a gentle voice.

"Wh-where am I?"

"You're in a hospital, dear."

"A hospital?"

"Yes, you've been hurt pretty bad, but you're going to be all right."

"There was a man, he was with me."

"Yes, why were you there with him? You weren't cheating on me, were you?"

"No, no. He was trying to help me."

"Listen, we'll talk about this later. I've got to go let the doctors know that you're conscious."

Joseph Klein got up and left the hospital room feeling hurt and confused. *I gave her everything that money could buy; I know she cheated on me,* he thought. Joseph went to the nurses' station to explain the situation. After walking down the hall, Joseph found the station.

"Excuse me, nurse! My wife just came out of her coma. Her name is Jessica Klein. She's in room 204," Joseph explained to the nurse on duty.

"I was just getting ready to check in on her," the nurse told him.

The nurse working at the station was an appealing, young African-American woman whom others had referred to as "Nurse Williams." Nurse Williams followed Mr. Klein to his wife's room. Jessica was in distress. Jessica called out to the nurse when she arrived with her husband.

"Nurse! Nurse, please, the pain. I can't bear the pain," Jessica cried out.

"Sure, Miss. I'll get you something for the pain, but I can't give you a sedative," Nurse Williams said.

"Why not, nurse?"

"Now that you're conscious, the police will want to question you. I've got to let them know," the nurse said as she left the room.

Officer Rose had been stationed just outside of her room to protect her. Chief Brady chose him since he was the first one on the scene. Brady thought that Rose would be able to jog her memory, if she had any recollection problems.

A middle-aged woman with short, salt-and-pepper-colored hair walked into Jessica's room, after the officer left to relieve himself.

"I see you're awake now," the woman said to Jessica.

"Wh-who are you?" Jessica asked.

"My name is Adinah, Mrs. Adinah Rosenberg. Does my last name sound familiar to you?"

"No, I'm sorry, it doesn't."

Joseph was looking at this strange woman inquisitively, wondering who the hell she was.

"My husband's name is Ishmael. Now does it ring a bell to you? You home-wrecker! You ruined my life," Adinah said as she sobbed.

"I'm sorry, Miss, but I don't know of any Ishmael, and I still don't know what you're talking about."

"Perhaps, I may be of some assistance, Miss," Joseph said to her.

"And who might you be, sir?"

"I am her husband."

"Oh, my, isn't this nice? Maybe, maybe *you* could explain why your wife was with my husband in his car when they crashed?"

"No, I can't. She hasn't told me yet."

"I never knew his name," Jessica stated.

"Oh, and I suppose that makes it all right?"

"No, you don't understand."

"That's right, I don't understand. I gave my Ishmael the best thirty years of my life, and this is what I get in return?" Adinah said while she wept.

"Your husband tried to help me."

"I bet he did. What were you doing to him in his car when he crashed?"

"Nothing! I swear to you; I didn't do anything to him!"

"Miss, if my wife says she didn't do anything, I would be inclined to believe her."

"You stay out of this, Mister! It's obvious *you* believe her, even though she cheated on *you, too.*"

"Mrs. Rosenberg, please listen to me! Your husband tried to save my life! I was attacked at the train station. He offered to bring me to the police station, and then we were shot at by the one that attacked me," Jessica struggled to say from the pain.

"Are you telling me the truth, Miss?"

"Yes. He was hurt and lost control of the car. After that, we crashed. Is he all right?"

"No, no he is not. He's…he's dead. My Ishmael is dead," Adinah said as she broke down and cried.

"Oh, my God! I am so, so very sorry, Mrs. Rosenberg."

"It just sounds like something he would do. My husband was a gentleman. He would always try to help anyone. Now, look at what it got him; it cost him his life. I must go now."

Adinah got herself together and left the hospital room, still clutching a very wet tissue in her hand.

"I feel so bad, honey. That man died trying to save my life," Jessica said to her husband.

"It still doesn't explain one thing, Jess," Joseph said.

"What's that, honey?"

"What were *you* doing there at that train station that night?" Joseph asked her in an accusatory manner.

Jessica said nothing. She knew she had been caught in the act. Joseph was staring at her, waiting for an answer, but Jessica had nothing to say. The nurse had come back with Officer Rose. He took out his little black book and was ready to question her.

"Mrs. Klein, I'm Officer Rose. I was right there at the train station where you and Mr. Rosenberg had crashed. I just want to ask you some questions if that's all right with you?"

"Sure," she said.

The officer turned to look at Joseph.

"Excuse me, are you related to Mrs. Klein?" Officer Rose asked him.

"Yes I am, I'm her husband," Joseph replied.

"Then, you won't mind me asking her some questions?"

"By all means, please proceed."

"You don't mind your husband being present here, do you, Mrs. Klein?"

She looked at her husband and thought, it would be an admission of guilt to kick him out now, even though, she really would prefer him to be absent during the questioning.

"No, I don't mind," she said after a bit.

"Now, Mrs. Klein, can you please tell me, for the record, exactly what happened on Saturday night, November 2, at the Allen Park train station?" Officer Rose asked.

Jessica decided to choose her words very wisely before she answered the officer's question. Jessica was still struggling with the pain, and she felt like she was in the hot seat with her husband present in the room.

"I had gotten off the train and…well, I just walked down the platform to the payphone…" she started to sob as it began to come back to her.

"I know it must be painful for you, but it's important that you try and recollect as much as possible. Please continue," Officer Rose told her.

"I was…at the payphone…looking for change in my bag, when all of a sudden…" Jessica started crying again.

"Please continue, Mrs. Klein."

"This man. This man tried to strangle me from behind. He, he put a rope around my neck and was pulling it tighter and tighter," she managed to say in between her sobs.

"How did you break free?" Officer Rose asked.

"I, I reached for my can of mace and sprayed him in the face," Jessica said while choking back her tears.

Joseph Klein was feeling sorry for his wife, thinking of the ordeal she's been through, but it still didn't explain what she was doing there in the first place. *Jessica should have been home instead. She must have been having a rendezvous with someone before she was attacked,* he thought to himself.

"Did you get a good look at your attacker, Mrs. Klein?" Officer Rose asked her.

"No! I was being choked! I just reached up from behind my neck and sprayed him."

"What happened next, Mrs. Klein?"

"He released his grip on me and then he screamed."

"Then what happened?"

"I, I ran! I ran for my life!"

"So you never got a good look at your attacker, did you?"

"No, I didn't."

"Are you quite sure your attacker was a male?"

"Yes, I am. I heard him scream, it was the scream of a man. I'll never ever forget it," Jessica said with tears streaming down her bandaged face.

"How did you go meet up with Mr. Rosenberg?"

"I just ran down to the parking lot screaming when this nice man overheard me. He called me to his car and I went to him."

"Then you two drove off and crashed?"

"He was going to take me to the police precinct when we were being shot at by that crazy maniac. The next thing I knew, we crashed. That's all I can remember, aside from waking up here."

"Ok, Mrs. Klein. If you do remember anything else, please give me a call. Here's my card," Officer Rose told her as he gave Jessica his card.

"Officer, one thing, please…"

"Yes, Mrs. Klein?"

"Could you please send the nurse back in here for me?"

"Sure, Mrs. Klein, right away."

"Thank you so much."

The officer walked out of her room, while saying goodbye to her and her husband. Joseph looked dearly at his wife, while he sat in the chair next to her bedside.

"Honey, I still need to know. What were you doing there at a train station far away from home that night?"

"I was visiting a friend, that's all."

"Who? Was it anybody I know?"

"Mrs. Klein, you called for me?" the nurse said as she walked into the room.

"Yes nurse, I'll take that sedative now, please," Jessica said while feeling like she was saved by the bell.

"Mr. Klein, you may want to say goodbye to her now. Your wife will soon be going to sleep after I give her the sedative; besides, visiting hours are just about over."

"Yes, I understand. Goodbye, dear, we'll continue this conversation tomorrow," he said while leaving the hospital room.

The next day; Friday, November 8, Angelo was getting ready for his hot date with Carla. It was twelve noon, Angelo had six hours to go. Carla had gotten her car back from the repair facility and was coming over at six p.m. She was shocked to find out that Angelo didn't own a car, while he was living in the suburbs. He offered to cook dinner for her in an intimate setting, but she wanted to go to a particular Italian restaurant, instead. Angelo went to the main upstairs bathroom to shave. When he looked in the mirror, it wasn't his face he saw, it was Carina.

"You're still going out with Carlita Gomez, aren't you? After I warned you," Carina's spirit said in her ghostly voice.

"Yes, I am," replied Angelo.

"Is there anything I can do to change your mind, Angelo?"

"No, there isn't. Look Carina, I love you, but please let me try to have a good time. Don't you think I deserve it after all the shit I've been through?"

"Yes baby, you do, but not with her. Carlita will hurt you. She will use and abuse you. I have seen her do it to so many people, long before you. You've got to trust me on this, my love," her spirit said so sincerely.

"Yeah, well, you could be wrong about her this time. Besides, I'm a big boy now. I can take care of myself. Now, will you please leave my mirror so I can shave?"

"Ok. I will leave you now, but don't say I didn't warn you."

After that, Carina's image vanished from the mirror. Angelo was now able to see his own reflection in the mirror again. He finished shaving and then he took a quick shower. The telephone rang just as Angelo was getting dressed. Angelo ran over to answer it.

"Hello?" Angelo asked.

"Hello, Conductor, are you almost ready?" Carla asked.

"Yes, I'll be ready by six."

"I'm running a little early and was wondering if you would be ready sooner."

"How soon? It's not even five o'clock yet."

"I could be there in thirty minutes, if that's all right with you, Angelo?"

"Sh-sure. I'll be ready, come on over!"

"Cool, because I'm hungry. I can't wait to take you to that Italian restaurant I told you about."

"Ok! I'll see you soon, baby!"

"Baby? Boy, are we moving fast!" she said with a chuckle.

Angelo hung up the telephone and proceeded to get dressed in his navy-blue suit. He wanted to make a good first impression with her. *Wow! I get a hot date, and she picks me up and drives me to the restaurant. How cool is that?* Angelo thought to himself.

About a half an hour later, Carla was there ringing Angelo's doorbell. He went downstairs to let her in.

"Wow! You look smoking hot, Carla," Angelo told her.

Carla was in a sexy, beautiful, low-cut, bright red dress, with a large string of genuine pearls wrapped around her neck. The dress accentuated her shapely figure, especially her large breasts and well-formed hips. She also wore a mink jacket over her dress. Angelo was awed by her high-class style and expensive clothes. Carla even donned a bright red pair of Prada shoes.

"You don't look so bad yourself, Angelo," she said to him.

"Come on in, Carla."

"Oh, I was hoping we could just go. Are you ready?"

"Sure! Let me just get my jacket and we can leave," he said.

Angelo grabbed his suit jacket and left with Carla. When he saw her car, his jaw dropped.

"Is that your car?" Angelo asked.

"Why yes, is there anything wrong with it?"

"No, no. It's not every day I see a Mercedes Benz parked in my driveway."

Angelo got in the black Mercedes sedan with his hot date. He realized his girlfriend had much more money than he did. She was also doing a very good job at flaunting it.

"So, you live in that house all by yourself now?" Carla asked him while driving off his property.

"Yes, I do. My parents died in a car accident a few months ago."

"That's right; I remember hearing about it on the news. I heard about your sister too, Carina, that was her name, right?"

"Yes, she was murdered shortly after that."

"I'm sorry for your loss, Angelo. Do you have any other relatives?"

"No, that was it."

"Your sister told me about you when we were in college together, but she never introduced you to me. You must feel so all alone now."

"Yes, I do, but not tonight."

"You must be making good money at the railroad to…well, I mean, to pay your mortgage and stuff, right?"

"There is no mortgage on the house. My folks had it paid off a while ago and yes, I'm doing all right at the railroad."

"So consider yourself lucky, Angelo. It really sounds like you've got it made."

"Yeah, I guess I do."

"Word around town has it that you know who the Railway Butcher is. Do you?"

"I wish I did. The witness they had didn't see him, she just ran away. I've got a score to settle with him for killing my sister."

"How do you know he did it?"

"I saw what was left of her body. The police said it fits his method of killing. She was beheaded."

"Oh, shit! Ok now, Angelo, TMI, that's just way too much information. Not before dinner, please."

"I'm really sorry. I didn't mean to get too graphic. I wouldn't want to spoil your appetite now."

"Apology accepted. We're here," Carla said while parking the car in the restaurant's parking lot.

A little further uptown, the Railway Butcher was on the telephone with Muhammad, the killer's favorite customer.

"My boss is not very happy with you," Muhammad said over the phone.

"What's the problem?" the butcher asked.

"The heart you sold us was no good. It was spoiled."

"That is *your* fault. You took so long to meet me. Hearts have a very short shelf life. They are only good for about six hours. You came too late, so it died."

"My boss needs a good heart, or you shall refund his money. You charged us $120.000."

"I know what I charged you. I'll get you another heart."

"Make sure it is fresh, or else."

"It will be fresh. Just make sure you meet me on time, next time."

"How soon can you have it?"

"Just give me a couple of days. I will let you know," the killer said as he hung up the phone.

"What a dopey bastard he is," the butcher said to itself.

"He screws it up, and I have to friggin accommodate him. Shit! Now I got to go find me another victim. I was going to take a break. Shit!"

The killer was getting its tools together for his next kill.

Meanwhile, back at Angelo's home, Carla was just saying goodbye to Angelo.

"I had a wonderful time, Angelo," Carla said.

"Do you want to come in for a nightcap or something?" Angelo asked.

"I would love to, but I have to work tomorrow."

"But it's only ten o'clock, the night is still young!"

"I really have to go. I get up early in the morning to go to work."

"Ok, but I have just one question."

"What's that?"

"Is your name really Carla or Carlita?"

Her smile turned into a frown. She became very upset at his question.

"What?! I told you my name is Carla! Where the *hell* did you hear that from?"

Angelo felt belittled and embarrassed. Clearly, he touched upon a nerve with her. She became so angry with him that he no longer wanted to be in the same car with her.

"My sister," Angelo finally managed to say.

"Your sister? Carina? Why, she's dead! What the hell kind of games are you playing with me, Angelo?"

"No game, but you're right, you should go."

Angelo opened up the car door and left her, without even saying goodbye. He walked right into his house and closed the door behind him, feeling upset and hurt.

"Carina! You were so damn right about her!" Angelo yelled up the stairwell.

Carla had raced her Mercedes out of Angelo's driveway so fast that her tires screeched. She flew down the road going twenty miles per hour above the posted speed limit. Her face had turned beet red. *How the hell did he know my real name?* Carla angrily thought to herself.

After driving twenty minutes, Carla arrived at her destination, Crane Park. Her boss was waiting there for her in a black Ford pickup truck. He blindfolded her and took her in his truck. Carla had left her own car there at the park.

After driving a while, they arrived at a beautiful, large, L-shaped ranch house in the middle of nowhere. The home was covered with cedar siding. He parked his truck in the long driveway and escorted Carla inside. Once they got inside, her boss removed her blindfold. Carla walked into the spacious home, while the man closed the door behind her. The big house was beautifully decorated with expensive artwork. The walls were covered in mahogany wood planking. There were large oil paintings, each with their own picture light, hanging on the walls. There were also exquisite statues everywhere, all highlighted by spotlights. The wood floors were covered with imported designer rugs. Closed circuit TV surveillance cameras were everywhere. Carla had thought she stepped into a museum.

"You look disheveled," the man said.

"I feel like it, too," she responded.

"Do you have any information for me?"

"Do you have my money?"

"Yes, I do, right here in this envelope. But first, tell me what I need to know."

"He doesn't know shit. He was bullshitting all along."

"Are you sure?"

"Yes! A girl can tell these things, you know."

"So, all this time, Mr. Angelo Russo was lying. What about the witness in the hospital?" he asked her.

"I heard she never got a look at the killer. She just ran away. Now, can I have the money, please?"

"Here it is, five thousand bucks. Now, don't go and spend it all in one place, honey," he said while handing Carla the payment envelope.

"Why do you care so much about this serial killer?" Carla asked.

"Who says I do?"

"Well, you seem to want to know a lot about him being spotted and shit. So, I assume you care about what happens to him if he's caught and whatever."

"My dear, first of all, you know what happens when you assume. Secondly, I'm merely writing a book about what goes on inside a criminal's mind. Thirdly, for what I'm paying you, I *don't* expect to be grilled. Now, do we have an understanding, or what?"

"Yes, we do."

"Good. It's been a real pleasure doing business with you, Carla."

She walked back to the front door.

"I'm ready to go back to my car. Are you going to blindfold me again?" she asked.

"But of course, dear, let's go," the man had said as he blindfolded her again.

The butcher was happy. He didn't have to worry about the so-called witness, or Angelo Russo. *She performed her task admirably well. I think I'll use her again,* the killer thought while rubbing his hands together.

A few minutes later, the slaughterer dropped her off at the park and removed her blindfold.

"Ok, we're here, dear! We'll be doing business again, someday," he told her.

"Good, I could sure use the money," Carla said as she got out of his truck.

Carla got back into her car and drove off. She was very happy with her payment, but Carla began feeling guilty. *I shouldn't have gone off on Angelo like that,* she thought. But it still bothered her. *How the hell did Angelo know my real name?* It bothered her so much that she decided to head back to Angelo's house. Carla wanted to apologize to Angelo, but more importantly, she had to know how he knew her real name. There were very few people around there that knew her name. Carina was one of them, but she promised she would never tell anyone else her real name. Carla also hadn't seen her in years since college. Now, Carina's dead…or is she?

After a while of driving, Carla was pulling back into Angelo's driveway. She got out of her car and walked up the pathway. It was after eleven o'clock at night. Angelo didn't leave the pathway lights on because he wasn't expecting any company. Angelo also wanted to keep the electric bill down. It takes a lot of energy to run a house and he knew that. Carla had to use her own flashlight to see where she was going. As she approached the front door, Carla began to hear voices emanating from inside the house. She decided to look through the sidelight window. Carla couldn't believe what she was seeing. Angelo was having a conversation with Carina's translucent ghost. They were both unaware of Carla's presence outside. Carla thought she was seeing things.

"Carina? It can't be…she's…she's…dead," Carla softly said to herself. "What kind of trickery is this? What the hell is going on here?" she whispered to herself.

Carla became scared and upset. She quickly ran down the pathway and back into her car. She started up her vehicle and drove off, feeling even more confused and lost in her own thoughts. *What the hell did I just witness back there? Is Carina still alive or what? But that's impossible…I could almost see right through her. What the hell is going on there?* The scene was playing over and over in her mind like a recording.

Meanwhile, Angelo was trying to get ready for bed. He was so upset that even Carina's ghost couldn't relax him. She had told him, "I told you so," and he didn't want to hear it. Angelo knew that Carina was right about Carla. He wondered how such a lovely girl like her could be so damn mean. *What made her go off like that? What set her off? Why was she so ashamed of her Spanish name and heritage, and why would Carla pretend to be something that she wasn't?* Angelo asked himself.

He finally got himself cleaned up and ready for bed. Angelo decided to sleep in Carina's old bedroom tonight. He wanted to be close to the only woman who really loved him. Carina was the only girl that ever completely understood him. *God, I wish she were still alive,* he thought. The girl he grew up with, his so-called "sister," was really the only one for him. Unfortunately, Carina was gone. Angelo got into her bed and pulled the covers up over himself. Unbeknownst to him, Carina's spirit was watching over him with a big smile on her face. She wanted him back. She wanted to be alive again and to be a big part of his life. Carina wanted to touch him again, to feel him again, and to hold him in her arms once more. Carina so desperately wanted to make passionate love to Angelo, but how? She needed another living body. Carina needed a body to possess. *I must be with him once more,* her spirit thought. *I need to be with my beloved Angelo. We shall be together somehow. I must find a way.*

"Pleasant dreams, my sweet love, pleasant dreams," Carina whispered to him before she disappeared.

Angelo slept peacefully that night. His sister made sure of that. She was his guardian angel, watching over him. Carina's ghost would haunt him every day and night, until they were together again.

12

THE DERAILMENT

It was early on Tuesday morning, November 12, just after a three-day weekend for most people. The sun was starting to rise, but it was only thirty-five degrees outside. The calendar said fall, but winter was what it really felt like. People everywhere had donned all of their winter clothing.

Railroad Engineer William Hunter and Conductor Angelo Russo were in the Hyde Road yard, making up a train for service. They were the first crew in the morning to bring a train into passenger service. Engineer Hunter looked at his watch and noticed it was already 5:40 a.m. The engineer knew they didn't have enough time to finish checking out the train. He had just finished removing all of the handbrakes on the train, but Hunter hadn't checked out all of the couplers yet. The crew had to be at the Hyde Park terminal by six in the morning, in order to make their 6:05 interval. Hunter wasn't happy about working with Angelo. William knew Angelo was a rookie and all rookies were slow and inexperienced. William Hunter was an average height, slim African-American. He worked his way up from being a porter, conductor, and then engineer. After about twenty years with the railroad, Hunter was well-seasoned. However, William Hunter was only an engineer for five years. He did have an attitude problem. Hunter thought he knew it all and didn't like anyone telling him how to do his job. Hunter had decided to call Angelo over the public address system.

"Hey, Russo, you finished yet?!" Hunter called out.

"Yeah Mr. Hunter, I'm done," Angelo replied over the microphone.

"All right then, close down the doors and let's go. We've got to be at the station in fifteen minutes. The only way that's going to happen is if we fly, so hang on."

"Ok, let's do it," Angelo replied.

Angelo closed down the rear section of the train first and then the front section. He turned his master door controller key to run and removed the key. Angelo then gave his engineer the proper proceed signal by passing him two long buzzer signals. Engineer Hunter released the air brakes and then he put the train into forward position. The train started to proceed down the tracks. Hunter was revving up the diesel engines. *We're gonna have to do eighty if we're going to get there on time,* he thought to himself. The train was cruising along the tracks as it left the yard. Once they reached the main line, the engineer wrapped up the controller to pick up the speed. Soon, they were speeding by at eighty-five miles per hour.

"Shit, we hauling ass now," William Hunter said to himself in the cabin.

Angelo was getting very nervous. He was hanging on for dear life. Angelo wasn't used to going this fast on a train before. He thought about complaining to the engineer to slow it down. Clearly, this was an excessive speed. *I should just pull the emergency brake cord to stop the train,* he thought. *That's what they told us to do in school in this type of situation.* Angelo knew the rules, but he didn't want to rock the boat. *It's tough being a rookie. You're constantly being torn apart between what's right and what's wrong,* he thought to himself. The train was approaching ninety miles per hour. Hunter was smiling in his cabin.

"We're gonna make it! Only three more miles to go," Hunter said to himself.

But Engineer William Hunter forgot about that sharp turn up ahead. He also didn't notice the big, black garbage bag on the track within the turn, until it was too late.

"Oh, shit!" Hunter screamed out.

Engineer Hunter desperately tried to stop the train. The locomotive flew over the large black bag around the turn. William realized his train could not make that turn, at that speed, especially after going over that filled bag. The engine, plus half of the train, kept going straight. The steel cars cried and squealed in agony, while derailing onto the ground with a thunderous thud. Engineer Hunter was thrown from his seat when his locomotive landed on its side. Three other railcars followed with him. Angelo was spared since he was riding in the last car. The rule was, when operating a train in non-passenger service, the conductor had to ride in the last car, in case the train pulled apart.

Conductor Angelo Russo started making his way up front toward the engineer. He could not get passed the fourth car, since the rest of the train was separated and lying on the ground. Angelo put his safety vest back on and climbed down on the road bed.

"Oh, my God!" he said while observing the derailment.

"I knew he was going too damn fast. Shit!" he said to himself.

Angelo kept walking along the tracks while watching for any other trains. He kept his flashlight on since it still wasn't that bright out yet. Angelo couldn't believe what he was seeing with his own eyes. The train wreck looked like a bunch of toy trains being thrown all over the place. There were bits and pieces of the railcars scattered everywhere. Angelo cautiously kept walking until he reached the head locomotive.

"Hunter! are you all right?!" he called out loud. "Hunter! Where are you?!"

But there was no response at all. When he finally got to the locomotive, Angelo noticed it was leaking diesel fuel. He spotted the train engineer lying unconscious, leaning on the shattered side cab window. There was blood all over his face. Angelo decided to call for help on his two-way radio.

"Hello, Command Center, come in to the zero five hundred yard put in, out of Hyde Road yard," Angelo called.

"Who's calling Command Center?" the supervisor replied over the radio.

"Command, this is the zero five hundred put in, out of Hyde Road yard."

"Zero five hundred; state your location and problem, sir."

"Command, we've had a derailment while leaving the yard!"

"Did you say a derailment, sir?"

"Yes sir, I did."

"Is this the engineer, zero five hundred?"

"No, sir, I'm the conductor."

"Where's the engineer, Conductor?"

"He's unconscious and trapped in the head locomotive, sir."

"Does he look like he needs medical assistance, Conductor?"

"Yes, sir, he does!"

"And you said you just left the yard, heading into the terminal, sir?"

"Yes, we're past that sharp turn, not far from the terminal, sir."

"All right, Conductor, stay with him. We'll send a train service supervisor out along with medical assistance."

"That's a copy, Command," Angelo said while wondering what he was going to tell the supervisor.

Angelo Russo tried to climb up into the locomotive to see if he could help the engineer.

"Shit! I can see the cabin door, but how the hell am I going to get up there?" he said to himself. "I need help," Angelo said while starting to walk away.

Angelo noticed a torn up black plastic garbage bag near the tracks. He walked over to check it out. As Angelo got closer to the bag, he began to get sick. There was a bludgeoned arm sticking out of the torn garbage bag.

"Oh, shit!" he said aloud.

Angelo thought about calling it in to the Command Center. He reached for his radio and then he spotted a train coming from the opposite direction. The train blew its horn as it approached him.

"Conductor Russo?!" the man yelled out of the locomotive's window.

"Yes, that's me, sir!"

"I'm TSS Moriotto, stay right there!" the supervisor said.

The engineer stopped his train right near Angelo and the supervisor disembarked.

"Thanks for the lift, Mr. Hudson," the supervisor said to the engineer as he climbed off the train.

The supervisor began walking toward Angelo. Once TSS Moriotto was cleared from the train, the engineer moved his train again. It was common for rail crews to use trains as taxis in the yard.

Train Service Supervisor Moriotto was a relatively new supervisor. Moriotto was around forty years old. He was short and stocky with a full head of black hair. The Asian supervisor was always accused of being overzealous.

"What the hell happened over here?" TSS Moriotto asked.

"We were just coming around the turn and the next thing I knew, we stopped short. I started to make my way up front to see what had happened. When I got up front, I realized we had derailed," Angelo replied.

"Was the engineer speeding?"

"I, I couldn't tell, sir, I was all the way in the back of the train. It seemed to me that we were moving pretty fast, but I couldn't really tell if he was going over the limit. The engineer is hurt, sir. He needs medical assistance."

"EMS is on their way. Where is he?"

"He's still in the locomotive sir, over there."

Angelo pointed to the locomotive lying on its side by the trees.

"Let's walk over there while I get your names and pass numbers," the supervisor said to Angelo.

"I'm Conductor Angelo Russo. My pass number is 762265."

"What's your engineer's name and pass number?"

"His name is William Hunter. I don't know his pass number, sir. This is the first time we've worked together, sir."

TSS Moriotto began taking pictures of the accident scene with his smartphone. He looked up at Engineer Hunter with his bloodied face leaning up against the shattered cab window. Moriotto knew he was going to be there for a while.

"Sir, there is just one more thing," Angelo said to the supervisor.

"What is it, Russo?"

"There's a bag over there you need to see," Angelo said while pointing to the tracks.

"What's so special about a bag, Russo? Can't you see this man is hurt?"

"It looks like there's a body, or body parts in it, sir."

"Jesus! Are you sure?"

"Yes, sir. I didn't look in it, but there's a bloodied arm sticking out of it."

"I have to call it in. We can't touch it. It would be like tampering with evidence. I'll call Command Center and they'll contact the proper authorities," the supervisor said while making a call on his smartphone.

Within a few short minutes, an ambulance was cautiously approaching along the road near the tracks. TSS Moriotto went to meet the ambulance crew. A paramedic and an emergency medical technician emerged from the ambulance.

"Hello there, I'm Paramedic Avila. Where's the injured employee?" the paramedic asked TSS Moriotto.

Paramedic Avila was a husky, middle-aged, tall, dark-skinned man of Puerto Rican heritage. His new partner was EMT Rhodes. Rhodes was a young male Caucasian of slender build with short, brown hair. TSS Moriotto went and showed the ambulance crew where the injured engineer was. Angelo followed close behind all the men. When they arrived at the locomotive, the paramedic asked TSS Moriotto where the access point was.

"Follow me, men, I'll show you an easy way to get inside the locomotive," TSS Moriotto told them.

They all climbed up the railing and up to the cabin door. It took two of the men to gain access into the damaged cabin. TSS Moriotto unlocked and opened the door, while Angelo struggled to hold it open for the men. The medical team followed the supervisor into the cabin. The paramedic checked out Engineer Hunter's vital signs.

"I'm sorry, but this man is dead," the paramedic stated to TSS Moriotto.

"Shit, I was afraid of that," Moriotto replied.

The medical team placed the engineer's body onto the stretcher. They struggled bringing the body down to the ground.

"Is he going to be all right?" Angelo asked.

"I'm afraid not; he's dead," Moriotto answered.

The medical team then took the engineer's body into the ambulance. A police car was now arriving on the scene. Two officers stepped out of the patrol car.

"Who's the supervisor in charge?" one of the officers asked.

"I am, Officer. I'm Train Service Supervisor Moriotto," the supervisor replied.

"Where's the body?" the officer asked.

"Right this way," Moriotto said, while taking the men to the site.

*
**

It was almost seven o'clock. An hour had passed since the derailment. The sun was shining brighter now, but it didn't add much more warmth. The police officers followed TSS Moriotto and Conductor Russo toward the black bag. Officer Paul Flanigan took out his pocket knife and began to cut open the bag.

"Holy shit," Officer Flanigan said under his breath.

Inside the plastic bag, there were cut up remains of what was once an attractive, young woman. The victim had long, light-brown hair, average height, and a slender build. She had brought back very uncomfortable memories for Police Officer Flanigan. He instantly thought about Kathy Rivera, the stunning young female officer that recently died in his arms. Flanigan had vowed to avenge her death.

"Are you all right?" Officer Ireland asked.

"Yes, yes I'm ok," Flanigan replied.

"She reminds you of Officer Rivera, doesn't she?"

"Yeah, she does. We have to catch this sick bastard, soon!"

They didn't know who the mystery woman was. She had no identification on her at all. The woman was sliced open. Her heart, liver, and pancreas had been removed. The killer had cut both of her legs off, to make her fit in the industrial garbage bag. The body was also torn up from being struck by the train.

Later on that morning, Angelo was downtown in the chief trainmaster's office. TSS Moriotto had brought him down to be interrogated. The chief was an elderly white male with snow-white hair. Chief Trainmaster Murphy could have retired five years ago, but he chose not to. He really loved his job and enjoyed putting his subordinates in the hot seat. Murphy was sitting in his plush office behind his big mahogany desk when Moriotto arrived with Angelo.

"I just got a call from the yardmaster, Mr. Russo," the chief said.

"Yes, sir?" Angelo said.

"They've hooked up the locomotive's data recording box to the computer. It appears that your engineer was flying by at eighty-eight miles per hour. You claimed that you didn't know if he was speeding or not. How the hell can you not know that, Mr. Russo?"

"Where I was, sir, there was no active speedometer for me to look at."

"That has got to be the lamest excuse I have ever heard. You don't need to look at a speedometer to tell if you're speeding, unless, of course, you were sleeping. Were you sleeping on the job, Mr. Russo?"

"No sir, I wasn't. It's just…"

"Just what, Mr. Russo? If you're trying to cover up for the man, forget about it. He's dead. It'll go a lot easier on you if you tell the truth. now, out with it!"

"Ok, sir. He was going rather fast, especially around that turn," Angelo nervously said.

"So, we have now determined that Engineer Hunter was speeding. Is that correct, Conductor Russo?"

"Yes, sir, I guess so. Can I have a union representative here with me, sir?"

"I already told you, Mr. Russo, there wasn't one available at this time. I've got a good mind to put you up for dismissal."

"But, sir!"

"Don't you 'but, sir' me, young man. You know the rules. If you find that your engineer is operating erratically, in this case speeding, what are you supposed to do?"

"I'm supposed to pull the emergency brake cord."

"Correct! You failed to do that! If your train were in passenger service, people could have lost their lives! Now, what have you got to say for yourself, young man?"

"I'm sorry; it will never happen again, sir."

"Yeah, well, I'm afraid 'sorry' doesn't cut it, Conductor Russo. You *are* right about one thing, though."

"What's that, Chief?" Angelo hesitantly asked.

"It *won't* happen again. I will put all of the necessary paperwork right through to Labor Relations. This is *certainly* grounds for your dismissal, Russo, and *that* is going to be my recommendation! Case closed."

"No, no, sir! Can I please get another chance? I really need my job, sir!"

"You should have thought about that before, young man; you were on probation."

Just at that very moment, Moriotto's cellphone rang.

"Yes? Yes, I'm at his office with Russo. Ok, hold on," TSS Moriotto said to the man on the phone.

"Excuse me, Chief?"

"What is it, Moriotto?" the chief asked.

"It's Superintendent James. He wants to talk to you, sir."

"Ok, give it to me," the chief replied.

"Hello James! How's it going? Yes, he's here… I've already recommended dismissal… I see. I see. Ok, if you say so. I'll do it for you. Say, are we still on for that golf game on Saturday? Great! See you then, take it easy." The chief gave TSS Moriotto back his phone and looked at Angelo.

"Mr. Russo!"

"Yes, Chief?" Angelo solemnly replied.

"It appears you have some friends in high places. So, I'm going to change my recommendations for you."

"You are, sir?"

"I'm retracting my recommendation of dismissal for you."

"Really, sir?"

"Yes, I am. Instead, I'm giving you thirty days' suspension, *without pay.*"

"Thirty days without pay? But, sir, I've got bills to pay!"

"Well, Would you rather the alternative: dismissal, Mr. Russo?"

"Uh, no, sir, I wouldn't."

"Good, then it's settled, thirty days' suspension it is. Oh, and by the way, Mr. Russo…"

"Yes, Chief?"

"There are strings attached with this offer. Remember, *you* are still on probation here."

"I'm well aware of that, sir."

"Good! Because if you pull that crap again, or if you get into any other kind of trouble, you'll be dismissed…permanently. You understand what I'm telling you?"

"Yes, sir, I do."

"I'm also going to extend your one-year probation, effective today, and you will have a train service supervisor riding your train for one week. Make sure you're on point and stay focused. Do you have any questions, Russo?"

"No, sir, I don't."

"Good, case dismissed," the chief told Angelo.

"So, what do I do now, Chief?" Angelo asked.

"What do you do now? You sign these papers and go home, Russo."

"Go home, sir?"

"Are we on the same page or what? Maybe I'm speaking a foreign language or something, is that it, Mr. Russo?"

"No, sir, you're not."

"Ok, then. Your time has been cut as of zero six hundred hours. Go home, Russo. See you in thirty days. Do I make myself clear?"

"Yes, sir."

"And we're on the same page now, Russo?"

"Yes, sir."

"Good, I'm glad. Now go home, Russo, and think about what you've done here today. Don't ever let it happen again, because next time, you won't be so lucky. Next time, no one will be able to save you."

"Yes, sir," Angelo said while leaving the chief trainmaster's office.

A few miles away in an exam room, the medical examiner was trying to identify the body of the female victim that was found on the tracks. Richard Weiss had been the medical examiner for Morton Town for over thirty years. At age sixty-two, he was about ready to put in his papers and retire. The tall, gray-haired Jewish man had seen more murdered young victims in eight months than in his whole lifetime. It was more than he could bear. *What is this quiet little town coming to?* Richard thought to himself. He turned on his recorder and proceeded to do the autopsy of the young body lying on the cold stainless-steel table. The medical examiner thought her killer was the Railway Butcher. It was the same type of work from the previous victims. The examiner had determined the young woman to be about twenty-four to twenty-six years old. She was of slim build, brown eyes, and light-brown hair. Her torso had been sliced wide open. The victim's heart, liver, and pancreas were surgically removed and her legs had also been amputated. Her lividity showed that she had been moved from her original place of murder. It was also determined that the victim had been dead for approximately six to eight hours. The victim's head was partially severed from her torso. Her face and upper torso had been ripped up, due to the wheels of the train. There were only two possibilities to identify the victim: fingerprints and dental records. Both were being explored.

"So many young victims. What a shame. When will it all end?" the medical examiner said to himself.

After the autopsy was completed, Mr. Weiss turned off his recorder. The medical examiner put all of his paperwork together and then proceeded to staple the body back together again. He hoped there wouldn't be any more victims for a while, but Mr. Richard Weiss knew better than that, he knew there would be more.

***

Later on in the afternoon, Angelo was coming down the stairs to answer the door.

"What the hell are you doing here? How did you find me?" he said to Conductor Taylor Parker.

"Listen, we got off to a bad start. Can we just start over again? I just wanna talk, that's all," Conductor Parker asked Angelo.

"What's there to talk about?"

"Well, by now you've probably figured out that I was responsible for saving your job. You *do* know that, right?"

"Yeah, I figured that out since the chief changed his mind right after that phone call from Superintendent James. I remembered you telling me that you were really tight with Superintendent James. So, I guess I owe you again for that?"

"Only if you want to. Look, I really do have feelings for you, but can we just be friends?"

"Well, as long as you don't try anything funny."

"Bet! Can I come in for a bit, just to talk? That's all, I promise."

"Ok, just for a bit."

Angelo reluctantly let the blond drag queen conductor into his home. He brought him into the family room and asked him if he wanted anything to drink.

"Nah, I'm fine," Taylor replied.

They both sat down on the sofa and talked about what had transpired today with Angelo.

"You know; it's so messed up about what happened to me today. Shit! I don't look for trouble, but it sure knows how to find my ass," said Angelo.

"It's hard to maintain a balance of what's right and what's wrong down there. You're constantly being torn between what's in the rule book and trying not to get yourself, or anyone else, in trouble. You're new there, Angelo, you'll learn."

"Yeah, the hard way, like today. Look, don't get me wrong, I really do appreciate you saving me my job like that, but it shouldn't have happened. Now, I'm out of work and out of money for a month. That really sucks."

"Listen, Angelo, if you need to borrow any money, I can lend you some, you know. No strings attached, really."

"Thanks, but no thanks. I already owe you enough. Besides, I can always hock some of my parents' jewelry if I needed to."

"Are you sure?" Taylor sincerely asked.

"Yeah man, really, it's all good," Angelo replied.

"Well, ok. I just wanted you to know that I would do *anything* to help you out, really!"

"I *bet* you would, but like I said before, it's all good," Angelo said with a smile.

"Hey, you know what?" Taylor asked.

"What?" Angelo replied.

"You could go down to Labor Relations with a union rep and ask them to spread it out!"

"What do you mean 'spread it out?'"

"Well, instead of you taking all thirty days off consecutively, you could take one or two every week until you've paid it off. That way, you could still get some kind of a paycheck every week."

"I could do that?"

"Sure could!"

"All right then, tomorrow I'm going to go downtown to Labor Relations."

"Whenever you do go, just don't forget to bring a union representative in with you."

"I won't. Thanks for the tip, man."

"Don't sweat it."

Taylor was so happy to be near his love, Angelo. He was already getting aroused just talking to him. What Taylor *really* wanted to do was to blow him right then and there on the sofa. He watched Angelo intently; that long, curly blond hair and those bright green eyes of his were definitely turning him on. Taylor watched Angelo stand up from the sofa and turn around. *My, he's got such a sweet ass, I would love for him to sit down on my lap,* Taylor thought to himself.

"Listen, I just wanna be square with you, Taylor. I know you like me and all that, but, I'm not gay. I like girls. I could never give you what you really want in return. I just wanted you to know that, that's all."

"It's cool, man, I'll deal with it."

"Good! We could be friends, but that's it," Angelo added.

"It's cool, man, really," Taylor regretfully replied.

Taylor wanted Angelo really bad. He was falling in love with him, but he'd never tell him that. *Friendship was better than nothing at all,* Taylor thought.

"Get him o-u-t!" Carina's ghostly voice exclaimed.

"What the hell was that?!" Taylor shouted.

"Get him out of here, A-n-g-e-l-o, now!" Carina shouted as she appeared right in front of them dressed in her white gown.

"What is that thing?!" Taylor fearfully asked Angelo while he jumped up from the sofa.

"It's my sister…or should I say her ghost?"

"A ggg-ghost?!"

"Get out of my house!" Carina's ghost shouted while she pointed toward the front door.

"Carina, what's up? He's ok!"

"No, he's not! I want him out of here, now!"

Angelo had turned around to reassure Taylor that it was all right, but he had already run out the front door.

"Look what you did, Carina! You scared him away!" Angelo shouted back.

"I don't ever want him back here again!"

"What's wrong, baby? Why don't you want Taylor here?"

"I have my reasons."

"Oh, come on now, Carina. It's my house, too, you know. Just give me one damn good reason why you don't want him around here?"

"My hair!"

"Your hair? What about your hair?"

"He's got my hair! He's the one! He's the one that killed me and cut off my head!" Carina's apparition screamed out in her ghostly voice.

13

THE SUSPECT

Angelo was happy he worked everything out with Labor Relations. He was going to work three days a week for fifteen weeks, in order to fulfill his thirty days' suspension. Angelo had decided to call Lieutenant Collins.

"Hello, Lieutenant?! This is Angelo Russo."

"What is it, Russo? My time is short," the lieutenant replied.

"I found a real suspect for you. I'm more than one hundred percent sure that he's the one who killed my sister. *In fact*, he's probably the one who killed them all," Angelo stated.

"And *who* might that be, Mr. Russo?"

"You're not gonna believe who it is."

"Who is it already?! Stop wasting my time, Russo!"

"It's Conductor Taylor Parker, sir."

"You're right, *I don't* believe it."

"But it is, Lieutenant, it really is."

"And what makes you so sure, Russo?"

"I just know that's all."

"You've got to give me more than that before you start accusing anyone of murder. You could get yourself in big trouble, you know."

"Well, sir, I have a very reliable source."

"And just *who* is this 'very reliable source,' Mr. Russo?"

"I can't tell you that, sir. She wants to remain anonymous."

"Well then, I can't help you out."

"But, sir!"

"You tell your girlfriend that when she comes forward, then we'll proceed, but until then, goodbye, Russo," the lieutenant said while hanging up on Angelo.

Angelo didn't know what to do. He didn't believe it himself, but he remembered his sister's hair. Angelo loved to brush Carina's long, beautiful hair. Taylor's long, blond hair, it was the same exact color and texture of Carina's. *I'll bet if they did a DNA test on it, it would show his hair belonged to Carina,* he thought. But how was Angelo going to convince Lieutenant Collins to do that? He could see it now: *Lieutenant, my sister's ghost said that Taylor killed her.* Angelo thought they would have him committed in an insane asylum with that remark for sure. He had to find another way. In the meantime, Angelo was steering clear from Taylor Parker; *that* was a given. *To think, I invited him into my own home…a murderer,* he thought. Angelo went upstairs to consult Carina. He went into her room and called her.

"Carina! Where are you?!" he shouted. "Carina! Carina?!"

"I'm here, A-n-g-e-l-o," she said in her ghostly voice while appearing in front of him.

"Are you positively sure that Taylor is your killer?" Angelo asked.

"That's the face I saw when he came to slash my throat."

"I just want to be sure. We all want to be sure, Carina."

"He has my beautiful hair. He cut off my head and scalped me. I know my own hair anywhere, Angelo."

Just then, the doorbell rang. Angelo left Carina's ghost and went downstairs to see who it was. *I hope it's not that lieutenant again,* he thought. Angelo opened the front door and was shocked to see Carla standing there.

"Well, what a surprise. I didn't expect to see *you* again," Angelo sarcastically said.

"Hello, Angelo. May I come in, please?" Carla said with a smile.

"What for? I mean, you chewed my ass up over nothing, really, and now you want to come in?"

"I'm sorry. I guess I just lost it. I get pretty defensive about my heritage. It's something you wouldn't know about. I really would like to try and make it up to you if I could. Please, may I come in for a minute?" she asked sincerely.

He looked at her sincere, blue eyes and just couldn't resist.

"Come on in, Carla," Angelo said while letting her into his home.

"Wow! Nice place you have here. Did you decorate it yourself?" Carla asked as she followed Angelo into the family room.

"No, actually, my parents did."

"Oh, I must compliment them."

"They're dead…remember, I told you?"

"Oh, yes…I'm sorry, Angelo, I guess I forgot."

They both sat down next to each other on the sofa.

"I'm really very sorry, Angelo. Can we just start over again?"

"Well, all right, just as long as you don't go off on me again."

"I won't, I promise. You really are a nice guy."

"Thanks."

Angelo felt a little awkward around her, ever since she blew up at him that day. He knew he didn't deserve that treatment after just asking her if "Carlita" was her real name. What was she so ashamed of? Carla was a beautiful young girl, like his sister was. She could easily have her pick of men.

"Angelo, can I just ask you something, please?"

"Sure, what is it?"

"Well, after our little fight that night, I decided to come back and apologize."

"You never came back."

"Oh, yes I did. I came back later on that evening, but before I rang the bell, I saw something unbelievable in your house."

Angelo was getting nervous; he knew where this was going. Carla must have seen him talking to Carina. She had spied on them.

"What did you see, Carla?" he asked her.

"Well, I don't want you to think I'm spying on you, because I'm not."

"What did you see?"

"Is your sister still alive?"

"Ha, ha, ha. No! I told you she's dead, remember?"

"Yes, I do, but, I saw her, Angelo! I saw you and Carina talking, right through the window, but she looked weird."

"You mean, like a ghost?"

"Yeah…a ghost. Sounds silly, doesn't it?"

"Nope. That's because, *she is a ghost!*"

"But, that's not possible, Angelo!"

"Oh, yes, it is."

"Are you serious?"

"Yes, it *is* possible, Carla."

"Oh, come on now. Are you telling me that you were carrying on a conversation…with a ghost?"

"Yep, that's exactly what I'm saying."

"Boy, and I thought I was nuts. Can you make her appear for me?"

"I can try, but I must warn you, she doesn't particularly like you. She was the one that told me your name was really Carlita."

"Well, if she's still holding a grudge, I just won't talk to her."

"You chicken shit bitch!" Carina's spirit said in her ghostly voice as she appeared before them.

"Ca-Carina, how nice to see you again," Carla nervously said.

"Cut the shit, Carlita," the apparition replied.

"If I didn't see it with my own two eyes, I wouldn't have believed it."

"Never m-i-n-d all the bullshit. Get out of my house!"

"Wait, Carina, she just came by to apologize," Angelo said in Carla's defense.

"No! It's a trick! Don't trust her. She has broken too many hearts before!"

With that last warning, Carina used her powers to slam open the front door for Carla's exit.

"I said: get the hell o-u-t!"

"Ok, Carina, I can take a hint. I'm leaving."

"Wait, Carla!"

"No, Angelo, I'm going. You can call me later if you want to."

Carla walked out of the family room and out through the open front door.

"And stay out, bitch!" Carina yelled as she slammed the front door closed with her powers.

Angelo was upset, but he knew there would be a feud if the two of them ever got together.

"Why were you so damn nasty to her, Carina?"

"I told you, she's no good for you, A-n-g-e-l-o."

"No one's good enough for me in your book. You're not my mother! I'll see whoever I damn well please!"

Carina shook the whole house like a spoiled child, sending dishes and glasses flying in the kitchen.

"Stop it before you wreck the damn house!" screamed Angelo.

Carina finally complied. Angelo started to clean up the mess on the floor. Carina felt sorry for him. She made the mess disappear by floating things back to where they belonged. Carina apologized to Angelo and then, she too disappeared.

The next morning, Angelo called the lieutenant back up and told him about Taylor's hair.

"It's my sister's hair," he said. "All you need to do is to take a DNA sample and you'll see if it's a match," Angelo told the lieutenant.

After thinking about it for a little bit, Lieutenant Collins finally agreed to do it. Collins assured Angelo that he would have Conductor Parker in this afternoon for the sample. Angelo hung up the phone feeling very satisfied. He thought this would not only get him off the hook, but finding his sister's killer would give him closure. Angelo decided to sit down, relax, and have a bowl of cereal before getting ready for work. *I sure miss Carina's ham and eggs breakfast,* he thought.

The next day, Conductor Taylor Parker was at his home, feeling hurt and very angry. *I can't believe I had to give a hair sample to the police. Why? They are so stupid. I'm not the killer,* he thought. Suddenly, a horrible thought came to his mind. *I wonder if Angelo could have had anything to do with this. Yes! I was just at his house the other day, and now all of a sudden, the police show up at my door? Maybe he was just pretending to be nice to me that day. Angelo never really cared for me. He always wanted to humiliate me. Angelo was always so ungrateful. I was so good to you, Angelo. I loved you, and this is how you treat me? This is how you repay me, you little shit?* Taylor thought. *I'll get even with you yet.* Whatever love Taylor had for Angelo, had now turned into resentment.

"No more 'Mr. Nice Guy,'" he said under his breath.

Taylor kept thinking about all the good he did for Angelo. He thought about how Angelo wouldn't even have that job if it weren't for him. *I just saved his ass from being fired. Now, I'm the number one suspect!*

"Shit! I hate you! I hate you! I hate you!" Taylor screamed out loud.

***
****

Not too far away, Carlita Gomez was stepping out of her Mercedes sedan. The car was mainly for show. Carlita wouldn't tell anyone she bought it second hand. The Mercedes was over ten years old at the time. Carlita really didn't have any money. The jewelry and clothes on her back were all second hand, too. Carlita had just gotten laid off from her job at the real estate office, since business was so slow. She was now worried about finding work. The young woman walked over to the old ranch house that she rented. Carlita disliked the old house; in fact, she found it revolting, but it was all that her salary could afford. The landlord never fixed the leaking pipes under the kitchen sink. There was always a puddle of water on the floor right near the sink. Carlita had also asked him to call the exterminator, for the ant and field mice problem that was abundant in the house. There were times when she felt safer sleeping in her own car in the driveway. The phone rang as she walked into the house. Carlita picked it up on the second ring. She was hoping it would be Angelo.

"Hello, Angelo?" she asked, thinking it was him.

"Angelo? Huh, were you expecting him, dear?" the butcher asked.

"Well, I thought it might be him."

"Well, it's not. It's me. Listen up; I got another job for you if you're interested."

"Does it pay the same as the last one?"

"No, it's double."

"Double? What do I have to do?"

"Your friend, Angelo, is starting way too much shit. I want him out of the way."

"What do you mean, 'out of the way?'"

"For ten thousand dollars, I shouldn't have to explain it to you, woman. What do you think I mean?"

"You mean that…you want me to…kill him?" she asked nervously.

"Whoa, you're a damn genius!"

"But, but, I've never killed anybody before in my life. I don't know how to!"

"What's to know? You come over here and I'll give you the weapon of your choice."

"I-I just can't do it, I'm sorry."

"Yeah, all right, forget it. It was just a thought anyway."

"You mean, I'm off the hook?"

"Yeah, I guess you really don't need the money, do you?"

"Oh, I need the money, all right, but not like that."

"Nah, you don't need the money, or else you would just jump at the chance to make *fifteen thousand bucks.*"

"Wait a minute; I thought you said ten thousand bucks?"

"That was before I heard you freaking cry like a baby. Now, do we have a deal or what?"

"It sounds tempting, but I just don't know. Can I sleep on it?"

"Listen up here, bitch, I don't have time for games! Twenty thousand dollars is my final offer. If not, I'll go find someone else who *really* needs the money."

"Twenty thousand dollars, cash?"

"Nah, I'm gonna give you food stamps. Of course, I'm giving you cash! Shit, what are you stupid or something?!"

"Ok, ok, you've got yourself a deal."

"All right then, it's about time. Now get your skinny little ass over here and we'll work out the details," the killer said.

He hung up on her and started laughing at how gullible she sounded over the phone.

"That bitch ain't getting shit! After she kills his ass, I'll waste her. I ain't leavin' no stone unturned," the butcher said to himself.

Carlita Gomez, however, had feelings for Angelo Russo. She really didn't want anything to happen to him, but how was she going to get out of it? Carlita had already accepted the killer's offer; there was no turning back now. *Maybe this is a joke, or maybe a test or something,* she tried to convince herself. Nonetheless, Carlita was going to have to get back in her car, go there, and find out, one way or the other. She was now unemployed. *Twenty thousand dollars would sure come in handy, if it were for real,* Carlita thought. She *still* could not see herself killing anyone, especially Angelo Russo.

Later on in the afternoon, Carlita had finally arrived at Crane Park to meet up with the butcher again. She didn't know who this strange man was; if Carlita did, she would have hightailed herself out of there. Carlita was blindfolded once again as she got back into his truck.

"Come on, let's go," the killer said as he took her.

*
**

Soon, they had arrived back at his L-shaped ranch house. He brought her back inside and he removed her blindfold just as before.

"Well, I noticed that you have cameras everywhere," Carlita said.

"You just noticed that shit, sister? I've got this place all wired up. Why, there ain't *nothing* that can go on outside or inside without me knowing about it first. Also, everything gets recorded on tape."

"Wow! No, I really didn't pay attention."

"You're not very observant, are you?"

"I guess not. Hey, I have noticed you don't have anyone else here, do you?"

"Oh, *that* you notice."

"No wife or girlfriend?" she asked him.

"Hell no! I'm free and single, just the way I like it."

Carlita thought about the prospect of all this. She thought about being set for life. Truly, she preferred Angelo much more, but *this* guy clearly had the bucks. *I wouldn't have to work if I hooked up with him. I could get out of that crummy old house and move in here with him,* she daydreamed for a bit. Carlita approached the man. She started kissing his face while massaging his neck.

"You're flattering yourself. It won't work, baby. I'm gay," the butcher said.

"Gay?" she asked while feeling the blow to her plans and her womanhood.

"That's right. I like men only. If you *don't* have a dick, then don't even bother. Now, can we please proceed with business?"

"Yeah, I suppose so. What did you have in mind?" Carlita apprehensively asked.

"Like I said, I want Angelo Russo out of the way. Follow me to the kitchen table and I'll show you where you can pick your poison, literally."

The butcher led Carlita into the kitchen to show her the weapons of her choice. There were cameras everywhere in and out of the house. It was like Fort Knox. The killer had also taken the liberty to soundproof several rooms in the house, including the basement.

When they arrived in the kitchen, he showed her the kitchen table that was loaded with weapons to do the job. On the table, there was a fully loaded forty-five Magnum with a silencer, a switch blade knife, two different kinds of poison, a Taser, and last but not least, a stun gun. Carlita realized that this man wasn't playing. This was for real. She started to get nervous.

"Do you like what you see, girl? I'm anxious to know what your weapon of choice will be, honey," the killer said.

"I-I really just don't know," Carlita said nervously.

"Let me enlighten you on the goods here. *My* weapon of choice would be this forty-five Magnum; it's got a silencer on it, that way no one would ever hear it fire."

"I've never fired a real gun before. I'm scared of them. Is that a stun gun?" she asked while pointing to it on the table.

"Yes, it is; however, it's been modified, so has the Taser. These units won't just stun you, they're guaranteed to stop your heart within fifteen seconds flat, ha, ha, ha," the killer said with a big grin.

"What's in those two tubes?" Carlita hesitantly asked.

"I'm glad you asked that, baby. Over here in these two vials, we have two different kinds of poison: a fast-acting and a slow-acting one. The fast-acting and more potent one, requires just five drops in any kind of liquid. It'll have Mr. Russo down in less than two minutes flat. The slow-acting one will need the full amount of approximately one-half ounce to work. That one will need much more time, about two to three hours to work. I'll tell ya this though; both of them are quite painless, and effective. If he ingests any one of them, it'll appear like he died naturally of a heart attack. There'll be no trace of them in his blood stream, so you'll be off the hook. By the way, I've taken the liberty of taking out a little insurance policy just in case you screw up in any way. Does the name, 'Serenity Station Care' mean anything to you?" he asked her.

A cold chill came over Carlita's body. She suddenly felt like the walls were closing in on her. The man had thought of everything. Carlita was going to have to play stupid.

"Serenity Station Care? Why, I've never heard of the place," she nervously replied.

"Yes you have. It's where your mother is. I know all about you and your screwed-up mother."

"What do you mean by that remark?"

"I know how she tried to kill herself after your father had left her for a younger woman. He had left the two of you all alone for that hot young Russian blonde babe. Your mother's suicidal, so they stuck her ass in that mental institution."

"And just what are you getting at? Are you threatening me with my own mother?" Carlita said angrily.

"Well, I see you're pretty smart after all. I have a man placed in that institution, just waiting for my word. If you back out on me, or even call the police, your mother is History! You get it, bitch?!"

"Yes, yes, I get it all right."

"Good! Now, tell me, which one of my tools would you like to use to do the job?" he fiendishly asked her.

**

One week later, Angelo was sitting down in his kitchen having breakfast when the phone rang. He put his spoon back down in the cereal bowl and got up to answer it.

"Hello?" Angelo asked.

"Russo, it's Lieutenant Collins. I've got some news for you," the lieutenant replied.

"Did you find out that Taylor Parker was the killer?" Angelo excitedly asked.

"On the contrary there, Mr. Russo, you were wrong…dead wrong."

"What do you mean I was wrong?"

"It's exactly what I just said, wrong. The DNA test came back from the lab with negative results. Parker's wig *is* from human hair. It's also a very good quality one, I might add, but it's *not* from your sister. That means, you're *still* my number one suspect, Russo. Have a nice day," the lieutenant said while hanging up on him.

Angelo was so disappointed. *How could this be?* he wondered. *Was Carina wrong?* He didn't know what to do. Angelo was a prime suspect all over again.

"Shit!" he said out loud.

"It is my h-a-i-r," Carina's apparition said in her ghostly voice.

"Carina? Where are you?" Angelo asked.

"I'm right in front of you, love," her ghost replied as she appeared in front of him naked.

"Wow! Are you trying to turn me on again or what?"

"You like my body, don't you?"

"Yeah, but I'd like it much better if I couldn't see right through you, and if I could touch you and hold you in my arms again," he said disappointedly.

"I'm working on that, sweetheart."

"Lieutenant Collins just told me that the DNA test shows that it wasn't your hair on Conductor Taylor Parker's wig."

"He's full of shit, Angelo. Don't you think I know my own damn hair?"

"Do you think he's lying, Carina?"

"I know he is."

"But why? Why would he lie about that, just to frame me? Does he hate me that much?"

"I don't know, A-n-g-e-l-o."

"Unless, something happened with the DNA test, or the sample."

"Anyway, I have to get ready for work, baby. *I hope* I don't see Conductor Taylor Parker anymore, especially today."

"Good luck, Angelo; remember, I love you," she said as she faded away.

Later that day, Carlita received a phone call from the butcher.

"It's been a damn week already! When the hell are you going to kill his ass, new year's?!" he yelled over the phone.

"I'll call him tonight, I promise," she said reluctantly.

"You better, or else!" the slaughterer yelled while hanging up the phone on her.

Carlita hung up her phone and just wondered what she was going to do. She really liked Angelo, but she was worried about her mother. Carlita had also thought about that twenty-thousand-dollar bounty. Her money was dwindling away. Carlita decided to call Angelo up for a date. The young woman was going to use the fast-acting poison she acquired from the butcher. Carlita didn't want Angelo to suffer.

Later that evening, Angelo was back with Carlita Gomez, in her favorite Italian restaurant, A Little Slice of Italy. The waiter had just come by and brought them two glasses of red wine. Angelo excused himself to go to the men's room. This was the perfect opportunity for Carlita. She took the vial of fast-acting poison out of her purse. Carlita poured half of the poison into Angelo's wine when no one was looking. After that, the woman mixed it up with her fork and stuck the vial back into her purse. Carlita sat there at the dinner table and waited for him to return.

***

Angelo Russo was in the bathroom stall, listening to the guy in the next stall yelling on his cellphone, apparently, to his woman.

"Listen up, bitch, I told you it's over! Now stop calling me, all right?!" the man said on his phone.

(Splash).

"Oh, shit, my phone!" the man yelled as he dropped his smartphone down in the toilet bowl. "I paid over nine hundred dollars for that shit, damn!"

Angelo couldn't stop laughing. He tried his best to be quiet, but he just couldn't. Angelo knew he had to leave before the man came after him for laughing. He was coming out of the restroom when someone very familiar to him was walking in.

"Well, well, well, look at what the cat dragged in," Conductor Taylor Parker said.

"What are *you* doing here? Are you following me or something?" Angelo asked.

"You'd like that, wouldn't you? Well, don't flatter yourself, Angelo. I came here to eat, like everyone else."

"Well, fine. Excuse me."

"Ah, not so fast, honey. I missed you today at work. In fact, I kind of got the feeling that you were avoiding me."

"I don't know what the hell you're talking about."

"Oh, I think you do and by the way, thanks for *trying* to get me in trouble with the cops, but it didn't work, honey."

"My sister says you stole her hair and killed her."

"Your sister is *dead*, but I didn't do it. I don't know what the hell that thing was in your house, but I *still* don't believe it's your sister. Maybe, it's some sort of trick, but *I don't believe in ghosts!*"

"It's no trick. Her ghost haunts me every day and night."

"Yeah, right, whatever. Hey, how about a nice blowjob right here in one of these stalls?" Taylor whispered to him.

"Like I told you, I don't swing that way. Excuse me, but my date is waiting," Angelo told him as he walked out of the men's room.

Taylor still had very strong feelings for him. His massive, throbbing hard-on proved it, as he was checking out Angelo's ass. He wanted revenge, but Taylor couldn't bring himself to kill Angelo; someone else could, but it wouldn't be him. He decided to go into one of the empty stalls and masturbate while thinking about Angelo.

Angelo had returned to the dinner table where Carlita was sitting and waiting for him.

"I was getting worried," Carlita said.

"I'm sorry baby, but I ran into someone I knew in the men's room," he replied.

The waiter returned and asked them if they were ready to order. Angelo ordered spaghetti and meatballs and Carlita ordered baked ziti. Angelo pulled out a long, thin box from his jacket pocket.

"I have something I want to give you, Carlita. May I call you Carlita? It's such a pretty name," he asked her.

"Yes, but, you don't have to give me anything, sweetie. You don't owe me anything," she said sincerely, while getting all choked up.

"Oh, yes I do. For the first time in a long time, I really feel happy and you're the cause of it. You're sitting right in front of me, looking like an angel with your beautiful, white dress and long, blonde hair. I want you to have this," he said while handing her the box.

Carlita opened up the box and began to cry. Inside was a beautiful, long necklace made of genuine pearls.

"Oh, my God, are they real pearls?"

"Yes, they are; they belonged to my mother. I just wanted you to have them, angel."

"Oh, God, I can't accept them, Angelo. I'm no angel, trust me."

"You are to me, and I want you to have them."

Angelo got up from his chair to put the long string of pearls around Carlita's neck. Carlita was so touched, she just sat there and cried. Angelo sat back down and raised his glass of red wine to her.

"I propose a toast: to the most beautiful girl in the world."

"Noooo!" she screamed hysterically while knocking the glass of wine from his hand.

There was wine all over the table and some spilled onto Angelo. Nearby customers were staring at them.

"What's with you, Carlita?!" Angelo yelled out.

"I'm so, so sorry, baby. I thought I saw a bug go into your drink."

"A bug? You freak out like that because of a bug?"

"Yeah, well, with all those diseases they carry nowadays, you know—Lyme disease and shit. Here, let me clean you up."

Carlita got up from her chair and then proceeded to wipe Angelo's dark gray suit with her napkin. Good thing it was a cloth napkin and not a paper one. Angelo got so turned on by this, he grabbed her and tenderly kissed her. Carlita kissed him right back, while she fell into his lap and wrapped her loving arms around him. They were both falling in love with each other. The nearby patrons that were originally staring at them began to applaud. She pulled back away from him and gazed into his bright, green eyes.

"I think I'm falling in love with you, Angelo Russo."

"I'm feeling the same way about you too, Carlita. But let's take it slow, please. The last girl I fell for was, well, she passed away."

"Oh, I'm so sorry to hear that," Carlita genuinely said.

Angelo almost told her the truth about his last girlfriend, but he didn't want to frighten her and he didn't want to spoil the mood. This was not the time and place to talk about murder and death. This was a time to enjoy each other's company, and if it led to love, so be it.

Carlita got up from Angelo's lap, turned around, and sat back down in her seat again. Through the corner of her eye she spotted a very familiar face; it was an angry face. It was the face of her boss. The Railway Butcher was staring intently at them both, wondering when she was going to make her move on Angelo. A cold sweat came over Carlita; she knew she had double-crossed him.

"Angelo, let's just go," she hurriedly said.

"Go? We haven't even got our food yet," he said while looking surprised.

"Please, baby, I'm not feeling well at all."

"You're shaking; what's wrong, love?"

"Please, can we just leave now?"

"Can't you just tell me what's wrong, Carlita?" Angelo asked her while feeling concerned.

"I just want to leave here. I'm not feeling good, please?"

"Well, if you really want to go."

"Yes, yes, I do!"

"Ok, then, let's go," Angelo told her.

Angelo and Carla both got up and left the restaurant as quickly as possible. The butcher was pissed off. He threw his napkin down on the floor. The killer got up from his seat, and then he followed them out of the restaurant. The slayer was crazed with anger as he watched Carlita and Angelo drive off together. He knew he had been double-crossed. *It's time for revenge,* he thought. *It's time to get even.*

"They won't get away with this shit, no fuckin' way," he said to himself while gritting his teeth. "They will both pay for this shit, mark my words, they will *both pay!*" he said in front of the restaurant while shaking his clenched fist in the air.

14

RETALIATION

The next morning, Carlita woke up all alone in her bed again. She thought about last night. The young woman thought about Angelo and how she wanted him so bad. They both went back to her house after the restaurant. Angelo was still confused. Carlita wanted to tell him everything, but she was really worried about her mother. Carlita remembered what her boss had told her: I have a man placed in that institution, just waiting for my word. *If you back out on me, or if you call the police, your mother is history,* he had said. Angelo was such a gentleman. He had made her some tea to calm her down. They both talked that night until she became tired. Angelo tenderly kissed her good night and then he left through the front door. Carlita felt so bad because it was such a long walk to the train station. She knew Angelo didn't own a car. Carlita's telephone began to ring; she cringed, thinking it was her boss. The woman leaned over on the bed to answer it.

"Hello?" she asked.

"This is Serenity Station Care calling. Is this Miss Carlita Gomez?" the female caller asked.

"Yes, yes it is," Carlita replied.

"Hello, my name is Nurse Robinson. We have a situation here with your mother, Angelica Gomez."

"What kind of a situation, nurse?"

"Well, we don't know how, but it appears that your mother has escaped."

"Escaped?! How?!"

"We don't know, but she must have had help. Is there something you may want to tell us, Miss Gomez?"

"Are you accusing me of helping her escape?"

"No, ma'am, I just want to get all the facts, that's all."

"Well, I'm sorry to disappoint you, but this is the first time I'm hearing about this. You must find her; she's all I've got."

"We're working on it, Miss Gomez. The police have been notified."

"Please, please keep me informed, Nurse Robinson," Carlita told the nurse as she hung up the phone.

Carlita suspected her boss. *He must have kidnapped my mother,* she thought.

"Shit! What am I going to do?" Carlita said while she began to sob.

Within a few minutes, her phone began to ring again. She pulled herself together to answer it, hoping it was Angelo.

"Hello?" Carlita asked.

"Hello yourself, you stupid-ass, double-crossing bitch," the butcher sarcastically said.

"Oh, God, it's you."

"Yeah, that's right, it's me again. You screwed up, royally! You were supposed to kill the sonofabitch, not screw his ass."

"I didn't screw him."

"Yeah, well, you didn't kill his little ass either."

"What did you do with my mother? I know you have her."

"Ha, ha, ha. It's time for retaliation. It's payback time, baby, ha, ha, ha."

"Is she…dead?" Carlita hesitantly asked.

"No, not yet, but she will be if you don't cooperate."

"What do you want?" she was afraid to ask him.

"You know *damn well* what I want. I'm giving you just two weeks to kill Mr. Russo."

"Two weeks?"

"That's right, honey. If Angelo Russo is *not* dead by Thanksgiving, your mother will be. Do I make myself clear, dear?"

"Yes, yes, you do."

"Good, now go have your fun with Angelo, screw him if you want to, but by Thanksgiving, his ass better be gone, or else."

The butcher hung up the phone without waiting for a response.

A few miles away, Angelo was waking up in his own bed. He had Carlita on his mind.

"Man, I must have walked about two to three miles to the train station last night, just to get home," he said to himself. "I'm gonna have to get me some wheels."

Angelo yawned and stretched before getting out of bed. He went to the bathroom to take a piss. Angelo flushed the toilet and washed his hands in the bathroom sink.

"I miss having that in me, A-n-g-e-l-o," Carina's spirit said in her ghostly voice.

"Good morning, baby," he told her while looking at her image in the mirror.

"I know where you were last night. You were at that bitch's house. Weren't you?!"

"Yes, I was. She wasn't feeling well, so we left the restaurant early."

"I'll *bet* she didn't feel good."

"No, really, we didn't even get a chance to eat."

"Yeah, right. I bet you wanted to eat her. You screwed her, didn't you?!"

"No I didn't and that's none of your business. But for the record, I made her some tea and we just talked until I left."

"You wanted to screw her, didn't you?"

"Yes, I did, but I told her I didn't want to move that fast. I knew she wanted me, too. I just want to take it slow, that's all."

"Don't you want me, love?"

"Yes, but I've accepted the fact that I can never, ever have you again. You're dead, Carina. You can't come back to me again."

"I can try," she said sadly.

"Look, Carina, there will always be a special spot in my heart for you, but I need someone. I need someone real. I have needs like any other man does. You understand, right?"

"Yes, Angelo, I do. I will go now."

Her apparition faded from his bathroom mirror. Angelo felt bad, he really didn't want to hurt her, but he had to deal with reality first. Angelo pulled open the small bottom drawer of the bathroom cabinet, grabbed his shaver, and began to shave.

A few hours later, Angelo was now back at work on a southbound train. It was a cool, brisk day for late autumn, even though the sun had been shining all morning. The damp, cold air was cutting through everyone. All of the leaves had finally fallen from the trees; it looked like winter was coming early. Angelo was checking tickets while trying to take in the colorful scenery from the windows. He made his way back to his operating position to get ready for the next stop.

"One hundred twenty-fifth is the next stop, 125th Street will be next," Angelo said over the public address system.

The train began slowing down as it approached the station. All of the passengers were lined up on the platform, waiting for the train to stop so that they could board. Angelo turned the master door key controller to the "on" position. Then, he pressed the "door open" buttons to let the passengers on. Angelo was surprised by the amount of people getting on to get to work at eleven thirty in the morning. Surely, rush hour was over and there were no more express trains running. Of course, some people did have odd hours, like himself. Once all the passengers boarded, Conductor Angelo Russo made his safety announcement.

"Please stand clear of the closing doors," he said over the train's public address system.

Angelo proceeded to close down the doors on the train. He turned the master door key switch to run, then the engineer started moving the train again. Angelo enjoyed looking out of the open window at the scenery, even though the rules were completely against it. He remembered the train service supervisor in school stating that you could lose your head out there.

All of a sudden, the train came to a screeching halt. The emergency brakes were activated, but by whom? Some people had fallen out of their seats.

"Attention, attention conductor and passengers, we have an emergency situation here. Everyone, please remain calm and seated. Conductor, please come up front," the train's engineer announced over the public address system.

Angelo hurried through the train, opening and closing the storm doors of each car as he walked through them. He was wondering what the hell had happened. *It must have been something really serious that the engineer didn't want to put it out over the radio,* he thought. Angelo finally arrived at the head locomotive. The engineer was waiting for him.

The train engineer was a well-seasoned Caucasian man that was a little older than the railroad really wanted to have around, but he had great experience operating a train. He went by the name of John Holms. John had been working for the Morton City Railroad for over forty-eight years. At seventy-two years old, John was finally going to put his papers in and retire at the end of the year. His health was starting to deteriorate, mainly his heart. John should have retired a long time ago, like everyone else did, but he was bored living at home alone. The job was all he had. John almost had a heart attack with what the man had just seen. If his hair weren't already snow-white from age, it would have been after today, along with his long beard.

"Hey, John, what's up? What the hell happened?" Angelo asked.

"Get in the cab and close the door," the engineer said.

Angelo got into the cabin and looked at his partner. He could see that the man was visibly shaken.

"Are you all right?" asked Angelo.

"I am, but someone else ain't."

"What do you mean, 'some else ain't?'"

"I mean, there was a woman on the tracks and I just hit her!"

"Holy shit! Really?!"

"Yeah, really, and you know what else?"

"What?!"

"She just got thrown right in front of me."

"Really, just now?!"

"Yeah, I was riding around the corner there and someone just rolled her down the hill onto the tracks. I couldn't get a look at him, it just happened so damn fast."

"Are you sure it was a woman?"

"Sure as shit! It was a woman with long blonde hair. If she wasn't dead before, she is now!"

"Where is she now?" Angelo asked the engineer.

"She's under this here train. I hit the dead man emergency brake when I saw it happen. I tried not to hit her, but you know, wheels don't stop, they just roll."

"We have to call this into Command Center you know."

"Yeah, I know, but let me go down on the road bed to check it out first."

"Ok, in the meantime, I'll make delay announcements to the passengers over the PA."

Angelo got back on the public address system to make an apologetic delay announcement, while the engineer put on his safety vest and went down onto the road bed to investigate. The passengers were getting very angry; they were tired of hearing: "Sorry for the inconvenience" over the public address system. It seemed like there was always some sort of unavoidable delay. The railroad was doing its best to replace its aging fleet of trains, but this was not an equipment breakdown issue. Some of the passengers were complaining to their bosses on their cellphones, explaining why they were going to be late, while others were trying to see what had happened.

Engineer Holms was down on the tracks with his flashlight in his hands. A cold wind was blowing up at him, while he checked under the carriage of the locomotive and the adjoining cars. John finally found the woman under the third car. The woman was cut in half, mid-section. Her face was pale white; like she had been dead for a while already. John was physically shaken. *Who would do that to such a good-looking woman?* he thought. There was no blood anywhere, because the lip of the train wheels had sealed the halves of the body up, like a zipper-lock-type bag. John took a good look at her face; she appeared to be in her late forties or early fifties. The woman looked vaguely familiar to him, like he'd seen her somewhere before, but he didn't know where or when. The engineer knew not to touch or move her in any way. This was definitely a police matter and John was now a witness to a crime. *Damn,* he thought. *I only got one more month to get the hell out of here. Now I got to get involved with the police? There goes my clean record. Shit!*

Engineer Holms started making his way back up to the locomotive to call Command Center. He needed to sit down for a bit. John was breaking out into a cold sweat. His heart had been working overtime, coupled with his high cholesterol. John refused to take any medication; he thought he could control it with proper diet alone. *Doctors, what the hell do they know? They just want to sell you some drugs,* he thought to himself, and now, John was paying for his stubbornness. John tried to climb up onto the locomotive when his heart gave out. He could barely scream with the agonizing pain in his chest. It felt like a freight train was crushing him. His breathing had become extremely labored. John couldn't hold on any longer. He lost his grip from the grab bars on the locomotive and collapsed back down onto the tracks, hitting his head hard onto one of the track rails.

Angelo stepped out of the cabin to look for his engineer.

"John! Where are you?!" he yelled out.

Angelo decided to put on his safety vest and go down on the tracks to look for him.

"John! Where the hell are you?!"

Suddenly, Angelo spotted him on the tracks. He quickly ran over to him.

"John, are you all right?!" Angelo screamed at him.

Angelo tried to wake him up, but there was no response. Angelo panicked; he didn't know what to do, except to call the Command Center on his radio.

"Hello, command center, come in to the ten o' five local out of Hyde Park Terminal!" Angelo called.

"Who's calling Command?" the desk supervisor asked.

"Command, this is the ten o' five local out of Hyde Park terminal."

"Ten o' five out of Hyde Park, state your location and problem, sir."

"Command Center, we have our brakes in emergency just outside of 125th Street. My engineer is injured, sir."

"Your engineer is injured. I take it you're the conductor?"

"Yes, sir, he claimed there was a woman on the tracks, but I didn't see her, sir."

"Wait a minute, Conductor, back up. How was your engineer injured?"

"I, I don't know, sir. He's lying down there on the tracks, unconscious."

"All right, Conductor, listen, please make all the appropriate announcements to your passengers and we'll send assistance out there."

"Ok, Command, that's a copy!"

Twelve minutes later, Angelo finally observed a supervisor approaching him. The man had a safety vest on and a flashlight that had been illuminated. It was Train Service Supervisor Moriotto, the same supervisor Angelo had seen in the last incident he had.

"You're the ten o' five local out of Hyde Park, right?" TSS Moriotto asked.

"Yes we are, sir," Angelo responded.

"Well, well. Conductor Angelo Russo, we meet again. You remember what the chief told you about staying out of trouble, right?"

Angelo was getting ticked off. Clearly, this was not his fault, but he sensed this supervisor was out for his ass, along with the chief. It was bad enough that Angelo Russo had to worry about Lieutenant Collins, but now, he had to worry about supervision on the job, also.

"I had nothing to do with this, sir," Angelo retorted.

"I know; I'm just testing you. Where's your engineer?" the supervisor asked.

"Just follow me, I'll show you. By the way, where are the medics?"

"They're on their way."

Angelo led the supervisor over to where the engineer was laying on the ground. TSS Moriotto attempted to check the man's pulse.

"I'm not a doctor, but I'm not getting a pulse."

"Oh, no!"

"You said he hit a woman?"

"I didn't say that sir. What I did say over the radio was that he claimed there was a woman on the tracks, but I didn't see her."

"Let's go see, shall we?"

TSS Moriotto led Angelo around the train to find the body. When they got to the third car, the supervisor detected half of the woman's body. Moriotto called the incident into Command Center, then he explained to Angelo what they were going to do with the passengers on board the train. By now, the passengers were getting extremely agitated. They wanted to get to their destinations.

"All right, Russo, this is what we're going to do. I want you to move all the passengers past the third car. Put them into the last five cars, and I'll cut the train there," Moriotto told him.

"You're going to cut the train in half?" Angelo asked.

"Well, almost. After I decouple the train, we're going to wrong-rail the half with the passengers to go back north into 125th

Street. Of course, that's if Command Center will give us permission to do so."

The supervisor got on the radio and explained what he wanted to do. Moriotto had also told Command Center that it was possible since they had already cleared the switch. After checking with train traffic and the towerman, Command Center gave them permission to proceed with the procedure. Angelo started moving the angry passengers toward the rear of the train. By this time, the medical team had arrived to check on Engineer John Holms. The team had declared him deceased.

The police finally arrived with another train service supervisor to investigate the deceased woman on the track. One of the two officers stayed with the body, while the other officer went looking for the conductor to ask him questions about what happened.

"Ok, TSS Moriotto, I've got all of the passengers into the last five cars," Angelo told him over the radio.

"All right, Conductor, I'm coming up to the north locomotive. The train has been cut. I'm going to change ends and we're heading back north into 125th Street, is that a copy?" TSS Moriotto asked him over the radio.

"Yes, sir, that's a copy."

"One other thing, Conductor. I have Officer Richards with me; he wants to ask you some questions."

"That's a copy, sir."

Train Service Supervisor Moriotto made his way up to the northbound locomotive after dropping Officer Richards off with

Angelo. Moriotto checked with the towerman to make sure the switch was set for northbound traffic. The partial train started to move back north, leaving the other half there. Officer Richards was asking Angelo questions about the incident. The supervisor pulled the train back into the station and he told Angelo to discharge the passengers. Angelo assured the passengers that there would be another train coming shortly to take them into the city; however, it would have to be going express to bypass the other half of the train that was still on the local track. Angelo made sure everyone was off the train, then he closed the doors and keyed himself off with Officer Richards. TSS Moriotto recoupled the train and he waited for clearance from the other officer before bringing the train into the yard.

Angelo had to go downtown to fill out an accident report. He didn't know what had happened to his engineer. Angelo kept thinking about the woman that was cut in half by the train. "There was a woman on the tracks and I just hit her, and you know what else, she just got thrown in front of me," those were the last words he had heard his engineer say. Angelo thought that the woman looked familiar to him, like he'd seen her in a picture somewhere, but he wasn't sure where.

Later that day, Carlita was watching the evening news while she ate her frozen dinner. The female news reporter was talking about a passenger injury on the train tracks. The incident had turned out to be a homicide.

"The body was identified as Angelica Gomez, who was found after being declared missing from the Serenity Station Care mental institution just yesterday," the news reporter said while showing Angelica's picture on the screen.

Carlita dropped her dinner on the floor and wept. She felt like her whole world had just come to an abrupt end. Carlita wanted to introduce Angelo to her. *This is the man I'm going to marry, Mom,* she thought to tell her. But now, it was too late. Her mother would never be able to dance at her wedding. *My beautiful mother! She didn't deserve this! Why, oh, why, Lord?* Carlita thought while she cried. Her telephone rang. Carlita tried to pull herself together to answer it.

"Hello?" she said with a cry in her voice.

"Hello Carlita? It's me, Angelo," he said over the phone.

"Angelo? Oh, my God, I, I'm so, so glad you called me. I need you so much right now," she barely managed to say.

"I guess you were watching the evening news?" he somberly asked.

"Yes, yes I w-was. My m-mo-ther—" Carlita couldn't finish her sentence. She merely broke down and cried.

"I'm coming right over, babe," Angelo stated as he hung up the phone.

Carlita felt a little more at ease, as she started to clean up the food she dropped on the floor. All of a sudden, her phone rang once more. Carlita wondered who it was this time.

"Hello?" she asked.

"Hello you double-crossing bitch. Did you see the evening news?" the butcher asked.

"You! You killed my mother! Why?! You told me I had until Thanksgiving!" Carlita screamed.

"I lied, just like you did. How does it feel, dear? How does it fucking feel?"

"I'll get you for this."

"You and who the hell else? I wanna know, who?"

"I don't owe you *shit* anymore."

"Oh, really? Yes, you do. You still have a big job to do, remember?"

"Well, I won't do it! I love him! Do you hear me?! I said: I love him and he loves me!"

"I heard all right, but it's too damn bad, baby, 'cause I can easily get someone else to do it for me."

"You sonofabitch!"

"Oh, name calling, huh? Let me tell you how this is going to play out: you kill him, like we agreed, and I'll graciously let you live. If you screw up again, you'll both die. You see, this is an offer that you can't possibly refuse. I'm giving you until Thanksgiving. Think about it, bitch."

Carlita heard a click and then the line went dead. She dropped the phone and cried some more. The poor girl didn't know what to do. Carlita was afraid of going to the police and there was no way in hell she could tell Angelo.

Carlita had thought about killing her boss, but she really didn't know where he lived. Carlita was always blindfolded when he took her there after they met in the park. Also, his house was like Fort Knox. The man had cameras everywhere, not to mention the metal detectors at the entrance, so there really was no way of sneaking in a gun, even if she had one, without him knowing about it first. Carlita knew she was a very desirable young woman. Carlita thought about using her femininity to her advantage, but her boss was gay. He had made that perfectly clear to her the last time she was at his house.

An hour later, Angelo was getting off the southbound train. He dreaded the long walk to Carlita's house and cursed the fact that he didn't have a car. *I'm gonna have to save up for a car,* he thought. Angelo had never turned down a damsel in distress before and he wasn't about to do it now. Angelo knew that he had strong feelings for Carlita. The young man also knew that Carlita felt the same way for him. He finally arrived at Carlita's front door. Angelo rang the bell and was greeted by a very emotional young woman.

"Oh, my God; come on in, Angelo, please come in," she said teary-eyed.

Angelo could see that she had still been crying. Her eyes were all red and puffed up. Carlita hugged him real tight as they walked into the house together. She closed the door shut and was all over him in an instant. Carlita wanted to make love to him right then and there in the foyer. The young woman started to unbutton his shirt. When she started to unzip his pants, Angelo stopped her.

"What's wrong? I thought you wanted me, like I want you," Carlita asked so innocently.

"I do, but not like this. What you need more than anything else right now is a shoulder to cry on. Come, let's go sit down on the sofa and talk," Angelo said, while acting like the perfect gentleman.

The two of them went into the living room and sat down together on the old sofa. Carlita cried on his shoulder, but she never revealed the problem of her "boss" to him. How could she? If Carlita told him the truth, it would incriminate her and break Angelo's heart at the same time. The last thing the woman wanted to do right now was to hurt Angelo in any way. Carlita didn't plan on falling in love, it just happened. She enjoyed being independent, but not anymore. If something bad were to happen to Angelo, Carlita would simply just give up on life. Angelo had now become the center of her world; there was no one else in her life. She had no more family members; they were all gone now.

Later in the evening, after Angelo had left her, Carlita needed some stress relief, since Angelo wasn't willing to give it to her. She went into her bedroom and removed all of her clothes. Carlita grabbed her smartphone and searched her mp3 collection. She was looking for her favorite love song, "Wicked Game" by Chris Isaak. The song was older than her, but she loved the cryptic melody and the lyrics of it. Carlita put her earbuds in and listened to the song while thinking about Angelo. She started rubbing her nipples with her left hand, then Carlita placed her right-hand fingers in between her legs and masturbated, until she climaxed at least three times. Afterwards, the woman pulled the covers up over her and fell asleep. Carlita had dreams of Angelo; she wanted him to be her man, she needed him.

15

CAUGHT

Thanksgiving was only a little more than a week away. The Monday morning sky was overcast and ominous. It was damp and raw outside. A thunderstorm was coming in from the south that would leave up to three inches of rain in the area and flood zones were being cautioned.

The medical examiner had determined that Engineer John Holms had died of a massive heart attack, brought on by stress and two severely blocked arteries. John Holms had also sustained a concussion from falling onto the track rails. The medical examiner also determined that the woman, identified as Angelica Gomez, had been dead for at least four to six hours before she had been pushed in front of the oncoming train. There were no body parts removed from Angelica Gomez's body, but Chief Brady still suspected it to be the work of the Railway Butcher. The chief couldn't understand why the killer would go through all that. *Why kidnap the woman, before killing her, and then just throw her onto the tracks of an oncoming train? It seemed to be a pretty elaborate way of killing someone,* he thought. Brady considered that the killer was trying to hide the fact that Gomez was murdered. The other thing that bothered Chief Brady was that this was the oldest female victim yet, coupled with the fact that this victim had none of her organs removed. It was a totally different MO for the butcher. Miss Gomez was singled out for some other reason, or else, why would he go through all the trouble of snatching her from a mental institution? He decided to have the woman's daughter, Carlita Gomez, brought in for some questioning.

Angelo Russo was just coming out of the shower when he saw his sister's spirit staring at him. Carina was giving him a ghostly wolf's whistle, as she stood there right in front of him wearing a white negligee. Angelo thought she still looked hot, even though her body was translucent.

"I'm glad that you approve," he told the ghost.

"I'll bet C-a-r-l-i-t-a a-p-p-r-o-v-e-s, t-o-o," the apparition replied in her ghostly voice.

"I don't know that yet."

"What do you mean by that?"

"Carina, Carlita hasn't seen me naked yet."

"Oh, come on now. Tell that story to someone else."

"It's true, honey. Carlita is special to me. I don't want to rush it with her. Besides, she just lost her mother. Right now, Carlita needs a friend more than anything else."

"I'll bet she does; however, I am sorry about her mom. When did it happen?"

"It was about a week ago."

"And you're just telling me now?"

"Because I know that you're not really interested in what happens to Carlita Gomez."

"I liked her mom; she was always nice to me, for the few times I saw her. Was her mother ill?"

"Yes, and no, but that's not what she died from."

"Well, how did her mother die?"

"She was murdered."

"Murdered?"

"Yes. Her mother was thrown in front of my train and my engineer saw it happen."

"Oh, my God! The poor lady."

"Yeah and dig this, I overheard the cops saying that she was dead already!"

"Did your partner see the killer's face?"

"No, he didn't, and they couldn't ask him any questions."

"Why not?"

"Because he's dead, too."

"Are you serious, Angelo?"

"Yes, I am. He dropped dead of a heart attack. He was old, so I guess it was a little too much for him."

"I'll bet it was the same one that killed me and all the others."

"That's what the police are trying to find out now, Carina."

"I knew something was bothering you, Angelo. You should have told me that right away. You know I worry about you."

"I know you do. But, please, try to be just a little more sympathetic to Carlita, especially if I bring her here for dinner or something."

"I will try, but I'm not going to promise anything," Carina's specter said as she faded away.

A while later in the afternoon, Angelo was boarding a southbound train. He was dressed in blue jeans, a tan sweater top, and a brown leather jacket. Angelo had Mondays and Tuesdays off this month. Since it was Monday, he was going to visit Carlita. The two of them were going to hang out together for the rest of the day. Angelo thought about what Carlita had told him over the phone: "When I'm lonely, I think of making love to you with my favorite song, 'Wicked Game' by Chris Isaak," she had said.

When Angelo finally arrived, she was already there at the train station waiting to pick him up. Carlita wore a tight white shirt that accentuated her breasts. She also had on a tight pair of blue jeans that flattered her buttocks. Carlita screamed when she saw someone very familiar to her on the train. It was her boss, the one who killed her mother. He was sitting right by the window. Carlita ran into Angelo's arms, screaming.

"What's wrong, sweetheart?!" Angelo asked.

"That's him, that's him!" Carlita screamed out.

"Him? Who? Carlita, who?" he asked her.

"He's the one who killed my mother!" Carlita yelled as she broke down and cried in his arms.

Angelo quickly turned around to see who is was, but he couldn't believe it. Conductor Taylor Parker was sitting by the window as the train pulled out.

"Are you sure that was him?" he asked her.

"Yes, I'm sure of it. I, I would know him anywhere," Carlita stated in between her cries.

"I know him, he's Conductor Taylor Parker."

Angelo took Carlita to her car and sat her down in the passenger seat next to him. He took out his smartphone and called

Command Center. Angelo had explained the situation to the desk supervisor on duty. The supervisor said he would have the police hold the train at the next station stop, while Angelo would meet them there with the witness.

"We're going to meet the police at the next train stop, honey. They're going to hold the train for us," Angelo told Carlita.

"Ok, can you drive?" she asked him.

"Yes, it's been a while, but I can drive. I just don't own a car."

Angelo took the car keys from her and started up the old Mercedes sedan. Within seconds, they were on the road racing to catch up with the train at the next station. The couple was very lucky that there was a road adjacent to the train tracks.

After a few miles, the train pulled into the Court Square station. Angelo was pulling into the parking lot of the train station. The police were already there holding the train and waiting for them. Angelo and Carlita went to the train platform and spoke to the police officers at the scene.

"Which one of you is the witness?" asked Officer Ireland.

"I am," Carlita replied.

"Ok, can you describe him, Miss?"

"Yes, I can."

"So can I officer, he's a male conductor that wants to be a woman. His name is Taylor, Taylor Parker," Angelo said.

"I know who he is; he's got long blond hair, probably a wig, right?" Ireland asked.

"That's correct officer," Angelo replied.

Officer Ireland boarded the train. Angelo and Carlita stayed on the platform with the other officer. Ireland was scanning the angry passengers while walking through the train. The operating conductor was making the usual apologetic announcement: "Sorry for the inconvenience," adding that they had police action on board. No one really cared as they sat there complaining to themselves and to the train conductor. The passengers just wanted to get to their destinations without any further delays. Officer Ireland finally spotted Parker in the fourth car. Officer Ireland went over to the Parker. He asked him to stand up and turn around. The police officer proceeded to place handcuffs on the suspect and he escorted him off the train.

"But wait, what did I do, Officer? What's this all about?" the blond man asked.

"You know perfectly well what you did and don't try anything funny, Mister. We've got men all over here," Officer Ireland stated.

The two of them got off the train. Officer Ireland gave the conductor the "proceed" signal. The conductor closed down the doors and the train started to pull out of the station. Ireland stared at his prisoner for a moment and tried to analyze him.

"I have a right to know what I'm being arrested for!" the suspect shouted.

"A woman claims that you killed her mother," Officer Ireland stated.

"What woman? I don't know what you're talking about?"

"Sure, mister, that's what they all say. Now, let me see some ID."

The man handed over his railroad identification pass to the

officer.

"Yep, I was right, you work for the railroad?"

"Yes, I do."

"Well, it looks like you just blew your career, Mr. Parker."

Officer Ireland proceeded to read him his rights. Carlita had stayed in the car so she wouldn't be seen by Parker. Angelo was still on the platform watching Officer Ireland bring Taylor Parker into the squad car.

"Yo, Angelo, help me please! I didn't do anything, I swear it!" Taylor shouted while he was being escorted into the police car.

"Looks like my sister was right about you all this time, Taylor!" Angelo yelled back at him.

"I need the two of you to come down to the station house for an affidavit before we book him," the other officer told Angelo and Carlita.

"Sure, Officer, anything that will help put that scumbag away," Carlita said.

The two police cars led the way to the station, while Angelo followed close behind with Carlita. Angelo loved the way the Mercedes handled; it was the best car he'd ever driven. *I could sure get used to this,* he thought to himself as he drove. Carlita was falling asleep; she was all worn out.

After driving down the road for about twenty-five minutes, they finally arrived at the police station. The officers took Taylor Parker inside; Angelo and Carlita were following behind them. Chief Brady was waiting there to see the suspect.

"Well, well, well, Mr. Butcher, you've finally been caught," the chief said with a smile on his face.

"You've got the wrong man, sir, the name's Parker not Butcher," Taylor replied.

"Sure, it is. Put him in one of the holding cells until I'm ready for him!" Chief Brady said to the officers.

"You got it, Chief," one of the officers replied.

The two officers took Parker to one of the empty holding cells. The chief wanted to interview the witness, personally.

"Come with me, Miss Gomez. I was going to bring you down here for questioning anyway," Brady told her.

"You were?" she asked.

"Yes. Please step inside my office."

"Can my boyfriend come with me?"

"Well, this is a surprise; sure he can. Come in, Mr. Russo."

They all went into the chief's office; Officer Ireland went inside with them, too. He stood guard at the door. Angelo and Carlita sat down on the two available chairs in front of the chief's desk.

"Now then, tell me everything from the beginning, Miss Gomez," Chief Brady stated as he sat down behind his desk.

Carlita Gomez explained to the chief of police everything that had happened to her. She told him all about her encounters with the suspect, how they met, and where they met. Carlita had even mentioned the fact that the man threatened her own mother. When she got to the part about her being hired by the suspect to kill Angelo, Carlita put her head down in shame. Angelo Russo couldn't believe his own ears. He just stared at her in complete shock and disappointment.

"That's why you acted so weird in the restaurant. You were trying to poison me with the wine, weren't you?" Angelo asked her.

"Yes and no, I-I spilled your wine so-so you wouldn't drink it, remember?" she said while choking back her tears.

"And all this time…all this time I, I thought you really loved me. My sister was right about you all along," Angelo said while feeling hurt and betrayed.

"But, I do love you, baby!"

"What?! Don't you dare call me 'baby!' You…you…you're just as bad as he is!"

"Angelo, can't you see?! That's why I spilled your wine, because I love you! I couldn't do it! I just couldn't do it! I really do love you," she pleaded with him.

"Miss Gomez, in light of all this, I'm afraid we're going to have to arrest you for attempted murder," Chief Brady stood up and stated.

"But…but…I didn't do anything! I was under pressure!" Carlita begged for mercy.

"Officer Ireland, lock her up, please," the chief said.

The officer took Carlita Gomez away. Angelo sat there, teary-eyed. He couldn't even face her as she was being handcuffed and taken away by the officer.

"Mr. Russo, it looks like we owe you a bit of an apology," Brady told him.

"Maybe *you* don't, Chief, but Lieutenant Collins sure does," Angelo replied.

"He would if he were here, but he's not. It's his day off."

"I still say Taylor's got my sister's hair."

"The DNA test came back negative on that, Mr. Russo."

"I don't care, it's wrong. Check his wig out again. I know my sister's hair; it's got to be hers. Do you know that Taylor has harassed me on the job, too?"

"No, I didn't know that. Sit right there for a minute, Mr. Russo."

The chief made a call to make sure everything that just happened in his office was still being recorded. He then called in another officer. Within minutes, Officer Paul Flanigan entered the chief's office. Flanigan was waiting patiently to take his revenge out on the butcher for killing Officer Kathy Rivera. Flanigan had never forgotten about how helpless he felt while she lay there dying in his arms that evening.

"You called me, Chief?" Officer Flanigan asked.

"Yes, I did. It appears that we've finally captured the so-called butcher. He's in holding cell number three. I want you to bring me his blonde wig," the chief stated.

"His wig, sir? That's all? Just his wig? 'Cause I can bring you his heart out on a silver platter. I'll never forget what he did to Officer Rivera, plus everyone else, sir."

"Calm down, Flanigan. His wig will do just fine for now, understood?"

"Understood, sir."

Angelo realized that the officer must have been really tight with this Officer Rivera. The name sounded familiar to him, and then he remembered. Officer Rivera was that beautiful cop that was on his train a while back. The butcher had murdered her when she got off the train.

* *
*

Officer Flanigan hurried over to the holding cell. He couldn't wait to see the sonofabitch that killed his girl. When Paul Flanigan arrived at holding cell number three, Taylor Parker was sitting on the bed with his head down in his hands.

"Hey, you, Butcher!" the officer yelled out while unlocking the cell gate.

"My name is Parker. Why does everyone around here call me 'Butcher?'"

"Cause that's what the hell you are, a damn butcher," Officer Flanigan said while stepping into the cell with Parker.

"The chief wants your wig; give it up," Flanigan said while having his right hand on his gun.

"No way, man! This is my hair!" Parker said while standing up in front of the officer.

Paul pulled his gun out of his holster and aimed it at Taylor.

"Don't give me another reason to use this on you! Now, sit the hell back down and give me the hair piece."

Taylor Parker started to shake. He never had a gun pulled on him in his whole life before. Taylor put his hands up and sat back down on the bed.

"All right, all right, man, it's cool; you can have it," Parker said while taking off his blonde wig and holding it out in front of the officer.

"I knew you would see it my way, baldy," Paul said while

grabbing the wig from him.

Taylor Parker had shaved his head, so it would make it easier for his wig.

"Ain't I entitled to a lawyer, man?"

"Yeah, you'll get one, eventually, but first, you'll be going into the interrogation room."

"The interrogation room, why?"

"So you'll get your chance to confess."

"I got nothing to confess about. You guys got me in here on some trumped up charges, for what?"

"Go ahead and play stupid if you want to; you'll only make it harder on yourself," Officer Flanigan said while stepping out of the cell and locking the gate.

"By the way, you looked like a fag with this wig; at least now, you look more like a man, baldy." The officer laughed while walking away from the holding cells.

A few minutes later, Officer Flanigan was back in the chief's office with the wig in his hands.

"Here you go, Chief; here's his rug," Flanigan said while handing the blonde wig to the chief.

"It sure looks like real hair, doesn't it?" Chief Brady stated.

"That's because it is, sir. It belonged to my sister. I know her hair," Angelo stated.

Chief Brady turned the wig inside out and was horrified. There was dried up blood on what looked like a human scalp.

"Oh, Jesus H. Christ! *Flanigan*, send this down to the lab and have forensics look at it on the double!" he said while feeling disgusted.

"Yes, sir," the officer said while grabbing the hair piece and leaving the office.

"Mr. Russo, we're going to get to the bottom of this; I promise you that. Why don't you just go home and relax? We'll call you with any new developments, all right?"

"Sir, there's just one more problem."

"What's that, Russo?" the chief asked.

"Well, sir, the car that I used to get here belongs to Carlita Gomez. I gave her back her keys."

"Well, you certainly can't drive that thing; it's going to have to be impounded. I'll have one of the officers take you back home in their squad car, all right?"

"Thank you, sir, I really appreciate that," Angelo happily stated.

The chief got back on his phone to see who was free to take Angelo Russo back home. Angelo just kept thinking about all that had happened today. It certainly was not the day off he'd planned. He was all alone again. He lost Carlita. She was going to have to do some jail time; that was a fact. Angelo didn't even know if he could ever forgive her for what she did to him…maybe someday…but certainly not now. Not for a long time.

The next morning, Angelo woke up in his bed with tears in his eyes. Thanksgiving was around the corner and he was supposed to spend it with Carlita. Angelo had no relatives nearby. His parents were dead. His sister was dead, too, with the exception of her ghost that haunts him every day and night. Angelo's smartphone began to ring; it was the police precinct. *Man, maybe they've confirmed that Taylor's wig was my sister's hair,* he thought before answering the call.

"Hello?" he asked.

"Oh, Angelo, it's me, Carlita," she said sounding desperate.

"I don't really want to talk to you, Carlita."

"Oh, please! They've given me only one phone call; you're the only one I want to talk to, please!" she pleaded with him.

"I'm sorry, but you've wasted your call. You really hurt me. Goodbye, Carlita," Angelo said while pressing the "end" button on his smartphone.

Back at the police precinct, Carlita broke down and cried at the phone. Her only love just hung up the phone on her and she couldn't accept it. The officer took the phone away from her. Police Officer Jones took a hysterically crying Carlita Gomez back to her holding cell, where she just cried the rest of the day away.

16

I'M INNOCENT!

Wednesday morning, November 20. Thanksgiving was in just eight days. It sure felt more like early winter than late fall. The temperature was only about thirty-five degrees outside with a sky that threatened a possible snowfall. Some people weren't waiting for Black Friday; they were doing their Christmas shopping earlier.

Lieutenant Collins had just returned from his regular days off. Chief Brady was waiting for him to return. He wanted Collins to interrogate Conductor Taylor Parker, personally. The chief briefed the lieutenant on what had transpired while he was away. Parker was handcuffed and locked up in the interrogation room. There was a camera and microphone monitoring and recording him while he waited.

"Are you ready for him?" the chief asked the lieutenant.

"As ready as I'll ever be," the lieutenant replied.

Police Lieutenant Collins unlocked the interrogation room and stepped inside, closing the door behind him. Collins sat down at the table, facing Taylor Parker. Chief Brady went into the station monitoring room to observe the interview in progress.

"I'm Lieutenant Collins. I'm going to be conducting your interview today. For the record, state your name and occupation, please," Collins declared.

"My name is Taylor Parker. I've been a conductor for the Morton City Railroad for over ten years," Parker stated.

"Do you know what you're being charged for, Mr. Parker?"

"Some woman claimed that I killed her mother. I don't even know her, or her mother."

"That's not the only thing you're being charged for. You're being charged for *all* of the murders that have been happening around here lately."

"What?!" Parker yelled while standing up from the table.

"Sit down, parker!"

"I didn't kill anybody, I swear it," Taylor said somberly while sitting back down in his chair.

"Miss Gomez claims that you threatened her."

"I didn't even know who the hell she was until the day I got arrested on the train."

"Yeah, well, she claims that you told her you were going to kill her mother, unless she killed Angelo Russo for you."

"That's bullshit!"

"That's not all, Parker. Mr. Russo claims that you killed his sister and scalped her."

"Come on, man, I'm being framed!"

"Where the hell did you get that blonde wig from?"

"It was a gift from someone."

"Oh, come on now, you've got to do better than that."

"Seriously man, it came to me in a big brown box. The mailman dropped it off in front of my door."

"Where did it come from? Who sent it to you?"

"I really don't know. There was no return address on the box, just a strange note inside with it."

"What did the note say?"

"It said: 'I can't wait to see you with this on. Love, your secret admirer.' That's it, man."

"I take it that you still have this alleged note?"

"Nah man, I threw it out long ago; besides, it wasn't signed or anything like that, it was printed, like from a computer."

"Did you know the hair came from a human?"

"What? What are you saying, man?"

"I'm saying that supposed wig you've been wearing is really a human scalp."

"Holy shit! Are you serious, man?"

"Didn't you ever look inside of it?"

"Nah man, I just grabbed it and put it on me. I liked it; it was really cool. Heck, I even slept with it on, but you're really creeping me out, man. Are you sure it's from a real live person?"

"Sure as shit, Mr. Parker. It's from a real person, most likely a woman."

"Is that why you had me come down here for a DNA sample?"

"That's right. You claim you know nothing about Miss Gomez or Mr. Russo's sister?"

"That's right, man. I don't know them."

"Come on now, Parker, cut the shit! Tell the damn truth, will ya?!"

"I am telling you the truth! I don't know any of them!"

"But you *do* know Angelo Russo, don't you?!"

"Yeah man, we work together at the railroad, that's all."

"Really, that's all? Mr. Russo claims that you've harassed him on the job. He says you've been hitting on him."

"Nah man, it ain't like that at all!"

"Well, are you willing to go through a polygraph test to help prove it?"

"A what test?"

"A lie-detector test."

"Sure man, bring it on! I'm innocent, you'll see, I'm innocent!"

Back in the monitoring room, the chief was not at all impressed with the interrogation he was watching. Chief Brady felt that Collins had gone soft on Parker. The lieutenant had just walked into the room to confront the chief.

"He wants a polygraph test to verify his innocence," Lieutenant Collins said to the chief.

"I heard. A polygraph? Really, Collins?" the chief asked.

"That's what he wants, Chief."

"No, that's what *you* want! You were so damn quick to send Mr. Russo up the river, but *now* that we have a *real* suspect here, you wind up going soft on him. What the hell is your problem, Collins?"

"No problem, sir. I just think it's a possibility that he's telling the truth, that's all."

"The truth, my ass. You know what I think? I think I want his damn house searched! As a matter of fact, I'm gonna order up a search warrant right now!"

"Nothing for nothing, but, do you really think that's necessary, Chief?"

"What?! Are you doubting my call?!"

"Well, I just thought—"

"You just thought. You know what I think, Collins? I think maybe you need a break from this case."

"No, I'm good."

"Really? You're off the case, Collins!"

"But, sir—"

"No buts. As of now, eleven hundred hours, you're off the damn case."

"But, but, Chief! I can do this, really!"

"You're pushing me, Collins, and I don't like that at all. Nobody questions my authority around here, not even you! You can't break the chain of command. Put in the paperwork for your vacation."

"But, Chief!"

"Do it now!"

"Yes, boss." The lieutenant walked away from the chief, feeling like a dog with his tail between his legs.

Carlita Gomez was in her cell, sitting on the bed, twirling her hair. She had become depressed, withdrawn, and near suicidal. All Carlita wanted was to be set free and to be with Angelo Russo.

"Miss Gomez, I brought you some food and cool water," Officer Flanigan said as he approached her cell.

"I'm not hungry," she said in a barely audible voice.

"But Miss Gomez, you haven't eaten anything since you've been here and that was two days ago. You've got to eat something."

"I said I'm not hungry," she said while raising her voice.

"Maybe, I'll just leave this here, in case you change your mind."

The officer opened up her cell gate and placed the tray of food on the floor next to her, then Officer Flanigan closed the gate and left Carlita all alone in her cell. She just stared at the ham and cheese sandwich, and then Carlita turned away in disgust. Carlita didn't care if she died in prison. The depressed young woman was helplessly in love with someone, that didn't even care about what happened to her. Carlita was truly hurt, but so was Angelo.

Chief Brady had secured a search warrant for Taylor Parker's home. He had sent Officer Flanigan and Officer Smith over there to search the whole place. The two officers had just arrived at Conductor Parker's home early in the afternoon.

"This is it, 15 Park Row Avenue in Morton. Let's go!" Officer Flanigan told Officer Smith as they exited the police cruiser.

Parker's home was a raised ranch house that he had rented with the option to buy it. The house was in good shape, with white vinyl siding, and it was only nine years old. There was a two-car detached garage with it. The home sat on a corner lot in a quiet neighborhood.

"You got the keys, Smith?" Flanigan asked.

"Yep, let's go on inside," Smith replied.

The two officers walked up to the front of the house. Officer Flanigan unlocked the front door with the key he got from Taylor Parker. They both walked inside and started to look for incriminating evidence.

"Remember what the chief said, look for any kind of body parts," Officer Flanigan told Officer Smith.

"We'd do better if we split up," Officer Smith replied.

"Yeah, you're right, I'll start from the basement and you check the upstairs, and don't forget the fridge."

"All right, let's do this!"

The two police officers checked the entire house from top to bottom, but they didn't find anything that would convict Taylor Parker. They didn't find any weapons, body parts, or even any kind of a security or surveillance system that Carlita Gomez was talking about. The officers wondered if they had the right house, or if Miss Gomez was making it all up.

"Hey, Smith, we forgot to check out the detached garage," Officer Flanigan stated.

"Right, let's do it, man!" Officer Smith replied.

The officers left the house and went straight out to the garage. Officer Flanigan unlocked the door handle and raised the door. They looked through all of the junk on the shelves and on the floors. The last thing the police officers searched was Parker's car, an old, black, four-door sedan.

"Well, that's about it. There's nothing here," Officer Smith solemnly said.

"The chief's not going to like this," Officer Flanigan answered back.

"Let's go," Officer Smith said.

Officer's Smith and Flanigan were both disappointed when they left the premises. They were both worried about how the chief was going to handle it. The question now remained: was Conductor Taylor Parker innocent or guilty?

A few miles away, Angelo Russo was feeling guilty about hanging up on Carlita. *She did sound desperate,* he remembered. Angelo decided to call the police station to see how she was doing.

"Morton Town Police Precinct, may I help you?" the female officer asked over the phone.

"Hello, my name is Angelo Russo. I'm just checking on a prisoner that was brought in two days ago," Angelo asked.

"Who's the prisoner, sir?"

"Her name is Carlita Gomez."

"Are you a relative, sir?"

"No, I'm her boyfriend, Miss."

"I'm sorry, sir, but unless you're a family member, I can't divulge any information about her to you."

"Oh, I see, but, she really sounded so distraught when she called me from there, so I…"

"You said your name was Russo, Angelo Russo?"

"Yes, we were brought in together for questioning and then she was arrested for trying to kill me."

"Yeah, I remember now, Mr. Russo, but I can't imagine why you'd care about what happens to her after all that."

"She hurt me, but I still love her."

"Well, if you really wanna know the truth, Mr. Russo, she's understandably depressed. She's not eating anything at all."

The tears started to well up in Angelo's eyes. He knew now that Carlita really loved him; she had given up her will to live. But Angelo wanted to know for sure, to see if this was genuine, or just a trick. He had to see her.

"Miss, I was wondering if I could see her, may I?"

"Sure, Mr. Russo, you could come down and visit if you want to."

"Thanks, I'll be there soon."

"Ok, Mr. Russo, we'll see you later," the female officer told him as she hung up the phone.

*
**

"Why are you visiting that damn bitch?! Are you stupid or something?! She just tried to kill you, A-n-g-e-l-o! Remember?!" Carina's spirit yelled at him.

"I know that, Carina, but she's so depressed. She hasn't eaten anything in two days. Carlita was only allowed to make one phone call and she wasted it on me. I hung up on her while she was crying and I feel really bad."

"Don't be a sucker or her little boy-toy," Carina's ghost said as she finally appeared.

"Oh, there you are! I was wondering when I could see you again in that sexy, white negligee," Angelo sarcastically replied.

"Oh, you're impossible! Can't you see she's just using you?"

"At first, I thought that, but now, I'm not so sure. I want to see her in person and then I'll know for sure."

"Again, she tried to *kill you!*"

"She was being forced to! It was kill or be killed. He was going to kill her mother, and then her. Can't you see that?"

"No! I don't!"

"This is ridiculous. I'm standing here, half-dressed, arguing with a ghost."

"I'm your sister!"

"Not anymore, Carina. You're dead and I'm going."

Back at the police precinct, Officers Flanigan and Smith were explaining to the chief that there was nothing incriminating in Taylor Parker's house. There were no body parts or weapons of any kind. Chief Brady was livid; he was so sure that they had their man. Taylor Parker had taken the polygraph test and passed with flying colors. Without any hard evidence, they were going to have to set Parker free. There was, however, the matter of Parker's wig.

Forensics confirmed that it was, indeed, a human scalp. The chief had decided to send a sample of it out for another DNA test. He wanted to determine if it really was from Carina Russo.

Angelo arrived at the police precinct at three o'clock in the afternoon. He stopped by the florist to pick up some red roses for Carlita. Angelo waited at the counter for the officer to get off the phone.

"I'll be right with you, sir," the female officer told him.

Angelo recognized her voice; it was the woman he had spoken to on the phone. He noticed her name tag: "Officer Sager." Angelo admired her; she was very attractive, much too pretty to be a cop. Officer Sager had long, shiny black hair, with hazel-colored eyes. Her face was sweet with a perfectly shaped nose and mouth. Sager had finally hung up the phone.

"May I help you, sir?" Officer Sager asked him.

"Hi, I'm Angelo Russo. I'm here to see Carlita Gomez," Angelo replied.

"Oh, yes of course, we spoke over the phone. Are those flowers for her?"

"Yes, they are, Officer."

"I'll need to check them out first, Mr. Russo."

"Sure, but they're just flowers, that's all."

Angelo handed the officer the bundle of flowers to inspect. She checked out the plastic wrapping paper around them and then sniffed them.

"They're beautiful, Mr. Russo. I wish someone brought me a dozen red roses like that," Officer Sager said while handing them back to him.

"As beautiful as you are? You should have a hundred guys buying you flowers!"

"Thank you, you're sweet. Let me get an officer to take you back to where Miss Gomez is being held."

"Thank you, Officer Sager, I'd appreciate that."

"I hope Miss Gomez appreciates you."

Sager got back on the phone to call another officer to bring Angelo back to the holding cells. She told Angelo that someone would be out shortly to escort him to Carlita's cell. Little did Angelo know that Taylor Parker was coming toward him.

"Well, well, fancy meeting *you* here, Angelo. Are those for me?" Parker asked him.

"What are you doing out?" Angelo asked him.

"They've got *nothing* on me! It looks like *you* and your *little girlfriend failed!*"

"There's no justice if you're getting out."

"You're so damn sure I'm guilty, huh? Tell me, why is your girl locked up here while I'm being set free? Huh? Did you ever think that maybe *she's guilty??*"

"No! Never!"

"Maybe she orchestrated the whole damn thing, Mr. Russo. Maybe she's the killer!"

"Stop it! Shut up!"

"Maybe you *both* deserve each other! Take her, Angelo, and the two of you can live in your own private hell, together!"

"Enough! I won't hear anymore from your mouth!"

"Excuse me! You guys need to keep it down, especially *you*, Mr. Parker, or do you want to go back to your cell?" Officer Sager said angrily.

"I'm sorry, officer," Angelo said.

"Yeah, I'm sorry, too," Parker added.

"Ok, you're cleared for now, Mr. Parker, but don't leave town. Do you understand?" Sager stated.

"Yes, I do, but what about my hair?"

"You're not getting it back, Mr. Parker. It is now police property and considered evidence. Now, go before I change my mind."

"I'm going. See you around, Russo."

Angelo glared at him with eyes full of hatred. He truly believed that Parker was still guilty.

"Mr. Russo?" Officer Sager asked.

"Yes, I'm truly sorry for that outburst," Angelo replied.

"Apology accepted, sir. Officer Jones is coming by to escort you to Miss Gomez's cell."

"Thank you, Officer."

Angelo was trying to calm down; he didn't want Carlita to see him all upset. A tall, husky African-American police officer came by the police counter; his name tag read: "Officer Jones." Angelo assumed he was the one that was going to take him to see Carlita.

"Mr. Russo?" Officer Jones asked.

"Yes, that's me," Angelo responded.

"Come with me, sir. I'll take you to see Miss Gomez."

Angelo happily followed the police officer to see his beloved lady. They both walked down the corridor and then turned right. Carlita Gomez was at the last cell at the end. Officer Jones unlocked her cell gate and let Angelo inside. The officer locked them both in and he waited outside. Carlita Gomez looked disheveled, withdrawn, and disconsolate.

"Hello, Carlita," Angelo said.

But Carlita didn't hear him; she just stared at the ceiling while lying in her bed. Her spark was gone. The young woman's will to live was absent. Carlita's once beautiful, blonde mane was now a tangled mess. There was a stale, uneaten ham and cheese sandwich on a tray, which was left for her on the floor. It broke Angelo's heart to see her this way. He went over to her and kissed her on the cheek. Carlita finally snapped out of her trance. She slowly turned her face and looked at her beloved, while tears fell down from her eyes like falling raindrops from the sky.

"Angelo, is it really you?" she asked with a tremble in her weak voice.

"Yes, my love, it's really me," he replied softly.

"You've come back to me, darling. Oh, how I've missed you, my love. Please hold me," she cried out while putting her arms around him.

Angelo dropped the flowers and climbed into the bed with her. He wrapped his arms tenderly around her. Nothing felt more right to them both than this one tender moment in time. Angelo regretted ever doubting her. How could this wonderful woman ever hurt him? The thought was now a distant memory. Carlita truly adored him. If he needed any more proof, this was more than enough. Little did they know that high above them on the ceiling, Carina's ghost was watching them in disgust. She wanted Angelo all to herself, and no one was going to take him away from her, especially Carlita Gomez.

"I brought you some red roses, honey," Angelo softly said.

"You did?" she asked.

"Yes, let me go and pick them up for you."

"No! Please don't ever let me go, Angelo!"

"Ok, baby, I'll get them for you later."

The officer was watching them all along. Officer Jones looked at his watch and grabbed his keys.

"Ok, guys, you need to break it up. Visiting hours are over," Officer Jones stated as he unlocked the cell gate and went inside.

"I have to leave now, honey," Angelo told her.

"No! I need you!" Carlita pleaded.

"I have to," Angelo struggled to say while looking into her teary, heartfelt blue eyes.

"Promise me you'll come back for me soon!"

"Yes, I will, but you have to promise *me* something."

"Anything, my love."

"You have to eat your food. I don't want to ever see you withering away like this again, ok?"

"Anything, anything for you, Angelo."

Angelo kissed his beloved goodbye and regretfully walked out of her holding cell. He turned around and said one last thing to her, as the officer locked her back up.

"I'm going to get you out of here if it's the last thing I do. I promise, Carlita," Angelo told her, as he struggled to choke back his own tears.

Angelo walked back out through the corridor with Officer Jones. While Angelo walked, he finally let go of his tears. Angelo and the officer ran into Chief Brady along the way.

"Mr. Russo, fancy meeting you here!" Chief Brady said with a surprised look on his face.

"I came to visit Carlita Gomez," Angelo said while wiping the tears from his face with his right hand.

"I see she's had some effect on you, Mr. Russo."

"I still love her, sir."

"Even after she tried to kill you? I'm afraid that's way beyond my capacity."

"She was pressured into doing it! Taylor was going to kill her mom! Can't you see that, sir?"

"Can we talk in my office, Russo?"

"Sure, anything, if it would exonerate her, sir."

***

The three of them walked into Chief Kevin Brady's office together. Officer Jones stood guard by the door. Angelo sat in the same chair he did last time when Carlita was with him. The chief sat back down behind his desk and grabbed some papers before he spoke to Angelo.

"Mr. Russo, there seems to be some inconsistencies in what Miss Gomez reported and what really happened," the chief stated.

"Why did you let Taylor Parker go and not Carlita?" asked Angelo.

"Because we had no real evidence against him, with the exception of his wig."

"Isn't that enough?"

"I'm afraid not, Mr. Russo. I had our forensics team check out his wig and it is a human scalp. However, Parker claims he received it in the mail as a gift."

"Oh, that's bullshit!"

"Calm down, Russo. The problem is, he took a lie-detector test and passed it with flying colors. Now, I know they're not infallible, but still, there is nothing else that we have on him."

"He killed my sister and then he scalped her, I know it!"

"I've taken the liberty to send another sample over to check the DNA. I suspect something may have happened to the first sample, but I'm not sure yet."

"Did you check his house, sir?"

"Yes, we did. There was nothing there, no body parts, no weapons, nada. Your girlfriend claims that Taylor Parker had a sophisticated security system, with cameras and metal detectors; I mean, the whole nine yards! My guys didn't find any of that, whatsoever. Miss Gomez had also claimed that Parker had an extravagant collection of artwork, including expensive statues and paintings. There was none of that, either. Now, it's entirely possible that we either got the wrong man or Miss Gomez is making this all up. I don't know. I'm going to need your help to find out the truth, Mr. Russo."

"*My* help? What can *I* do?"

"I'm going to order Miss Gomez back to the interrogation room. I want to question her, personally, with your help; that's if you agree."

"Sure, sir, I will do anything for her, anything at all."

"Good. After that, I'm going to submit her to a lie-detector test."

"So, just to be sure I understand you, Chief, you want me to be with her while you question her in that room that looks like a recording studio, right?"

"That's correct, Mr. Russo."

"Question, sir: what about Lieutenant Collins?"

"He's on vacation for two weeks."

"Ok, I'm game. Let's do it!" Angelo said.

"Ok, Mr. Russo, can you be here at nine in the morning tomorrow?"

"I'll try. I don't have a car and you're not near the train station, so I have to call a cab. That's how I got here today, by cab."

Angelo looked at his smartphone to see what time it was.

"Oh, no, shit, man, it's almost five o'clock! I have to be at work at five thirty tonight. I'll never make it!"

"You will if I can find someone to drop you off. Where do you have to be?" the chief asked.

"I have to be at the Hyde Park terminal, sir."

"All right, that isn't far. Let me see what I can do," Chief Brady said while making a call.

"Thank you, sir, I really do appreciate it," Angelo said.

17

THE TRUTH?

Thursday morning, November 21. Angelo was just waking up to his alarm clock at seven o'clock. Angelo had set the alarm to wake himself up early, so that he could have time to go to the police station before going to work. Unfortunately, Angelo hit the snooze button on his clock, he wasn't ready to get up yet, but doing that was going to set him back a few minutes. Ten minutes later, the alarm went off again. This time, Angelo flew out of his bed. Angelo looked right outside of his bedroom window and was flabbergasted. There was a coating to an inch of snow on the ground.

"Shit!" he shouted. "I hope I can still get myself a cab. I better hurry up," he said to himself.

Angelo quickly went to the bathroom to shave and to take a shower. He was hoping Carina's spirit wouldn't pop in because he had no time to make idle chit-chat with a ghost. Angelo grabbed his smartphone and called a cab.

Twenty minutes later, Angelo Russo arrived at the Morton Town Police Precinct. He paid the cab driver, got out, and walked into the precinct. Angelo got to the counter and saw Officer Sager again. Angelo blushed when she smiled at him.

"Good morning, Mr...." she tried to remember his name.

"Russo, Angelo Russo," he helped her say.

"Yes of course. No flowers today?"

"No, but I'm hoping to get her out of here. I'm here to see Chief Brady."

"Oh, I'll let him know you're here," Officer Sager told him while she grabbed her phone to call the chief.

About five minutes later, Chief Brady appeared at the police reception counter. The chief had a cup of coffee in his hand, but he still looked tired. Brady had been handling a heavier work load since he sent Lieutenant Collins on vacation. The chief wanted to go on vacation himself, but not until the serial killer was caught.

"Good morning, Mr. Russo," Chief Brady said.

"Good morning, sir!" Angelo replied.

"Are you ready for this?"

"Yes, I am, sir."

"You know, I don't know what it is that you said to your lady friend in there, but whatever it was, it seemed to have a positive effect on her."

"Really?"

"Yeah, really. For one thing, Miss Gomez is finally eating her food."

"Good! I told her I didn't want to see her that way again."

"You should have seen her this morning when she found out that you were coming here. The lady asked for her hair brush and makeup that was in her bag, obviously we couldn't give it to her, so she did the best she could with her hands to get all dolled up for you, Mr. Russo."

Angelo felt a warm sensation in his heart. He was really glad to have made a positive difference in someone's life, especially Carlita's. The chief offered Angelo a cup of coffee, but he turned it down. They both walked into the interrogation room. Chief Brady made a call to have Miss Gomez brought in with an extra chair, since there were only two chairs present in the room.

A few minutes later, Officer Jones brought Carlita Gomez into the interrogation room. Officer Smith was right behind them with an extra chair in his hands. Smith put the chair down by the table next to the other one, and then he walked out of the room. Officer Jones remained as a guard just in case there were any problems. The chief sat at one side of the table, while Carlita and Angelo sat together opposite the chief on the other side. There was a microphone on the table, with a pitcher of water and three glasses. A camera was pointing down at them recording the entire event.

Angelo was impressed with Carlita's appearance. She looked much better than the last time he had seen her. Carlita was all cleaned up. She had makeup on and her hair was brushed neatly. Carlita gave Angelo a great big smile. They both wanted to kiss each other right there, but each one knew it would be inappropriate.

"Excuse me, Chief!" Angelo said.

"Yes, Mr. Russo?" the police chief asked inquisitively.

"Are these really necessary?" Angelo asked while pointing to Carlita's handcuffs.

"I see no harm in removing them. Jones, take Miss Gomez's cuffs off, please."

"Sure, Chief," Officer Jones replied while coming over to remove Carlita's handcuffs.

"Are we all ready to begin?" Chief Brady asked them.

"I'm ready," Miss Gomez replied.

"So am I, sir," Angelo added.

"Ok. Miss Gomez, you identified Mr. Taylor Parker as your mother's killer. Do you *still think* that he is the one?" the chief asked her.

"At the time, I thought he was, but now, I'm not so sure about that. I started thinking, remembering, and then trying to piece all the things together, but they just don't fit," Carlita replied.

"Why's that, Miss Gomez?"

"Well, for one thing, sir, the man I dealt with seemed a little taller."

"Taller than Mr. Parker?"

"Yes, and the other thing was his voice."

"His voice? Was it different than Mr. Parker's, Miss Gomez?" the chief asked her.

"Yes, sir, the man I used to deal with had a deeper voice. It was kind of a smoker's voice."

"But you did identify his face, didn't you, Miss Gomez?"

"Yes, but that's another thing. His face seemed like it was cold and, I don't know, sort of rubbery."

"How did you determine that, Miss Gomez?"

"I kissed him on the cheek; that was before I knew what a monster he was."

Angelo shot her a dirty look. Carlita knew she had hurt his feelings again, but Carlita wanted to tell the truth, the whole truth.

"It was nothing, Angelo. He meant absolutely nothing to me at all, I swear it," Carlita told him.

"It's possible that the killer was wearing a disguise. But why would he want to look like Taylor Parker?" Chief Brady asked.

"That's a good question, Chief," Angelo said.

"Miss Gomez, what ever happened to the rest of this alleged poison?" the chief asked her.

"I threw it out. I knew that I couldn't do anything to hurt Angelo, or anyone else for that matter, so I just threw it out. I'm not a killer."

"So there's no evidence of any kind, is there, Miss Gomez?"

"I guess not, sir."

"Well, on account of these new findings, I'm going to order up your release, Miss Gomez."

"Really?" she excitedly asked.

"Don't get too excited now, I may need your help to identity this sonofabitch," Chief Brady added.

But Carlita Gomez *was* excited. In fact, the young woman was so overjoyed that she gave Angelo a long, sensual kiss. The two of them were extremely happy to be together again.

"All right, break it up you two lovebirds," the chief told them. "I just want to make sure you're telling me the whole truth, right, Miss Gomez?"

"Yes, yes I am, sir!" Carlita exclaimed.

"Then you wouldn't mind submitting yourself to a lie-detector test before you go, would you?"

"No, of course not. When can we do it?"

"Right now, if you don't mind?" Chief Brady asked.

"That'll be just fine with me, sir," Carlita answered.

So, they all walked right out of the interrogation room. The chief had told Officer Jones to bring Carlita Gomez over to the room where the lie-detector machine was set up. Chief Brady brought Angelo back to the front counter and asked him to wait there until the test was completed.

About an hour later, the chief returned with Carlita Gomez. She ran right into Angelo's awaiting arms and hugged him tight.

"Did you pass the lie-detector test?" Angelo asked her.

Before she could answer, the police chief replied for her.

"With flying colors, I might add. Officer Sager here will give you all of your personal belongings at the counter. Your car is in the back lot behind the precinct. Remember, if you think of anything else, please, give me a call. Good luck out there, Miss Gomez," Chief Brady told her as he gave her his card.

The two of them left the police precinct together, holding hands along the way. Angelo asked Carlita to drop him off at his job location, since he already had his work bag and uniform with him. Carlita didn't mind at all, she was so happy to be back together again with Angelo.

"Are you gonna be all right while I go to work, baby?" Angelo asked her.

"As long as I know you're coming back to me, darling?" Carlita questioned.

"Of course I am, love."

"What time do you have to be at Hyde Park, Angelo?"

"I have to be there a little earlier than yesterday, two o'clock. I'm working two until ten tonight, babe."

"I'll pick you up tonight."

"Oh, you don't have to."

"I want to. Please, let me do that for you. You've done so much for me already; I don't know how I can ever repay you."

"Like this, honey," he said as he grabbed Carlita and kissed her again.

"I love you, Angelo; you're all I have now. My mother's gone and my father went to Russia with that woman. Please, promise me you'll never leave me again," Carlita pleaded.

"I promise, babe," Angelo said as he kissed her again.

After they peeled themselves apart, Carlita and Angelo got into her Mercedes and drove off. Carlita made sure to drive within the speed limit. She wasn't going to risk getting pulled over or getting arrested again. The woman didn't ever want to go back to prison. She was going to be really good, especially for Angelo.

"Here, take this, babe," Angelo said as he gave her a twenty-dollar bill.

"What's that for?" she asked.

"It's for gas. I know you're out of work and this car doesn't run on air, so take it, please?"

She reluctantly took the money at the stop light and put it in her blue jeans pocket. When the light changed, Carlita took off and then placed her right hand on Angelo's left thigh, near his crotch. She started to squeeze and massage his crotch, until she felt his member growing in his pants. Angelo was getting a massive hard-on. He gave her a loving look, and then Angelo took his left hand and started rubbing *her* crotch. Carlita sighed. They were both in heat for each other. The couple finally arrived at the Hyde Park terminal. Angelo kissed her goodbye and she stared at him with a dreamy look in her eyes. Carlita watched him walk. She liked his gait. *He has such a cute ass,* Carlita thought. After Angelo disappeared from view, she took off and headed home.

Angelo signed onto his job for the day at the dispatcher's office. When he walked out of the office, Angelo ran right into Taylor Parker. Taylor was wearing a new blonde wig; this one had bangs in it.

"Whoa, look at what the cat dragged in," Taylor said sarcastically.

"Hey, man, I guess I owe you a bit of an apology," Angelo replied.

"Damn straight you do! That was a *really shitty thing* that you and your girlfriend did to me. Man, I could have lost my job, my life...*everything,* because of you!"

"I know and I'm truly sorry, Taylor. She thought it was you. Someone sure went through a lot of trouble to make himself look like you."

"You mean someone dressed up like me?"

"We think the person may have had a mask and wig on to look like you!"

"Shit, man, are you for real?"

"Yeah, man. Do you know of anyone that would want to do that to you?"

"No…but you know what? It's kind of flattering. Someone wants to look like little ole me."

"It ain't flattering if they want to frame you for murder."

"Yeah, I guess not…hey, I wonder if it's the same one that sent me that wig."

"It could be. I see you got yourself a new wig."

"Yeah, man, but it's not as nice as the other one. Look, I really didn't know it was your sister's hair. I'm sorry, Angelo. I really do want us to be friends."

"It's all good, man. We still don't know for sure if it really is her hair."

"Yeah, well, it creeped me out when they told me it was from a human scalp. To think I had that shit on me almost all the time…ugh!"

"You guys better get on your trains on time!" the dispatcher ordered.

"Yeah, all right, sir, we're going," Angelo said as he told Taylor goodbye.

Later that night, Carlita was getting ready to pick up Angelo from the Hyde Park train station. It was almost nine o'clock at night. She knew he was getting off at ten o'clock. The trip itself was only about a half an hour, but Carlita wanted to get there early without feeling rushed. She left the house, got into her car, and started up her engine. Carlita pulled out of her driveway at about five after nine. Another vehicle on the street had also started up its engine and turned on its headlights. It proceeded to follow her, staying far enough behind to avoid any suspicion. Carlita went down Route 22, which was a two-lane road with one lane going in each direction.

Traffic was fairly light at that time of night. She started to notice a vehicle behind her that seemed to be getting closer. All of a sudden, the vehicle put on its bright lights. Carlita wondered what this fool wanted from her; clearly, there was nowhere else for her to go. She was already doing sixty miles per hour, which was five miles over the speed limit. Carlita vowed not to exceed the speed limit any more than that. She didn't want to be pulled over, but the vehicle was now almost riding her tail. It came closer and closer until it could almost touch her bumper. Carlita started getting nervous. *Well, if he wants to pass me by going in the opposite lane, he better do it now before another car comes,* she had thought to herself. Then, without any kind of warning whatsoever, the vehicle struck her from behind.

"What the hell?" Carlita shouted as if the person could hear her.

The vehicle bumped her again. Carlita was frightened. She didn't know what was going to happen next. Carlita decided to floor it, but the vehicle kept up with her. She glanced at her speedometer.

"Oh, shit! I'm doing eighty miles per hour and he's *still* on my ass!" Carlita shouted in disbelief.

Carlita could tell that the vehicle behind her was bigger. *It must be some kind of truck,* she thought. Once more, the vehicle struck her from behind. The young woman was so terrified that her bladder emptied all over herself. There was a car coming from the opposite direction, in the other lane. This time, the big, black, Ford pickup truck went around her on the shoulder. The driver in the truck rolled down his window and shouted: "die, bitch, die!" She knew that voice. The butcher side-swiped Carlita so hard that she got pushed into the other lane and crashed, nearly head-on, into the oncoming car. The killer kept on going, laughing all the way.

Angelo had just gotten off his train at ten p.m. He ran down the stairs taking them two at a time, rushing to the station parking lot. He couldn't wait to see Carlita again. When Angelo got there, he was disappointed. He did not see Carlita's car. Angelo thought she was just running a little late. *I told her I would be getting off at ten; she's never late for anything,* he thought to himself. Angelo looked at his watch a few minutes later. It was now ten twenty. *I guess I've been stood up,* he thought. Angelo called her cell and got her voicemail. The young man left her a message, then he waited some more. By eleven o'clock Angelo decided to take the next train back home, feeling disappointed and confused.

"What happened to her?" Angelo softly asked himself on the train.

18

ALL ALONE AGAIN

The next morning, Angelo woke up to the sound of the doorbell ringing. He still wondered what happened to Carlita last night. Angelo looked at his clock to see what time it was.

"Shit, it's only six in the morning. Who the hell is ringing my doorbell this early?" he mumbled to himself.

Angelo put his light-blue robe on and went downstairs to see who it was. He turned on the outside light and opened the door; it was Officer Ireland. Angelo recognized him from the last visit when he came over with Lieutenant Collins.

"You're Angelo Russo, right?" Officer Ireland asked.

"I didn't do it," Angelo suspiciously answered.

The officer briefly smiled.

"No, sir, it's nothing like that," Officer Ireland replied, while now looking serious at Angelo.

"Well then, what's up, Officer?"

"I'm afraid there's been an accident, sir," he gravely replied.

"Accident? What kind of an accident?" Angelo nervously asked.

"You know a Miss Carlita Gomez, Mr. Russo?"

"Oh, no! What's happened to my baby now?" Angelo asked as the tears started to well up in his eyes.

"She had a very serious car accident. It was a near head-on collision on Route 22 last night."

"Is she all right?"

"She's in critical condition; they don't expect her to survive. I'm sorry, Mr. Russo," Officer Ireland said while removing his hat.

Angelo was terribly distraught; he was even trembling. If Carlita died, Angelo would be all alone again. He looked right at the officer and managed to ask him for some more details.

"What hospital is she at, Officer?"

"She's at Morton Medical Center, in the ER."

"I know where that is, it's at the South Park train station."

"Yeah, that's right, Mr. Russo, South Park. The chief said she has no family here, just you, is that true?"

"Yes, it's true. Her father left the country with another woman and her mother was recently killed. Carlita was an only child, she doesn't have anyone else."

"What about her grandparents?"

"From what I understood, they're dead, too."

"And I guess she was never married, right?"

"Right. Hey, listen, I've got to get dressed and go visit her."

"Ok, Mr. Russo. I hope everything turns out all right for you."

"Thanks, Officer."

"Oh, I almost forgot, the chief wanted to talk with you about this. He's there at the hospital waiting for you; he's been there since they brought her in last night."

"Ok, Officer, thanks," Angelo closed the front door and went upstairs with tears in his eyes.

Carina's ghost had appeared behind him watching his every move. She wanted to comfort Angelo, but she thought it was best to just give him his space right now. He went to the bathroom to shave, but Angelo just collapsed over the sink and cried.

A few miles away, the butcher was out stalking his next victim. A good-looking, young woman with long, light-brown hair was heading into the Hyde Park train terminal. She was obviously going in to work. The killer knew he was running out of time. It was still fairly dark out, but it wouldn't be long before that morning sun came around. He started walking closer behind her, trying to maintain her stride. *I got an order for a new liver and pancreas; she'll fit the bill just nicely,* the butcher was thinking while he followed her, but he also wanted her hair. *A change in hair color would sure be nice,* he thought. The killer walked behind her, closer and closer, getting ready for the kill. *I've got to reach her before she gets to the stairs of the train station,* he thought. The woman kept walking down the street, unaware that she was now being followed by a ghastly serial killer. The butcher clenched a tight rope in his hands as he got ready to strike, but he wasn't aware of what was really going to happen next. The slaughterer jumped up from behind her and tried to lasso the woman, until she turned around and shot him with her gun. The bullet entered right into his abdomen. He dropped to his knees screaming in agony, while the woman ran away. The young female was so traumatized that she dropped her gun while running. She did manage to get a good look at her assailant, thanks to the train station lights. The butcher struggled to get up. He knew he had to get out of there before the police came to arrest him. The woman was hysterically crying while she called 911 on her cellphone. After acquiring all the necessary information from the woman, the 911 operator told her the police were on their way. The butcher finally made his way back to his black pickup truck, like a wounded animal struggling to survive. The police had finally arrived on the scene, but it was already too late. The killer had gotten away. They decided to interview the young woman; her name was Julie Berlin. Julie had become so distraught that she could barely answer the two officers' questions. All Julie could say was, "It was the conductor, the conductor on the train!" The two police officers asked her if she wouldn't mind coming down to the station house. They wanted the woman to look at some mugshots, and Julie agreed to go.

"I want him arrested, as soon as possible," Julie told the officers.

Later on at the hospital, Angelo was trying to find out where Carlita was being treated. He was extremely worried about Carlita's condition. Angelo went to the hospital main entrance, and then to the information desk where he was greeted by Chief Brady.

"Mr. Russo, how are you?" Chief Brady asked him.

"Where is Carlita?" Angelo anxiously asked.

"She was just brought up to surgery, Mr. Russo."

"How is she, sir?"

"I'm not going to sugarcoat it, Mr. Russo. Miss Gomez is hurt pretty bad. She's got multiple fractures and she's in a coma. Carlita Gomez may not even make it; her condition is grave. Are you prepared for that?"

"She's got to make it…I love her," Angelo said with tears streaming down his face.

"The doctor will fill you in more when he comes out of surgery. Mr. Russo, there's something else I wanted to tell you."

"More bad news, sir?"

"Witnesses claim that she was pushed into the oncoming vehicle by a black pickup truck. Now, if this is true, we're looking at an attempted homicide case. Unfortunately, we haven't got much to go with here. We don't have a license plate number, just that description, that's all."

"She should have had police protection from that animal out there! He wants her dead because she can potentially identify him."

"I'm sorry, Mr. Russo, but I just didn't have enough manpower to do that. However, as a result of these new findings, I'll have an officer stationed here for her. By the way, there's just one more thing I really wanted to mention to you, Mr. Russo."

"What else is it, Chief?"

"A woman was attacked earlier this morning near the Hyde Park train station. She managed to shoot the perpetrator before he attempted to kill her, assuming that's what he was trying to do to her."

"Was it the butcher?"

"We think so."

"Good! I hope he friggin dies!"

"Unfortunately, he got away; we never found him, but the woman identified him as a railroad conductor. She's down at the station house right now looking through mugshots. If she confirms it's Taylor Parker, well, we're back to square one again."

"I guess her Mercedes is totaled. She loved that car."

"Yes, Miss Gomez's car was totaled and so was the Chevy hatchback she hit. The two drivers, Miss Gomez and Miss Melinda Stokes, tried their best to avoid hitting each other, but there just wasn't enough room on the road."

"The other driver; is she…?"

"She didn't make it, Mr. Russo."

The two of them talked some more while drinking coffee and sitting in the waiting room.

*****

Two hours later, a doctor had come into the waiting room looking for them. The doctor, who went by the name of Jerold Foster, was a neurosurgeon with a long-time residency there at the hospital. Doctor Foster was tall and thin, but at only fifty-five years of age, his bright white hair, from stress, no doubt, had made him look much older than he was. The doctor approached the chief and Mr. Russo, while he was still wearing his hospital scrubs, to give them an update on Miss Gomez's condition.

"Chief Brady?" the doctor asked.

"Yes, that's me," the chief replied while standing up from his seat.

"I'm Doctor Foster. I just wanted to inform you of Miss Gomez's condition."

"How is she, doc, is she going to be all right?" Angelo asked.

"And you, sir, are you her husband?"

"Not yet, sir, but I'm going to marry her as soon as she's well."

"So, you're not a member of her family, is that correct?"

"It's ok, doc. Mr. Russo here is the only family she's got," Chief Brady attested.

"All right, then, Miss Gomez has been moved to the intensive care unit upstairs. She has a fractured disk in her vertebrae;

it's a C2 fracture. Because of this, she has to be in traction. Miss Gomez has now been fitted with a halo to stabilize her neck."

"What's a halo, doc?" Angelo asked.

"Well, it's sort of a cage that is bolted to her skull and held in place by a vest. She'll have to wear it for at least three months if all goes well. Miss Gomez also has a fracture in her left femur, that's her thigh bone, Mr. Russo. And because of that, the orthopedic surgeon has inserted a titanium rod into her femur bone. She will have to keep that in her for the rest of her life."

Angelo was getting all choked up. The tears were literally streaming down from his eyes like a waterfall. He was doing his best to maintain all his composure, but it was sure evident that the young man would not be able to do so for long.

"There is one other thing that I should mention," Doctor Foster added.

"And what's that, doctor?" Chief Brady asked, while Angelo was struggling to keep himself together.

"Well, we really don't even know how successful we were in treating Miss Gomez. You see, Miss Gomez has remained in a coma ever since she arrived at this hospital; actually, since the accident itself, from what we know. We just don't know when or if she'll ever come out of it."

Angelo couldn't hold it in anymore. He collapsed back down in his seat and wept uncontrollably.

"Mr. Russo, you really do have a lot to be thankful for!" Doctor Foster tried to explain to Angelo.

"What?! What could I possibly be thankful for?! You tell me, doctor!" He yelled as his voice cracked.

"Well, she's still alive! As long as she's alive, there's hope. Please keep that in mind, Mr. Russo, for your sake, and for hers," the doctor told him.

"Can I visit her, doc?"

"Yes, you may, but only for just a few minutes. Come, I'll take you to her."

The doctor escorted Angelo and Chief Brady to the elevator. They went up to the fourth floor and into the intensive care unit. Angelo was nervous; he didn't know how he was going to handle seeing the love of his life in her present condition.

*
**

Meanwhile, back on the other side of town, the butcher was struggling with his pain and blood loss. The killer was lucky that the bullet didn't pierce any major organs. The bullet had come right out on the other side of him.

"Shit, it hurts! It's a good thing I was a paramedic for two years so that I could treat myself," the slaughterer said to himself.

The butcher knew going to the hospital was way out of the question. They would know who he was. The police were on the lookout for a male that's been shot. They were also looking for someone that fit the description furnished by the woman he attacked. The Railway Butcher was going to have to treat himself and hope for the best. He wanted revenge; revenge against Angelo, Carlita, and now, the woman that shot him. The assassin cleaned and bandaged himself up to the best of his abilities. This was going to set him back. He had an order to fulfill. The killer never did get the liver and pancreas that his customer wanted. Time was running out for him.

"I must find more prey, soon!" he said to himself. "I can't let this shit hold me back!"

But the pain was much too great. He decided to pour himself a good strong drink, hoping the alcohol would ease the pain. The butcher was worried.

"I know they're looking for my ass, I've got to be careful," he said to himself while drinking his scotch and soda, wishing that he had something much stronger.

Meanwhile, back at the hospital, Angelo Russo and Chief Brady were being brought into the intensive care unit by Doctor Foster. When Angelo spotted Carlita Gomez on the hospital bed, he was totally shocked. Carlita had a cage-type apparatus bolted to her head and connected to a vest. It was the halo the doctor had mentioned. Her left leg was in a cast and she had bruises on her face and arms. There were numerous tubes and wires hooked up to her, from all of the associated monitoring and life support equipment in the room.

"Jesus, my poor little angel," Angelo said in a weak voice, while trying his best to choke back the tears once again.

Angelo carefully approached her, and then he turned to look at the doctor.

"Tell me, can she even see or hear me, doctor?"

"See? No, she hasn't opened her eyes up since the accident. However, Miss Gomez *may* be able to hear you, Mr. Russo. Talk to her, let her know just how much you love her, it may help to bring her back," Doctor Foster told Angelo.

"Baby, can you hear me? It's me, Angelo. Honey, you've got to pull through this; you've got to come back to me. I love you. You're all I've got right now. I want to marry you, darling. I need you, please come back to me, Carlita," Angelo managed to tell her in between his weeping.

Carlita didn't move. She didn't even flinch a muscle. No one knew if she even heard his words at all; there certainly wasn't any indication of it on any of the monitoring equipment. Even Chief Brady felt bad, especially for Angelo.

"We must go now and let her rest," Doctor Foster said.

They all walked out of the intensive care unit, leaving Carlita alone with the nurse. The chief had received a phone call from the police station before he walked out of the hospital. Julie Berlin, the young woman that was attacked earlier at the train station, had positively identified Conductor Taylor Parker from the mugshots. Chief Kevin Brady had ordered him back downtown for further questioning, but the train dispatcher said it couldn't have been him. Conductor Parker was operating his train at the time of the incident.

Angelo Russo decided to call in sick for the next two days. He was too emotionally disturbed to work; plus, he wanted to be with Carlita. Angelo originally wanted to take more time off, but the man knew that he couldn't take more than two days off, without having to get a note from a doctor.

The next day, Angelo went back to visit Carlita in the hospital again. He brought a book with him to read to her. The doctor told him that she may be able to hear him. Angelo hoped it was true. He sat down next to her and began reading from his book, not knowing Carina's apparition was in the room with them, watching and listening to everything that was going on.

19

I SEE RED

Monday morning, November 25. The notorious Railway Butcher was getting ready for his next kill. He felt better now and knew it was time to get back to work. Although the killer wasn't completely healed, he was well enough to make his next move.

"I see red, red as in blood, but I also see green, mean green, as in money," the butcher said to his reflection in the bathroom mirror.

It had been about a week since the butcher was shot by the last woman he attacked. The killer still had that order to fulfill. His customer needed a pancreas and a liver. He was willing to pay big bucks for both parts. The slayer really didn't need the extra money; not right now, anyway, but he had a big taste for more blood. The murderer had enjoyed killing, especially beautiful young women. The predator was getting everything ready for tonight. He was out of practice for a while, but stalking and killing had become second nature to him. *It was like riding a bike, you never forget,* he thought to himself. The butcher got his tools together and made sure they were all sharp, then the killer got his coolers out. He washed them all out thoroughly. Next, the butcher made sure he had enough ice in the freezer to fill the coolers up, leaving just enough room for the organs. The slaughterer was going to wait until the last minute before leaving to fill them up with ice.

A few miles away, Angelo was getting ready to go to work. He really didn't want to go to work, the only thing Angelo had on his mind was Carlita. Carina's ghost had appeared in the bathroom mirror again as Angelo began to shave.

"Good morning, darling," Carina's spirit said to him.

"Good morning, Carina," Angelo replied.

"Getting ready for work again?"

"Yes, I am."

"Are you coming straight home tonight?"

"No. I'm going back to the hospital to visit Carlita."

"That's what you've been doing every night since she's been there."

"And, is that a problem?"

"Well, it's just that I think it's a waste of time. I mean, she can't hear you or anything, you know. I thought you and I could spend a quiet evening together."

"Well, aren't we being a little bit selfish? That girl is in there fighting for her life and all you can think about is yourself!"

"What do you see in her, Angelo?"

"Well, for one thing, she's alive and you're not! But the main thing is I really do love her. You're going to have to learn to accept that, Carina!"

But Carina could not accept it; she vanished from his mirror with a loud bang. Angelo knew that Carina was envious of Carlita, but she was going to have to get over it. Angelo wanted to make a life with Carlita *if* she survived. Thanksgiving was in three days and he was going to spend it with Carlita at the hospital. This was going to be the first time in his life that he would be spending the holidays without his family. If Carlita dies, he will have no one, except his sister's ghost.

Two hours later at the police station, Chief Brady was trying to figure out a way to trap the serial killer. He was beginning to regret sending Lieutenant Collins on a two-week vacation. The chief sure could have used his help now. Lieutenant Collins would not be back to work until after Thanksgiving. Chief Brady wondered why the killer would go through such an elaborate scheme as this. *Why would he create a mask of a specific person to commit murder? What did the butcher have against Conductor Taylor Parker? The killer obviously wanted to frame someone for his massacres, but why Taylor Parker? What did Parker do to him?* He decided to have Taylor Parker brought back down to the station for additional questioning.

Later that evening, the butcher was ready to leave his house. He had filled up his two coolers with ice and loaded them and his tools into his truck. The killer was heading back down to the South Park train station to claim his next victim.

"This time, there better be no slip-ups," he said to himself.

The killer got into his pickup truck and drove off with the thirst for blood in his mouth.

About twenty minutes later, the butcher arrived at the South Park train station. It was eight thirty in the evening. *This seems dark enough,* he thought. The butcher sat in his truck and waited for the train to arrive. A few minutes later, a northbound train was pulling into the station. The butcher left his vehicle, taking his knife and rope along with him. He scanned the platform after the train had left the station. There were two passengers that had gotten off the train; one went down to the parking lot and the other one stayed there. The killer could tell it was a woman talking on her cellphone, probably calling for a ride. He got closer to get a better look at her. She started to walk down the station platform while still talking on the phone. The killer didn't have to approach her; she was coming to him. The train station lights were bright enough for him to get a decent look at his new target. The woman was a little older than what he had wanted. The lady appeared to be in her early forties. *Shit, she's a little older than I thought, but screw it, she'll do,* the butcher thought. The slayer started to position himself to get behind the woman. She was still yakking on her phone.

"How soon are you coming?" he overheard her ask the other party. *That's right, keep talking, baby; it'll be easier for me,* the butcher thought. The woman had shoulder-length, curly black hair, which didn't appeal to him. He liked long, straight-flowing hair. The killer was only interested in her liver and pancreas. The slaughterer couldn't decide which weapon to use on her: the knife or the rope. She finally put her phone into her purse. He waited for her to pick up her head and then, like an executioner, he threw the rope around her neck and proceeded to choke the life out of the woman. The lady tried to plead for her life while she was being strangled, but her cries fell on deaf ears.

"Please! My...children," the woman cried out.

Finally, the killer tightened the rope even more until the mother of two breathed no more. The woman gave up her fight and collapsed right in front of him, onto the cold concrete station platform. The butcher went back to his truck to get his two coolers. He returned to his victim and proceeded to slice her wide open with his scalpel. The murderer removed her liver and placed it into one of the two coolers he had, then he removed her pancreas and placed it into the other cooler. The killer walked back to his truck, leaving the poor victim lying there on the platform with blood everywhere.

Back at the hospital intensive care unit, Angelo assumed his regular spot, sitting in a chair beside Carlita's bed. As usual, he started to read from one of her favorite thriller novels. Angelo kept glancing up at her in between paragraphs. He was wishing, hoping, and praying that Carlita would open up her eyes, but she just laid there in a coma. Carlita had planned to cook him a nice big Thanksgiving dinner for the holiday, and then they were going to go Christmas shopping for each other. The two of them made some really nice plans together, but the Railway Butcher sought to put an end to all of that. The trail of blood that he spilled was getting longer. The butcher won't stop. He won't ever stop killing until he's caught.

Angelo looked at all of the life support and monitoring equipment that was in the room, not knowing what their displayed information meant. The doctor came around and asked him if he would consider taking her off life support. Angelo refused. He knew what that meant. Angelo was not ready to give up on his beloved girlfriend, not now. He still had hope, even if no one else did.

A few miles away at the Morton Town Police Precinct, Chief Brady had just received a phone call about another murder. He sent Officer Smith and Officer Ireland down to investigate it. The chief had hoped that it wasn't the work of the butcher, but he knew better than that. The squad car carrying police officers Smith and Ireland had finally arrived at the South Park train station. When they got there, the two officers were met by the train station cleaner.

"Hello, Officers, my name is Robert James. I'm the one who phoned it in," the cleaner said.

"Do you work for the railroad, sir?" Officer Ireland asked.

"Yes, I do, Officer. I'm the head station cleaner. I just discovered the poor woman about an hour ago. Who would do such a horrible thing to a woman?"

"You'd be surprised. Where's the victim, Mr. James?" Officer Smith asked.

"Right this way, Officers; she's laying on the northbound platform."

The station cleaner led the two police officers to the woman's body. Officer Smith was starting to get sick to his stomach as he approached her. He recognized the woman immediately.

"Oh, Jesus, Mary, and Joseph! It's Mrs. Fields!" Officer Smith said.

"You know this woman, Smith?" Officer Ireland asked.

"Yes, I do. Her name is Jessica Fields and she's my next-door neighbor. She's married with two children. Shit, how am I going to tell her husband and the kids?"

"Well, it sure looks like the work of the butcher to me. We got to call the chief," Officer Ireland stated.

"Listen, do you have any red tape lying around here, Mr. James?" Officer Smith asked the cleaner.

"Yes I do, Officer."

"Good. I need you to close up all the entrances, exits, and stairwells to this station. This is officially a crime scene. Nobody comes in. Nobody goes out. Ok?"

"Well, what about the trains coming in and going out, Officer?"

"I'll tell the chief to call the Command Center. They can have all the trains bypass this station until further notice."

"Ok, Officer, I'll start taping up the exits and entrances."

Officer Ireland called the chief over the radio and explained the situation to him. Chief Brady told them to hold tight, while he sent a forensics team out there. Officer Smith was deeply saddened.

He and his wife were very good friends with the victim and her family.

***

Twenty minutes later, the butcher was pulling into his driveway with the victim's body parts. The killer knew he had $300,000 coming to him, but his thirst for blood was not completely satisfied.

"She was the oldest female I have ever attacked, with the exception of Angelica Gomez. But this one had strings attached. Shit, I didn't know the bitch had kids…the hell with it," he said to himself.

Still, the butcher was used to getting fresh, young meat; young, single girls. This was all new to him. He didn't get that excitement, that rush of adrenalin he would normally get when killing a beautiful young woman.

"The nerve of her, begging for mercy just because she had kids! Shit, too late, too bad," the heartless killer said.

This was a rush job. He did it just for the money. The killer knew his client had been waiting for those parts, but he didn't expect to get shot at by some young woman with a gun. He made a call to his customer and told him where to meet him.

"You better have the money, all of it in cash, or you get nothing," he said over the phone.

The butcher had an hour before he met his contact. He went to the bathroom to relieve himself and wash his hands, then he made himself a peanut butter and jelly sandwich, grabbed a soda from the fridge, and left with the body parts.

***

Taylor Parker was just getting home. He had worked some overtime by making an extra trip. Conductor Williams didn't show up for work. The crew office didn't cover his job, so the dispatcher asked Conductor Parker if he would pick up the job. Parker told him, "I'll work half of the job, but not the whole thing." Taylor had told the supervisor that he was tired, but he'd still help out.

Taylor went to his mailbox to get the mail on the way to the front door. There was a package waiting there for him. Taylor grabbed the box and brought it inside. There were no markings or labels on the mysterious package. He put it up on the kitchen table and looked at it, wondering what it was and who sent it. Parker grabbed a knife from the cabinet drawer and proceeded to cut open the box. When he finally removed all of the Styrofoam packaging from inside the box, Taylor was shocked. Inside, there was a beautiful, long red wig. Taylor took it out of the box and flipped it inside out. The wig turned out to be a human scalp, similar to the blonde wig that he had received before, the one Angelo claimed was his sister's hair. There appeared to be some dried blood on the inside. Taylor dropped the wig and screamed. A note was also inside the box:

Try this on for size, baby. It will look much nicer than that fake blonde shit you're wearing now. Love forever and always, your secret admirer.

The scalp came from the butcher. The killer had taken it from Joanna Helms when he killed her last spring. The slayer wanted Taylor, badly, but he sure had a weird way of showing it. Taylor Parker freaked out. He now knew that this was another gift from that crazy serial killer. *He's sweet on me, I know that now. But why is he disguising himself like me?* Taylor thought to himself. *Is he knowingly trying to frame me, or is this a sincere form of flattery?* Either way, Parker knew that this man was a dangerous killer and was not to be toyed with. Taylor repacked the scalp back in the box with the note. He was going downtown to the police station tomorrow morning with the package. If the chief of police needed any more evidence, this was surely it. Taylor knew the chief didn't believe him before, but now, he had proof.

⁎⁎⁎

The next morning, Chief Brady had just received the DNA report. It had confirmed Angelo Russo's suspicion. The blonde wig that was confiscated from Taylor Parker was, in fact, a human scalp that once belonged to Carina Russo.

"Russo was right; it was his sister's hair, but how did he know that?" the chief said to himself.

Chief Brady decided to call Angelo Russo to let him know the findings of the DNA test.

"Chief Brady, you've got a visitor," Officer Smith came in and announced.

"Who is it, Smith?" the chief bellowed.

"It's Parker, Taylor Parker, sir," Officer Smith told him.

"Send him in, Smith," the chief stated.

The officer went back and brought in Taylor Parker to the chief's office. Parker was in full uniform and he was holding the package he received yesterday. Taylor just couldn't wait to show it to the chief.

"Hello, Chief. I just wanted to show you a package I received yesterday, before I head on over to work," Taylor told him.

"It's not a fricking bomb, is it?" the chief asked.

"No, it's another scalped wig, sir, and this time, I saved the note and everything so that you'd know I'm not making this up."

"All right then, let's see it, Parker."

Taylor opened up the box and took out the wig to show the chief. The chief was horrified to know that this wig was another female scalp. Brady was pissed off.

"This damn sick bastard must be caught! I'm tired of his shit!" Chief Brady shouted as he stood up from his desk, spilling his coffee everywhere.

Officer Smith escorted Conductor Taylor Parker out of the chief's office, leaving the package on his desk. Chief Brady sent the scalped wig down to forensics. He also asked them to send a sample out for DNA testing. They were going to have to find out who the unfortunate victim was that the scalp had belonged to.

20

SHE'S BACK

Thursday late morning, November 28. Thanksgiving Day arrived with typical fall-like weather, cool with bright sunshine. Everyone had finally picked up all of the pesky leaves, otherwise known as "Mother Nature's litter." People everywhere were looking forward to spending their Thanksgiving feast with their family and friends. Most people were going to enjoy a four-day weekend. Some folks were eager to go Christmas shopping right after they finished their dinner; others were going to wait for tomorrow for the Black Friday sales.

Angelo had Wednesdays and Thursdays off this month, so he was lucky to have Thanksgiving Day off. He went to take a shower and then have breakfast. Angelo wanted to eat his turkey dinner at the hospital with Carlita. They finally moved her out of the intensive care unit and into a semi-private room. Carlita was still in a coma, but Angelo still hoped for the best.

Angelo went down to the train station and waited there for the train. He knew it was a holiday schedule, so the trains were far and few. After waiting for thirty minutes, the southbound train was pulling into the Morton Town train station. Angelo waited for the train to stop and open up its doors, and then he got on board. Conductor Taylor Parker was on board checking tickets. Angelo spotted him. *Shit, I just can't seem to get away from his ass, can I?* he thought to himself.

"Tickets please!" Conductor Parker shouted.

The local train was barely filled with passengers. Most people either took the earlier trains, or they drove to their families with their own vehicles. Parker finally got to Angelo and smiled.

"Yo, Angelo! What's up?" Taylor asked him.

"Same ole, same ole. I'm just going to the hospital to visit Carlita," Angelo replied.

"Oh, ok."

"Hey, I heard you got another scalped wig in the mail."

"Yeah, I did. I brought it to the police station," Taylor said.

"Chief Brady told me the DNA test had confirmed that your old wig was from my sister's scalp."

"Wow, I'm really sorry, man…I had hoped that it wasn't. I knew how upset you were about it, especially after losing your sister in the first place."

"I'd sure like to catch that sick bastard. I'd like to scalp him, so he would know what the hell it felt like."

"Watch out, man, he's dangerous. I'm serious; you need to be careful out there. Let the cops do their job. I'm sure they'll catch him soon."

"Yeah, right, they thought I was the murderer, remember?"

"Yeah, well, they also suspected me, too. The cops ain't perfect, but they're all we have in the line of defense. Anyway, I've got to get back to work. I'll check back with you later, man," Taylor told him.

After a while, the train was arriving at the South Park train station near the hospital. Angelo was getting ready to exit the train. When the train finally stopped, he waited impatiently for the train doors to open, and when they did, Angelo flew out before anyone else did. He ran down the stairs and briskly walked over toward the hospital.

Angelo went to the hospital cafeteria and picked up the Thanksgiving dinner for one that was on the menu. He took his dinner and went over to Carlita's room. When he arrived there, Angelo was surprised to see that the doctor was standing by Carlita's bedside, with a tablet in his hands. *I thought Doctor Foster would be off for Thanksgiving,* Angelo thought.

"Hey, what's up, doc?" Angelo comically asked.

"Mr. Russo, I was just waiting for you," Doctor Foster said to him.

"Me? Why were you waiting for me, doc?"

"First of all, happy Thanksgiving to you, Mr. Russo."

"Happy Thanksgiving to you, too, doc. Now, what's this all about?"

"Miss Gomez has been on life support now for a little over a week, with relatively no improvement in her cognitive state, I might add. Since she has no other family member available, then *you* must make the right decision for her, Mr. Russo."

"What do you propose I do, doctor?"

"Mr. Russo, there's no delicate way for me to tell you this, so I will be blunt with you. I really think we should remove Miss Gomez from life support, with your permission, of course."

"No! Never! There's still hope; I have to believe in that. I've been praying every night!" Angelo said with a cry in his voice.

"Mr. Russo, why let her suffer like this? Surely, you'd want to give her some sort of dignity. Look at her, Mr. Russo, would you want to be in her shoes?"

Angelo knew the doctor was right, but he just could not let her go. Angelo had flashbacks of everything they've been through. Carlita could have killed him to save her own mother, but she didn't. Angelo remembered what Carlita had told him: "I love you, Angelo. When I'm lonely, I think of making love to you with my favorite song, 'Wicked Game' by Chris Isaak."

"No, doc, not yet! Please, let me spend Thanksgiving with my girl," Angelo pleaded with him.

"This is highly irregular, Mr. Russo. You really should reconsider."

All of a sudden, Carlita opened up her eyes and began choking and gagging on the oxygen tube that was down in her throat.

"Doctor, look! She's coming out of it!" Angelo exclaimed.

Doctor Foster slowly removed the intubating tube from Carlita's mouth, while she gagged and coughed. He checked her vitals and asked her how she felt.

"I…feel…pain," she said in a barely audible voice.

"Where are you feeling the pain, Miss Gomez?" the doctor asked her.

"All…over," she replied in a low, raspy voice.

"I'll have the nurse come by and give you something for the pain."

Angelo was so overjoyed; he had tears of happiness in his eyes. Angelo kissed her cheek through the halo apparatus that was still on her head.

"Angelo…I missed you."

"Carlita, my love, I knew you would come back to me," Angelo tearfully said to her.

Doctor Foster called the nurses' station and asked to have some pain medication for Miss Gomez.

"She's back! I knew she'd be back, doc, I knew it," Angelo said happily.

"Yes, Mr. Russo, it's nothing short of a miracle," the doctor replied happily.

Doctor Foster watched Angelo and Carlita holding hands and smiling at each other. He was still befuddled and amazed at her sudden, miraculous recovery. *It's as if Carlita Gomez knew she was going to be taken off of life support. She had to respond quickly. Nonetheless, it's nice to have a happy ending,* the doctor thought.

"Mr. Russo, I'm sending the nurse in to give her something for her pain. You may talk with her for a bit, but soon she may be going back to sleep," Doctor Foster told him.

"Ok, Doctor, and thank you very much for everything."

"Don't thank me, thank her, Mr. Russo. She's a very lucky girl."

"Angelo, I'm thirsty," Carlita said in a low, croaky voice.

"Oh, let me prop her up in the bed, first," the doctor said just before pressing a button on the electric hospital bed. "Ok, that should do it. I'll just leave you two alone for now," the doctor said with a smile just before he exited the room.

"Here, baby, have some water," Angelo said while gently bringing a cup of water with a straw to her lips.

Carlita slowly took a sip of water, while spilling some of it all over her face and neck. Angelo grabbed a tissue from the box and gently wiped her clean. He looked at her with such loving eyes.

"I'm so, so glad you came back to me, honey. I don't need anything else for Christmas. I have *you* now and that's all I need."

Carlita started crying tears of joy. She squeezed his hand and told him that she loved him with all of her heart. Within a few minutes, Nurse Candy Smith came in to the room. The nurse was a young, heavyset African-American woman, who genuinely cared about the patients in the hospital. Nurse Smith gave Carlita some pain medication through her IV, and then she looked at Angelo.

"She may be falling asleep soon, Mr. Russo," the nurse told him.

"May I stay and watch her while I eat my dinner?" Angelo asked.

"Sure, Mr. Russo," the nurse replied.

Nurse Smith walked right out of the room feeling touched, wishing she had someone devoted to her like that. *It's rare to find a guy like that nowadays,* she thought. Nurse Smith was always a sucker for love stories, and she thought that this was a real-life love story at its best.

Angelo was happy there was no one else in the room now. He sat there and ate his now-cold Thanksgiving turkey dinner, while he was watching his beloved Carlita fall asleep. Angelo felt like he had a lot to be thankful for.

Back on the train, the Railway Butcher was waiting for Conductor Taylor Parker to come and check his ticket. He had just boarded the train at the previous stop. Taylor was finally walking into his car. *Ain't he got the sweetest ass you've ever seen?* the butcher thought. The killer had disguised himself so that Taylor wouldn't recognize him.

"Tickets please," Parker said as he went to the passengers.

When he finally got to the butcher, Parker gazed into his eyes, while handing him the ticket.

"You look familiar; do I know you from somewhere?" Taylor asked.

"No, you must be mistaking me for someone else, but I'd sure like to get to know *you*. You've got to be the prettiest conductor I have ever seen, seriously!"

"Really? Well, I'm kind of spoken for, but thanks for the compliment anyway. Have a nice day, sir."

As Taylor walked away, the butcher grabbed his ass. Parker was startled and pissed off at the same time.

"Hey, what the hell is wrong with you?! I got a good mind to kick your ass right here and now!"

"But you won't, because people are watching!"

There weren't that many passengers on board, but the few that were there had all turned around to look at the scene unfolding.

"Look, Mister, I don't want any trouble!"

"Neither do I. Now, keep your damn voice down. You've got such a sweet ass that I just lost control, that's all. I'm sorry, ok?" he said in a low-toned voice.

"Don't ever do that again or I'll throw you off this train. I said I was spoken for, do you understand that, Mister?"

"You said you were 'kind of spoken for.' That's different, you know."

"Look, Mister, I'm warning you; keep your damn hands to yourself. Do I make myself clear?"

"Perfectly. Now, I'll tell *you* what you always tell us: sorry for the inconvenience."

Taylor walked away from him in disgust.

I'll get you. I'm gonna make you mine, you skinny little bitch, just you wait, the killer thought. He knew there was no one in Taylor's life, but the killer also knew that Taylor was sweet on Angelo. *Angelo's not gay. He could never have him, but he could have me,* the butcher was thinking. *Shit, I need to get Angelo out of the way. I need to kill his ass.* The slaughterer thought about it for a while, but realized he couldn't do it. Much as he despised Angelo, the killer just couldn't do it himself; he'd have to get someone else to do it for him. Deep down inside, the assassin had thought Angelo was very attractive, but again, he knew Angelo only liked women.

At the Morton Town police station, Chief Brady was trying to figure out why there were two different results on the scalped wig that once belonged to Carina Russo.

"Someone must have switched the sample, but why?" Chief Brady said to himself.

The chief thought there was some sort of cover up going on. The serial killer was trying to frame Taylor Parker, but someone else was trying to protect him. The questions that he thought of were, who and why?

"It could be an inside job and if so, that's going to be a major problem," the chief said bitterly to himself.

He sat in his office thinking, while drinking his coffee. The forensics team had confirmed that the red-haired wig obtained from Taylor Parker was indeed a human scalp. The question now was:

who was it from? The chief would have to wait until the DNA test results came back from the lab.

"Happy friggin Thanksgiving to me," Chief Brady said to himself.

It was almost four o'clock in the afternoon. The chief was getting ready to leave. *I shouldn't even be here,* he thought. Brady couldn't wait to get back home to his family and have Thanksgiving dinner. The chief was thinking about the spread of food his wife was making: turkey with all of the trimmings, including his favorites, homemade apple pie and peach cobbler.

At the Morton Medical Center, Angelo had finished his turkey dinner in Carlita's room. He threw his garbage in the can and gave Carlita a kiss on her cheek. Angelo thought it was a little tricky kissing her through her halo. They were both going to have to deal with it for the next three months. This was surely a small price to pay after what the poor girl went through. Angelo was extremely grateful for having her back in his life. He wasn't about to lose her again. *This sonofabitch serial killer has got to be stopped, if it's the last thing I do,* he thought to himself. Angelo watched Carlita sleep; she looked so frail and vulnerable, but still, like a Sleeping Beauty.

Angelo walked out of the hospital room waving goodbye to the police officer that was stationed outside of Carlita's room. He felt at ease knowing that she at least had police protection. *The killer would have to have balls to come here and finish her off,* Angelo thought.

Angelo was back on the train going home. He started thinking about how to protect the love of his life from this crazed serial killer. Angelo thought about getting a gun for protection. *I bet*

I could find one online. You could get just about anything you wanted on the internet, he thought to himself while riding the train.

"Next stop, Morton Town. Morton Town is the next stop!" the conductor announced over the train's public address system.

"Oh, shit, that's my stop!" Angelo said loudly.

There was no one else in the car but him. Everyone else on board had reached their destinations already. Everybody was at home eating their Thanksgiving dinners with all of their family and friends…everyone, but Angelo. He got up from his seat and made his way toward the exit doors, waiting for them to open as the train was slowing down. Angelo disembarked the train, walked down the stairs, and walked to his home.

When Angelo finally arrived at his house, he walked inside feeling happy and relieved. The young man was eager to share the good news with Carina about Carlita.

"Carina, I'm home!" Angelo shouted. "Carina, guess what?! Carlita's out of her coma! She's going to be all right! Carina? where are you?!"

But Carina's ghost never appeared and never answered. Angelo thought that it was strange. Carina's apparition always greeted him when he came home, but she didn't this time. Angelo thought that she might be in a bad mood. He knew Carina detested Carlita. Angelo had also detected jealousy from her whenever he spoke of Carlita.

"She'll be back, have no doubt of that," he said to himself.

Angelo went to take a shower. Afterwards, he sat in front of the TV for a while. *Man, it's awfully quiet and lonely here without Carina,* Angelo sorrowfully thought to himself. After doing some channel surfing, he turned off the television set and went straight off to bed.

*
**

A few miles away, the butcher was just walking into his L-shaped ranch home. He didn't need to take the train; the slayer had his own transportation. There was only one good reason for him to take public transportation: the killer knew Conductor Taylor Parker would be on that train at that time. The butcher knew Parker's work schedule…he knew everything about Parker.

"I'll get you, baby, you'll see. I'll get you in the end," he said while rubbing his thigh.

The Railway Butcher turned on his television set. He was hoping to catch the eleven o'clock news. A female reporter came on with the top stories.

"After one week of being in a coma, attempted murder victim, Carlita Gomez, finally regained consciousness today in her hospital room. Her doctor says it's nothing short of a miracle," the reporter stated while showing Carlita's image on the screen.

The butcher was livid with what he'd just seen and heard. In a fit of rage, he threw his remote controller right at the TV set, smashing its glass screen.

"That bitch is *still* alive?! Shit! Shit! Shit! What the hell?! Does she have nine fricking lives?!" the butcher yelled at the broken television set.

The news was the icing on his cake; his evening was ruined. It was bad enough that he didn't get his love, Taylor Parker, to like him; but now the killer finds out that the woman he thought was dead by his own hand, had completely survived.

"Sonofabitch! This is too damn much!" the slayer said.

I've got to find someone to kill her and Angelo, thought the killer.

The slayer knew that Carlita could still potentially identify him. He needed her out of the way. *The double-crossing bitch was supposed to kill Angelo; instead, she winds up falling in love with him,* he thought. Also, as long as Angelo was around, he didn't stand a chance with Taylor Parker. Taylor was in love with Angelo, that much he knew.

"Shit, now I have to go out and get me another TV set. I've got to learn how to control my temper. This shit is gonna cost me now," the butcher bitterly said to himself.

The executioner began looking through the contact list on his smartphone. He was searching all of the possible hitmen he dealt with in the past.

"One of these suckers is going to get the job done," he said to his phone.

The murderer looked at the time on his phone; it was eleven thirty. He realized it was way too late to call any of them, and besides, he was tired. Tomorrow was Black Friday; the killer was going to have to pick up a new television set. *I hate going out to the stores on Black Friday,* he thought. *But maybe I can catch a good sale on one of those new 4K sets.* The butcher wrote down some names to call for the hit jobs. He had seven to choose from.

"Wow, look at that, the lucky seven," he said to himself.

After that, the murderer decided to turn in for the night. He first took a quick shower, then he put on his underwear and went off to bed. As the killer slept, sexual dreams of Taylor Parker filled his head.

21

TIME TO GO HOME

After being a patient in the Morton Medical Center for over three weeks, Carlita Gomez was being discharged. Angelo was at the hospital talking to her and Doctor Foster. Angelo was hoping that Carlita would come and live with him, but ultimately, the decision was Carlita's.

"Well, Miss Gomez, it's time for you to go home. Are you ready?" Doctor Foster asked her.

"Yes, I am!" Carlita said with a joyful smile on her face.

"Well, then, the question is: which home do you want to go to?"

"I want to go home with Angelo."

"So, you want to stay with Mr. Russo, instead of going back to your home?"

"My home? Well, my home is with you, Angelo," Carlita said while looking at him.

"Of course, you can stay with me, babe; I wouldn't have it any other way," Angelo replied.

"Ok then, it's settled. Miss Gomez will be going to your home, Mr. Russo. We'll have a special hospital van bring her right over as soon as you sign the necessary release forms," Doctor Foster told him.

"All right, doc, you got it. Can I ride with her in the van?" Angelo asked.

"Well, I don't see why not," the doctor responded.

"Cool, I'm ready. Give me the forms so I can sign them, doc."

"There are a few things I must mention to you both."

"What's that, doc?" Angelo asked.

"For starters, Miss Gomez will have a visiting nurse for the next three to four months. The nurse will clean under her halo vest and the pins securing Miss Gomez's skull to it. She will also assist her with getting in and out of her wheelchair, also with some of the chores around the house. This is especially useful while you are at work, Mr. Russo. Of course, afterwards, Miss Gomez will need some physical therapy," the doctor stated.

"Sounds good to me, doc," Angelo said.

"Me too," Carlita added.

"Good, then it's settled," Doctor Foster stated.

On the other side of town, hired hitman Paul Graves was receiving a phone call from the butcher. He wondered who was calling him. Paul didn't recognize the phone number on his cellphone display.

"Yeah, what's up?" Paul asked.

"It's me, your friend till the end," the butcher replied.

"Hey, how you doing, you got some work for me? 'Cause that's the only time I hear from ya."

"Yeah, I got a couple of pain in the asses I want you to waste."

"All right, now you're talking. Who the hell are they and where do they live?"

"The first one is Carlita Gomez; she's at the Morton Medical Center."

"Whoa, man, I ain't touching that with a ten-foot pole. That bitch is a hot commodity. She's been all over the news with what happened to her. She's got police protection around the clock."

"Oh, come on, man, ten thousand bucks says you can!"

"Sorry, I wouldn't do it for twenty. Who's the other one?"

"Her boyfriend, Angelo Russo."

"Oh, hell no! That's another one I'm not touching, not even with a ten-foot pole. Ain't you been watching the news, dude? It's all over the place about how his *love* helped her come out of a coma, just before her doctor wanted to pull the cord on her. Shit, I wouldn't be surprised if they made it into a movie."

"Man, you suck! You were my last hope. I just can't believe you'd turn down twenty thousand bucks!"

"What the hell good is it if I can't spend it? Nothing for nothing, man, but I ain't going back into the slammer, ya dig?"

"Yeah, I dig all right, chicken shit," the butcher said while hanging up his phone.

The killer had exhausted his whole list of hitmen. He called all seven men and each one of them turned down the job for the same reason. If the butcher still wanted Carlita and Angelo dead, he was going to have to do it all by himself. *If you want something done right, you've got to do it yourself,* he thought, but the slayer also remembered what happened the last time with Carlita. *The bitch was supposed to die, instead, she survived…shit!*

The next day, Lieutenant Collins had returned to work. Collins walked down the hall of the police station. The lieutenant was going to the locker room, but decided to check in with the chief, first.

"How was your vacation, Collins?" Chief Brady asked him.

"Eh, it was all right, Chief," the lieutenant replied.

"Did you go anywhere?"

"Nope, I just stayed home for two whole weeks."

"Are you feeling refreshed?"

"Refreshed?"

"Yeah, you know, are you bright-eyed and bushy-tailed?" the chief asked with a chuckle.

"Well, I guess so, but there really wasn't anything wrong with me to begin with, Chief."

"We won't go there, Collins. Let's just say I need you here now one hundred percent, all right?"

"Yeah, all right, you got me, Chief," Collins responded.

"Good, because we still have a psycho serial killer to catch," Chief Brady stated.

"Hey, Chief, what ever happened to Carlita Gomez?"

"What do you mean, what happened to her? She finally came out of her coma. She's gonna be all right."

"I know all that, but she's not in the hospital anymore."

"No Lieutenant, she's not. Miss Gomez was discharged yesterday. Tell me something, Collins, why all the sudden interest in Miss Gomez? I thought you were after Mr. Russo."

"I am, I was just curious, that's all. I was gone for two whole weeks and I'm trying to gather up all the facts."

"Really?"

"Yeah, really. You want me to be really thorough in my investigations, right?"

"Yeah, I do. Listen, don't mind me if I get a little too defensive when it comes to Carlita Gomez. That girl has been through hell and back."

"I'm sorry if I ruffled up your feathers, boss."

"Look, let's just both do our jobs here and concentrate on catching this sick-ass bastard, ok?"

"You got it, Chief!" Lieutenant Collins said.

At four thirty in the afternoon, Angelo was just getting home from work. This was the first day he's worked since Carlita had moved in with him. Angelo noticed a white four-door sedan parked in his driveway. *Who the hell could that be now?* he wondered. As Angelo approached the car his memory came back to him. *Of course, now I remember, the visiting nurse, that's whose car it is,* Angelo recalled. He unlocked the front door of his house and was greeted by Nurse Cassandra Rosado. Nurse Rosado was a middle-aged woman of Mexican heritage. Her hair was long, wavy, and jet black. Angelo thought she was pretty and had a nice build. Nurse Rosado was petite, but still, she was strong enough to do her physically demanding job.

"Hello, Señor Russo!" Nurse Rosado said in her Spanish accent.

"Well, hello, Nurse…" Angelo said, not knowing her name.

"You may call me, Cassandra."

"Ok, Cassandra it is," Angelo said while walking into his home.

Carlita overheard Angelo's voice and wheeled herself into the room to greet him.

"Angelo, you're home!" Carlita had exclaimed.

"Carlita, my love!" he happily replied while bending down to give her a kiss through her halo.

"Señor Russo, since you are home now, may I go?" Cassandra asked him.

"Sure, Cassandra, but you'll be back tomorrow, right?"

"*Sí*, I will be back tomorrow. *Muchas gracias.*"

Nurse Rosado went to get her things together so that she could leave. Angelo looked at his girlfriend sitting in the wheelchair. She looked so helpless. Her halo was a scary thing to behold, knowing that it was responsible for keeping her head still and supported, so that her neck vertebrae would heal properly, but it looked like a cage around her head. Angelo loved her dearly, but he also felt sorry for her.

"I'm gonna find the bastard that did this to you and make him pay, if it's the last thing I do, honey," Angelo told her.

"I want you to be careful. I can't afford to lose you, Angelo. I love you," she replied.

"Ok, Señor Russo, I will see you both tomorrow,"

Cassandra had said while leaving through the front door.

Angelo closed the door and then locked it back up. He turned around toward Carlita. The young man gazed at his love, sitting in her wheelchair, with loving eyes.

"I love you too, baby," Angelo said to Carlita.

"Even though I'm damaged goods?" she asked him.

"Oh, stop it. You'll get better; just give it time."

"Do you think I could still be a model when this cage comes off of me?"

"Of course, but, why would you want to be a model?"

"You don't think I'm pretty enough?"

"I didn't say that, it's just, well, that's what my sister was and look what happened to her."

"Carina didn't get killed because she was a model; she got killed because she was in the wrong place at the wrong time."

"I suppose so."

"If you didn't have that fight with her that night, she wouldn't have left here. Carina may still be alive today if it weren't for that."

"How did you know about that? How did you know about our fight that night?" Angelo asked her while feeling freaked out.

"Um, she told me."

"She told you? She told you that night before she got killed?"

"Well, yeah. Carina called me on her cell; she was very upset about it."

"What else did she tell you?"

"That was it."

"She didn't tell you what our fight was all about?"

"Na-nope."

"I just find it so damn strange that she confided in you, that late at night, especially since she loathed you."

"Like I said before, Angelo, Carina was upset and she just wanted to talk to someone; that's all there is to it."

It was Christmas morning and Angelo had everything he needed and wanted. It's been over a month now since Carlita had survived that horrific auto accident caused by the butcher. Carlita had been doing much better, but she still needed the nurse to help her get in and out of her wheelchair, plus, Carlita needed her help with certain chores around the house.

Angelo had switched days off with someone so that he could be at home with Carlita. Angelo was very gracious in giving Nurse Cassandra Rosado the day off since he would be at home. Angelo pulled out the old, artificial Christmas tree from the basement a few days ago, placed it in the family room, and decorated it all by himself.

That Christmas morning, Carlita was calling Angelo for help. She needed assistance getting into her wheelchair. Angelo was in such a deep sleep that he didn't hear her calling him for a while.

"Angelo?! Angelo, help, help me, please!" Carlita yelled out.

"Huh? Carlita? I'm coming, babe!" he yelled.

Angelo jumped out of his bed and into his slippers, and then he went downstairs to the living room where the rented hospital bed was. Carlita wanted to be downstairs, so that she could easily roll in and out of the kitchen and family room. Carlita had been sitting up in the bed when he walked in.

"I have to go to the bathroom, now!" she pleaded to him urgently.

"Ok, babe, I'm sorry. I guess I was in such a deep sleep that I didn't hear you calling me."

Angelo helped her into the wheelchair, rolled her into the downstairs bathroom, then he helped her onto the toilet seat. He waited outside for her to finish. When she was done, Angelo rolled her into the family room. The old Christmas tree was standing near the fireplace. There were presents all around it.

"Merry Christmas, baby!" Angelo exclaimed.

"Oh, my! Is *this* why you didn't want me in here?" Carlita asked him.

"Yup, I didn't want you to see it till I was finished decorating it. Next year, we can both do it together."

Carlita began crying tears of joy as she grabbed his hand. Angelo picked up some presents and put them on her lap. Some of the gifts were from Angelo and his co-workers, others were from strangers that heard about her miraculous recovery. The good-hearted strangers had dropped off gifts at the hospital where she had been recuperating. It was as if Carlita Gomez was a celebrity. She was one of the lucky three that had survived the wrath of the serial killing butcher. Some of the gifts contained cash. There was one gift, however, that really shocked Carlita. It was a diamond engagement ring from Angelo.

"Oh, my God! Is this what I think it is, Angelo?" Carlita

asked.

"Yes, it is. Will you marry me, Carlita?" Angelo nervously asked her while he went down on his knee.

"I-I don't know what to say."

"Say yes."

"Angelo, you know I love you, right?"

"Yes, so say you'll marry me."

"I-I can't, not now anyway. I need time, baby. You're sweet and everything, but, I'm not ready yet. I like what we have now, you understand, don't you?"

"No…I don't. You told me you loved me, but you don't want to marry me," Angelo said.

"But I *do* love you, more than anything else in this world," she pleaded, not wanting to hurt his feelings.

"Yeah, sure, but just not enough to marry me. Ok, it's cool…whatever."

"You're not mad at me, are you?"

"Nah, it's all good."

"Listen, if you help me, I can make you breakfast," she told him.

"I'm not hungry. I just want to go take a walk, that's all," he replied.

"A walk? It's fricking snowing outside! Where are you going?"

"I'm just going out for a damn walk! Why the third degree?!

You ain't my wife…you don't wanna be!"

Angelo went and put on his winter coat, grabbed his hat, and left. Carlita sat there in her wheelchair, crying. She realized that she had broken his heart, but Carlita Gomez just wasn't ready for marriage, not now, that was certain.

Angelo decided to walk over to the train station. While walking, he started thinking: *merry friggin Christmas to me. Maybe it wasn't such a good idea to have Carlita stay with me after all,* he thought. *I gave up my privacy and everything…for what? She doesn't even want to marry me.* Angelo kept thinking about the rejection he just got from Carlita. He wondered what happened to her. Before her car accident, Carlita was willing to marry him; she was willing to spend her whole life with him. Now, Carlita was sending him mixed messages. *What am I going to do with her?* Angelo thought to himself. The young man decided to turn around and go back home. It was too damn cold and snowy out. *It's my damn house, not hers. As far as I'm concerned, she is a guest in my house. I'm not getting kicked out of my own damn house for anybody,* he thought while walking back home.

When Angelo got back in his house, Carlita was in the family room watching *Miracle on 34th Street,* probably for the umpteenth time. Angelo walked right past her, without announcing his return. He went upstairs to his room and closed the door.

A week had gone by; it was now New Year's Eve. Angelo was waking up to the smell of breakfast being cooked. He looked at his clock: it said nine thirty a.m. Angelo went downstairs in his pajamas just in case the nurse was there. Carlita was in her wheelchair in the kitchen with Nurse Rosado.

"Well, good morning, dear!" Carlita said.

"Good morning, Señor Russo," Nurse Rosado added.

"Good morning. Did you let Cassandra in, Carlita?" Angelo asked.

"Yes, I did. I didn't want her to wake you up. I saw her car coming through the window, so I just let her in before she got a chance to ring the bell," Carlita replied.

"You can get into your wheelchair with your cast and halo all by yourself?" Angelo questioned.

"Well, it's not easy, but I'm trying to be a little independent. I know it's been hard on you, love."

"She's doing really, really good, Señor Russo," the nurse happily said.

"I see, I see," Angelo replied.

"I just made you breakfast, dear, with Cassandra's help, of course."

"It smells good. What is it?"

"It's your favorite, dear: ham and eggs, just the way you like it, with basil, cayenne pepper, chopped tomatoes, and garlic," Carlita said.

Carlita had made direct, intense eye contact with him all along. Angelo nearly collapsed right there on the floor upon hearing what Carlita had made him. He just couldn't believe it.

"Señor Russo! Are you feeling all right?" Cassandra asked him.

"Yes, I'll be all right. How…how did you know that was my favorite, Carlita?" Angelo nervously asked her.

"Your sister, Carina, she told me that was your favorite dish,

Angelo, darling."

"Carina hasn't been around for a while now."

"Silly boy, when she was alive, she told me what you liked."

But Angelo didn't buy it. Carina and Carlita were enemies. He just couldn't see his sister confiding in her; at least, not from the way Carina's ghost had talked about Carlita.

22

I'M SO CONFUSED

Two months later, it was now Monday morning, February 24. It had snowed the day before and left around three inches on the ground. The air was bitterly cold. Everyone had finished shoveling the snow and they were already preparing for the next storm. After three long months of wearing a halo and a cast on her left leg, Carlita was now ready to have them removed. Angelo was at the hospital with her.

"Why are you staring at me?" Carlita asked him.

"I was wondering why you're wearing Carina's old, rose-colored blouse and her blue jeans," Angelo said.

"Well, your sister had great taste and her clothes fit me like a glove," Carlita replied.

Angelo was perplexed. He had rented a truck to get her things from her old house; he even spent his money to have Carlita's clothes cleaned and pressed. But she preferred to wear his sister's old garments…even her makeup. Carlita grew out her bangs and parted her hair in the middle, just like Carina did. It was like Carlita was trying to be like Carina.

They had taken a cab to get to the hospital since Carlita hadn't replaced her car yet. She told Angelo that they didn't need a car, which he found very strange. Carlita loved to drive, but not anymore. Doctor Foster was with them looking at her X-rays. The doctor had a promising look in his eyes. He turned off the lighted screen and looked at her with a smile.

"Miss Gomez, the X-rays have confirmed my findings; your neck and leg fractures have all been healed. You're young, so you've healed quickly. Are you ready to have both your halo and cast removed?" Doctor Foster asked her.

"Oh, hell yeah! I'm ready, Doctor! Please remove this contraption from me," Carlita begged him.

"Will she still need a nurse, doc?" Angelo asked him.

"That's up to Miss Gomez to decide," the doctor replied.

"Well, how will I be getting around, Doctor?"

"You won't need the wheelchair anymore or the hospital bed. We will send you home with a walker, a pair of crutches, and a special collar for your neck to help build up your neck muscles. You'll also have to go through about one and a half months of physical therapy."

"Ok, Doctor, I have Angelo to help me out when he's home, but when he's not, well, let me see how it goes. I may choose to keep the nurse for a week or so if that's all right."

"Sure, Miss Gomez, whatever you need. Now, let's get your halo off first," the doctor told her as he started to remove Carlita's halo.

Angelo was wondering how much this was all going to cost him. So far, Carlita's auto insurance was paying for it, via her no-fault coverage, but what happens when it all runs out? Angelo took the liberty of forwarding all of her mail to his house. Carlita had utility bills that were piling up, plus her rent had been past due for over two months now. When he asked her about the house she rented, Carlita drew a blank: "What house? My home is with you," she replied. Angelo wondered if the accident may have affected her memory. She clearly wasn't herself at times.

That evening, Melody Gray was walking toward the Williams Port train station. Melody knew it was very cold outside, especially at nine thirty at night, but she didn't care; she had a sizzling date tonight. Her boyfriend was waiting for her; they were finally going to get together. The cold wind was blowing in her face, making her wish she were almost there.

Melody was only twenty-five years old. Most of the men she worked with in the music store thought that she was really hot. They especially liked her warm, cheerful smile and that lovely, waist-length straight brown hair of hers. Jimmy Style in the acoustic guitar department thought that Melody was a complete knockout; he especially liked her gregarious personality. But Melody had a thing for older guys, one of whom she was meeting, Dave Singer, the store's manager. Dave had hired her to be the store's checkout girl, but he didn't think they would actually get together. Dave was over twenty years older than her, but clearly, Melody wanted a father figure. Melody's old, red, goose down coat was barely keeping her warm. It was missing so many down feathers that it had gotten thin in certain areas. She was too cold to run to the train station. *I'll just have to deal with it,* she thought to herself while walking. Suddenly, Melody was grabbed from behind. A black gloved hand covered her mouth before she had a chance to vocalize a scream. With one quick twist, the butcher completely snapped her neck. The gorgeous, young girl collapsed in the snow, right in front of her assassin, with her eyes still open. It happened just before the southbound local train was arriving at the station. This time, the killer didn't have any orders for body parts. This time, it was all for fun and practice. The butcher wanted only one souvenir for himself. He grabbed his long, sharp, stainless-steel knife, the one with the serrated edge, and proceeded to cut the girl's head off.

"Won't she look pretty on one of my mannequins? A living doll," he laughingly said to himself.

The murderer left the headless body near the steps leading to the Williams Port train station. The snow under the female's decapitated body began to turn a bright red. He wrapped up the victim's long, brown hair with its disembodied head and placed it into a plastic bag. After a short walk back to his vehicle, the butcher left in his black pickup truck with the head belonging to Melody Gray. He was exhilarated. *It's been a while since I killed someone like that. I've got to stay in practice, because practice makes perfect,* he thought while driving back home.

The next afternoon, Angelo was sitting in the pizza parlor with Taylor Parker. The two conductors were having lunch together, not knowing they were being spied on.

"I'm so confused," Angelo told Parker at the dining table where they were sitting.

"Whoa, do I detect a problem with the renowned love birds?" Taylor asked him.

"Oh, yeah, there's a problem all right, a problem with *her!*"

"Man, I told you, you'd have been better off with me. Women are high maintenance, you know."

"Oh, stop it already, will ya?"

"All right, love, you know I'd do anything for you. What's up with her this time?"

Taylor reached for Angelo's hand, but Angelo retracted his.

"Well…it's like I'm living with two people…she's kind of like a split personality. Sometimes, Carlita doesn't remember shit about her past. But other times, she knows things that only my sister would know. It's weird."

"Yeah, that is messed up, man. Maybe something happened to her head in the car accident, you know what I mean?" Taylor said while pointing to his head.

"That's just what I thought."

"You might want to consider taking her back to the doctor, maybe even taking some X-rays of her head. Who knows? Not to scare you or anything, but she may have some kind of a brain tumor…or something."

"Wow, thanks, you really are scaring me, man."

"I'm sorry, man, but she's been through a lot; anything is possible, you know."

"Yeah, I guess so," Angelo responded in dismay.

The two of them finished their pizzas and sodas and stood up from the table. Taylor gave Angelo a hug and told him not to worry. They left the pizza parlor and went back to work.

From the corner of the dining area, the butcher had been sitting at a table, watching them intently. He had become so furious when Taylor hugged Angelo that he crushed his soda can, spilling all of its contents all over the table. *Why that greedy little sonofabitch! A woman's not enough for him; he's got to have my man, too,* the killer angrily thought.

Back at the police precinct, Chief Brady was highly upset about the recent murder and decapitation of another young woman. He was clearly running out of patience. *This shit has got to stop and stop now,* the chief had angrily thought.

"Hey, Chief?" Officer Ireland said.

"What is it, Ireland?" Brady asked him.

"We've found out whom that female body belonged to."

"I heard she had no ID on her."

"Yeah, but she did have a smartphone in her coat pocket, and guess what?"

"What?"

"It was unlocked and turned on!"

"Really? Well then, who the hell was she already, Ireland?" Chief Brady questioned him while sounding annoyed.

"Her name was Melody Gray; she worked at the Musician's Palace as a cashier."

"That's that music shop down the block from here. I know where the hell it is."

"That's right, Chief!"

"And you got all that information from her smartphone?"

"Well, not exactly, sir. I remembered her when I would go in there."

"*You* went to the music store, Ireland?"

"Yes, sir, I play keyboards, bought a couple from them, too!"

"Well, who would have thought…you a musician, huh? Funny, I kind of pictured you as a computer geek. I guess I was wrong."

"Computers? No sir, I hate 'em."

"All right, now that we know who she was, we have the unpleasant task of notifying her family," the chief stated.

"We still have to find her head, Chief."

"I'm well aware of that, Ireland."

"There's a selfie picture of her on her smartphone. She was very pretty with her long, brown hair. It's a damn shame, Chief," Officer Ireland somberly stated.

"I'm sick and tired of this scumbag; I want his ass already!"

"I hear you, Chief."

"Where the hell is our elusive lieutenant, already?"

"He's out to lunch, sir."

"Feeding his face again, huh?"

"I guess so, Chief."

"Well, when you see him, tell him I want to see him in my office, pronto."

"You got it, boss," Officer Ireland told him as he stepped out of the chief's office.

***

Later that evening, Angelo Russo was walking back home from the Morton Town train station. He was tired after working his first day back at work. Angelo thought long and hard about what Taylor had told him: *You might want to consider taking her back to the doctor, maybe even taking some X-rays of her head. Who knows? She may have some kind of a brain tumor…or something,* he remembered Taylor saying. Angelo didn't know how he was going to deal with her. It was cold outside and trudging through the snow was no fun, even though it was only three inches. Angelo was too tired to shovel and he didn't want to bother with the snow thrower yet. Angelo turned the key to unlock his front door, wondering how Carlita was going to act.

Things just changed so much with her after the car accident. He walked inside, expecting to find her around, but she was nowhere to be found.

"Carlita, I'm home!" Angelo shouted. "Carlita!" Angelo shouted again.

But there was no response. Angelo went upstairs. He went to her room; it was empty. Angelo noticed Carina's old, pink vibrator on her bed.

"I thought I threw that shit out when she was killed. What the hell does she need that for when she's got me?" he said to himself.

Angelo looked in every room, but the house was completely empty. He started to worry.

"Where could she have gone?" Angelo said to himself.

Angelo looked out the window and noticed a vehicle pulling up in his driveway. He immediately recognized the red Jeep, it belonged to Michael Alfonzo, Carina's old boyfriend.

"What the hell is *he* doing here?" Angelo asked himself.

The vehicle doors opened up. Michael grabbed the crutches for Carlita and helped her out of his Jeep. She kissed him goodbye and walked up to the front door, as Michael Alfonzo drove off.

"Well, well, well, what the hell do we have here?" Angelo sarcastically asked her as he opened up the front door.

"Angelo? I didn't know you were home," Carlita nervously said to him.

"Where were you? I've been worried sick about you!"

"I-I was out with an old friend, that's all."

"An old friend? His name wouldn't happen to be Michael Alfonzo, would it?"

"Why are you giving me the third degree out here? Can I at least come inside the house?"

Angelo stepped aside and let her walk into the house. He was livid. Angelo slammed the front door behind her and gave her dagger eyes. He could tell Carlita was nervous.

"Why are you looking at me like that? You look like you want to hurt me!" Carlita said to him.

"I want to know, what are you doing hanging out with my sister's ex-boyfriend?" Angelo angrily asked her.

"In the first place, I knew him way before your sister did. In the second place, nothing happened between us."

"Really?"

"Yes, really. I was just lonely and wanted the company of an old friend, that's all there is to it."

"An old friend? I don't believe you and furthermore, I think you've been lying to me all this time."

"I'm telling you the truth, really, Angelo, whether you believe me or not."

"Then why didn't he just come here and visit for a bit? Why did you have to go out riding with him in his Jeep in the snow?"

"I simply wanted to get out of the house for a while. I was tired of being cooped up in here all alone. Can you not see that?"

Angelo started to feel sorry for her, but at the same time, he was still very angry. *Why the hell did she have to hang out with Carina's old boyfriend? Didn't she have any girlfriends to hang out with?* Angelo wondered.

"Look, I'm sorry. I guess I just got a little jealous, that's all," he told her begrudgingly.

"Apology accepted. Now, may I go off to my room and rest?" Carlita asked him.

"Aren't you hungry? I could fix us up some sandwiches or soup," Angelo asked her.

"No, thanks; I already ate."

"What did you eat?"

"Michael took me out to eat at the Café Mexicana, you know, that Mexican place that's about five miles away from here."

"Oh, excuse me! I'm surprised you didn't go to your favorite Italian restaurant."

"What Italian restaurant?"

"Oh, come on now, you know, the one you've always taken me to: A Little Slice of Italy."

"Uh, no, I wanted Mexican food."

"Yeah, all right, whatever."

Carlita climbed up the stairs with her crutches. She was now sleeping in Carina's old bedroom. Angelo wondered why she chose *that* room to sleep in, instead of sleeping with him in the master bedroom, where his parents used to sleep. "We're not married yet; besides, Carina's room feels so safe and cozy," she had told him. It all felt so weird to him. Carlita had changed so much since her car accident. He was going to talk to her about seeing a doctor, maybe even a specialist.

*
**

A few miles away, the butcher was in his basement removing the head on one of his mannequins. He had completely soaked the head that once belonged to Melody Gray in some formaldehyde. After it had dried up, the killer had mounted Melody's head on his model, then he draped her hair all around the life-size doll.

"There now, doesn't she look lovely? It's perfect; a woman that won't talk back to you, ha, ha, ha," the butcher said to his dummy.

The slaughterer hadn't heard from his customer, Muhammad, in a while. He had wondered what happened to him. *I guess he doesn't need any more body parts for now,* the slayer thought. The killer realized he should have taken some more body parts from Melody Gray, besides her head, just in case.

"Oh, well, it's too late now. I can always kill another bitch if I really need to," he said to himself.

The heartless killer stood there in his basement, in front of the mannequin he just retrofitted with the head of Melody Gray. He admired his work. *I think I'll take a selfie with her,* the butcher happily thought to himself.

The next morning, a thin, middle-aged man with black hair walked into the police station. The man went by the name of Dave Singer. He walked over to the female officer at the front counter.

"May I help you, sir?" Officer Sager asked.

"Yes, ma'am, I came here to report a missing person," Dave told her.

"How long has this person been missing, sir?"

"She was supposed to come into work yesterday and she never came in. We were also supposed to meet the night before and she never showed up, Miss. I've tried to call her several times and all I ever get is her voicemail."

"Ok, are you a family member or her employer, sir?"

"I'm her employer, but also her friend."

"What's the woman's name, sir?"

"Her name is Melody Gray."

"Did you say 'Melody Gray,' sir?"

"Yes, she worked with me down at the Musician's Palace. It's the music store down the block from here."

"And your name, sir?" she asked him.

"My name is Dave, Dave Singer; I'm the manager of the store."

"Ok, sir, give me a minute. I have to call the chief."

Officer Sager picked up her phone to make the call. Dave was worried about Melody; he knew it wasn't like her to just disappear like that. Dave stood at the counter while the officer called her chief. *She's gorgeous, much too stunning to be working down here,* he thought to himself. She finally got off the phone.

"The chief will be right out, sir," Officer Sager told him.

"Thank you, Miss," Dave responded.

Within a few minutes, Chief Brady was out to greet him. The chief looked at him, wondering if Dave was more than just an employer to the victim. He obviously wasn't her father, although he could have passed for that.

"Hello, I'm Chief Brady," the chief said while extending his right hand out to Mr. Singer.

"Hello, sir, I'm Dave Singer from the music store," Dave replied without shaking his hand.

"I know, please, won't you step into my office, sir."

The two of them walked down the hall to Chief Brady's office. Dave was getting bad vibrations about this. When they arrived at the chief's office, Brady sat behind his desk and asked Dave to sit down.

"We have been trying to contact Miss Gray's parents, but they haven't been home. Do you know where we may be able to find them, Mr. Singer?" Chief Brady asked him.

"They're away on vacation, at least, that's what Melody had told me," Dave replied.

"Do you know where they went, sir?"

"What's this all about, Officer?"

"Miss Gray has been murdered and it's chief, not officer," Chief Brady sternly added.

"Oh, my God, are you serious?"

"I'm very serious. Her body was found yesterday morning by the Williams Port train station. She was decapitated."

"Oh, shit! What a waste. She was such a wonderful and beautiful young girl! Who would do that to her?" Dave said sounding genuinely upset.

"That's what we're trying to find out, sir. You didn't hear anything about this on the news, Mr. Singer?"

"I've been so busy lately with inventory, you know, getting

ready for new products and trying to move the old stuff out. I thought I heard something on the radio about a murder, but I didn't think it would be Melody."

"We really need to get in touch with her parents. Do you know where they went, Mr. Singer?"

"From what she said to me, they're out of the country, Chief."

"Out of the country?"

"That's correct; I believe they went to Rome for two weeks. Melody was kind of happy that she had the whole house all to herself," Dave replied.

"Do you know when they might be returning?"

"I believe by the end of next week, sir."

"Thank you for your help, Mr. Singer," the chief said as he stood up from his desk.

Dave Singer got up from his seat and left the chief's office feeling gloomy. He never got a chance to get together with Melody. Dave thought he got stood up that night. *What a hottie she was,* Dave thought to himself. *I'll never really ever know just how hot she was…damn, that really sucks!*

Dave headed back to the music store. He was going to have to tell his employees what happened to their cashier. *I'm gonna have to hire another girl, that's for sure,* he thought.

The sky had turned gloomy and snow was starting to fall. It was that fine snow, the type that signified a big, intense snow storm was approaching. The meteorologists had declared that a big blizzard was coming. It was also predicted that it would dump up to eighteen to twenty-four inches of snow on the ground by morning. The snow was going to be mixed with sleet, which would make traveling on all the roads extremely dangerous. Shoppers were already lining up in the stores to go purchase food, water, snow shovels, gasoline, and snow throwers. All of the radio and television stations were already announcing the school closings for tomorrow.

Angelo was in the garage checking to see if the snow thrower had gas and oil in it. This was going to be the first time it would be used since his parents died last winter. There wasn't enough snow this winter to try it out. His father finally showed him how to use it last winter before he died, but Angelo never got a chance to try it out for himself. What little snow they had either melted away by itself, or it was light enough to be shoveled by hand. Angelo didn't mind shoveling snow, he enjoyed the exercise. Angelo was also very frugal with his money, he had to be. The young man didn't want to waste money on gas, knowing it would expire if it wasn't used right away. After pulling the starter cord several times, the engine on the old snow blower started right up. Angelo was surprised the old machine started up, but he remembered that his father maintained all the yard equipment. *It pays to be handy,* he thought. The other thing that surprised him, was the fact that the gas in the can was almost a year old. *It must have been that stabilizer stuff Dad would put into the gas can,* he remembered. Angelo heard Carlita calling for him; she was wondering where he was. He shut down the snow blower, left the garage, and walked into the house. Carlita was in the family room, yelling out of the window for him.

"Where were you?" Carlita asked him.

"I was in the garage checking on the snow thrower," Angelo replied.

"The snow thrower?"

"Yeah, I had to make sure it was working for the upcoming

snow storm."

"You don't know how to use that thing; that was Daddy's job!"

"How the hell would you know about that?!"

"Carina told me long ago. She said your father didn't trust you with it, that's why he always gave you the shovel to help out."

"You know something, Carlita? You're *really* creeping me out."

"I'm sorry," she replied.

"Yeah, well, sorry just doesn't cut it right now. Excuse me," Angelo said as he walked away from her, feeling confused again.

Angelo went up to his room to think. He really just wanted some space away from her. *I shouldn't have to feel uncomfortable in my own damn home, but I do,* he thought. Angelo wanted to call a doctor about her. *Maybe Doctor Foster could help,* he thought, *but obviously, it will have to wait until the snow storm is over and the roads are all cleaned up.*

"Thank God I'm off tomorrow," he said to himself.

Of course, Angelo still had to worry. If the railroad called it an emergency situation, he would probably have to go in to work. All Angelo could do now was to hope for the best. He knew being a rookie was hard. Rookies were always the ones to go in first for any little thing. Rookies were always being tested for their loyalty. It sucked, but that's the way it was. The young man didn't mind the job, but he just didn't like going in to work in bad weather. The man knew he was going to have to keep a keen eye on Carlita. *That girl is not to be trusted,* he thought. Carlita had really become way too unpredictable and unbalanced. Angelo never knew what to expect from her. It seemed that Carlita was slowly becoming more and more like his dead sister, Carina Russo. *She dresses up in Carina's clothes, wears her makeup and tries to act like her. Why is she so obsessed with my dead sister?* Angelo asked himself. *Maybe Doctor Foster would know, maybe he could run some tests on her,* he hoped. Once the storm was over and the big cleanup was completed, Angelo was definitely going to call Doctor Foster and make an appointment for Carlita. Until then, he was going to watch every move that she made like a hawk. The young man knew it wasn't going to be easy, but it had to be done and without creating any suspicion in Carlita's mind.

23

THE END OF THE LINE

Almost four months had passed since Carlita's attempted murder. It was now early March, early in the afternoon. The groundhog had been right in its prediction, the animal had seen its shadow and winter was sticking around for an additional six weeks. There were six additional inches of snow on the ground from yesterday's storm. Angelo was tired of breaking out the snow thrower; the novelty of it had worn off long ago. The young man wondered why he even bothered to clean the driveway; Angelo didn't own a car, and neither did Carlita anymore.

Carlita had completely healed up. She no longer needed crutches or the special collar for her neck. All she had now, besides her memory of the incident, was a small scar on her left thigh. The scar was made from the incision when they inserted the titanium rod into her leg.

Angelo had taken the day off from work today to bring Carlita in to the doctor's office. Doctor Foster's office was at an inconvenient area; it wasn't near any train station stop. The only way they could get there was by car, so Angelo and Carlita were going to have to take a cab ride. He had finally convinced her to go see Doctor Foster about her mental condition. "There is nothing wrong with me, Angelo, but if you really feel that concerned, then I'll go," she had told him. Angelo went ahead and made an appointment for her at three o'clock to see the doctor.

The two of them were still sleeping in separate rooms. Angelo wondered if she would ever marry him. They still haven't had any sexual relations together; whenever they tried, it always turned out to be a fight instead. It would seem that sometimes there were two people living inside of Carlita's body, fighting to take over. The last time Angelo was kissing Carlita, it was on the family room sofa. She had started getting undressed right in front of him; it was the first time he had ever seen her completely naked. They began to caress one another, and then Angelo started to take off his clothes. He kissed her breasts, rolling his tongue gently around one of her big hard nipples. All of a sudden, Carlita screamed and pushed him away, yelling, "No, you can't have him! He's mine!" Angelo became so freaked out by her that he never attempted to make love to her again. The two of them had been getting ready to leave. Angelo looked up at the clock upon the wall; it was one forty-five. He wanted to leave by two o'clock.

"Hey, Carlita, are you ready to leave?!" Angelo yelled up the stairwell.

"Almost, dear, I just have to fix my hair!" she loudly replied.

"Ok, dear, I'll call a cab now!"

Angelo got on the phone and called for a cab. The car service told him that they would be there in about thirty minutes. That was cutting it kind of close, he thought. Angelo had informed Carlita when the cab would arrive. Since he was ready, the man decided to sit down and wait for Carlita. Angelo wondered what tests Doctor Foster would order up for her.

At the police precinct, Chief Brady was trying to put the pieces of the puzzle together. The chief finally had an idea who the serial killer was, but he didn't want to believe it. Brady started going through all the evidence, until Officer Ireland stepped into his office and interrupted him.

"Hey, Chief!" Officer Ireland said to him.

"What is it, Ireland, can't you see I'm busy?" the chief angrily asked him.

"We just got an anonymous caller."

"Please don't tell me someone else found another body."

"No, not exactly, sir."

"Then, what may I ask was it all about?"

"An unidentified man said he thinks he knows who the butcher is."

"Oh, Christ, another crank call?"

"I don't think so, Chief; at least, not the way he was talking, sir."

"Well, what did he say already?"

"The man said he thinks the one that was selling him body parts is the killer."

"Jesus H., body parts? Now, *this* sounds like a *real* lead! You spoke to him personally, Ireland?"

"Yes, I did sir, but he wouldn't give his name, sir."

"Well then, let's hear the tape."

"I'm sorry, Chief, but I got so caught up in it, I forgot."

"You *forgot?* What do you mean you forgot? You did record the call, right?"

"No, sir, I forgot to activate the recorder. I'm sorry, sir."

"You, you forgot?! You're sorry?! There's no recording, at all?!"

"No, sir, none whatsoever."

"You asshole! I got a good mind to fire your ass! How could you?! Of all the stupid things to do!" Chief Brady roared.

"I'm really sorry, sir."

"I can't believe you, Ireland! Something that important! now, we have nothing!"

"Not exactly, sir, I can tell you pretty much everything he told me over the phone, Chief."

"Well, out with it already, Ireland."

"Well, for starters, sir, the man had a very thick accent. He sounded like he was West Indian or Pakistani."

"Go on, Ireland, what the hell did he say about body parts?" Brady anxiously asked.

"The man said he was buying fresh body organs from this guy. The thing that made him suspicious was he always wanted cash. He said he'd call this guy up and order whatever organs that were needed, and within just a few days, the man would have the parts, for a hefty price."

"So, our notorious Railway Butcher is killing young women, stealing their organs, and then selling them on the black market."

"That's what it looks like, Chief."

"Did he give you his contact's number?"

"Well, he rattled off some numbers really quick, but the guy's thick accent made it real hard to understand, sir. I only picked up about three or four numbers. Sorry, Chief."

"Shit! You suck, Ireland. Had you done the right thing and recorded the conversation, maybe we could have had something solid to decipher."

"I'm sorry again, Chief."

"Well, 'sorry' doesn't cut it. My only question is: why kill only young attractive women? Why not kill men, too? I mean, a body organ is a body organ, that's what puzzles me."

"You're forgetting something, Chief."

"What, Ireland? Enlighten me."

"He did kill two young men, Chief. They were conductors, remember?"

"Yes, I do remember. Conductor Josh Vincitore, Angelo Russo's best friend, and Conductor James Mitchel, but those were hate crimes, weren't they, Ireland?"

"Yeah, but maybe they were really killed because they were getting in the way, or something."

"That's plausible. Did this caller give any kind of description of our killer?"

"Yes, he did. He said the man was tall, with long blond hair."

"Well then, it appears we're right back at square one now, doesn't it?"

"Not exactly, sir. At least, we now know what he's doing with the body parts—selling them."

"Yes, but there has to be another motive. Why then is this sonofabitch only slaughtering pretty, young women?"

"I don't know, Chief."

"Please, tell me you put a trace on the call, Ireland."

"No, Chief, I didn't."

"I did!" Officer Sager said as she walked into the chief's office.

"You did, Officer Sager?"

"Yes, sir. I received the call first before I patched it through to Officer Ireland. The way the man was talking, I thought it would be important to do so, Chief."

"Well, will you look at that? She's got brains *and* beauty. What's your excuse, Ireland?!"

Officer Ireland remained quiet. He knew he wasn't in the chief's good graces now. Officer Sager handed the chief a cup of coffee that was in her hand when she walked in.

"Here, Chief, I thought you could use this. I heard you yelling and…" Officer Sager trailed off.

"You thought it would pacify me, right?"

"Well, yeah."

"You're all right, Sager. Now, just tell me, Officer, where did the call come from?" the chief asked her.

"It was from a payphone at the Williams Port train station, sir."

"A payphone? Shit! How long ago was it, Sager?"

"It was about fifteen minutes ago, sir."

"Oh, Christ, he's probably gone by now. Ireland, make yourself useful; you and Smith get down there and see what you can find!"

"You got it, Chief!" Ireland said as he briskly walked out of the chief's office.

"Ok, gorgeous, although I don't mind having you around here, you'd better get back to your post before someone misses you," the chief told Officer Sager.

"All right, boss, you got it," Sager replied as she walked out of the chief's office.

Chief Brady started to think about what just happened. *The sonofabitch is not only killing innocent young women, but he's selling their body parts on the black market. This shit has got to stop,* he thought. Brady began writing notes in his notebook. He had been collecting the evidence from all of the victims.

Angelo and Carlita had finally arrived at the doctor's office. Doctor Foster's office looked like an old, two-story home that was converted into a business office. The outside of the building had yellow vinyl siding on the upper half, while the lower half had brick facing on it. There was a ramp near the stairs to make it wheelchair accessible. At the front entrance was a white metal sign with black letters above the door that read: DOCTOR FOSTER on it. Angelo paid and tipped the cab driver as he and Carlita got out. They walked inside the office and marveled at how modern it looked on the inside. There were big flat-screen TV sets on most of the walls to keep people entertained. A kiddie corner with small tables, chairs, and toys to keep the little ones busy, was also provided. The room was painted white and had bright fluorescent ceiling lighting. There were rows of comfortable seats and two tables filled with magazines to read. Over on the left side of the entrance there was a large reception counter with three receptionists to greet the doctor's patients. Angelo and Carlita went to one of the receptionists. The one that greeted them was an attractive young female with long red hair. Angelo thought that she reminded him of Sharon White, his old girlfriend and co-worker that was murdered. Her nametag read: Terri Roberts.

"Hello, may I help you?" the receptionist asked them.

"Hello, I'm here to see Doctor Foster," Carlita stated.

"Your name Miss, please?" Miss Roberts asked.

"Carlita, Carlita Gomez. I have a three o'clock appointment with him."

"Yes, you do. Have you ever been here before?"

"No, but he was my doctor at the hospital."

"Which hospital, Miss?"

"The Morton Medical Center."

"Ok, Miss Gomez, since it's your first time here, please take this tablet, have a seat, and fill out all of your information. Don't forget to include all of your insurance coverage, allergies, current medication, your date of birth, and home address."

"Ok, Miss."

Carlita took the orange tablet from the receptionist and sat back down with Angelo. After she finished filling out all of her information, Carlita brought the tablet back over to the reception desk. Ten minutes later, she was called into the exam room. Angelo went with her.

Doctor Foster had run the usual tests on Carlita while she sat up on the exam table. He had also taken a sample of her blood to be analyzed. Angelo had painted such a bleak picture of her condition; the doctor wanted to rule out all of the possible ailments. Finally, Doctor Foster relayed his findings to both of them.

"Her blood pressure and heart rate are normal. She's not running a temperature or anything," the doctor told them.

"It's her memory and personality that's changed, doc," Angelo stated while he pointed to his head.

"Miss Gomez, are you experiencing any kind of headaches associated with your memory loss?" Doctor Foster asked her.

"I can't say that I have, Doctor, not particularly anyway; although, I did have a headache last night," Carlita replied.

"All right, then, I'm going to order up some X-rays of your head to see if we can find anything."

"Ok, doc, sounds good to me!" Angelo exclaimed.

"But there's nothing wrong with me! Why run expensive diagnostic tests on me when I feel fine?" Carlita asked.

"I just want to be sure. We all want to be sure. Don't you agree, Miss Gomez?" the doctor asked her.

"Well, I suppose so. I just think it's an unnecessary expense, that's all."

"Young lady, I beg to differ with you. There is nothing unnecessary when it comes to your health," Doctor Foster sternly told her.

Angelo was happy; the doctor was seeing it his way. *Finally, someone's agreeing with me,* he thought to himself. Angelo sat in the doctor's office while Carlita Gomez was being brought into the X-ray room. *Maybe now we'll find out what the hell is really wrong with her,* Angelo thought.

A few miles away, the Railway Butcher was calling his customer on his burner phone. The disposable phone was the only one he would use for his unpleasant business. If the call ever got traced, he would simply throw it away and purchase another one using cash. After four rings, his client answered.

"Hello?" Muhammad asked.

"Hey, Muhammad; it's me, your favorite body parts store!" the butcher replied.

"What do you want?"

"I haven't heard from you in a while, what's up?"

"Nothing is, as you say, 'up!'"

"I was just wondering if you needed anything."

"No, nothing from you, my ex-friend."

"Whoa, *ex-friend?* What happened to you?"

"Nothing to me, but you are in big trouble."

"What do you mean I'm in trouble?"

"My people found out where you were getting all those body parts from. You are a dangerous murderer."

"Dangerous murderer? This is just a business, that's all, man. You are a customer looking for a product and I supply the demand. That's it! What do you care where I get the organs from?! As long as it suits your needs, that's all you should be concerned about!"

"Oh, but we do care, my ex-friend. We do not want to do business with cold-hearted killers. You had better be careful; the police have been informed. Goodbye, forever!" Muhammad yelled as he hung up the phone on the butcher.

"Shit! You stupid sonofabitch, you ratted me out?!" the butcher yelled to a now-dead line.

The killer started to feel like the walls of law were closing in on him. He now knew why Muhammad didn't call him to place an order. *I have to be really careful now. The cops are going to be watching everyone and every place like friggin hawks*, the butcher thought.

"I *still* have a score to settle with Mr. Angelo Russo and his bitch, Carlita Gomez!" he said to himself.

The slayer had decided to do some cleaning up around his basement. He didn't want any evidence lying around to incriminate him. As much as the butcher had liked having the mannequin with the head of Melody Gray in his cellar, the killer knew it had to go.

"I'll bury the head in the back yard and throw out all the mannequins," the murderer said to himself.

Back at the doctor's office, Angelo was consulting with Doctor Foster about all his findings.

"Well doc, how do her X-rays look?" Angelo asked the doctor.

"Miss Gomez's X-rays are normal, Mr. Russo. However, X-rays wouldn't show if she had a lesion in her brain, specifically in the temporal lobe," Doctor Foster replied.

"You think that's what she has, doc?"

"I'm almost certain of it. That could be the cause of her split personality or strange behavior. She could also have a brain tumor, or maybe a clot that was brought on by her car accident."

"But how could we know for sure, doc?"

"With her permission and also with the approval of her insurance company, I would like to do a CT scan of her head, Mr. Russo."

"Ok, doc, you check with her insurance company and I'll talk to her."

"Mr. Russo, I cannot stress enough the urgency of this matter. If it is a clot or tumor, she may not have much time at all."

"I completely understand, doc."

At that moment, Carlita was brought into the examination room by the nurse. She looked at them both, dumbfounded. Angelo wondered just how much she heard of the conversation he had with the doctor.

"Am I going to die?" Carlita asked them both.

"No, honey, you're not going to die. The doctor just wants to run some additional tests on you, that's all," Angelo told her reassuringly.

"I heard him tell you that I don't have much time at all," she said.

"Miss Gomez, I would like to run a set of tests on you to help determine your ailment," Doctor Foster told her.

"More tests? What sort of tests, Doctor?" Carlita asked him.

"Mainly, a CT scan of your head."

"What's a CT scan, Doctor?"

"It's a computerized axial tomography. We call it CT or CAT for short. The CT scan will allow us to see inside your head. It uses a combination of X-rays and a computer to help create pictures of all of your organs, bones, and tissues. You see, Miss Gomez, it will show us greater details than a regular X-ray can do."

"Ok, Doctor, if you really think that it's necessary, let's do it."

That was music to Angelo's ears. He didn't think Carlita would go through with it. The way Carlita was acting, you never knew what to expect from her lately.

"Great, I'll put the necessary paperwork through to your insurance company and hope for the best," Doctor Foster told them.

"Ok, doc, so we can leave here now?" Angelo asked him.

"Yes, but please stop by the receptionist on your way out in case you have a co-pay. My nurse will let you know when you can make an appointment for her CT scan, that's if her insurance covers it," Doctor Foster told them.

Back at the police station, Chief Brady had finally put two and two together. He finally figured out who the infamous Railway Butcher was, or so he thought. The chief had written down an address on a piece of paper and reached for the intercom.

"Hello, Sager?" he said on the intercom.

"Yes, Chief?" Officer Sager replied.

"Send in Officers Flanigan and Smith, please."

"You got it, Chief."

Within minutes, the two officers stepped into Chief Brady's office. Brady asked the men to sit down. They both had puzzled looks on their faces, knowing this must be serious.

"Men, I'm going out on a hunch," the chief stated.

"A hunch, sir?" Officer Flanigan asked.

"That's right, a hunch, and I want one of you men to accompany me, while the other one stays here and mans the fort."

"What kind of hunch, Chief?" Officer Smith asked him.

"I think I know who our infamous serial killer is," the chief replied.

"Well, who is it, Chief?" Officer Flanigan anxiously asked him.

"Now, it's just a hunch, so I'm not saying anything else till I'm one hundred percent sure, all right?"

"Yes boss," Officer Smith replied.

"Now, the question is, which one of you wants to come with me?"

"I'll go with you, Chief," Officer Smith replied.

"Ok, Flanigan, you stay here and man the fort. This is the address of where we'll be at," Chief Brady said as he handed the paper to Officer Flanigan.

Flanigan looked at the address: 15 Park Row Avenue in the town of Morton. He suddenly remembered whose house it was. Flanigan and Smith had recently been there to search the premises.

"But, but Chief, that's Conductor Taylor Parker's house!" Officer Flanigan exclaimed.

"Brilliant deduction there, Flanigan," the chief sarcastically replied.

"But Smith and I were just recently there searching the place, and we didn't find anything!"

"Yeah, well, let's just say I planted a seed and now, I'm gonna watch it grow, all right?"

"Ok, Chief, whatever you say; you're the boss," Flanigan replied.

"Yeah, that's right, and don't you forget it. Listen, if we're not back in an hour, you send every man we've got over to that address. Do I make myself clear, Flanigan?"

"Yes, Chief, perfectly clear."

"All right, Smith, let's go," Chief Brady told him as they left together.

A few miles away, Angelo and Carlita finally arrived home from the doctor's office. He paid the fare and tipped the driver of the cab. As they left the car, Angelo noticed there was a text on his smartphone. He read the text: "Angelo, please meet me at my house at 15 Park Row Avenue in the town of Morton, it's very important, Taylor." *Man, how the hell did Taylor get my number?* Angelo wondered.

"What is it, honey?" Carlita asked him.

"I just got a text from Taylor; he wants me to meet him at his house. He says it's important," Angelo told her as they walked toward the house.

"And you're going?"

"I don't want to, but I owe him a favor. Will you be all right while I'm gone?"

"You're not staying long are you?"

"No, I promise. I just want to go to the bathroom really quick before I call a cab," he said while they walked into the house.

A few minutes later, Angelo was heading out to the cab. He gave the driver the address and they left. Angelo didn't realize how close Taylor's house was to him. It took only fifteen minutes to get there. When they arrived at Conductor Parker's house, Angelo paid the fare and tipped the driver of the cab. Angelo rang the doorbell of Taylor's home. *It's not a bad house at all; I remember him living in an apartment when I delivered his pizza, he must have moved,* he thought while waiting for Parker to open the door. Angelo rang the bell again; this time, Parker yelled out for him to come in. He turned the knob on the front door and walked inside. Parker was sitting on the sofa in the living room, waiting for him.

"Hey, Taylor, what's up?" Angelo asked him.

"Come here and sit down," Taylor said to him.

"You're not gonna try any funny stuff, are you?"

"No, I'm not, just please come here, will you?"

"All right," Angelo said as he closed the door behind him.

Angelo sat down on the sofa, but not too close to Taylor. He still didn't trust him. Angelo noticed he was nervously shaking.

"Ok, now, what is it already and how did you get my number?" Angelo asked him.

"Chief Brady gave it to me," Parker replied.

"Chief Brady…why?"

"He wanted me to contact you. Angelo, I'm scared."

"Scared? Scared of what, Taylor? Tell me, will you?"

"Angelo, we're in big trouble. This is a setup."

"A setup? What do you mean a setup?"

"The chief told me he thinks he knows who the killer is."

"He does?"

"That's what he says. He asked me to do him a favor and to contact you to come over here."

"For what? Do they still think I'm the killer? Well, I'd hate to disappoint them, 'cause I ain't."

"No, Angelo, don't you get it? The chief thinks the butcher is on his way here!"

"Why? I still don't get it!"

"Chief Brady thinks the butcher is sweet on me!"

"Oh, shit! Now, I get it! This is a trap! I'm out of here!" Angelo yelled as he stood up and got ready to leave.

"No, Angelo! Please, please don't go! The chief said that he would be here before anything bad happens," Taylor said as he started to cry.

Angelo couldn't resist anyone crying, not even a young man. He turned around and saw Taylor crying so much that his feminine makeup was running all over his face. Angelo looked around for a tissue and gave one to him.

"I-I'm s-sorry. I didn't mean to get you involved in this shit, but if it will help to catch this asshole, it will also clear you. Please, say you'll stay," Taylor said as he blew his nose.

Angelo felt sorry for Taylor. He sat back down on the sofa next to him and placed his left arm around Taylor, to comfort him. Then, all of a sudden, the door burst wide open. The butcher was standing in the doorway, furious, with a gun in his hands.

"Why you little bitch! Get your fucking arm off of my boy, now!" the killer yelled while pointing his gun at Angelo.

The two of them were shocked. Taylor felt like he was looking into a mirror. Angelo quickly removed his arm from Taylor.

"Y-yes, sir, anything y-you say," Angelo stammered.

"You! You really *do* look like me!" Taylor exclaimed.

The butcher removed his blonde wig, and then his mask. Angelo and Taylor couldn't believe what they were seeing. All this time, the butcher was right under their noses.

"You! You were the one that grabbed my ass on my train! You're that cop, too!" Taylor said.

"I can't believe it! Lieutenant Collins?! Why?! Why'd you do it?!" Angelo shouted.

"None of your damn business, bitch! I'm gonna put an end to your sorry ass right now!" Lieutenant Collins said while cocking his gun.

"No! I love him!" Taylor said as he jumped in front of Angelo while the gun fired.

"No! You stupid ass!" the lieutenant screamed.

Taylor Parker collapsed right on the floor in front of Angelo. The bullet from the forty-five Magnum pierced his heart, killing him instantly. Lieutenant Collins bent down and cried over him while cradling Taylor's body in his arms. He put Parker's body gently back down on the rug, stood back up, and turned toward Angelo.

"You're gonna pay dearly for this shit, Angelo!" Collins said while once again pointing the gun at him.

"Drop the gun, Collins! It's the end of the line for you!" Chief Brady warned him as he entered through the open door with Officer Smith.

The chief and Officer Smith both had their guns aimed at the lieutenant. Collins was surprised. He didn't expect to get caught. He didn't realize this was a trap.

"Never! This scumbag has got to pay!"

"Let this be your final warning, Collins! don't make me do this! Drop the gun, for God's sake!" Brady warned him again.

"Nooo!" Collins shouted.

All of a sudden, shots rang out from both the chief and Officer Smith's guns. The crazed lieutenant collapsed from the multiple gunshot wounds right in front of Angelo Russo. Angelo was shocked. He still couldn't believe that the man who was trying to hang him all along, turned out to be the infamous serial killer, the one responsible for his sister's death and everyone else that got close to him.

"Chief, is he finally dead?" Angelo asked.

Chief Brady checked both of the bodies. He looked at Angelo and Officer Smith and shook his head yes. Chief Brady felt sorry for both of them.

"They're both gone. What a waste. I warned him. Lieutenant Collins was a great detective, but he got caught up in his own crazy world," the chief said.

"Taylor sacrificed his own life for me, even though I was mean to him. He really did love me. I'll never forget that," Angelo solemnly said.

"Chief, I got only one question…" Officer Smith said.

"What's that, Smith?" the chief asked him.

"How the hell did you know it was Lieutenant Collins…I mean…what tipped you off?"

"It was a lot of little things that finally added up. For starters, Collins had a problem with women, especially beautiful women. He really disliked Officer Sager and Officer Rivera. Collins seemed very elated when Officer Rivera was murdered, now we know by his own hand. The lieutenant seemed threatened by attractive women. He wanted them all dead, and Collins couldn't just murder them, he had to destroy them."

"But what about the body parts, Chief?"

"That was his little side business that allowed him to live like a king. Collins figured he could make some money off of the victims' organs. Collins worked as a paramedic before he came to work for the police department, which is how he knew how to surgically remove body organs."

"How did you know he had a crush on Conductor Taylor Parker?" Angelo asked the chief.

"That was the other thing. I found out that Collins was gay, and he seemed really easy on Parker when we brought him in as a suspect. You should have seen him in the interrogation room with Parker; he felt so sorry for him. When Collins asked if we could give Parker a lie-detector test, I knew something was up. Believe it or not, Russo, Collins had a thing for you, too. He could have killed you long ago, but Collins couldn't bring himself to do it."

"Was there anything else that tipped you off, Chief?" Officer Smith asked him.

"Yes, there was. That last gift that Taylor Parker received, the red-headed scalp, it came from the post office nearby the lieutenant. However, the last thing that was the icing on the cake, was that Lieutenant Collins became increasingly interested in the whereabouts of Carlita Gomez, your girlfriend, Mr. Russo. I just knew right then and there that he was responsible for her accident and wanted to finish the job."

"Wow, I just can't believe it… It sounds so surreal, Chief," Angelo said.

"Mr. Russo, I'm sorry we took so long to get here, but we also had a stakeout at the lieutenant's house going on. I wanted to be sure before we barged in here. My men found some blood and formaldehyde on a headless mannequin in the lieutenant's basement. They followed the trail of blood to his backyard. There was a half-ass, makeshift shallow grave there. When my men dug it up, they found the missing head of his last victim, Melody Gray. There were also pictures of all of his victims with X marks on them, on his basement wall. The last thing they found were mug shot pictures of Taylor Parker and pictures of you, Mr. Russo. The pictures had, what appeared to be, semen stains on them, probably from the lieutenant himself. That was all the proof I needed to justify my findings," Chief Brady stated.

"Chief, I do have one more question," Angelo said.

"What is it, Russo?"

"How did you know the lieutenant would be coming here, now?"

"I planted bait, that's how. I called your friend here, Mr. Parker, and told him to call you over here. Then, I told the lieutenant that you were going over to visit Parker; oh, you should have seen the look in his eyes. I knew right then and there that I had my man. For Christ's sake, Collins loved Parker enough that he even had a face mask made to look like him. What a sick-ass puppy he was. I'm sorry about your friend. I'm also sorry about putting you in the police line of fire, Mr. Russo, but it had to be done," Chief Brady sincerely added.

"It's all right, Chief, I'm just so glad that it's over," Angelo replied.

"Hey, Smith, please make a call and have those bodies removed, will you?"

"You got it, Chief," Officer Smith replied.

Officer Smith took out his smartphone to make the phone call for the chief.

24

I KNOW WHO YOU REALLY ARE

Chief Kevin Brady had Angelo Russo taken back home by Officer Smith in his squad car. It was the least the chief could do for him after he had helped them capture the Railway Butcher. Angelo got out of the car and then thanked the officer. He was still shaking as he approached his front door. Carlita was waiting for him; she opened up the door and let him in.

"Angelo, are you all right?" she asked him while sounding concerned.

"Not really," he replied as he walked into his house.

"I was worried sick about you; it's nine o'clock at night. You were gone for such a long time."

"It's that late?"

"Yes, it is. Why were you brought home in a police car? Is everything all right?"

"Yes and no. Come, let's go and sit down in the family room and I'll tell you all about it."

The two of them walked into the family room and sat down on the sofa. Carlita gave him a curious look. She wanted desperately to know what happened with Angelo.

"Well, tell me what happened!" Carlita anxiously asked.

"Well, the good news is, the butcher was finally caught and killed by the chief and Officer Smith."

"That's great! Now, we can all finally relax. But why are you so glum?" she asked him.

"Conductor Taylor Parker was shot and killed."

"He was the butcher? I knew it all along! Shit, that's why he had my...I mean...Carina's hair on him."

"No, he was not the killer and how did you know about that?!" Angelo yelled at Carlita.

"I-I heard it from someone...I think it was you," she said while being on the verge of tears.

"Look, I'm sorry I blew up at you like that, but a lot of shit has happened tonight."

"Well, then, tell me. I'm right here for you, honey."

"Like I said before, Taylor was shot and killed. He was killed accidentally by Lieutenant Collins. Taylor jumped in front of me to protect me from being shot. He took the bullet for me. Taylor saved my life, Carlita."

"But...who was the butcher, then?"

"Lieutenant Collins."

"What? Police Lieutenant Collins was the killer?"

"That's right. Lieutenant Collins was the Railway Butcher all along. He wore a mask and a wig that looked like Conductor Taylor Parker. It seems that the lieutenant was in love with Taylor. They were both gay, but Taylor was in love with me."

"Holy shit! This is just way too much for me to digest, Angelo. You're not in love with Taylor...I mean...you're not bi or gay, are you?" Carlita asked him feeling worried.

"Of course not!" Angelo exclaimed. "I just feel bad that he had to die because of me, that's all. That was just the ultimate sacrifice. Nobody has ever given their life away for me. When I think of all the times I cursed him out and told him to go get lost...I feel really, really guilty," Angelo solemnly said to her.

Carlita put her loving arm around him, then she gave Angelo a hug. He finally broke down and cried in her arms. Angelo felt totally responsible for Taylor Parker's death.

The next morning, Angelo woke up to Carlita talking on the phone in Carina's old bedroom. She was sleeping in Carina's room, which was right next to his room. Carlita finally hung up her phone and came over to Angelo.

"Good morning, dear. How do you feel?" Carlita asked him.

"I'm all right," Angelo said as he yawned.

"Guess what?"

"What?"

"That was Doctor Foster's office on the phone. The nurse said the insurance company is going to pay for my CT scan."

"That's great news, baby."

"They also made an appointment for me to have the test."

"When is the appointment, Carlita?"

"It'll be next Tuesday, March 17, at nine in the morning."

"It works out fine, then. I'm gonna be off Tuesdays and Wednesdays for the next month. Is it going to be at the doctor's office?"

"No, he doesn't have that kind of testing equipment at his facility."

"So where the hell are we going?" Angelo nervously asked

her.

"The doctor said it's going to be at the Morton Medical Center, where I was."

"The hospital? Cool, we could take the train and save some money since I get to ride for free," Angelo said happily.

"You do, but what about me?"

"Don't worry, babe, I got you covered. I'll pay your fare. It's still cheaper than taking a damn cab."

"Fine, would you like me to make you breakfast, love?"

"Sure, what are you making?"

"Your favorite, dear: ham and eggs, just the way you like it, Angelo," Carlita told him with a mischievous look in her eyes.

"You're really creeping me out, you know that?"

"I'm sorry, dear, I didn't mean to."

"Carlita, I have a question for you."

"What is it, Angelo?"

"You once told me you had a favorite song you would play when you were lonely and thinking of me."

"I did?"

"Yeah, you did. What was that song?"

"I don't remember."

"You don't remember the name of it, or the artist?"

"No, I really don't. I'll go start breakfast," Carlita said as she hurriedly walked out of his room.

Angelo started thinking again. *Wow, how convenient, she doesn't remember. She seemed rather nervous, too,* he thought. Angelo knew something was really up with her. He began thinking again until his smartphone started ringing.

"Hello?" Angelo asked.

"Mr. Russo, it's Chief Brady."

"Oh, hello, Chief, what can I do for you?"

"I have something here for you, Mr. Russo."

"I have no way of getting down there; you're not exactly close to any train station, you know," Angelo told him.

"You really ought to get yourself a car while you're living around here, Mr. Russo."

"I know, I'm working on that, but Carlita doesn't want one after what happened to her."

"I see. I'll have Officer Ireland come by and get you since you've helped me solve this case, all right?"

"All right, Chief, when will he be here?"

"Will three o'clock be ok?"

"That's fine, Chief; I'll be ready by then."

"Ok, Russo, see you then," the chief said before he hung up the phone on Angelo.

Angelo wondered what the chief had for him. *I hope it's nothing bad. Maybe it's some sort of reward,* he thought. He got out of bed and got dressed.

A few minutes later, Angelo was having breakfast with Carlita. *How strange this is—she makes my favorite dish, exactly the way Carina used to,* Angelo thought. He wondered whatever happened to her. Carina Russo's ghost hadn't been around since Carlita came out of her coma; that was almost four months ago. Angelo kept on thinking until Carlita broke his thought.

"You look like you're a million miles away, hon. Are you all right?" Carlita asked him.

"I'm fine, it's *you* I'm worried about," Angelo replied.

"Me? I feel fine."

"Are you really?"

"Yes, I am. Now, would you please stop staring at me?"

"Fine, listen, I have to go back to the police station for something."

"For what, Angelo?"

"I don't know; the chief says he has something for me. He's sending a patrol car over to pick me up."

"When are you going?" Carlita asked him.

"The chief said by three o'clock," Angelo replied.

"That's why you got dressed up so fast on your day off?"

"Yep, I'm curious to see what the heck it is. Maybe it's some sort of reward!"

"Yeah, that would be nice, but I doubt it."

"Boy, aren't we pessimistic? You're just like my sister was."

Carlita shot him a weird look. The two of them just stared

at each other for a brief moment. Angelo thought that she was hiding something. They both took a sip of coffee before speaking again.

"I'll do the dishes," Angelo said.

"No, that's all right, I can do them. You go finish getting ready for your visit with the chief," Carlita replied.

Angelo Russo got up from the table and finished getting ready. He took his smartphone off the charger and put it in his right front pants pocket of his blue jeans. Angelo grabbed his keys and waited for the police car.

Later that day, Officer Ireland was at the front door ringing the bell. Angelo kissed Carlita goodbye and left with the police officer. While riding in the police cruiser, Angelo kept wondering what the chief had for him.

Soon after, they were back at the police station in Chief Brady's office.

"Mr. Russo, welcome back!" Chief Brady exclaimed.

"Hello, Chief, I'm anxious to see what you have for me," Angelo said to him.

The chief handed Angelo a box he had on his desk.

"I believe that this belongs to you," Chief Brady told him.

"What is it, Chief?" Angelo asked.

"Why don't you just open it up and find out?"

Angelo opened the box, expecting to find an award. When he saw what it was, Angelo jumped. There was a blonde wig inside of the box.

"I thought you would want the last of your sister's remains. Since the case is solved, it's no longer evidence," the chief told him.

"So, this is Carina's scalp?"

"Precisely, it's yours to keep, Mr. Russo. Bury it, burn it, do whatever you want with it; just get it out of my sight, please," the chief said as he closed up the box again.

Chief Brady had Officer Ireland bring Angelo back to his home with Carina's scalp. Angelo rode in the back of the police squad car feeling disappointed. *So much for my reward,* he thought to himself. *Carlita was sure right.* They soon arrived back at Angelo's house. He thanked Officer Ireland for the ride and walked over to his front door. Angelo looked at the time on his smartphone before he unlocked the door; it was five o'clock. Two hours wasted for nothing. *What am I going to do with Carina's hair?* Angelo thought while walking into his home. Carlita had just come down the stairs to greet him.

"Hey, whatcha got in the box, baby?" she asked him.

"This…" he said while taking out the blonde scalp.

"W-where did you get that from?"

"It was a present from the chief."

"That's what he wanted you downtown for?"

"Yeah, that's my reward. You know what it is, don't you?"

"It-it's a blonde wig, right?"

"Not exactly, it's my sister's scalp."

"You should bury it with her."

"Oh, I should exhume Carina's body just so that I could bury her hair with her?"

"Well, yeah. I really think she should be completely whole again."

"I did that once when they found her head, I'm *not* going to do it again; besides, why do you care so much about Carina all of a sudden? Weren't you two enemies?"

"I just thought it would be the right thing to do, that's all."

"Yeah, right," Angelo cynically added.

"Well, I could keep it in Carina's room with me for the time being."

"No, thank you, I'll keep it with me," Angelo said as he took the scalp and the box upstairs to his bedroom.

A week had passed by; it was now Tuesday morning, March 17. Angelo got up at six o'clock in the morning to take Carlita for her CT scan at the hospital. He went next door to her room to wake her up. Carlita was sleeping in Carina's white negligee, the same one he would see her apparition in. Angelo noticed his sister's blonde scalp in the corner of the floor near her bed. *What's that doing in here? I had that in my room,* he thought. Angelo gently picked it up and put it back in his room. This time, he hid it in his dresser drawer. Angelo went back up to her room to wake Carlita.

"Good morning, Sleeping Beauty!" he said to her.

"What time is it?" Carlita asked him as she yawned.

"It's ten after six."

"In the morning?"

"No, in the evening…of course in the morning, silly! You have your test today, remember?"

"Oh, I forgot about that. Can't I sleep a little bit more?"

"No! We have to catch the seven fifty-five train if we're going to get there on time."

"All right, all right, let me get dressed."

Angelo walked out of her room so that she could get dressed. *I hope this test shows what's wrong with her,* he thought. Angelo went to one of the three bathrooms to shave and wash up.

Later that morning, Angelo and Carlita had just departed on the southbound express train. The two of them had made great time getting there. It was only eight thirty-five when they walked into the hospital. Angelo waited for Carlita in the waiting room. A technician had escorted her to the testing room. Carlita was very nervous. The massive CT machine, which resembled a large doughnut with a narrow table in the middle, seemed very intimidating to her. A nurse had given her an injection prior, since the test was going to be performed with contrast. The technician told Carlita to lie down on the table and remain perfectly still for thirty minutes.

An hour later, Carlita was brought back to the waiting room where Angelo was. They took the train back home and relaxed the rest of the day. Carlita was very quiet after her test, she seemed very uneasy. Angelo wondered what the test would reveal.

Three days later, Carlita had received a call from Doctor

Foster. The CT scan was negative. There was no abnormality in her brain, whatsoever. Angelo couldn't believe it. "It must be a mistake! I know there's got to be something wrong with you!" Angelo shouted out loud. Carlita stood her ground: "No more tests! I'm done!" she yelled back at him. Angelo knew his hands were tied. There was nothing else he could do, except to deal with it…or ask her to leave.

The next day, Angelo was coming back home from work; it was six o'clock in the evening. Angelo was very cold. He froze on the train ride coming back since the cabin heater was broken. Angelo decided to light up a fire in the family room fireplace. Carlita walked into the room wearing Carina's sexy white negligee.

"Well, hello there, handsome," Carlita said while putting her arms around him.

"Hello, babe," Angelo replied as he went to kiss her.

"Ooo, how romantic, a fire," Carlita said in a very sexy voice.

"Sorry to disappoint you, dear, but I wasn't doing it for romance. I'm burning it to warm myself up. I froze my ass for almost two hours because of a burned-out cabin heater on the train."

"Oh, I think I know how I can warm you up, baby."

Carlita started undressing Angelo right there in front of the fireplace. He was shocked; Angelo couldn't believe it. After four months of living together, they were finally going to make love. She threw his uniform on the sofa and aggressively laid him down on the carpet. Carlita pulled off her white negligee and then removed Angelo's underwear. She sat down on his genitals, facing him, and rubbed herself on his growing penis. Carlita had gotten herself all wet. Angelo Russo couldn't believe what was happening. *Is Carlita finally snapping out of it? Is she finally coming back to me?* Angelo asked himself. Then, Carlita bent over to him and whispered to him.

"I'll make a man out of you yet, little brother."

"W-what, what did you say?" Angelo fearfully asked her, not believing what he had just heard.

"You know what I just said. Why don't you lick your fingers and rub my nipples like you did before?" she said while laughing in his face.

Angelo was in complete shock. His big hard-on completely went away. *This isn't possible,* he thought. But all the pieces seemed to fit. Carina's ghost had disappeared when Carlita had become conscious in the hospital. Carlita didn't remember the song she played while thinking of him. Carlita no longer wanted to marry him. Her split personality issues…and hanging out with Carina's old boyfriend. She cooked his favorite breakfast just like Carina used to do. Carlita was wearing Carina's clothes, even acting like her. *There could only be one explanation,* he thought.

"I know now who you really are!" Angelo shouted as he pushed her off of him.

"You do?" she asked while continuing to laugh.

"I don't know how, but it's you, Carina, isn't it?!"

"That's right, baby brother, I'm back! I told you I'd be back!"

"But…how? Where's Carlita?"

"That bitch is history. Oh, she put up a good fight, but she's gone now."

"But, I still don't understand it. You're possessing her body?"

"Whoa, you just won the big booby prize, baby. When Carlita was far out of her body, in a coma, I simply just slipped on in and took it over. I'm a witch, remember? I can do that. But then, the bitch decided to try and come back when she saw you with me. She got really jealous of us, you know. But now, it's all over, lovey. But I must say, I'm a little disappointed in you, little brother."

"Disappointed? Why?"

"You never figured out who the hell the killer was. *I* did."

"You mean; you knew all along it was the lieutenant?"

"Well, not exactly. I first thought it was Taylor, but then later on I realized it was the lieutenant wearing a ridiculous mask."

"Why didn't you tell me?"

"I wanted to see if *you* could figure it out on your own, but you didn't. You are a simpleton, but I still love you; and now, you're mine again. I have a new body; a second chance at life. I can start my career as a model all over again, especially with all the contacts I know. Isn't it wonderful, baby? Of course, you know we could *never ever* get married; it wouldn't be good for my career, my image. I'll just keep you around as my boy-toy. I wanna play, now; I'm horny."

"No, Carina, it's not right. You stole her body, Give it back!" Angelo cried out.

"Never! It's mine, now!"

"I love you, Carina. I'll always love you, but this is all so wrong and you know it."

"No, it's not!"

"You lived your life; give Carlita a chance to live her life!"

"Never! My life was taken away from me, unfairly!"

"It's not right, Carina!"

"Are you gonna fuck me, or do I have to call Michael again?!"

That last remark infuriated Angelo. He knew it was time for drastic action. Angelo wanted Carlita back and there was only one way to do it. He had to destroy Carina's spirit. Angelo ran upstairs to his room.

"Where the hell are you going?! Come back here, now!" Carina screamed.

Angelo came back down with Carina's blonde hair and scalp.

"What are you doing with that, you silly little fool?!" she screamed.

"This?! This is goodbye, Carina!" Angelo yelled while throwing her scalp into the roaring fireplace.

"Noooo!" Carina screamed while she collapsed onto the floor right in front of the fireplace.

Angelo went over and held her in his arms. Angelo hoped that what he just did would bring back his beloved Carlita. Angelo didn't want to burn Carina's scalp, but it was the only way, the only chance he had at getting Carlita back.

"I'm sorry, Carina, I'll always love you," Angelo said while cradling Carlita's naked body.

All of a sudden, Angelo saw her eyes open back up. She stared right up at him. He didn't know who she was. Was it really Carlita Gomez? Did he succeed? Or was it his sister, Carina, playing a dirty little trick on him.

"Angelo, is it really you?" Carlita said in a faint voice.

"Carlita?" Angelo hesitantly asked her.

"Yes, honey, it's me."

"What was that song you used to play when you were all alone and missing me?"

"Oh, that's easy: 'Wicked Game' by Chris Isaak," she replied.

"All right!" he exclaimed.

"Oh, *my*! Why are we both laying here naked?" she timidly asked him.

"Baby, it's a long story, but you know what? I've got a great idea!" Angelo said as he carried her off to his bedroom.

EPILOGUE

Police Chief Kevin Brady finally got his long and awaited vacation. When Chief Brady returned, he had to make a big decision: who was going to be promoted to take over as the new lieutenant, now that Collins was dead? The chief had some candidates to consider.

Angelo Russo and Carlita Gomez were finally married in a small ceremony, since they didn't know that many people. The couple purchased a brand-new car; they had to since Angelo and Carlita were going to start a new family. Angelo had occasionally thought about his sister; he didn't want to completely remove her out of his life, but the young man knew that it had to be done in order to move on. Carlita got herself a job working in the Payroll Department of the Morton City Railroad.

A few miles away at the Morton Medical Center, a young mother was giving birth to a little girl. Carina's spirit was not destroyed after all; she knew that Angelo no longer wanted her. Carina knew that Angelo didn't need her anymore, but Carina still wanted to live again. No one was going to deny that from her ever again. Carina found a new host. She would just have to start all over again…in a newborn's body.

I hope you enjoyed this story.
Manuel (Manny) Rose

ABOUT THE AUTHOR

Manuel "Manny" Rose was born in Brooklyn, New York. He is the exclusive owner and CEO of MMRproductions.com. Manuel is an author of both children's books as well as adult thrillers. Manny started his own business in 2000, which has evolved and branched out into multiple avenues, including some of his how-to educational products. As an avid professional audio/video producer, writer, singer, and voice actor, he provided the screenwriting and narration for the instructional films that he produced, as well as character voice-overs for his line of children's audio books, including his project, "My Child Storytime VOL. 1," which is a CD that features all original stories and songs. Manny is also a proud member of ASCAP.

Please Visit His Websites at:

https://manuelrose.com/

http://mmrproductions.com/

https://twitter.com/ManuelRose

https://www.facebook.com/Manuel-Rose-Writer-101580988342731/

https://www.youtube.com/user/MMRPRODUCTIONS

https://www.amazon.com/Manuel-Rose/e/B078J5QKVX

https://soundcloud.com/user-112846907/a-murderers-music-box-demo

https://www.goodreads.com/ManuelRose

Thanks so much for reading!

If you enjoyed this book, please take a minute to leave a review on Amazon.com, BarnesandNoble.com, and Goodreads.com. Reviews make a huge difference to an author's sales and rankings—the more reviews, the more books I'll be able to write.

My readers mean the world to me, and I'd love to stay in touch. You can keep up with me on Goodreads.com https://www.goodreads.com/author/show/17650713.Manuel_Rose
and Amazon.com https://www.amazon.com/Manuel-Rose/e/B078J5QKVX/ref=dp_byline_cont_pop_ebooks_1

Also from Manuel Rose

A Murderer's Music Box

Avalina
A Mystical Thriller

Coming Soon:

Time Enough for Murder
A Science Fiction Murder Mystery

www.ingramcontent.com/pod-product-compliance
Lightning Source LLC
Chambersburg PA
CBHW020912110726
47900CB00001B/113